THE ANATALIAN KING

REBECCA MIKKELSON

AUTHORS 4 AUTHORS PUBLISHING
Marysville, WA, USA

Published by Authors 4 Authors Publishing
1214 6th St
Marysville, WA 98270
www.authors4authorspublishing.com

Library of Congress Control Number: 9781644771808

E-book ISBN: 978-1-64477-178-5
Hardcover ISBN: 978-1-64477-180-8
Paperback ISBN: 978-1-64477-179-2
Audiobook ISBN: 978-1-64477-181-5

Edited by Renee Frey
Copyedited by Lisa Borne Graves
Proofread by Brandi Spencer

Cover design ©2023 Brandi Spencer. All rights reserved.
Interior design and map of Aratia by Brandi Spencer.

Authors 4 Authors Publishing branding is set in Bavire. Titles and headings are set in Beguns and Goudy Twenty. Correspondence is set in IM Fell and Gothic Ultra. All other text is set in Garamond.

THE ANATALIAN
KING

REBECCA
MIKKELSON

Authors 4 Authors Content Rating

This title has been rated 17+, appropriate for older teens and adults, and contains:

- brief implied sex
- graphic violence
- rape
- strong language
- frequent negative alcohol use
- alcoholism and depression
- child death
- parent death

Please, keep the following in mind when using our rating system:

1. A content rating is not a measure of quality.

Great stories can be found for every audience. One book with many content warnings and another with none at all may be of equal depth and sophistication. Our ratings can work both ways: to avoid content or to find it.

2. Ratings are merely a tool.

For our young adult (YA) and children's titles, age ratings are generalized suggestions. For parents, our descriptive ratings can help you make informed decisions, but at the end of the day, only you know what kinds of content are appropriate for your individual child. This is why we provide details in addition to the general age rating.

For more information on our rating system, please, visit our Content Guide at: www.authors4authorspublishing.com/books/ratings

DEDICATION

For my friend Kelley,

Thank you for believing in me more
than I believe in myself.

WORKS BY REBECCA MIKKELSON

"The Measure of a Princess"

The Anatalian Series:
The Anatalian Soldier
The Anatalian Countess
The Anatalian Throne
The Anatalian King
The Anatalian Queen
The Anatalian Heir

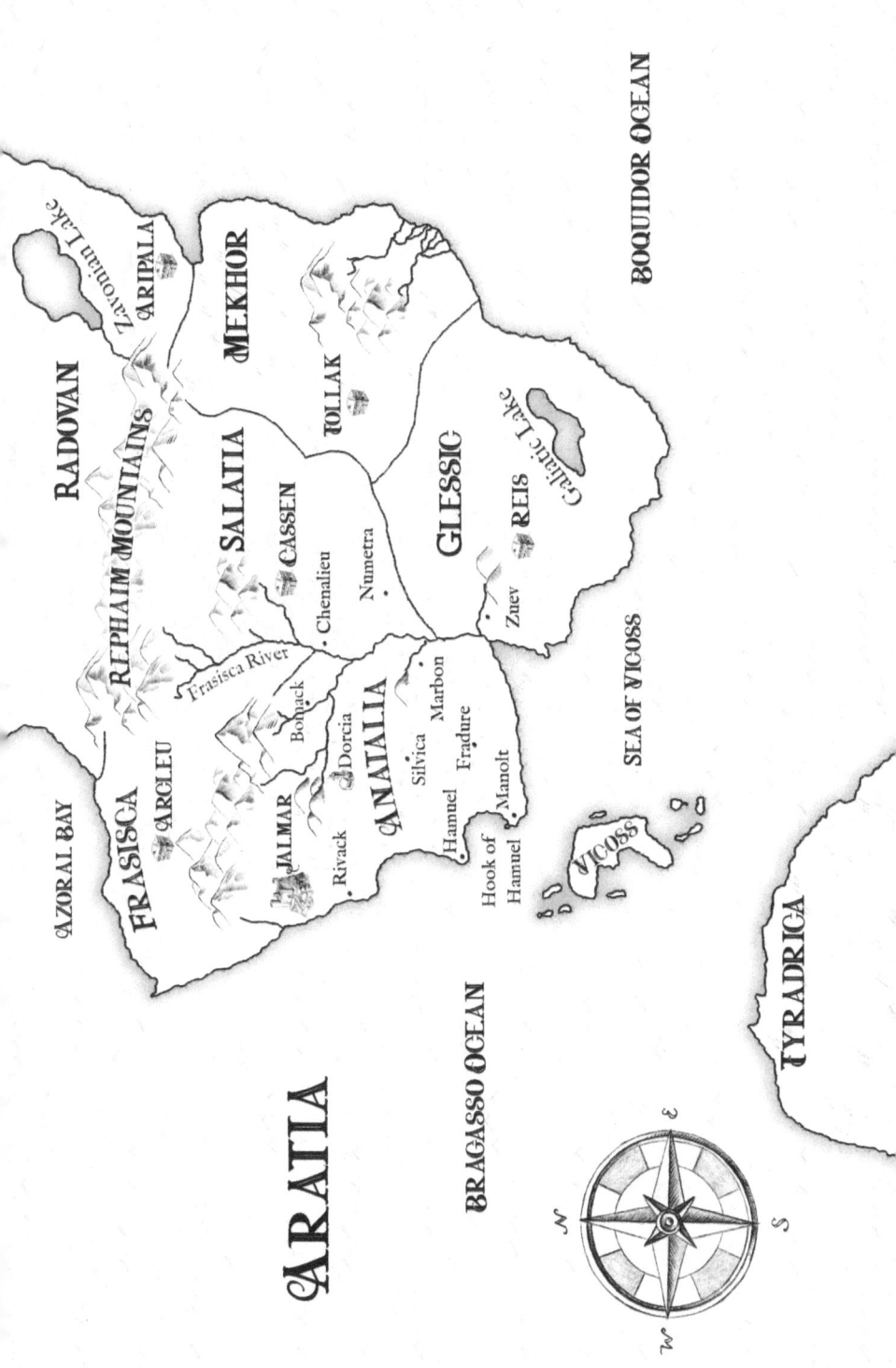

TABLE OF CONTENTS

1

Margaret inhaled deeply, filling her lungs with a hopeful breath for what felt like the first time in years. She was finally out from under Sorren's thumb—if only for a little while—after giving assurances that she would frequently update him with their progress. Even with the restrictions imposed on her, it was a taste of freedom she couldn't wait to immerse herself in. She delighted even more in knowing the king couldn't deny her the trip. With him finally granting Margaret her title, and even more lands, she had no choice but to take a tour.

She leaned back in the carriage seat, her eyes closed. The farther the carriage rode from the palace, the more her shoulders loosened. When she turned to look out of the small slotted window in the back of the carriage, the palace was barely visible. Smiling, she turned back to Rowan, who was sitting opposite her.

"You look happy." His lips twisted slightly. It wasn't quite a grin yet. He was still in mourning for his wife after all. His gray suit was the lightest she'd seen since she had met him, but she was sure it would take some time before his mourning colors turned to white.

Margaret looked down at Samuel snuggled into her side. She wrapped her arm around him, rubbing the soft velvet on his shoulder with her thumb. "I am," she confessed. "Being away from the palace will do me good."

"It will do us all good, I think." Rowan reached across the carriage and squeezed her hand. "I have written a note and sent it with one of my men to the Count of Reung, asking him to host us for a time."

"Do you think he will?" Margaret raised her brows. "It isn't much notice for us to arrive and send for the extra food."

Rowan leaned back with a nonchalant shrug. "Hosting a duke would be a great honor for him. The chance he'll say no is low."

"I hope he will." Margaret looked out the clear window in the side of the carriage. "I would like for this trip to last as long as possible."

The longer she was away, the longer the rumors of her affair with the king would have to die down. She was lucky Rowan didn't believe them. Especially since they were true. When she had returned to court, the king had given her a choice of being executed as a traitor or becoming his mistress, and she had chosen her life. Not that it was much of a choice, or much of a life.

Rowan smiled, eyes softening. "We can make it last as long as we can get away with."

1

A slow smile spread across her face. There was nothing she would have liked more.

"Your Grace!" The call was quiet, but it caught their attention.

Margaret and Rowan both looked out the window of the carriage. A man was riding toward them, his wind-bitten face red.

"Is that who you sent to the Count of Reung?"

"It is." Rowan unlatched the window in the door of the carriage, opening it for the rider.

Margaret was relieved—they'd find out one way or another if their week's travel toward the Count of Reung's lands was for naught.

"Your Grace." He handed the note to Rowan through the carriage window, bowing his head to the both of them.

Rowan broke the blue wax seal, quickly reading it. "The count would be happy to host us. He says his children are looking forward to seeing Samuel again."

Letting out a sigh, Margaret slumped back against her plush seat in the carriage. "Good news, then. I was beginning to worry when we hadn't heard anything back."

"Elias probably stayed a day to rest his horse and himself," Rowan said. "Which we should probably do. Samuel is getting restless as well." He slapped the side of the carriage for it to pull to a stop.

"I'm sure we could all do with stretching our legs a bit." Margaret looked down at Samuel, his legs kicking against the seat. Once Rowan got out, she followed suit. "I'll have Sarah arrange a light lunch for us."

"Thank you." Rowan pulled Samuel out of the carriage and set him to run with a light pat on his shoulder. "Go straight to Diana!"

It was a pleasant place to stop. They were surrounded by trees on one side to give them cover and could see anyone approaching on the flat plains to the other side. No doubt, Captain Vojvo would be pleased with its built-in safety. Margaret inhaled deeply, closing her eyes. Wind blew across her face, filling her with a freshness that could only be brought by nature.

She couldn't believe she was really away from the king and the palace. It almost felt like a dream; she would wake up from at any moment and find herself next to Sorren once more. She opened her eyes again when Rowan touched her arm lightly.

"You look relaxed." The wind tossed his wavy hair in front of his crinkling eyes.

Margaret reached up and brushed it from his face. "I am." She smiled, linking her arm with his. "Shall we join everyone?"

Rowan took her hand and squeezed it gently. "I think I'd like a few more moments of time with you before we have to deal with anyone else."

Margaret looked up at him, taken aback by the way his eyes had gone soft. "Oh?"

"We have so few moments of being truly alone." He gently cupped her cheek, slowly dragging his thumb across it. "I hope that will change soon."

A shiver went down to her stomach as she leaned her cheek into his hand. "I hope so too." She watched him swallow as he looked down at her and started to lean closer.

"Father!" Samuel ran up and shook the bottom of Rowan's jacket, jolting them out of their trance. "Come play with me!"

Margaret stepped back, turning her head away as she rolled her lips between her teeth. The last time he had tried to kiss her, the king interrupted them before he could. It seemed Samuel had the same talent. "I'll ask Sarah to oversee our lunch."

Rowan looked at her regretfully. "Thank you."

She walked to where the servants were starting to set up a temporary camp, hands on her hot cheeks to cool them. A small canopy was being erected over the seats Margaret would share with Rowan and Samuel, their guards hammering in the stakes to ensure it stayed there through lunch.

"My lady?" Sarah asked when Margaret approached. "Are you all right?"

"I am." She debated telling Sarah about the near kiss. "His Grace would like for lunch to be served shortly." Margaret would keep that for herself a little while longer.

"Right away, my lady."

Margaret's stomach tightened as they pulled up the drive to the Count of Reung's home. She had never been before, and it was far grander than she had expected.

The stone walls grayed in different shades, weathered over the years. It looked like it would withstand the ages, and already had. Ivy climbed on parts of the

3

house, aiding in its presence rather than detracting. Windows lined the front, the glass being clear flat panes like the palace, instead of thick and rippled like a droplet had fallen into a glass pond. They must be very well off—even Margaret had not taken the plunge in replacing the remaining rippled glass in her family home, due to the expense.

There was a single walkway made of gravel to the front of the manor through a stone gate. The household staff fanned the front door, hands clasped in front of them, while the family stood in the middle. The lady of the house looked particularly severe, her mouth in a firm line.

Margaret looked to Rowan when the carriage came to a stop. "Are they nice?"

"Very," Rowan said. "You'll love each other." He got out when their butler opened the carriage door and then turned to offer his hand to Margaret. "Ready?"

Margaret nodded, clasping his hand tightly. She was nervous—this was the first time she visited anywhere with her title of countess intact.

Rowan brought Margaret in front of the count's family, her hand still in his. "Lord Reung, Lady Albwin, may I present to you Lady Dorcia?"

A smile erupted on Lady Albwin's face. "Lady Dorcia, it's a pleasure to finally meet you."

A thrill went through her, being called Lady Dorcia. "Lady Margaret will be fine." It wasn't exactly proper with her being the Countess of Dorcia, but she was unmarried, and unmarried ladies were rarely called by their surnames.

"You both honor us with your presence, Your Grace, my lady." Lord Reung bowed his head to them. "Please, come in, and the servants will get your bags unpacked."

Margaret looked back to Sarah and Vojvo, who were already taking some of her trunks off one of their wagons. "My lord, we have quite a large party—is there space for them in the servant's quarters, or should we have some of the guards set up tents a distance from the house?"

Lady Albwin, the Countess of Reung, surveyed their group, the smile once again gone from her face. "We only have room for a few—we certainly didn't think you'd have such a large party."

Margaret supposed that Rowan hadn't mentioned anything other than they were traveling. "Once we know where, I'll have my captain oversee the set up and manage the men to ensure they don't disturb the house."

"My apologies, Lady Albwin," Rowan said, "I should have said how large our party was."

They followed the family into the house, and Margaret had to refrain from gasping. The inside was as lavish as the outside suggested. It reminded her of the palace in the overwhelming wealth hanging from the walls. She supposed that's what centuries of having a title afforded a family—amassed wealth that could be displayed.

Margaret once again felt the newness of her family's title; even though she was richer than them by far, it would take her five years of total income to even come close to purchasing the wealth dripping from the walls. One day, she would make sure her family could stand next to the ancient houses with no discernible difference.

The housekeeper came to stand by Margaret's elbow. "My lady, Your Grace, if you'll follow me, I'll show you to your rooms."

"Dinner will be served at eight," Lord Reung said. "We're sure you'll want to rest until then. Samuel can stay in the nursery with the other children. Nanny won't mind an extra child, and his caretaker can have a few hours to herself."

Margaret followed the housekeeper. She was led to her rooms first and let out a sigh, thankful to be in the plush room. Everything from the pillows to the chairs looked like it was stuffed to the brink of explosion. Her feet and back suddenly ached, being pulled toward the promised comfort. It was tempting to flop onto the bed and fall asleep right then, but she knew to wait for Sarah to take her out of her clothes before falling asleep. The last time she hadn't, she was stiff for several days.

Sarah arrived shortly after, followed by several footmen with a few of her trunks. "Let's get you out of those traveling clothes, my lady."

Margaret didn't need to be told twice. She was ready to be cut out if it meant getting into something more comfortable for her rest period. She started removing the pins holding her hair in place, letting out a breath as her locks tumbled down. "Will you bring me my writing supplies when we're done?"

"Of course." Sarah started at the bodice, methodically working until Margaret was out of her riding clothes and into a housecoat. "Will there be anything else you need, Your Ladyship?"

"Something to keep me awake until dinner—whatever they have ready." Margaret looked longingly at the bed. "I'll need it if I'm going to be in here until then."

"I'll see what they have." Sarah gave her a quick curtsy before leaving the room with Margaret's dusty clothes.

Margaret yawned as she stood at the window. She watched some of the men setting up their camp for the duration of their stay. It looked like all of the guardsmen would be roughing it here. She would have to ask Sarah if there had been room for them or if they elected to stay together in solidarity.

Sarah returned quickly with a tray, setting it down on the small table by the windows. "All they had was the coffee that the servants were drinking, my lady."

Margaret tried not to laugh. The last time she had drunk coffee had been with Liam, and they'd had an argument over it. "It's perfect. I remember it being rather pleasant."

Sarah poured a small cup of black liquid and added a small amount of cream. "I'll be back in a few hours to ready you for dinner. Call for me if you need anything before then."

"Thank you, Sarah." Margaret sat in front of the tray, pulling out a piece of parchment as her lady's maid left. It was time to write to Sorren again.

It was her least favorite task, but it was worth doing to be away from the palace. Margaret would send him platitudes, as always, and tell him where they were and how long they anticipated they would stay before moving on—even when it was them camping for a day or two to rest the horses and the party. She didn't want to leave any chance he would find her letters insufficient and request her return.

She wouldn't ruin her chance at freedom.

 **2**

ueen Lillian was furious.

She watched her husband mope around publicly, pining for Lady Margaret like a lovesick boy, now that she was on her travels. Lillian was humiliated by the public attention he was giving that harlot.

Lady Margaret was a festering thorn in her side. Her husband normally tired of his mistresses but had yet to tire of this one. Lillian knew the reason why: Lady Margaret reminded the king of his former lover, Lady Catherine Doremis. Catherine had been the only woman that Lillian was scared Sorren would leave her for. At least, until Margaret had come back to court a grown woman, looking much like her mother.

Lillian sneered at the thought of Catherine. Whoring must run in that family.

She was happy Lady Margaret was gone. It would give Lillian a chance to get her husband back into her bed and away from his mistress.

She had done everything she could to thwart their relationship, even going so far as to ruin the celebrations for Sir Adam by telling him what Lady Margaret had done to get him into his chivalric order. But nothing seemed to faze her; the whore just kept getting more and more for her troubles. His Majesty had given the harlot her title and more lands to supplement her income, and even given her jewels from the Queen's own collection. It had made Lillian sick every time she saw Margaret wearing them. Lillian just couldn't seem to be rid of the stupid girl.

The queen had to get rid of that woman as soon as possible—more permanently than a tour of her lands.

Lillian went to her husband's private chambers to speak with him. "Your Majesty?" she called out gently as she entered the room.

"What do you want?" Sorren demanded of her from the plush wingback chair he sat in, a crystal goblet filled with an amber drink in one hand and a crumpled letter in the other.

Lillian's lip curled. Lady Margaret had left only two weeks ago, and her husband was already wallowing in drink. She was sure he felt this was Catherine leaving him all over again. She went to her husband and took the drink from his hand. "It is too early in the day for such things."

Sorren stood, his eyes flashing. "Give me my drink back."

"You have things to do," Lillian chided. "Lands to rule over, not sitting here wallowing in your mistress's absence."

He sneered at her. "Do not presume to tell me what to do. I am your husband, and I am your king."

"Then act like a king and not a lovesick commoner," Lillian told him coldly.

Sorren raised his hand for a moment before bringing it down to his side in a clenched fist. "Don't you dare speak to me that way."

Lillian hesitated before setting his drink on the table next to him. "I'm sorry."

Sorren flopped back into his chair with a heavy breath, caging half of his face with one hand. He rubbed his forehead with his middle finger, his thumb digging into his cheekbone the longer he did the motion. The letter remained tightly in his other hand.

"May I see it?"

"What?" He furrowed his brow at her.

Lillian motioned to the parchment. "The letter. May I see it?"

Sorren sighed, holding it out for her. "It doesn't say anything important. None of her letters do."

Letters? Lady Margaret had barely left! How many had she sent?

Lillian skimmed through the contents. There were a lot of flowery sentences that said absolutely nothing of substance. Maybe she could convince Sorren he meant nothing to Lady Margaret one day—there was certainly zero indication she had any feelings for him in this letter. The only interesting thing in it was where they were staying.

Rubbing her lips together, Lillian looked over the letter at Sorren. He had picked up his drink again and was sipping it. "Lady Victoria—my Lady of the Bedchamber—her husband has family by the Count of Reung."

Sorren squinted at her, his mouth in a slight grimace. "And?"

"That is where Lady Margaret will be for some time if this is to be believed." Lillian handed him back the letter. "You could send Lady Victoria and Lord Hargrave to 'visit their family' and have them check on Lady Margaret for you. Give you a real report, not just platitudes."

Sorren took his hand from his face, a smile spreading. He stood and wrapped his arms around her, kissing her soundly. "A marvelous idea."

Lillian rested her hands on his chest. He hadn't kissed her like that in some time. It had been long before Lady Margaret came along—long before even Lady Catherine. "Is it?"

"It is." He rested his forehead against hers. "They're both in the palace?"

"They are." She closed her eyes, savoring the closeness.

"Summon them here." Sorren kissed her again before he pulled away, going to his writing desk.

Feeling dazed, Lillian shook her head. "Yes, of course." She went to the corner of the room where a black velvet rope hung and pulled it to summon a servant. "Shall I wait with you for them?"

"I would like that." He quickly wrote a letter, sealing it with the impression of his ring in the wax before she could come close to reading it.

Lillian frowned. It would be pushing too much now to ask him what he'd written. She had only just made a step forward with him for the first time in years. She poured herself a drink while she waited for a servant to appear.

When Christian arrived, Lillian told him where the couple would likely be and to bring them immediately. "And His Majesty's favorite lunch." She hesitated, looking back at her husband for a moment. "For two."

Christian coughed, heat creeping up his neck as his eyes went wide. "I—"

"Second favorite, Christian," Sorren called from his seat. "Bring the second favorite for two."

Lillian looked between the two, furrowing her brow at Christian's panic and then relief.

"Right away, Your Majesty." Christian wasted no time leaving the room.

"Am I missing something?"

"My favorite lunch is something you've never been interested in," Sorren said. He motioned to the chair opposite him. "Come, sit with me."

Lillian decided to let it go—not knowing was likely for the best. She was doing all of this for the sake of progress and saving her marriage, not to get into more fights. She went to him, picking up the drink she had poured earlier. She sat, waiting for him to speak first.

Sorren took a long sip of his drink, seemingly content to remain silent.

Trying to appear at the same ease as her husband, she gently swirled the drink in her hand to let it air. Lillian didn't want to seem too eager or discontent at the lack of conversation. It was a careful balance she always had to keep around her husband. There was no telling how he would react in any given situation.

As the moments dragged on in silence, the hackles rose on Lillian's neck one by one. She couldn't take it anymore.

"Do you—"

"Your Majesties, Lord and Lady Hargrave," Christian announced as he came through the door.

The pair followed him, bowing and curtsying to them both, murmuring their honorifics.

Sorren eagerly stood, his face the brightest she had seen since before Lady Margaret left. "Thank you for coming. I have a task for you both."

"A task, Your Majesty?" Lord Hargrave looked at Lady Victoria quizzically before turning back to them. "For us?"

"Her Majesty has ingeniously pointed out that you have family near where I have someone dear to me staying." Sorren grinned at her like she had given him a prized horse. "I want you to deliver this letter to her" —he pulled it from the table, holding it out to the lord— "and give me a report on how she is on your way to see your family."

"Sir, I don't think we have a visit plan—"

Lady Victoria put a hand on Lord Hargrave's arm, smiling warmly at the king as she took the letter from him. "We'd be honored to do it, Your Majesty. It's been far too long since we've seen Mother Hargrave, and this gives us the perfect opportunity."

Lord Hargrave looked at her sharply before plastering an obviously fake smile on his face. He couldn't hide the annoyance on the rest of his body, his back rigid as he said, "Yes, of course. It will be wonderful to see my family again."

"Good." Sorren waved his hand toward the door. "Now, go. You have packing to do. You'll be leaving in the morning."

Lillian couldn't be sure, but she could have sworn she heard a strangled noise escape Lord Hargrave as Lady Victoria assured the king they would bring back a thorough report. The pair backed out of the room, Lord Hargrave's face getting redder the closer to the door they got. She had put a hand to her mouth to keep from laughing.

"What's so funny?" Sorren asked when the door was closed.

Lillian inhaled deeply to compose herself. "Lord Hargrave hates his mother. I wouldn't be surprised if we hear news of her falling down the stairs by the time they return."

He let out an amused grunt. "A small sacrifice." Sorren took her hand in his, kissing her knuckles. "Thank you for your help."

A thrill went through her. "It was my pleasure."

"We still have some time before lunch will arrive," he said slowly. "Shall we make use of it?"

Lillian gave him a wistful smile. "We shall."

This would certainly be a wonderful first step in reconciliation.

3

After three weeks of exploring the lands, a hunt, and learning about the history of several of the artifacts in the home, Lady Albwin decided it was time they had a large dinner party. Margaret waited for Rowan at the top of the stairs so they could go down to dinner together. There would be several guests Margaret didn't know, and she wanted him with her to bolster her confidence. He was well settled into his title, whereas she had wrapped herself in airs that she had no right to until recently and faltered easily on her own. Sometimes, she still had trouble believing the king had finally granted her the title.

She smiled when Rowan came around the corner. "There you are."

"Were you waiting long?" Rowan straightened his light gray dinner jacket. "My valet found a hole as he was putting it on and had to fix it."

"No, not long." Margaret looked him over. He looked very fine in the plain suit, lacking the silver collar he would have worn at court with the king. "Shall we?"

"We shall." Rowan offered her his arm, escorting her down the wide curved staircase.

There were several people gathered around the fireplace, chatting. The conversation broke off when they approached, and they bowed or curtsied to Rowan. One of the footmen swooped in to offer them glasses of wine. Margaret certainly wouldn't decline—she would need it to get through a dinner with this many people.

Lord Reung motioned toward one of the women. "Your Grace, Lady Dorcia, may I introduce you to Lady Cecilia, wife to Sir Anthony du Burg?"

"An honor," Rowan said.

"Have you been enjoying your time here, Your Grace?" she asked.

"It has been a lovely respite away from the chaos of being a courtier." Rowan looked to Margaret, the corner of his mouth turning upward. "And I've enjoyed the company I've been keeping."

"And you, Lady Dorcia?"

"I have very much enjoyed getting to know Lord Reung and Her Ladyship." Margaret smiled at her hosts. "They've made us feel very welcome."

"It's been a pleasure having you here, Lady Dorcia," Lady Albwin said.

Margaret felt a small boost of confidence. She turned sharply when the doors to the dining room opened, and a footman stood on each side.

"Shall we go through?" Lord Reung asked, looking between his wife and Margaret.

Margaret was sure he was trying to figure out whom he was supposed to escort into the room since they were the same rank, but she was a guest.

Rowan made the decision for him, offering his arm to Margaret. "After you, my lord."

Lord Reung took his wife's arm, going first into the dining room and depositing Lady Albwin in her spot at the table.

Margaret and Rowan followed suit, and Margaret was dismayed to find that she and Rowan were seated on opposite ends of the table. She would do well enough, she supposed, as long as she listened more than she spoke.

The table filled quickly, except for two seats, and the footmen wasted no time in filling guests' cups and serving the first course.

Margaret furrowed her brow. "Is someone else joining us tonight?"

Lady Albwin looked to the empty chairs. "Ah, yes—they'll only be a bit late, so they asked we serve the first course without them."

"Who else is coming?" one of the other guests asked.

Lord Reung grinned. "It seems our table is to be graced with a fair few from the palace this week. Lady Margaret, you should recognize Lady Victoria and Lord Hargrave."

"Lady Victoria will be here?" Margaret clenched her hands in her skirt under the table and tried not to exude the panic within her. Lady Victoria and the now Dowager Duchess Cecily had been the worst of the ladies when Margaret was in the queen's retinue.

"It was quite the surprise to get her letter," Lady Albwin said. "We've only briefly spent time with them."

It was Sorren, no doubt, sending them to check on her and make sure she was behaving while she was away. Would this be a constant for her? Would she have to always look over her shoulder for the next spy?

Margaret's eyes met Rowan's. His narrowed as he watched them—seemingly disturbed as she was that people from the palace were following them. Maybe she was wrong, and it was just a coincidence, but she couldn't shake the feeling this would be normal for them. She would have to test her theory and choose someone of no importance to the king and stay with them next. If someone showed up after she told the king of their plans, she would never have any peace on this sojourn with Rowan.

"How long will they be staying?" Margaret asked.

"Just the night." Lady Albwin took a sip of her wine. "They're on their way to visit Lord Hargrave's family in Bomack."

Maybe it *was* just a coincidence then.

Starting to relax, Margaret listened to the conversation across the table. She could not follow much of it, but it was nice to hear something other than court gossip for once. She looked at Rowan again. He was enjoying himself, engaged in animated conversation with Lord Reung.

If she were being honest, she was jealous of how easily Rowan was able to talk to others. She felt she had been trained for only one thing by her mother—being a good wife to a high-ranking husband, not a conversationalist. Margaret was more skilled in arranging flowers and looking lovely, not bonding with others. Even once her mother abandoned them, it was just her and Papa, who couldn't talk to her any longer. And once she was with Liam and the Gollacks, she was content to let them do most of the talking. She mostly gave orders to everyone else.

The door to the dining room opened, startling her from her thoughts. Margaret paled when she saw Lady Victoria. The men stood until Lady Victoria and Lord Hargrave were seated.

"We're so pleased you could join us tonight." Lady Albwin beamed, a wide smile stretching across her face. "We've been truly honored by all the auspicious company."

Lord Hargrave nodded to her. "We're grateful you were able to host us on such short notice." He sounded pleasant despite the scowl on his face.

"Lady Dorcia, it's lovely to see you again." Lady Victoria smirked, brows quirking slightly. "We miss you in the queen's chambers."

Margaret doubted it. She disliked Lady Victoria as much as the older woman disliked Margaret. Regardless, she said, "It warms me to know that. Maybe one day I'll be able to rejoin you."

"Why did you leave, Lady Dorcia?" Lady Cecilia asked.

"I—"

"Oh, she didn't leave—she was asked to leave." Lord Hargrave guffawed, taking a sip of his wine. "I doubt she'll ever see the queen's chambers again."

Margaret's stomach dropped. She knew people gossiped about her, but this was malicious. "Lord Hargrave—"

"What?" He looked at her defiantly. "Is it not true? Were you not dismissed for sleeping with His Majesty?"

Blanching, Margaret stood. She looked at Rowan, wide-eyed. Would this be the moment he found out? He wasn't looking at her but at Lord Hargrave, his face stony.

Chairs scraped around her as the men of the table rapidly tried to stand with her as etiquette dictated they should. "Lord Hargrave, you're doing nothing but spewing scurrilous rumors, and I won't sit here and listen to it." She nodded to her hosts. "I'm sorry for ruining the evening. I think I'll retire to my room for the rest of the night."

"We'll send the rest of your dinner up to your room," Lady Albwin said, avoiding Margaret's eyes.

"That's all right. I can't say I'm hungry any longer, and I don't want to overwork your servants."

"I'll escort you," Rowan said, dropping his napkin on the table with little grace before circling the table to stand next to Margaret. "And if you could, I would like my dinner in my room, Lady Albwin. I do not wish to be in the company of Lord Hargrave any longer."

"As you like, Your Grace," she said slowly.

"And we'll be leaving as soon as we're able tomorrow." Rowan offered his arm to Margaret. "Goodnight to you, Lord Reung."

Margaret took Rowan's arm as though it was her lifeline—in fact, it was. He was supposed to be her way out of the trouble she had gotten herself in. She didn't know if she could keep her relationship with the king a secret from Rowan after this—not with so many people saying it. Honestly, she didn't know how he still disbelieved the rumors. She suspected he was being willfully ignorant.

Rowan led her to the stairs silently. She looked up at him, but he was looking straight ahead. Margaret swallowed hard—perhaps he was starting to believe. He stopped at her room. "Will you be all right?"

Margaret nodded, afraid to speak. After a moment with him not leaving, she asked, "Will you?"

Picking up her hand, he kissed it. "Don't worry about me. I'll see you in the morning."

She waited until he was out of sight before going into her room. Margaret leaned her forehead against the door. Was she losing him? She didn't know what she would do if he abandoned her as well. Accept her destiny to always remain at the king's side? That would be a fate worse than death for her. She'd rather fling herself from a balcony like she'd threatened him with.

Margaret pulled the bell in the corner to summon Sarah from the servant's hall, taking off what little she could without help before her lady's maid arrived.

"My lady, what are you doing up here?" Sarah's brow furrowed, looking over her mistress. "The dinner is only on its second course. Did you spill something on your dress?"

"Lady Victoria and her husband are here from the palace." Margaret sighed heavily. "Lord Hargrave wasted no time in telling everyone I was the king's mistress. They'd barely sat down before he just blurted it out."

Sarah blanched. "What did His Grace do?"

"Almost nothing. He requested the rest of his dinner in his room and took me to mine." Margaret covered her face. "We're leaving tomorrow now."

"I'll let everyone know." She started removing the pins from Margaret's bodice. "What are you going to do?" she asked hesitantly.

"I don't know." Margaret shook her head, letting out a heavy breath as her shoulders sagged. "Hope that His Grace doesn't change his mind about courting me."

"You could always secure his courtship in other ways." Sarah shrugged. "It's done all the time in Mekhor."

"And what would that be?" Margaret turned when her bodice was off, unlacing her skirts to step out of them.

Sarah started unlacing her corset. "The same thing you do with the king, but with the promise of marriage."

Margaret sighed heavily. "It's tempting, but that would only add credence to the rumors. I have to win over Rowan with nothing but flirtation."

"Do you think you will?" Sarah asked. "Does he still believe you?"

"I don't know." Margaret shook her head. "I'll see in the morning how he reacts to me."

"Let's hope he doesn't treat you any different." Sarah stripped her until Margaret was in her shift. "Would you like me to take down your hair, or would you like to do it yourself?"

"I can do it myself, thank you." Margaret pulled her robe from off the bed, putting it on. "You should take the rest of the evening to yourself. I know you've been working extra with us being away from the palace."

"Thank you, my lady." Sarah gave her a small curtsy before leaving the room.

Margaret sighed, taking the pins out of her hair before flopping onto the bed. She covered her face and groaned. If only she had gone with Liam. None of this would be happening to her—the constant worry of who would find out when, the humiliation that came with the whispers and looks. She could have been living a simple life on some farm with chickens and pigs, and the Gollacks could have moved onto their property to live their golden years in peace. She'd trade anything for that life now, but there was no escaping the king and her responsibility for her people.

The candles in her room were burning low when a knock sounded on her door. Margaret stood and answered it. She started when she saw Lady Victoria, the last person Margaret expected at her door. "What are you doing here?"

Lady Victoria pulled a letter from her skirts. "The king requested I pass this to you since he knew you would be here."

Margaret tried not to roll her eyes. This was the first letter she'd received from him with her constant barrage of letters to him. She hoped all of his wouldn't be delivered by a lackey. "Is that all?" she asked after she took the letter.

"I don't like this any more than you do," Lady Victoria snapped. "There wasn't a reason for us to be here, but the king wanted to make sure you got this letter."

Why this letter? Margaret looked down at it—seeing nothing special about it— the seal still intact. "I'll be sure to read it tonight."

Lady Victoria nodded before walking away.

Margaret wanted to toss the letter in the fireplace, but her curiosity got the best of her. She sat next to a candle, running her finger under the wax.

My dearest Margaret,
The sun has dimmed in your absence.
I cannot sleep without you here, and I long for the day you return to me. When is it you'll travel back? I cannot bear to have you away long.
I miss the way you—

Margaret threw down the letter. How dare he—how dare he write to her as though they were in love and their relationship weren't based on her self-preservation? It made her sick.

She picked up the letter from the floor. Even just touching it made her queasy. She briefly considered reading the rest but instead threw it into the fireplace, watching it quickly catch and burn. She would have to get Sarah or Vojvo to read them for her from now on to see if there was anything pertinent she needed to know.

Margaret rubbed her face before taking off her robe to get into bed. The sooner she went to sleep, the sooner she could see Rowan and see where they stood.

There was already a flurry of activity in Margaret's room when she woke. Rubbing her eyes, she asked, "What's going on?"

"We need to leave sooner than later," Sarah said, handing one of the housemaids a dress of Margaret's to pack away in her trunk.

"His Lordship is quite angry," the housemaid said. "Lord Reung was in such a tizzy according to his valet."

Margaret sat up quickly. "Did something happen after I went to bed?"

"Oh yes, my lady." The housemaid nearly chortled in excitement while Sarah looked at her reproachfully.

"It seems His Grace wasn't content to let things lie last night and confronted Lord Hargrave," Sarah said as she handed the maid another dress. "There are some bruised knuckles and scrapes to go around."

Margaret covered her face. "This is not at all how I wanted this trip to go."

"I know, my lady." Sarah grabbed one of Margaret's travel dresses and laid it out on the bed. "Anne, could you get Lady Dorcia a bite to eat while I get her dressed?"

Anne nodded, giving Margaret a quick curtsy before leaving.

"Do you know anything of what happened?" Margaret asked when the door closed.

"Only secondhand." Sarah grabbed the more comfortable stays from the trunk to put on Margaret. "His Grace confronted Lord Hargrave in the hall when the men went to bed and told him to recant his dinnertime accusations."

"And?"

"Lord Hargrave refused, so His Grace hit him."

"Rowan *hit* him?"

Sarah nodded, squatting with Margaret's skirt to let her step into it. "Lord Reung asked we leave before breakfast, so as not to cause any more trouble."

"Do you know where His Grace is now?"

"Outside with the party," Sarah said. "His man packed his things last night, so we're all that remains."

"Let's hurry, then. I don't want to let His Grace stew in his anger any longer," Margaret said as she secured her skirt. "Is there anything left in the room after this?"

Sarah shook her head. She looked at the door when it opened. "What took you so long?" she asked Anne when she walked in.

"I had to get Cook to make something fresh." Anne handed Margaret a boiled egg. "I'm sorry, my lady, it's all I could get her to make on the spot."

"Thank you, this will be plenty, Anne." Margaret smiled. "Would you ask one of the footmen to bring my trunks down?"

Anne bobbed and left.

Margaret nibbled on her egg while Sarah finished dressing her, putting her hair in a simple braid. "Shall we?" Margaret asked when Sarah finished.

"You go ahead—I'll check the room one more time." Sarah opened the door for Margaret.

"Be quick." Margaret walked out into the hall, pulling up short at the stairs when she saw Lord Hargrave leaving his room. His eye was a dark purple, and he'd be lucky if it healed fully before he saw his family.

When Lord Hargrave saw her, he turned and went back into his room.

She guessed that settled that then. Margaret hurried down the stairs and went into the back grove, looking for Rowan among the men. She encountered Vojvo first.

"Are you all right, my lady?" he asked. "The men told me what happened."

"I've faced worse." Margaret shrugged, shaking her head. "Have you seen His Grace?"

"He and Master Samuel are with the horses."

"Thank you," she said before going to their makeshift stable. It wasn't hard to spot them. "Your Grace?"

Rowan's head snapped around. His cheek was bruised and his lip split. "Margaret."

She was relieved he was still using her name. "Are you all right?"

"It's not much. Lord Hargrave has a weak arm." Rowan smiled at that briefly.

"He certainly looked worse than you," Margaret commented.

Silence settled between them. Margaret looked down at her hands, tugging at the bottom of her jacket. "Rowan—"

"I know people talk, Margaret," he said. "I know what the rumors are—people have loved to say them as close to me as possible since we started our courtship."

Margaret frowned. "I'm sorry, Rowan. I—"

"I know that rumors will always circle those close to the king, but I will believe what *you* tell me." Rowan picked up her hands, kissing each one. "Are you his mistress?"

Margaret squeezed his hands. "No." She certainly wouldn't call what he was doing to her being his mistress. It was purely a transaction to keep herself alive after helping Liam, the so-called traitor.

She took in a deep breath as she waited for his response. Margaret wanted to tell him. She wanted to tell him more than anything so that she could stop lying to him and constantly worrying what would happen if he found out. But she couldn't. Not now. Not until she was able to secure a proposal and an escape from the king.

"Then, that is the end of that, and we can continue on with our tour." Rowan smiled, letting go of her hands.

Margaret returned one of her own, relief flooding through her, tamping down the guilt she felt. Maybe she could survive this yet.

4

Liam smiled as he watched the pair across the table. Jamie sat close to his new wife, Ellie, arm around her waist and mouth close to her ear. Was this what wedded bliss looked like?

Liam looked to Gretta at his side. She was watching her son with soft eyes, looking up at Liam when he offered his hand on the top of the table. She took it, smiling. Would he want to take that leap with her? They were all but married in name anyway. Liam had thought about what life would have been like with Margaret in the same way, but those thoughts seemed further away the more time he spent with Gretta and her boys.

His boys.

They were his, and he was theirs as he'd promised when he had accepted Gretta.

Liam smiled back at her, lifting her hand and kissing her knuckles. Margaret hadn't needed him once in the years they'd been apart. Maybe he *could* settle. Maybe…he could have with Gretta what Jamie had with Ellie.

"Ma, Da," —Jamie pulled Ellie closer— "we have somethin' we'd like to tell ye."

"What is it?" Gretta squeezed Liam's hand.

Ellie blushed, a shy smile breaking across her face. "We're expectin'."

"Already?" Liam was taken aback. Jamie and Ellie were still children themselves—at least, to Liam they were. He'd watched Jamie grow and mature into the man in front of him over the last two years. "You've only been married two months."

Gretta hit Liam's arm with the back of her hand, frowning at him. "How quickly they want bairns is nae our business."

It was Jamie's turn to blush. "Aye…Ellie didna want to waste any time."

"We're happy for you, no matter when it happens." Liam lifted his glass. "To you and your child."

Gretta lifted her glass as well. "Aye, we couldn't be happier."

Ellie put a hand on her stomach as Jamie lifted his glass to them. "To the grandparents."

Warmth filled Liam's chest. He wrapped his arm around Gretta, squeezing her to his side. He was going to be a grandfather.

"I understand congratulations are in order," Jossnon said when Liam walked into the forge. He clapped him on the shoulder, a grin wide on the smith's face.

"News spreads fast." Liam gave him a shy smile. He was excited but cautious. Things often happened in the first few months.

"Gretta's been tellin' anyone an' everyone who stops by The Smiling Fox." Jossnon chuckled. "I couldna no hear it if I tried."

"She's excited." Liam pulled out a steel bar, looking over it before putting it into the coals. "We both are."

They worked for a time, the only sound between them was the hammers against steel. He hoped they wouldn't have many customers, or— He frowned, stopping his hammering. "Joss?"

Jossnon grunted, not looking up from his work.

"Have you thought of hiring someone to run the front of the shop so we don't have to stop our work?" Liam didn't know why he never thought of that before—especially since he was the one to stop and take orders. Jossnon could charge more if people were excited to order from the Hero of Chenalieu.

Jossnon stopped, looking at Liam. "I suppose we've done well enough to hire another."

"Where do we keep the heavy parchment?" Liam asked, setting down his tools. "I'll set a page out now."

"Same place as the small pouches," Jossnon said.

"Do you care who fills the position—man or woman?" Liam asked when he came back.

Jossnon shook his head. "I dinna care—whoever fits best."

Liam wrote out a few requirements, ending the call sheet by saying all are welcome to apply. He nailed it to the front of the smithy. When he came back in, he said, "I suspect we'll have a few applicants by the end of the day."

"I'm sure." Jossnon sighed, rubbing the back of his neck with a sad look. "There aren't enough jobs to go around as the town grows—not yet, anyway."

Liam talked to each applicant as they came. They needed someone personable, and Liam had yet to find one. Jossnon would have taken the first man who had walked in. He'd been knowledgeable enough but had a cold demeanor Liam was worried would scare away customers. A few others had only been looking for work and were unable to tell Liam what a few of the basic items they sold were for. A young lady Liam had never seen before walked into the smith holding the call sheet he had nailed on the wall.

Liam frowned. "You're supposed to leave that out there so others see it, young lady."

She handed it to Liam. "Nae need," she said. "Ye'll no be needin' to see anyone else."

Jossnon let out a surprised laugh. "Ye're a cheeky one, are ye no?"

She shook her head. "No, sir. I just ken my worth."

"What makes you think you'd be a good fit here?"

"I ken a bit about what ye do here from my brother-in-law's forge in Esmelar, and I ken what the women are askin' for if their husbands send them." She gave them a grin. "And I ken men are no opposed to buyin' more from a pretty wee lass."

Jossnon hid his laugh behind a cough. "Aye, that is true."

"What's your name?" Liam asked.

"Joanna McBrie, sir."

Liam looked back to Jossnon—he only shrugged and went about his business. "Well, Miss McBrie, let's start you off on a two-week trial and go from there? You'll need to be here no later than nine in the morning, and you'll be paid two silver stral a day."

"When can I start?"

"If you'd like to stay a bit now, I can show you where everything is, and you can start in the morning." Liam folded the call sheet and set it on their kindling pile. She had been right after all. "Or I can come in early in the morning once my boys go off to work."

"I can have a look around now," Joanna said hurriedly. "I wouldna want to impose upon yer mornin'."

Liam wiped his hands with the rag that was always stuffed in his apron pocket. "If you'll follow me?" He waited until she started to move before walking into the back where they kept most of their supplies. It was a short tour—the main portion of the space was where the forge was.

"Do you have any questions?"

Joanna scanned the room slowly. "Will ye be needin' me to clean all of this, or just the front room?" Her gaze finally settled on Liam. "An' will ye be makin' any improvements to the front of the shop to make it more appealin' to customers?"

"I, uh—" Liam was taken aback. He looked to the front of the shop. There was plenty there for the comfort of a customer—a chair to wait in if there was more than one person waiting, a table to set their wares on for measurement or while a customer paid. What more could they need? "Why don't you have a think on it and tell us ways you think we could improve the space, and we'll talk about it when you're ready?"

"And the cleanin'?"

"Just the front unless you decide you want to clean something else."

"All right." Joanna nodded. "I'll see ye in the mornin'."

Liam waited until she'd left before turning to Jossnon. "What's wrong with our front room?"

Jossnon shrugged. "She'll certainly tell us."

"I have a feeling she'll tell us a lot of things." Liam laughed. Joanna certainly had some gumption to her.

Joanna was already at the smithy when Liam arrived the next morning, counting the items already made and hanging on the wall, then recording them on a piece of parchment.

"What are you doing?"

"Ye have no inventory," Joanna said after she wrote something on the parchment. "I'll no be able to tell a customer what we have wi'out havin' to check each time."

Liam looked to Jossnon, who was starting to heat the forge—he only shrugged. "We didna need one when we spent the day in here."

"It is pretty smart," Liam admitted. "Do you need any help?"

"Och, no—ye go on about yer business," Joanna said, her eyes still on the inventory. "Jossnon's already checked my list before I started countin'."

Liam didn't suspect they would need the two weeks to figure out if they wanted to keep her on or not. She was going above and beyond on her very first morning.

When she was done with her inventory, she looked around for something to do. "D'ye have any way for an irregular customer to leave an order when they need it?"

"What d'ye mean?" Jossnon asked. "They can come when we're here an' ask for what they want."

"But what if they cannae come durin' the day an' miss ye?" Joanna asked. "If they had a way to order in the night, ye could get more work."

"Let's hold off on that for now," Liam said. "We don't want to change things too quickly."

A petulant pucker twisted Joanna's lips, and her brow furrowed. She opened her mouth to say something but paused, letting out a breath as her hands dropped to her waist. "As ye say."

Jossnon looked to Liam with his brows raised. Liam suspected the smith was thinking the same thing he was: they would likely have the order forms by the end of the week.

Liam set to his work as Joanna poked around the smithy. He hadn't realized how long they had been working until Joanna asked what she could get them for their midday meal.

"If ye take a few copper stral down to the Smilin' Fox, Gretta there will ken what we want," Jossnon said. "And ye get herself whatever ye want there."

Joanna did as she was bid, leaving the forge.

Liam waited until he was sure Joanna was gone before saying, "She's a force to be reckoned with."

"We'd best pray to Olam we dinna get run over by her grand ideas." Jossnon shook his head. "She'll have to take one idea at a time."

When she returned with three pasties wrapped in brown paper, Liam and Jossnon put down their tools. "If ye want, ye can leave after lunch, Joanna," Jossnon said. "It's no busy here."

Joanna looked between Liam and Jossnon, her brow furrowing. "Are ye no happy with my work?"

"No, we're very happy," Liam said quickly. "This is just our slow day."

Joanna still looked hesitant. "Are ye sure?"

"Yes, I promise," Liam said. "Now enjoy your lunch—Gretta always makes wonderful food."

After they started eating, Simon came into the smithy with a few bottles of something in his hands. "Da, Ma said ye forgot—" He stopped when he caught sight of Joanna. "She, uh… She said ye, uh…ye forgot…" he stumbled.

"Drinks?" Liam supplied.

"Drinks, aye." Simon nodded, not taking his eyes off Joanna. "Ye forgot yer drinks."

Liam looked to Joanna. She had a small smirk on her face as she kept her eyes down. "May I present to you Miss Joanna McBrie?"

"A pleasure," Simon said.

"Joanna, this is my son, Simon," Liam said. "Joanna is the new shop girl I told you about last night."

"I'm pleased to make yer acquaintance, Simon," Joanna said.

Liam waited for Simon to say something, but the boy just continued to stare at Joanna. Liam tried not to laugh—he had never seen Simon so struck before.

Jossnon cleared his throat. "Is there somewhere ye need to be, lad?" Startled, Simon looked to Jossnon. "I, uh…"

"Did Ma send you here on your way back to work?" Liam raised his brows.

"Oh, aye," Simon said. "I'll see ye at home, Da."

Liam waited until Simon was gone before turning to Joanna. "I'm sorry if he made you uncomfortable—I'll have a talk with him."

"Och, no." Joanna waved her hand, smirk sliding off and on her face as she tried to contain her amusement. "He seems harmless."

"He comes in fairly often. You let me know if he becomes a problem." Liam didn't want Simon to scare her off if he was going to be coming in and harassing her.

"I will." Joanna smiled. "I appreciate ye lookin' after me."

"Can we really?" Eli's eyes lit up as he slid off the chair.

Liam looked out the window. It was clear out, and it had been warmer than usual. "Yes, but go bundle up, just in case it gets too cold."

"Ye dinna have to," Gretta said after Eli ran upstairs. "It's yer only day off."

"I don't mind." Liam stood, taking in a deep breath as he stretched. "And he's been asking me to take him since before the weather turned."

Gretta rubbed his arm, smiling. "Then I suppose ye better bundle up as well."

He wrapped an arm around her waist. "Would you mind packing us lunch?"

"Aye, I'll have it ready by the time ye come back down."

Liam kissed her forehead. "Thank you, dearest," he said before he went upstairs to change. After he changed, he packed a small bag of things Eli might need while they were out. There was no end to the things Eli asked for when he was away from home. Liam supposed that was just the way of children.

"Now ye be on her best behavior fer Da, ye hear?" Liam heard Gretta say as he descended the stairs.

"Aye, I will," Eli said.

"Are you ready?" Liam asked as Gretta handed him a bag. When Eli nodded, he kissed Gretta. "We'll get our supplies on the way out."

They stopped by the smithy for hooks and grabbed fishing line from the general store. They could use some of their lunch as bait instead of having to pay for it. He didn't pick up rods—they were outrageously expensive when they could just as easily use a branch for the type of fishing they would be doing.

Eli ran ahead of Liam once they left the town. "Not too far ahead, Duck."

He stopped running, turning to look at Liam. "Duck?"

"My mother used to call me that when I was your age," Liam said. "Duck—like her duckling."

Eli broke into a grin, running back to Liam's side. He slipped his hand into Liam's.

Liam squeezed it, his own smile on his face. As they walked, Liam pointed out the edible plants one could harvest in the colder months. "Why don't we pick some on the way back and surprise Ma?"

Eli nodded excitedly.

Liam waggled Eli's arm when he caught sight of the pond. "Why don't you run ahead and find us some long sticks to fish with?"

Eli squealed as he ran to the tree line behind the pond.

Liam took his time walking to the water, letting Eli have the time to bring him several different branches. He proudly presented them to Liam, his arms barely wrapping around the bundle.

"Great job, Duck." Picking the best out of the bundle, Liam showed Eli how to tie the hooks and the knots needed to keep the line on their makeshift rods. Once Eli was finished with his, Liam stood him in front of the water.

"All right," Liam said, "you just need to flip the hook into the water like this." Liam pulled the stick back and flicked it forward into the water. "See? Now you try."

Eli took the stick, pulling it back over his shoulder the same way Liam did.

Liam looked to the water to see where the hook would land, jumping when he heard a scream from Eli. "What happened?"

Eli cried loudly, not answering.

"What happened?" Liam knelt next to him. "I can't help if I don't know what's wrong."

"The hook!" Eli screamed through his tears. "It's in my bum!"

Liam put his knee up. "Lean forward, and I'll get it out," he said. When Eli leaned on his knee, Liam grabbed the hook. It was firmly in there—he'd have to be careful taking it out. He cut the line, using it to leverage the hook while he pushed the end down. Blood welled around the metal, and Liam stopped to try another angle.

Eli wriggled and cried harder.

"I know, Duck," Liam soothed. "It's almost out." When he finally removed the hook, Liam stood Eli up. "It's all right now."

"I dinna want t'go fishin' anymore, Da." Eli sniffled.

Liam rubbed his back. "I know." Liam put everything away before picking up Eli. "We'll go home right now, and Ma can help us clean this up."

Eli wrapped his arms around Liam's neck tightly, nodding into his shoulder. Liam walked back home, holding onto Eli tightly.

"What are ye doin' back so soon?" Gretta asked when they came into the kitchen.

"We had a little accident," Liam said as he set everything but Eli down.

"What happened?" Alarm raised Gretta's voice.

"He managed to catch himself on the hook." Liam rubbed Eli's back before setting him down. "He wanted to come home after that."

"I never want t'go fishin' ever again."

"Ye dinna have to." Gretta swiped Eli's hair back. "Why dinna ye go up to yer room and have a lay down while I go and get somethin' to clean it with?"

Liam waited until Eli was upstairs before he turned to Gretta. "Is there anything you need me to do since I'm back?"

Gretta shook her head. "Ye go enjoy yer day, and I'll see ye after dinner."

Liam kissed her cheek. "I'll be in the back, likely," he said before walking to the door.

"Liam?" Gretta called.

Liam turned to her expectantly.

"Thank ye fer bein' so good to him."

He smiled. "It's easy when you love them."

5

R elief flooded Margaret when they crossed into her lands. They wouldn't see her home for several more weeks, having only just passed the boundary markers, but just knowing she was on land that was finally hers, something lifted in her chest. Only one thing laid heavy—Rowan had retreated into himself since they left Count Reung's.

Deafening silence hung between them. Even the wheels of the carriage on the bumpy road couldn't break the barrier. He told her he believed what she'd said, but she wondered if they were just words the longer he ignored her.

She looked him over—his blue eyes were illuminated by the light streaming through the carriage window. Samuel was with the servants because he wanted to be with the horses—and they needed a break from his incessant questions. Rowan only looked out the glass pane, his mouth turned slightly downward into a not-quite frown.

Margaret was hesitant to break the silence, but she couldn't stand it any longer. Her knuckles would bruise soon from how hard she was nervously pulling them. "Captain Vojvo said we should arrive at Mr. Persbrant's tomorrow afternoon provided we keep a good pace today."

Rowan turned his eyes to her, slowly blinking. "Who is this Mr. Persbrant again?"

"He's a former Lord General for Dorcia, and he invested in Papa's business when he first started it." Margaret started to pull her knuckles again but smoothed her skirts to her knees to stop herself. "I've never met him in person, so I'm not sure what we should expect."

Nodding, Rowan sighed as he went back to looking out the window. "Hopefully, this visit will be uneventful."

Margaret looked down at her hands. So, she did have reason to worry his words were just words. She wished she could tell him the truth, but she couldn't risk it. While they were with Mr. Persbrant, she would have to work hard to convince Rowan of her lies that she was what she was pretending to be. It would be her only chance.

"We should stop for something to eat soon," Margaret said, gauging the time by looking at where the sun was. "I'm sure Samuel is starting to get hungry."

The corner of Rowan's mouth lifted. "I'm sure we could all use a break from sitting." He tapped the roof of the carriage with his fist, it coming to a stop shortly after. He got out and offered his hand to Margaret.

Smiling, she took it, letting her hand linger longer than needed after stepping out. Margaret kept walking—she didn't want to ruin the effect. She had seen many a woman in court use that trick to pique the interest of their suitors, and she needed Rowan interested in her again. She couldn't lose his favor so soon into their courtship. Not when she needed his position.

Margaret went to Sarah and Vojvo, desperate to turn around to see what the trick had done to Rowan. "Is the duke looking this way?" She kept her voice low so he couldn't overhear her.

Captain Vojvo looked over her shoulder sharply. "He has his eye on you." He squared his shoulders and furrowed his brow. "Is there something I should be concerned about, my lady?"

"No," Margaret said quickly. "He hasn't done anything. I want to ensure his interest remains."

"Ah." The captain's lips pursed. "He seems interested. He's coming this way."

Sarah looked up at Vojvo, her dark hair tumbling over her shoulder, before turning her gaze back to Margaret. "Are you sure this will work?"

"No." Margaret shook her head. "But what other choice do I have?"

She resisted the urge to turn around immediately. Margaret waited until Sarah curtsied to Rowan before she finally did. "Is there something I can do for you?"

Rowan seemed surprised. "I— Well, I was wondering if you wanted me to arrange lunch today?"

It didn't seem like that was what he'd really wanted to ask her. Margaret figured it wouldn't hurt to have him off balance for a little while. "I don't mind making the arrangements. It'll give me a chance to go over our stores and see what we need to make an order ready once we reach Mr. Persbrant's."

Rowan nodded. "I'll attend to Samuel then."

Margaret watched him walk away. She hoped she was doing the right thing. She didn't want him to think she was actually pushing him away.

After they had lunched and the servants had put everything away, Margaret elected to ride on Duchess with Sarah and Vojvo instead of staying in the carriage with Rowan. He wasn't a rider, so she knew he wouldn't join her.

"Are you sure?" Rowan asked.

"It's been some time since you've had Samuel to yourself," Margaret said. "I wouldn't want to deprive you of that." She gestured around them. It was bright and breezy out, the branches of the trees gently tossing in the wind. Only a few clouds dotted the blue sky. "Besides, it's nice enough out, and I won't be too cold."

He hesitated. Rowan rubbed his lips together looking like he wanted to ask her again to join them. Instead, he said, "All right…don't hesitate to join us if you need a rest."

"I won't." Margaret squeezed his forearm before walking toward her party. "Will you have Duchess saddled for me, Captain?"

"Are you certain?" Vojvo furrowed his brow. "You'll be far more comfortable in the carriage with His Grace."

"I think a little distance will help revitalize our courtship," Margaret said. "Or, at least, I hope it will."

Vojvo looked dubious, his eyes squinting slightly. "What is your goal here, my lady?"

Margaret frowned. With a powerful husband behind her, she could leave court and stay away for good. Be as far away from Sorren as she pleased with no commitment to return. She didn't doubt that if she could get Rowan to fall in love with her, he would fight for her to get just that. "Freedom."

Margaret shivered on Duchess. The weather turned as they rode up to Mr. Persbrant's. Glancing at the sky, it looked like it could snow. It was an odd thing to see this far north—rarely did it even get cold. It hadn't snowed there for as long as she could remember. She was starting to regret staying on horseback but wanted to keep herself at a distance from Rowan—even if only for a little while.

She didn't know what she was expecting, but the house seemed to fit what Margaret knew of Mr. Persbrant. It was smaller by far than Lord Reung's home, containing maybe ten rooms in its entirety, made of stone with rounded ends. No doubt it was built to have a reinforced structure in the event of some sort of battle. She expected she'd see many things in the home that hinted at his previous position of Lord General for Dorcia.

Stables jutted out at each end of the home, which Margaret was thankful for. There would be enough room for at least half their horses, and they could build enough of their tents against it to protect the rest from the cold.

Mr. Persbrant was standing outside waiting for them. He hurried down the steps from the covered porch to greet her, his small stomach jiggling on each step. "Lady Dorcia, it's a pleasure to finally meet you," he said once she was helped down from Duchess.

"You as well, Mr. Persbrant." Margaret tried to keep her teeth from chattering while she spoke. "May I present to you His Grace, Duke of Fradure?" Margaret said when Rowan came to her side with Samuel in his arms.

"Let's get you inside, my lady." Puffs of breath surrounded him, blending against his white hair. "I wouldn't even let my servants out in this cold." He stepped aside to let her pass as his butler opened the door.

Margaret hurried inside, letting out a relieved breath when the warmth hit her face.

Rowan followed behind her, rubbing Samuel's back to warm him up. "You'll have a warm bed soon enough."

"We'll try to get as many of your people inside as possible," Mr. Persbrant assured them. "We only have three spare rooms after Your Grace and Your Ladyship are housed—and, of course, the young master."

"Samuel can stay in my room—as well as my valet—if that frees up any space," Rowan said.

"And my maid can stay in mine," Margaret said. "We don't want to have the men suffer the cold if they don't have to."

"How many do you have between you?"

"We're a party of thirty. Fourteen soldiers and the captain—and our servants, of course," Margaret said.

"That might be too many to fit in four rooms," Persbrant said slowly. "We'll keep the soldiers outside with large fires, and we'll split the three rooms between your servants so the young master can still have his own room."

Rowan nodded. "If we could be shown to them?"

"Yes, of course." Persbrant waved to his butler. "Please show our guests to their quarters." He turned back to them, saying, "We'll be serving dinner in an hour, but please don't feel the need to dress grandly for it."

"Thank you, Mr. Persbrant," Margaret said before she went upstairs. She let out a relieved sigh when the door to her room opened. It was far from grand, but Mr. Persbrant liked things simple. In her room was only a bed, a chair by the window, and a standing mirror with an attached basin stand. He would have liked their cottage in Silvica as much as her father had. "Sarah, could you help me take my hair down?"

Setting down her bag at the foot of the bed, Sarah turned to Margaret. "Of course, my lady. Would you like to dress for dinner as you would in Marbon with the Gollacks?"

"I think that would be a welcome reprieve—for me, and Mr. Persbrant."

Sarah took down Margaret's hair, brushing it out while they waited for her trunk. "Do you want it only down, or some out of your face?"

Margaret hesitated. "I think the same style as the last time I saw Liam." It was a sweet style, her hair out of her face save for a few strands to frame it.

Sarah rubbed her lips together as she thought. "It's a very innocent look."

"Exactly." Margaret smiled. "I want the first time Rowan to see me again as an innocent, simple girl."

Margaret's trunk came after Sarah had already finished her hair. Sarah immediately dug through it for a simple house dress. She held it up for Margaret to see. "This should do."

"Oh, yes," Margaret said. It was one of her blue dresses—one of her best colors. "This will do very well."

Sarah quickly undressed Margaret and poured water into the basin in the corner. She wiped down the grime gathered from the day's ride before helping Margaret into the house dress.

"How long until I need to head down?" Margaret looked over her jewels, deciding against it. The simpler the better.

"Only a few minutes." Sarah looked over Margaret in the mirror, pulling out one more strand of hair, curling it around her finger before dropping it.

"I'll head down now so I can have a moment with Mr. Persbrant." Margaret smoothed her skirt, looking herself over briefly. "I'm more than happy for you to stay in the room with me if you don't want to share with the other servants."

"Thank you, my lady," Sarah said. "I'll have my things directed here."

Margaret went back downstairs, finding Mr. Persbrant sitting in front of the fire, his hand in the man's standing in front of him. It looked pale and frail in the younger man's dark hand. She stopped, not wanting to intrude on a private moment.

"Lady Dorcia, please come in," Mr. Persbrant said, letting go of the man's hand as he stood. "May I introduce you to Mr. Vernon Rachne?"

"A pleasure to meet you, Lady Dorcia," he said, bowing his head.

They provided no other information, and it was none of her business. "You as well, Mr. Rachne," she said before turning to Mr. Persbrant as Mr. Rachne retreated to a chair across the room. "Thank you again for allowing us to stay with you. I know we're a much larger party than you expected."

Mr. Persbrant waved his hand. "Think nothing of it. I'm happy to welcome you into my home, and it's high time we met with your father being gone."

"I agree." Margaret smiled. "I plan on visiting the rest of the investors on this tour."

"Good." Mr. Persbrant gestured to a small table with decanters. "May I pour you a drink? I'm sorry to say we don't have any wine."

Margaret hesitated. The last time she'd had a stronger drink was with Lord General Crompton not long before his death, and it had burned her throat to the point of not being able to breathe for several seconds. "I'll have a little of what you're having."

He poured two glasses and added water to Margaret's. He clinked her glass after he handed it to her. "To your father."

Margaret gave him a halfhearted smile. "To Papa," she said before taking a drink with her investor. It was far more pleasant than the last time she had a drink like this. She sat on the small couch by the window with Mr. Persbrant, turning slightly so she could see him clearly. She only got a few sips in before her cheeks started to heat. "I was wondering if I might have an evening of your time to talk about the business. I have some hesitations about some people remaining."

Persbrant cocked his head, a smirk coming to his face. "Would that be a one Mr. Charles Luther you're referring to, my lady?"

Margaret sighed, her shoulders drooping. She was hoping it wouldn't have to come to this, but Charles had turned his back on her first after she kissed him and even more when he found out she was mistress to the king. "It is. I'm not sure what to do with him, and I need to find someone to replace him that can be my man instead of Papa's man."

He nodded along as she spoke. "Since you are meeting with the rest of your investors on this trip, I would ask each of them to suggest a man, and pick the one who is named the most."

It was a good idea. All of her investors had been involved with businesses long before she was even born—they would certainly know who in Anatalia would serve her. "And who would you recommend, Mr. Persbrant?"

Leaning back, he crossed his arms and put the rim of his glass against his mouth while he thought. "Nathaniel Ethum." Persbrant looked to Mr. Rachne, who nodded. "Mr. Ethum is young—perhaps only ten years your senior—but he has a mind for numbers."

When Rowan came into the room, introductions were made once more. He came to Margaret's side, looking her over slowly. "May I speak with you before dinner?"

Margaret looked to Mr. Persbrant, who nodded. "Of course." She stood. "Will you excuse us?" she asked without waiting for an answer before she led Rowan from the room.

"Can we step outside?" Rowan asked, stopping at the door.

Margaret's brow furrowed. "Won't it be too cold?"

"What I have to say won't take long."

Panic fluttered in Margaret's stomach. Maybe the distance she put between them hadn't been a good idea. "All right."

He held the door for her and followed behind. Rowan stopped short when Margaret turned to face him. "You look lovely in this light," he said, gently brushing aside a strand of hair that blew in front of her face.

Margaret smiled demurely. "Thank you."

"I—"

"Yes?" Margaret tried to keep her teeth from chattering, but it was too cold out.

Rowan grabbed her hands, warming them between his. "I don't like the distance that's come between us."

"I'm sorry, I—"

"I know." Rowan squeezed her hands. "I didn't help. I'm going to do better."

"The rumors—"

"They're hard to hear." Rowan looked down at their feet, rolling his lips between his teeth. "But I promise, as I said before, I will believe whatever *you* say about it."

Margaret let out a sigh, her breath clouding around them. "Thank you."

White flakes began to fall as Rowan kissed her cold hands. "Let's get you inside."

Margaret looked out the window, her shawl wrapped tightly around her. It had been snowing on and off for the last two months. She hadn't expected snow this far north—it was usually much warmer this time of year. "I'll need to tell His Majesty we've been delayed," she said when Rowan sat across from her.

Rowan looked dismayed when he looked out the window. "It was kind of Mr. Persbrant to allow us to stay so long."

"I think he's enjoying having all of the guards around." Margaret smiled. Mr. Persbrant had been spending more time with Captain Vojvo and the guard than with her or Rowan.

"I think you're right." Rowan gave her a sly grin. "I can't say I'm disappointed—it gives us plenty of time on our own."

"Especially since Mr. Rachne likes to keep to himself most of the time." Margaret let out a soft laugh, thinking of the pair. "Or with Samuel. He really seems to love him."

"It's quite the thing," Rowan said. "You're the only other person Samuel has so immediately bonded with."

"I'm glad he's getting time with someone who is not in his class, who's not a servant," Margaret said. "It will serve him well when he eventually becomes the next Duke of Fradure to take care of his people."

Rowan furrowed his brows at her. "I—"

"I'm not saying he won't do well if he doesn't, or that he won't be caring otherwise," Margaret said quickly, seeing the anger forming on Rowan's face, "but I've seen many of our peers who are entirely oblivious to anyone but their equals. It isn't right."

"He—"

"Father!" Samuel ran into the room with Mr. Rachne in tow. "Mr. Vernon made me this." It was an intricately carved deer.

"That's beautiful," Rowan said.

"He saw it yesterday on our walk," Mr. Rachne said shyly. "I thought he'd like it to remember his time here."

"You carved this in a day?" Margaret asked, eyes widening as she examined the figurine "That's incredible!"

Mr. Rachne nodded, a small smile on his face.

Margaret looked around the room. There were several carved pieces lining the walls she had never noticed. Surely, they were all thanks to Mr. Rachne.

"Thank you, Mr. Rachne—he'll cherish it forever," Rowan said as he examined the carving.

"These carvings rival what's at the palace," Margaret commented, her eyes now on the ceiling where there were even more carvings.

"Thank you, Lady Dorcia." Mr. Rachne cleared his throat. "I have actually done some of the carving at the palace. It's where Jedediah and I met."

Margaret turned to him, surprise running through her. Neither one of them talked about anything personal between them. "We'll have to look out for your pieces when we return."

"You'll have to let me know if any are still there," Mr. Rachne said quietly. "I would be surprised if they were."

It took a moment for Margaret to realize what he meant. His preferences would be frowned upon and his work not shown to hide any trace of him. "I'll look nonetheless."

The tightness around Mr. Rachne seemed to loosen. "Thank you, Lady Dorcia."

Mr. Persbrant came into the room followed by his butler. "Dinner should be ready in the next hour. Would anyone care for a drink while we wait?"

Mr. Rachne shook his head, sitting across from Rowan and Samuel. Samuel snatched his deer from Rowan's hand and went to sit with him.

"I'll take whatever it is you're having," Rowan said.

"No thank you." Margaret shook her head.

Mr. Persbrant poured Rowan and himself a glass of amber liquid. "One of your guards said he started to feel a warm wind and thinks the snow will finally stop."

"We promise as soon as it's clear enough to leave, we'll get on the road," Margaret said. "I feel like we've been taking advantage of your hospitality."

"Nonsense. It's been a pleasure to have you." Persbrant waved his hand, taking a drink. "In any case, it's nice to get to know whom I've invested in with your father's—and now your—business."

"I suspect the house will feel quite empty when you're gone." Mr. Rachne looked down at Samuel, eyes crinkling when Samuel made the deer run through the air.

Margaret looked out the window. It was no longer snowing, and she couldn't help feeling a little sad about that. She looked back to Samuel and Mr. Rachne, catching the droop in his shoulder as he looked to the window himself. It seemed she was not the only one who was a little sad.

6

ueen Lillian gasped awake when her door slammed open, bolting up onto her elbow. She put a hand to her chest, breathing heavily as her heart pounded.

"Do you know what your son has done?"

She shook her head, gently patting her chest to help her calm quicker after recognizing her husband's voice. "What?"

Heavy footsteps thudded toward her. "Your son," Sorren seethed, "stole a boat from the harbor while he was drunk and crashed it on the cliffs."

"Is he all right?" Lillian tried to shake the panic from her head as she sat up straighter.

Sorren roughly pushed his hand through his hair, a scowl on his face. "Only by dumb luck. He and three others survived—everyone else drowned."

"What was he thinking?" How could Gareth have been so reckless? Lillian swallowed hard against the bile gathering in her throat. "Who was killed?"

"A few crewmen who were sleeping in the boat, Sir Harold and his wife, and a few minor nobles." Sorren sighed heavily. "There are going to have to be consequences."

"He's the heir," Lillian protested. "What could you possibly do? Banish him?"

"I don't know." Sorren ran his hand over his tired eyes. "But it will need to be public."

"But—"

"Lillian," —Sorren grabbed her hand, squeezing it hard— "he's regularly alienated the nobility. It has to be public."

He was right—of course, he was right. They had let Gareth get away with too many things over the years because he was the heir. But if anyone was going to follow him when he became king, the people would need to see that Gareth was willing to take the consequences for his actions.

"When?"

"Tomorrow." Sorren flattened his lips. "It needs to be swift. Notices have already been sent."

Lillian lifted Sorren's hand to her mouth, kissing the back of it. "You should get back to bed. You'll need the sleep."

He tucked a piece of hair behind her ear before he stood. "You should sleep as well. I'll want you there with me as a show of solidarity."

"I'll be there."

Lillian sighed as her husband left. There was no telling what kind of punishment he would dole out to keep the nobles on his side. Even Sorren's pull with the nobles was tenuous with something this big.

She slid down into her silk sheets to sleep. Lillian would be lucky if she managed to get anymore after the distressing news.

Gareth crossed his arms, mouth in a tight frown. "Why are we even doing this?" He nodded his head toward two knights stationed against the wall in formal regalia. "What are they doing here?"

Lillian inhaled deeply, closing her eyes as she rubbed her lips together while she tried to calm her temper. "Because you have to face the consequences of your actions, Gareth."

"But why?"

Sorren let out a noise from the back of his throat, throwing his hands in the air. "You killed people!"

Gareth rolled his eyes. "It's not my fault they didn't know how to swim."

Her mouth dropped open. She knew that they hadn't done all they should have while raising Gareth, but how had he become this callous? She looked to the knights against the wall. Even they looked surprised.

"Theotes above." Sorren clenched his fists in front of him before spreading them out while he let out a frustrated growl. "Just come into the hall when the door is opened for you. I promise you, you won't like what happens if you don't."

Lillian let out another heavy breath before she walked into the hall on Sorren's arm. She nearly stopped when she saw the furious nobles. She'd never seen the throne room so crowded.

Outraged cries erupted, several of the nobles neither bowing nor curtsying to them as they walked past. She didn't doubt if they had food to throw, they would. Lillian could have sworn she heard someone spit.

She swallowed hard. This was not good. Whatever punishment Sorren had in store for Gareth, it would have to be worse to assuage the nobles.

The hall quieted to angry whispers as Sorren first deposited Lillian in front of her throne chair before going to his.

Lillian watched the crowd nervously. Several of the nobles glowered in their direction. Others continued yelling, fists shaking in their direction. She glanced at Sorren—his shoulders stiff as he waited for Gareth to enter.

When the doors opened, Gareth walked in, the two knights flanking him. He waved the gathered nobles, a grin on his face.

Dread weighed heavy in Lillian's stomach as some of the nobles jeered, and others hissed as their son walked toward them.

"Silence!" Sorren yelled, startling Lillian. When the room quieted, he continued, "It's clear based on your behavior that you've heard the tragic news of the boating accident."

"What are you going to do about it?" a nobleman yelled, sparking others to start shouting agreements.

Sorren held up his hand to quiet the room again. "That is the purpose of gathering you all today. My son will be held accountable for his actions."

Gareth scowled, flexing his fingers before clasping them in front of him. "I am ready."

Inhaling deeply, Sorren straightened his shoulders. "You are hereby ordered to pay a fine of five hundred gold tal to each of the deceased's family—"

"That's six thousand tal!" Gareth's face went slack. "That will bankrupt me!"

"You will lose your title as Theotes's Defender as you've taken the lives of several of this court, not through necessity but your recklessness,"—Sorren inhaled deeply with his mouth in a flat line— "and such a person cannot be tolerated among Theotes's chosen. You will also lose your knighthood in the Order of Saint Asesia because I will not inflict on them an agent of chaos when they stand for order and unity." Sorren nodded toward the knights behind Gareth. "Remove his collar."

The knights stepped forward, standing at Gareth's shoulders. They lifted their hands, reaching toward the order's collar.

Gareth slapped away their hands, glaring at his father. "This is too much. You cannot do this to your *heir!*"

The knights paused, looking to Sorren for guidance. Lillian looked between Sorren's back and Gareth. She didn't want to think of what would happen if Gareth refused his punishment, especially in front of the court.

Sorren inhaled deeply, his back becoming impossibly stiff. "Failure to comply with your punishment will result in your confinement in Theotes's Tower until I have deemed a reasonable period of time has passed."

Lillian let out a strangled noise. Stunned looks erupted throughout the gathered crowd. They were, no doubt, as shocked as she. Theotes's Tower was usually only occupied by noble traitors awaiting their executions. What would that say to the people? They would lose confidence in Gareth as the heir and could spark a civil war when it was time for succession.

Gareth stared at his father, shocked. He turned his gaze to her, but Lillian quickly lowered her eyes.

She couldn't help him now. Not without making things worse for him, for their family—for Anatalia.

"Fine." Gareth removed his collar of gold, decorated with sapphires at every interlocking loop, throwing it to the ground in front of him. "Take the titles. I don't care."

Lillian wanted to follow after him as he stormed from the hall, but she couldn't. She had to stand in solidarity with Sorren.

"It is my hope that this will prove to you that I hold you all in the highest regard," Sorren said. "And that I will not let acts such as this stand without swift and harsh punishment." He turned and held his hand out for Lillian.

She took it, letting him escort her back out of the throne room. She waited until they were close to his chambers before she spoke. "Do you not think that was too harsh?"

Sorren sighed, his shoulders drooping. "Some were calling for his banishment last night."

"Banishment!" Gareth was the heir. They couldn't banish him—not without inviting fights for the throne, or worse, invasion from other kingdoms. "How could they?"

"This was the compromise." He shook his head. "I didn't think they would react so poorly to him. Gareth is going to have to be on his best behavior from here on out, or we might have to start thinking about banishment."

Lillian swallowed hard. She didn't know if Gareth *could* be on his best behavior.

7

Margaret's stomach fluttered when she spotted the aged-black brass finials dotting the roof of her family home through the trees. They were almost there. She breathed in deeply, holding it as she tried to control her bubbling excitement.

Letting out her breath, a smile broke out onto her face. There it was. The sandstone had worn into a darker yellow since the last time she had seen it, but it still made her heart flutter. It was far grander than Papa had wanted, but her mother had insisted on building something that would match the other noble houses in splendor.

It had been nearly two years since she had been there last for her father's reburial and funeral service. Margaret had hardly been able to look at the house then, her days consumed with grief and being rushed around from this to that as she tried to catch up with the goings on. But this time was different. She took another deep breath, closing her eyes. She was looking forward to being home for a few months. They would stay for the harvest at the end of Mamonat so Rowan and Samuel could see what her father had started to provide for the Doremis family. It had the added bonus of being able to give the soldiers a well-deserved break in comfort after spending months outdoors in the cold while they were waylaid by the unexpected snow.

The home was only staffed by a dozen or so people when no one was there to keep the rooms and surrounding lands pristine. In the interim, Margaret had made arrangements for any nobleman to stay at the house to rest and replenish their supplies for a small fee, the excess going to the surrounding city to help the less fortunate in Dorcia. She had written ahead and requested the current renter vacate while she and her party were there.

A smattering of people came to the roadside to investigate their traveling party. Margaret smiled, tapping the top of the carriage to get the driver to stop. It slowed to a halt and more people gathered to glimpse inside.

"What are you doing?" Rowan asked. "We're nowhere near your home."

"I'm going to greet my people." Margaret got out of the carriage, looking around at the inquisitive faces.

Vojvo rode up to her when he saw that the carriage had stopped. "My lady, is there anything the matter?"

Margaret held a hand over her eyes to shade them from the sun when she looked up at him. "Not at all, Captain. I'll be honoring my father with alms to the poor. Which wagon was the chest of tholar loaded on to?"

"The second one, my lady."

Vojvo followed her as she grabbed Sarah to carry the chest for her. It would be nice to spend a little more time with her. Margaret felt like she had hardly seen Sarah for most of their trip. She went back to Rowan in the carriage. "I'm going to walk the rest of the way. You and Samuel can go on to the house without me. I'm not sure how long this will take."

Rowan wrapped his arm around Samuel, who was asleep against his father. "Not too long I hope."

Margaret smiled at them and went to the gathering crowd. Vojvo and a few other guards stayed behind with her to keep watch in case the workers got too rowdy. In turn, Margaret went to each of the workers that came out to see them.

"Theotes bless you, my lady," one of the workers told her, kissing her hands when she put the money in his.

Margaret smiled at the kindly old man. "And you."

She walked the rest of the way to her home, greeting the people who worked on her lands and giving alms until there were no more people and no more money. Margaret saw a new respect for her on Vojvo's face that made her pause.

He offered her his arm to guide her up the steps to the small courtyard in front of her home. "That was very generous of you, my lady."

"My father would have done the same." Margaret leaned on the captain's arm. She was tired and her feet hurt, but she didn't regret it for a moment.

When they topped the stairs, Margaret was surprised to see some of the servants still waiting for her. She would have thought they'd all go back to their duties with the rest of their traveling party having arrived before her.

"Welcome home, my lady." Her butler bowed his head to her, sweat beaded on his forehead.

"Thank you, Mr. Wallace." She nodded to each servant as she passed, smiling when she and Vojvo entered the home, pausing to look at the mural on the floor.

It was the one thing Papa approved of sparing no expense on. In the center was the crest he had designed for their family: three tobacco leaves overlapping each other in a trident shape, their stems twisted together, topped with a garland of the five-pointed flower that bloomed as tobacco grew. Surrounding that was a wreath of the same flowers in every shade they came, as a show of unity from their family.

The wreath's meaning had been tarnished over the years with her mother abandoning them when Papa was too sick, and then Margaret abandoning her father as he died. She hoped one day she could polish it with another show of unity with the family she would make.

They made their way up the grand staircase made of stone to the level where the bedrooms were held, passing several paintings she didn't remember. They must have been added by her mother throughout the years they were away at court.

Once they were in the familiar east wing of the home, Margaret started to relax. She was in her own space, among her own things that the king couldn't take away at a whim to get her to obey.

Sarah rushed ahead of them, opening the door to Margaret's room for her.

"I'll be settling the men in the west wing if you need me, my lady." Vojvo patted her hand on his arm before dropping it.

"Thank you, Captain." Margaret smiled, going into her room to change out of her dusty clothes. She was pleased to see some of her trunks were already there. "Sarah, will you grab the dark blue day dress?"

"Yes, my lady," she said, opening a few trunks before pulling it out. "His Grace seems to be enjoying himself on this trip."

Margaret sighed. "He does…though I thought we would have progressed further than we have."

"What do you mean?" Sarah started unlacing Margaret's dress, shaking out the skirts once they were off. Puffs of dirt came off them with each shake.

Pulling off her shift in favor of one that wasn't sweat-soaked, Margaret frowned. "I thought by now he would have started talking of marriage, but he's only tried to kiss me once since we left."

Sarah replaced the shift, straightening it before laying the skirts out for Margaret to step in to. "You could always kiss him, my lady."

Margaret laughed. "The last time I kissed a man, he refused to speak to me for a year and barely tolerates me now."

"His Grace isn't Mr. Luther," Sarah reminded her. "And he's a widower, not a married man."

"I'll consider it," Margaret said, though she wasn't sure she was brave enough to try it again—she hadn't had the best luck with men thus far. Nicholas had murdered her father. Liam could not be in the country without risking arrest and execution. Charles was married and had put her in her place for her recklessness. The king…he was the worst of all, giving her no choice in the matter.

She had pursued Rowan to get away from the king, and she had accomplished that. Margaret wasn't sure what she would do if he did not want her after all. She could not bear going back to the palace without at least a hint Rowan had any intentions for her.

"Would you like me to fix your hair?" Sarah asked.

"Please." Margaret sat at her dressing table, scrunching her nose when she saw a pile of letters from the king. No doubt they were brought to her room once the traveling party was seen. She owed him several letters from the travel to Dorcia—maybe the delay could set a precedent for fewer letters between them.

Reading them as Sarah worked, Margaret was surprised by the content. She couldn't believe what Gareth had done, and the punishment he'd received for it. It must have been the first time he'd ever faced anything so harsh. She was glad she wasn't there—no doubt, Sorren would be in a foul mood over the ordeal and would have taken it out on her.

When Sarah was finished, Margaret went to the drawing room to wait for Rowan. She sighed, running her fingers along the books that lined the walls. She had so many happy memories in this room, her father reading to her all the books he could in his spare time. Margaret would trade a thousand lifetimes to go back to those moments and stay there forever.

She pulled a random book from the shelves and sat with it on one of the plush sofas, her finger tracing the title embossed on the front as she had when she was a child. Margaret let out a soft grunt, smiling when she realized it was the one her father read to her the most.

"My lady, the Duke of Fradure," Wallace announced.

Margaret stood when Rowan entered the room. "How are you finding your rooms?"

"They're wonderful, thank you." Rowan circled the couch going to her side.

Margaret smiled. "Good. They were made for His Majesty when he would come visit my father."

"I'm sure I'll enjoy them just as much as His Majesty did." He motioned toward the couches, sitting once she had.

Margaret looked around, furrowing her brow. "Where is Samuel?"

"He was too tired from the journey to come down," Rowan said. "He's sleeping soundly in his room."

"Poor thing," Margaret cooed.

"That was a spectacular thing you did today with your people." Rowan poured two glasses of red wine from the decanter in front of them, raising his glass to her. "I haven't seen it done in ages."

Margaret picked up her own glass, a shy smile on her face. "Thank you."

Rowan gently lifted her hand, kissing her knuckles. "You look beautiful tonight."

The butler entered the room. "Your Grace, my lady, dinner is ready."

Margaret pulled her hand from Rowan's quickly. "Thank you, Wallace."

They followed the butler to the dining room, where Rowan was placed at the head of the table since he was higher in rank. He looked around the room before saying, "This is a beautiful home, Lady Margaret."

"Your Grace is full of compliments tonight," Margaret said teasingly. "I was hoping to show Samuel a bit of the surrounding village in the next few days if he's up to it."

"That's very thoughtful of you. I think Samuel would love anything he does with you. He loves you."

"Does he?" Margaret blushed.

"You're almost all he talks about when we're alone."

"Well, I love him too." Margaret gave him a shy grin, excitement flitting through her chest. "He's a sweet boy."

Margaret waited in the dining room for Rowan and Samuel with several stacks of paper in front of her. She held a cup of tea to her lips, not drinking, as she read. Her brow furrowed the longer she scanned the pages. Margaret was glad to have a steward, but she wished the information she was reading didn't confound her.

She would have a meeting with him after breakfast to discuss the ledgers and reports Margaret was left to peruse as she ate. She would much rather have been told what was going on—all of the papers might as well have been in Radovian for all she understood.

Rowan cleared his throat to announce his presence, smiling when Margaret looked up. Samuel sleepily blinked at his side. "Good morning, Lady Margaret."

Margaret tried not to laugh at Samuel's expression. He looked like he could sleep three more days and not wake. "Good morning. Did you sleep well?"

"Very well, thank you." Rowan helped Samuel into the chair next to him before taking a seat across from Margaret.

"I thought I might visit the village surrounding the house this afternoon if you and Samuel would like to join me." She set aside her papers, motioning for the servants to start their breakfast service.

"I think perhaps Samuel will stay here with his nursemaid—to get used to his new surroundings." Rowan swept a lock of hair out of Samuel's face and gently pushed him back into the seat when he sleepily tottered forward. "I would be happy to accompany you today, however."

"We will leave after luncheon then." Margaret tried not to let her excitement show too much. This would be the first time Rowan would be able to see her interact with her people in a productive way up close and be able to judge her mettle as a possible duchess for his duchy.

Rowan made a noise in the back of his throat to acknowledge he heard her, serving himself eggs and bacon when the plates came around. "What is it you have planned for this trip?"

"I want to see the condition of the village and the people to ensure they are prospering," Margaret said. "When my father was alive, he would make trips every few months to see them and inquire about their health."

Rowan furrowed his brow. "Is that not why you have a steward?"

"It is…" Margaret said slowly, trying to pick her words carefully. "But they are my people, not the steward's. I am responsible for their health and their prosperity. They should have an ultimate trust that I will always have their best interests in mind."

"You shame me, Lady Margaret." Rowan held his hands up in concession.

"My apologies, You Grace." She shot him a chagrined grimace. "I am overly excited for my first meeting with these people."

Rowan arched a brow. "These are not the same people we saw gathered on the side of the road coming here?"

"Some will be," confirmed Margaret. "Most will not."

Once they had finished their breakfast, she walked with Rowan to the library. It was the most central part of the home, and he could easily find his way to any other part from there.

"Please feel free to explore wherever." Margaret clasped her hands in front of her. "I'll meet you back in the dining room for lunch?"

Rowan slowly nodded, his brows knitting together. "Where will you be?"

"In Papa's…" Her shoulders fell slightly before starting again, "In my study meeting with my steward, Mr. Amali."

"I've no doubt you'll do well." Rowan picked her hand up, kissing her knuckles. "I look forward to hearing how it went."

Margaret gave him a small smile before she headed to the second floor to her father's study on the west wing. She hesitated at the door, her hand on the knob. It felt wrong going in and claiming it as her own. Closing her eyes, she twisted the knob and pushed the door open.

Cracking an eye open, she looked in. It wasn't any different than she remembered but very different at the same time. Margaret went to the desk, running her finger along the edge. It was obviously kept clean by the servants. She glanced around the room. It felt so…empty.

It lacked the presence her father had filled it with. It was just a room now.

Margaret's shoulders drooped as she circled the desk, sitting in her father's plush chair. She had always imagined one day her husband would take over this room, and she could have run of the house. Maybe one day, but for now it was hers.

She looked up at the sharp knock at the door. A short man with slicked back black hair stood in the doorway, a smile on his face. He was younger than she expected—she thought he'd be her father's age or older. "Mr. Amali, I presume?"

"You presume correctly, Your Ladyship." He bowed his head to her. "It's a pleasure to finally meet you."

Margaret gestured to the chair in front of her. "Please, have a seat."

Mr. Amali put the bundle of papers down on the desk before he sat. He leaned back comfortably, resting his interwoven fingers against his stomach. "What is it you would like to accomplish with this meeting, my lady?"

She paused for a moment, running her tongue along the back of her teeth as she thought. "I want to understand—how the house is run, the finances, what's being done for the people in the village—everything."

Smiling broadly, Mr. Amali said, "We can do that."

Unable to help it, Margaret smiled along with him. "Let's get started then."

Once they finished with lunch, Rowan and Margaret started their walk into the village. Margaret couldn't wait to see the state of the village after talking with Mr. Amali. He had assured her everything was running smoothly in her absence, there was nothing to worry over, and he would send her bimonthly reports to keep her apprised of the goings on.

Rowan pulled at his cravat, sweat dripping down his forehead in the Amonat heat. Margaret fanned herself beside him, cheeks hot. Her hair stuck to the side of her face. She regretted not taking the carriage now—and not telling Captain Vojvo she was going. He'd have told her she was being daft and would give herself sun sickness walking all that way, and then he'd have forced her into a carriage.

"It seems I forgot how long the walk was in my absence." Margaret let out a chagrined laugh when she caught him staring, a wry smile curling her lips.

Rowan smiled encouragingly at her. "Think nothing of it—the walk will do us good."

Nodding, Margaret entered the main street of the village. Several children scantily dressed only in their underclothes played in the street. They scampered off to their homes when they saw Rowan and Margaret. Parents replaced children and Margaret raised her hand in greeting. She slowed, shocked at the state. This was not what she had expected.

"Can I help you?" One of the women called, shading her eyes from the high noon sun.

"Do they not know who you are, Margaret?" Rowan whispered covertly to her.

Margaret rapidly waved him off, stepping closer to the woman. That certainly wasn't the first impression she wanted to give him, that her people had no clue who she was. "I am Lady Marg—Lady Dorcia, and I would like to speak with you."

The woman's eyes bulged in her panic, falling into a clumsy curtsey. "My lady!"

Smiling, Margaret touched her arm to get her attention. "May I speak with you, Mrs....?"

"Graham," she said hurriedly. "Mrs. Graham, my lady."

"May I speak with you, then, Mrs. Graham?" Margaret asked again.

"Of course, my lady," agreed Mrs. Graham. "I would be honored."

"How is life for you here?" Margaret looked around. It didn't look like it was good. Margaret saw the shift in Mrs. Graham's eyes from a look of excitement to one of hesitation. "Please, you have no fear of reprisal from me, Mrs. Graham," Margaret tried to assure her. "You may be as frank as you please."

"Well, my lady…" Mrs. Graham said slowly. "Since you and your father went away for good—may Theotes keep his soul at rest—things have not been quite the way they were."

Margaret looked at her expectantly.

"We're not getting quite the…support we used to," Mrs. Graham finally said.

That much was obvious by the dilapidated state of the homes they saw along the way, but she needed to know more. "How so?"

Mrs. Graham motioned to a few of the houses. "We ask the manor for supplies to fix our homes, and we can't get anyone to help us for months at a time. There have been families here forced to leave because they can't afford to live anymore. Mr. Amali will not talk to us anymore."

"Not one of you has been able to have a meeting with him?" Margaret asked incredulously.

Mrs. Graham shook her head. "Only one, Mr. Porter, was able to see him and was told there wasn't enough supplies to give out because the house needed repair."

There hadn't been any repairs made to the house she had seen. Margaret rolled her lips between her teeth as she thought. "You said some people had to leave?"

"Yes, my lady." Mrs. Graham nervously rubbed her thumb against her opposite palm hard enough Margaret could see it go red. "Mr. Amali said the rent must be raised to afford the repairs to the manor."

Out of the corner of her eye, Margaret caught Rowan watching her as Mrs. Graham spoke. Clearing her throat, Margaret pulled her shoulders back to stand straighter. "Thank you, Mrs. Graham. I will be speaking with Mr. Amali about these issues today and ensure they are resolved quickly."

"Oh—"

"Is there anyone else you think would be willing to tell me their experience with Mr. Amali?" Margaret looked on either side of her. The street had emptied while she spoke to Mrs. Graham.

"Anyone here, my lady." Mrs. Graham gestured to each side of her. "We've all been affected by Mr. Amali."

"Thank you, truly."

"Of course, my lady." Mrs. Graham hurriedly curtsied as Margaret turned to leave.

She talked to several others on each street of the village and the consensus was the same: Mr. Amali refused to work with them and actively made their lives harder. One villager had even mentioned her steward had stopped hearing petitions altogether more than a year ago, and several disagreements had become violent without a mediator.

Margaret breathed out heavily when they left the village, running a hand over her face. She couldn't believe she had let Mr. Amali fool her. She thought she was a decent judge of character, but it seemed she was not. First with Lord Nicholas tricking her into a courtship with gentlemanly behavior, then the king fooling her for years, and now being duped in a single afternoon by her steward.

"Stupid," she murmured to herself before letting out a frustrated growl. Margaret picked up her pace to get back to the manor faster.

Rowan pulled off his cravat when he caught up to her, dabbing his forehead with it. "What are you going to do, Margaret?"

"I'm going to find myself a new steward."

8

iam spent the morning making the nails he would need to start building the new addition for Jamie and Ellie. They would need a space of their own for their little one, and Jamie's room wouldn't be big enough for the three of them. Liam planned to change the attic to another level of the house for their family and add a new attic on top of that. It was the most ambitious build Liam had done yet.

He looked up when Joanna greeted someone in the front. It was Simon—again. Liam thought he had come by frequently before, but Simon's visits had tripled since Joanna was hired.

"I'll tell him when he has a moment," Joanna said.

Simon said something in return that Liam couldn't hear, but Joanna swiped her hair back behind her ear with a giggle. Simon grinned at her before leaving.

"You're gonna have to look out for that one," Jossnon said, raising his hammer to point at Simon's back.

"Don't I know it." Liam sighed. Simon had even started asking about her in the evenings. He didn't think Jamie had been *this* lovesick over Eleanor when they had courted. "She seems not to be bothered by him, at least."

"For now," Jossnon said. "He'll need to play his hand right so he's no harassing her."

Liam nodded. He'd have to talk to him about the time he spent talking to Joanna when they both had a free moment alone. He didn't want to embarrass Simon around his mother and siblings—and to be honest, Liam didn't particularly want to do it. It was only natural for Simon to want a companion when his older brother was married with a child on the way and no longer spending as much time with him, and Eli was over a decade younger than Simon's seventeen years. He needed someone around his age to spend time with, and Joanna was like a shining beacon for Simon—having just moved into Numetra a few months ago.

Joanna came into the back room. "Simon wanted to let ye know his Ma has requested ye bring home a new spoon."

Liam raised his brows. "A spoon?"

"Aye." Joanna nodded. "Simon said her stirrin' spoon broke."

He tried not to look at Jossnon incredulously and roll his eyes. Gretta's spoons were made from wood, not metal. Simon could have gone to the general store to get her one instead of stopping here. "Thank you, Joanna."

She smiled and went back to the front of the shop.

"Do you mind if I leave early?" Liam asked. "We're starting to build today."

"So that's why ye spent so much time on nails lately." Jossnon laughed. "I thought I missed an order. How long d'ye think it'll take ye to build it?"

Liam shrugged. "Three, four weeks if I can get some help from the boys—a month and a half if I can't."

"Why dinna ye take the time until it's finished?" Jossnon looked around the shop. "We're all caught up in our orders, an' I can handle a few weeks wi'out ye here."

"Are you sure?" It was a generous offer from Jossnon, but Liam didn't want to take advantage. "I can come in for the mornings if it takes longer."

"Oh, aye. Ye ken well Femonat and Marmonat are our slowest months." Jossnon nodded. "Ye take the time, an' we'll discuss it if ye need longer."

Joss was right. The cold kept most of the customers away. "I suppose I'll see you in a few weeks then," Liam said as he gathered his supplies.

"Try not to hurt yerself," Jossnon called after Liam.

The thought was nice, but Liam was sure there would be a few smashed fingers by the end of the build. He stopped by the general store to get a new spoon for Gretta before going home.

He found her in the larder and held up the spoon when she turned around. "I got that new spoon you asked for."

Gretta looked at him confused. "New spoon?"

"Simon came into the smithy and told Joanna you asked me to bring you a new spoon because yours broke."

"My spoon didna break." Gretta laughed. "He just wanted to talk to that girl."

"I guess now you have an extra." Liam sighed. "Joss gave me time off until the build is finished."

"That was nice of him." Gretta handed him a few things before turning back to the shelves. "Would you take that back to the kitchen?"

Liam tried not to roll his eyes. He would have to talk to Simon about wasting Liam's time just to see Joanna. He went to the kitchen and put the food onto the counter. He let out a noise when arms gripped him from behind.

"Da!" Eli yelled.

Bringing his hands behind his back, Liam hugged Eli to him. "Hey, Duck." He let go, turning to face Eli. "You ready to help me start building today?"

Eli nodded excitedly.

Liam clapped his shoulder. "Great. You can help me start taking things upstairs." He handed Eli the bag of nails. "Start with these."

Eli scampered up the stairs while Liam grabbed some of his tools. It would be good to have a helper who was excited to cart away debris. Today would mostly be making way for the new build, creating a new opening for the top level and a staircase for them to easily walk up. Liam hefted his ladder over his shoulder, carrying it upstairs with his saw and hammer in his other hand.

Eli met him at the top of the stairs, grinning excitedly. "What now?"

Liam held out his hand with the saw and the hammer. "If you'll put these in the corner?"

Eli took them from him, swinging the two around as he walked toward the corner.

"You can't swing them like that, Eli," Liam scolded. "Just put them in the corner."

Eli's shoulders fell, but he did as he was bid. "Sorry, Da."

Liam set the ladder against the wall, looking around while he chewed at his lip. He'd have to start with the ceiling, and then frame the stairs to the new opening. "Now, I want you to stay out of the way," he said. "I don't want something to fall on you, Duck."

Eli went to the far end of the room as Liam climbed the ladder.

Hours passed as he worked. Sweat gathered on his forehead, and Liam billowed his shirt to get some air on his neck. He'd gotten into the ceiling and framed the edges of the hole to support the stair frame. He'd need to start the frame from the ceiling to get the winder at the bottom in the correct spot. Liam didn't want the stairs to be too steep for anyone carrying an infant and increase their chance of falling with it.

Coming down, Liam missed the last step on the ladder, stumbling backward as the saw clattered to the floor. He let out a curse, stepping away from the saw.

"Da!" Eli ran to Liam, latching onto him.

"What's the matter?" Liam furrowed his brows, looking down at Eli.

"I dinna want ye to have an accident like my Da." Eli buried his face into Liam's stomach. "My other Da."

Liam was taken aback. He hadn't realized Eli's father's death had affected him so much. Gretta had told Eli his father died in an accident but confided in Liam he'd been killed by rebels. When Liam had first come into their lives, he'd met Eli after the boy had a nightmare about his father. But that was the last Liam had heard of any anguish on Eli's part.

"I'll be careful, Duck—I promise." Liam held him close, rubbing his back. "I'll have you here watching out for me, yeah?" Maybe letting Eli know Liam trusted him to alert Liam when something amiss would make the boy feel better and more in control of what was happening around him.

Eli nodded against Liam, holding on to him tighter.

"Why don't we take a break?" Liam asked gently.

Eli nodded again, loosening his grip on Liam.

Liam smiled when Eli carefully walked up to him with a mug of beer, foam spilling over the side. "What are you doing up here?"

"Ma said ye need a break."

The project had taken far longer than Liam anticipated. He was now in his third month of building and was increasingly frustrated by the day, but there was finally an end in sight.

"She heard the yelling, did she?" Liam laughed when Eli solemnly nodded. He took the beer, taking a large drink. It was still cold. "All right, then. Why don't you and I have a sit in the kitchen and see if Ma will feed us?"

Eli grinned. "I'll race ye downstairs."

"If you win, I'll let you have an extra-long break."

"Deal!" Eli ran down out of the room.

Liam sighed, slowly getting up. At least now he'd be able to work in peace without having Eli underfoot. Ellie was in the kitchen in front of the stove when he came down, wiping her forehead with a rag. Her pregnancy was finally starting to show on her small frame—he'd heard nothing from Gretta on the subject but about how late Ellie was in showing she was with child.

"I won!" Eli bent at the waist, pointing to Liam with a smug scrunch of his nose. "You lose!"

Ellie swatted at him with her rag. "Mind yer manners." She looked back at Liam. "Ye a'right, Da?"

Liam gave her an embarrassed grin. "The hammer just wanted to give my thumb a kiss. No harm done."

"When is it ye think ye'll be done?" Ellie asked as she dished up two plates for him and Eli. "I cannae wait to see it. Jamie willna let me up there."

Liam took another sip of his beer. "I'm hoping tonight after Jamie is home to help finish it."

Ellie broke out in a grin. "Really?"

He nodded. "You won't have any furnishings in there yet, but it'll be ready to move into it starting tomorrow—or the next day, depending on how everything has dried."

Ellie let out a squeal, kissing him on the cheek after she set down his plate. "Thank ye, Da!"

"What's this?" Gretta asked as she came in from the dining room, eyes crinkling as she looked between the two.

"Da says he'll be done with our new room tonight," Ellie said.

"Hopefully," Liam added before stuffing a forkful of food into his mouth.

"Ye and I will need to take a trip to the shops to make sure ye have everything ye need to move." Gretta threw her towel to rest over her shoulder and put her hands on her hips. "We'll make a day of it."

"Thank ye, Ma." Ellie put a hand to her burgeoning bump. "I dinna ken what Jamie and I would do without you and Da."

"It's our pleasure to do it." Liam finished the last bite of his food before standing. "When Jamie gets here, send him right up."

"Aye, I will."

When Eli started to stand, Liam stopped him. "You won an extra-long break, remember?"

"Oh, aye." Eli plopped back down onto his chair with a grin. "'Cause ye were too slow."

Liam caught Gretta's eye as she hid a wry grin behind the back of her hand and tried not to grin himself. She knew Eli had been particularly clingy the last few days and Liam needed a break from him. "That's right. You enjoy whatever your Ma has for you."

"I—"

Liam kissed her quickly before going upstairs to enjoy the time by himself. There wasn't much left to be done. The leftover materials needed to be hauled away and the last few boards nailed into place before he and Jamie could put down the wood oil.

He was able to get most of the items cleared before Jamie came up to join him. Jamie paused at the door, looking around. "Ellie is gonna be chuffed."

Liam smiled. "She was very excited when I told her we were almost done."

"It's all she's been talkin' about the last three days." Jamie laughed. "It's been a challenge to keep her from comin' in here."

"I believe it." Liam grabbed the hammer, bringing Jamie to a board under the window. He pulled two nails from his pocket. "I saved the last two for you. One to remember the support of the family you came from, and one to support the family you're starting."

This was Liam's first chance to pass what his father never got the chance to pass to him. His father had talked about one day helping Liam build a house for his own family one day because Liam's grandfather had helped his father finish his first house. It made Liam equal parts sad and happy as he handed Jamie the nails. At least the tradition would live on.

Jamie's mouth twisted as he nodded silently. He swallowed hard before saying, "Thank ye, Da."

Liam gripped his shoulder. "I'll get the wood oil while you finish up here."

He and Jamie opened the windows to get a breeze in the rooms before they laid down the oil. Hopefully, it would be dry enough to walk on by the time dinner was over. Anything longer and Ellie would likely throttle the both of them.

Jamie looked around the room, letting out a breath. "It's perfect, Da. Just perfect."

9

Margaret paced her study, arms crossed over her chest. She was still angry, at times verging on furious. "How much longer, Mr. Tevna?"

Neville Tevna pulled his eyeglasses down his nose to look at her. "I'm unsure, my lady."

"You've been at this for weeks!" Margaret exhaled sharply, closing her eyes. She shouldn't direct her anger at Mr. Tevna. He hadn't done anything wrong. "I'm sorry, but I want the evidence to be undeniable when I fire Mr. Amali."

"Your Ladyship, you could easily prosecute Mr. Amali on the theft from this year alone." Mr. Tevna sat back in his chair, lightly tossing his eyeglasses onto the ledgers in front of him. "You don't need me to go all the way through his tenure."

Margaret paused, looking him over. "Really?"

He nodded, gesturing to the ledgers. "There's more than enough evidence here. The only reason to go so far back is to get the exact amount he's stolen over the years, but it's enough that he would never be able to repay you in his lifetime."

The thought made Margaret sick. Not only had Mr. Amali stolen from her, he'd stolen from her people—her charges—whom she was meant to look after. He had forced her into failure before she'd even started.

Finally sitting in the plush chair behind the desk, she rubbed her lips together as she thought. "I have two questions I would like to ask you, Mr. Tevna."

"All right."

"Would you help me present this evidence to a magistrate to have Mr. Amali arrested?" Margaret rubbed her fingers together nervously before she continued on, "And would you be interested in becoming my new steward?"

He grinned. "I would be honored, my lady."

Margaret let out a relieved sigh. Now, she wouldn't be alone in this.

Margaret waited in the main hall of her home for her residents to come to her for petitions that morning. She hoped they would come—that the people would trust her now since she had Mr. Amali arrested for what he had done to her and the people of Dorcia and hired a more trustworthy steward to look after them when she had to leave. She inhaled deeply, rubbing her fingers together as her nerves grew more frenetic. She had watched her father several times, but this would be her first. It seemed simple enough—she would listen to the people and give her judgment to the best of her ability.

She had once asked her father why they weren't done in private, thinking it would be simpler. He had told her he always chose a public forum to show the people they would get equal treatment from him, and he had no tolerance for backroom deals meant to alienate those who didn't have the affluence behind them, deals that many of the other nobles allowed in their homes.

Margaret scanned the room for Rowan. She had invited him to join her, but he had yet to arrive. Only servants and guards lined the walls, prepared with either sustenance or protection—whichever the situation called for.

She twisted the signet ring on her middle finger, pausing when she realized what she was doing. Margaret had barely been able to look at the ring since she had slipped it off her dying father's finger so it wouldn't be lost. Now she must wear it to every official event. She fought the tears welling, closing her eyes. Margaret reminded herself this ring was her father still with her. She wouldn't allow the panic to haunt her forever.

Rolling her lips between her teeth in an attempt to calm herself, Margaret looked to her new steward, Neville Tevna.

He gave her a small smile, nodding.

She was sure it was meant to reassure her, but Margaret felt nothing but the electric wave of nervous energy fluttering in her chest. Taking a deep breath, she called to the guards at the doors, "Let them in."

The heavy oak doors opened, petitioners pouring into the hall like a flood come to drown her in her inexperience. They crowded the back and sides of the room.

Margaret waited until the room quieted before looking to her steward. "Mr. Tevna, who is our first petitioner?" she asked.

Clearing his throat, Mr. Tevna pulled out his list. "My lady, the first petitioner is a one Mr. Webster."

Margaret nodded, looking into the crowd.

"Step forward, Mr. Webster," commanded Mr. Tevna, "and tell Her Ladyship your plight."

A grungy man stepped forward, gripping his woolen cap nervously in his hands. His eyes darted between the steward and Margaret, unsure who to address. "Good mornin', milady," he started slowly.

Margaret smiled at him encouragingly, eyes crinkling. She was glad she wasn't the only nervous one in the room. "Good morning, Mr. Webster," she returned. "Please, tell me what brought you here today."

"Well, ma'am," he cleared his throat, "you see, I have yet to receive payment for repairs done to the fences around your cabbage to keep the deer out."

Nodding along, Margaret asked, "And how long ago were you supposed to be paid?"

"Two months, ma'am."

Margaret tried not to let her dismay show. She was sure she would hear many of the same sort of complaints today. It had all been laid out in black and white by Mr. Tevna how much Mr. Amali had stolen from her—and her people. "And how much were you supposed to have been paid?"

"Three tholar a day, ma'am. I worked for six days," Mr. Webster told her.

Margaret turned to her steward. "Do you have a record of why Mr. Webster was not paid for his work, Mr. Tevna?"

"An oversight by Mr. Amali, my lady," Mr. Tevna said quietly.

In other words, money lining Mr. Amali's pocket in her name. Clearing her throat, Margaret turned her attention back to her petitioner. "Well, Mr. Webster, in my way of apology, you will receive two months' interest on your payment, coming to three gold tal for your trouble."

"Thank you, ma'am!" Webster gushed, bowing back until he returned to the crowd.

Margaret looked at the steward expectantly. She caught movement over his shoulder and smiled when she saw Rowan slip in the door closest to her.

"Mr. Tolbert and Mr. Dillingham, please step forward," Mr. Tevna called.

The two men came forward, standing as far apart from each other as they possibly could. Both glanced at each other, not speaking.

Margaret raised a brow. "Mr. Tevna, would you care to tell me what their complaint is?"

"Of course, my lady," he said, bowing his head to her. "Mr. Dillingham alleges that Mr. Tolbert—"

"He stole my cow!" Mr. Dillingham shouted, interrupting the steward, pointing at the man standing with him.

"You stole my cow first!" Mr. Tolbert screamed back. "You lying thief!"

Mr. Dillingham lunged for Mr. Tolbert, almost reaching his neck before being pulled back by guards. He tried again but was forcibly separated from the other man.

Margaret's stomach tightened as she watched the two continue to try to get near each other, only to be thwarted by the guards holding them. It was no wonder petition days were her father's least favorite days when they had been in residence. She hoped, for her sake, that this would be the only time arguments nearly came to blows.

She wanted to scold them for their behavior but instead forced herself to take a breath. If she remained calm, they would also remain calm—hopefully. "Are you quite finished, gentlemen?" Margaret arched a brow at them.

"Yes, milady," Mr. Dillingham mumbled.

"Yes, milady," Mr. Tolbert followed suit.

"Good. Then we can proceed." Margaret nodded to the guards, who released the two petitioners but stayed close behind. "Mr. Dillingham, you said Mr. Tolbert stole your cow. When did that happen?"

"Two weeks ago, milady. He took my cow and branded her with his own mark to cover his tracks. I just bought her two days before he took her!"

Margaret held up her hand when she saw Mr. Tolbert preparing to yell at the other man. "You will have your chance to speak, Mr. Tolbert."

"Yes, milady." Mr. Tolbert sighed, his shoulders slumping.

"Do you have any proof that this is indeed your cow?" Margaret asked.

"She has my brand!"

"You said she also has Mr. Tolbert's brand. How do we know which brand to trust?"

"Mine, milady!" Mr. Tolbert yelled. "I bought her three weeks ago and put my brand on her the very next day."

"And do you have proof that she was your cow first?" Margaret asked. "And please don't say your brand. We will be turning in circles all day. A bill of sale, perhaps?"

Sighing heavily, Mr. Tolbert answered, "Then, I have no proof."

"And you, Mr. Dillingham?"

Looking as though some of the bluster had been taken out of him, Mr. Dillingham also answered, "I have no proof, milady."

How in Theotes's name had her father ever found solutions so quickly? She would have to figure something out that wouldn't be picking one side over the other just to solve the problem.

Margaret took a moment to think before finally speaking. "Gentlemen, I can see three solutions for you: the cow can be butchered and you split the meat equally, one of you can pay the other a reduced price for the cow, or I can buy the cow from you both and you each get half." She held a finger up with each proposal, searching their faces to see which appealed more. "Your decision must be unanimous, or I will decide for you."

The men looked at each other tentatively.

"I don't want to give her up," Mr. Dillingham said.

Mr. Tolbert scoffed. "I'm not going to pay you for *my* cow!"

"Then I will decide for you." Margaret sighed. "How much did you each pay for her?"

"Four tholar, milady," Mr. Tolbert answered.

"The same, milady," conceded Mr. Dillingham.

"Very well, I will purchase the cow for six tholar, and you will each receive three," Margaret ruled. "Whomever is now in possession of the cow will bring her here, and the payment will be dispensed."

"Thank you, milady," they both grumbled, eyeing the other, before returning to the crowd.

Margaret listened to the remainder of the petitioners, breaking briefly for everyone to eat, providing food for the petitioners that stayed during the hour. Rowan came to her side at the end of the day, gently touching her arm.

Margaret turned to him with a tired smile. "Did you stay here all day?" She wouldn't have blamed him if he left. It was a long day, and even she wanted to leave halfway through.

"I did," he answered. "Can I interest you in joining me for a drink in the library?"

"You certainly can interest me." Margaret lowered her lashes, hoping he would catch on to her double meaning. "Will you allow me to change first?"

He frowned, clearly debating if he could wait longer to be in her company. "Of course," he finally conceded. "I will meet you there."

Margaret grinned to herself as she went to her room and pulled the bell for Sarah. A thrill went through her that there had even been a debate inside Rowan.

She sat at her dresser, rubbing cream into her hands while she waited. While tiring and frustrating, it was thrilling having done the petitions—it had finally set in that she had authority, and her people would have to listen. They seemed to accept her rulings easily enough, though. There were no jeers from the back or cries of outrage when she'd dispensed them.

"You called, my lady?" Sarah asked when she came into the room.

"His Grace would like a drink in the library, and I'd like to change into something more comfortable," Margaret said as she stood.

"Perhaps the lilac dress?" Sarah suggested as she went to the wardrobe.

Margaret smiled. It was a flattering dress on her. "I think he would like that."

"Very good, my lady," Sarah said, pulling the dress out.

Margaret pulled down her hair, brushing it out into soft waves while Sarah unlaced the dress. She and Rowan hadn't been able to spend much time together today, and she hoped now that petitions were done for the week, they would have time to quietly relax together.

Sarah helped Margaret dress, smoothing out any wrinkles once it was on. "Is there anything else you need, my lady?"

Margaret shook her head. "No, I think this will be fine."

Rowan already had two glasses of wine poured and was waiting for them when she got there. He turned when she approached the couch. "You look lovely."

Margaret smiled. "Thank you." She sat next to him, her knees nearly touching his.

Rowan handed her her drink. "To you," he said. "You were impressive today."

Margaret smiled behind her glass before she took a sip. "Had I known you would be there all day, I would have tried harder."

Picking up her hand, Rowan straightened the signet ring on her finger. "Then I look forward to seeing you handle petitions again soon."

"I certainly look forward to you seeing me." Margaret looked down to their hands, slowly sliding hers from his.

Rowan cleared his throat taking a large drink. "Do you?"

"Oh, very much." Margaret tucked a hair behind her ear. "Though, I hope it won't be disappointing."

Rowan shifted, his leg against hers. "I don't think you could ever be disappointing."

Margaret let out a hum from the back of her throat. "That's good to know." She wound a curl from its tip around her finger. She knew she was pushing the limits of what was proper. There was some leeway for them being alone in her own home because servants surrounded them, but not much.

"What is it you would like to do tomorrow?" Rowan asked.

"I'd love to spend some time, just the two of us. " Margaret picked up his hand, sliding her fingers between his. "There's plenty for Samuel to do so we can be on our own."

He tightened his grip on her hand, pulling her toward him as he brought it to his mouth to kiss her knuckles. "It's just the two of us now."

Margaret inhaled deeply, wetting her lips before rolling them between her teeth. "It is, isn't it?"

"It is," Rowan breathed. He snaked his hand behind her neck, pulling her closer. "It is."

The door opened behind them. "My lady?"

Margaret gasped, jerking away from Rowan. "What is it?" she snapped.

The butler cleared his throat, averting his eyes. "There is a gentleman here that requires your immediate attention."

Margaret sighed heavily, standing and smoothing her skirts. She turned to Rowan with a frown. She didn't know if they would get the moment back, even if they tried. "If you'll excuse me," she said. "I'll see you at dinner."

Rowan stood, clearing his throat. "I look forward to it."

Regretfully, Margaret followed Wallace.

10

"**M**a!" Jamie yelled, barging into Liam and Gretta's bedroom, waking the two of them. "Ma, it's time!"

Liam groaned, covering his eyes. It was too early for yelling. "Time for what?"

"Ellie is havin' the wee lad!" Jamie told him excitedly before returning to his wife.

Gretta was already out of bed, starting to dress. "Will ye go an' get the midwife?" she asked, tying the front of her shift.

Liam rolled out of bed himself, quickly dressing as he tried to shake the sleep from his head. "Aye, where is she?"

"It's Mrs. Danes by The Heated Forge," Gretta called before disappearing.

Inhaling deeply, Liam stumbled down the street with blurry eyes. He found Mrs. Danes's door by the sign hanging next to it, pounding on the dark blue door. "Hello?"

Mr. Danes came to the door blinking slowly. "Can I help ye?"

"Ellie McWard's about to give birth at The Smiling Fox. Can you send Mrs. Danes when she is ready?" asked Liam.

"Aye, I will," Mr. Danes said before closing the door.

Returning to the eatery, Liam heard a loud groan coming from the upstairs bedroom. It was a good thing Gretta had closed down the eatery the day before last, telling customers they wouldn't open until Ellie had given birth.

"Where's the midwife?" Jamie asked. His eyes were crazed as another groan came from upstairs.

"She's coming as soon as she can." Liam gripped his shoulder. "Everything's going to be fine. Where's your Ma?"

"Upstairs with Ellie." Jamie looked to the stairs.

Liam felt the shift in Jamie. Every muscle leaned toward the stairs—he wanted to go up to be with his wife, but there would be nothing he could do up there. "She's the best person to be with her right now."

Jamie sighed heavily. "I ken it, Da."

"Have you had anything to eat yet?" Liam led Jamie to the table, gently herding him into a chair.

Jamie shook his head. "I cannae eat right now."

"You'll need it," Liam said. "We have no idea how long it'll take, and you'll need your strength for Ellie."

Liam looked around the kitchen for something he could shove at Jamie. He found a bannock and slathered it with butter and jam, setting it in front of Jamie, who only took a small bite.

"Eat the whole thing," Liam said. "Even if you don't want to. You'll need something to keep you on your feet today."

Jamie took another bite. "Where the hell is the midwife?"

Liam clapped Jamie's shoulder. It didn't bode well for Jamie if he was already agitated. From what Liam had heard, it could take most of the day, sometimes several days, for a woman to give birth. "I'll go wait outside for her, how's that?"

"Thank ye, Da." Jamie leaned back in the chair with a sigh, covering his face.

The stress Jamie was feeling now almost made Liam happy he hadn't had any children of his own. He couldn't even imagine the weight of Jamie's thoughts. He went outside to stand on the main street to wait for Mrs. Danes. He hoped for Jamie's sake that she arrived soon.

Simon stepped outside, eyes bleary. "Mornin', Da."

Liam nodded to him. "Sleep all right?"

"Nah." Simon shook his head. "Ellie was pacin' the floor the whole night."

"It was that long?" Liam furrowed his brows. He'd only heard a step or two. "Aye."

"Has anyone told Mr. and Mrs. Kaneh?" Liam hadn't even thought about them.

Simon shrugged. "I dinna ken."

"Can you stop by and let them know on your way to work?" Liam wouldn't deny them the chance to be there for their daughter, but he couldn't leave for the sake of Jamie."

"Aye." Simon nodded. "Will ye tell me all is well if she has the bairn while I'm workin'?"

"I will." Liam stood up straighter when he saw a flutter of skirts rushing their way. "That'll be the midwife."

"Where is the girl?" Mrs. Danes demanded, cheeks scarlet from her hurried walk.

"She's inside in her room, up on the top floor." Liam extended his arm toward the door. "This way."

Mrs. Danes scurried inside, passing Jamie at the table.

Jamie stood quickly, shoving his chair back hard enough it fell. "Is there—"

Mrs. Danes shook her head, holding up her hand. "Husbands stay downstairs," she said as she climbed up the staircase.

Jamie frowned at her back as Liam came to his side. "She doesna seem very nice."

"I imagine she gets a lot of angry husbands coming her way," Liam said. Mrs. Danes did seem excessively rude, but he didn't want it to color the day for Jamie. "She probably just wants to nip it in the bud."

"Aye." Jamie sighed. "D'ye think Ellie will be all right?"

"I think she has your Ma up there with her, and you know she takes guff from no one," Liam said. "And Simon is letting her parents know, so she'll have both her mothers soon enough to keep her safe for you."

Jamie picked up his chair and sat heavily. "I cannae stand feelin' so helpless."

"I know." He didn't, but Liam wanted to comfort Jamie. "Why don't we put up the chairs in the dining room for Ma? She'll be closed the next few days anyway." Plus, it would keep him occupied for at least a short while.

Jamie frowned. "D'ye think she wants us to?"

Hell if Liam knew. He just wanted to keep Jamie occupied today, and he wasn't going to let him near the logs that needed to be chopped. That was asking for an accident. "It'll keep the chairs from gathering dust, and she won't have to clean them off when she's ready to open up again."

Jamie jumped when Ellie let out a loud groan. "Aye, we can do that fer Ma."

"Good lad." Liam ushered Jamie into the dining room of the eatery. It was a convenient set up for Gretta to have her home attached to the eatery, but it had its hassles on later nights when patrons sometimes stumbled on their private dinners in their personal dining room.

Liam watched Jamie turn one chair upside down onto the table after another. Hopefully, the Kanehs would be there by the time they finished, and he would have help distracting Jamie. He kept asking Jamie questions as they worked, so the chore would take longer. Liam looked sharply to the door when he heard someone call out.

"That must be the Kanehs." Jamie abandoned the chair he was holding. He went through the door to the kitchen.

Liam followed closely behind.

"Where's my Ellie?" Mrs. Kaneh asked.

"She's upstairs with Ma and the midwife," Jamie said.

She didn't wait for him to say more before rushing up the stairs.

Mr. Kaneh held up a large brown glass bottle. "Ye ready to settle in an' wait, my boy?"

Jamie looked at Liam.

Liam wasn't quite sure why—Jamie was certainly old enough to drink on his own and didn't need Liam's permission. Still, he nodded, saying, "I'll get the glasses."

Mr. Kaneh poured drinks for the three of them before lifting his glass. "To becoming a father."

Jamie lifted his in return. "To my sweet Ellie."

Liam wasn't sure what to toast to, clinking his glass with the others. "To you both."

Jamie downed his drink in one go, letting out a sharp breath as he shook his head.

"Ye'll need to pace yerself." Mr. Kaneh clapped Jamie on the shoulder. "I remember my first. I nearly fell down the stairs drunk, I'd had so much."

Liam was relieved Mr. Kaneh had said that. With not having done this for himself, Liam wasn't sure how much he could advise Jamie on how to behave.

"Aye, ye're right." Jamie laughed. "I dinna ken if Ellie would ever talk to me again if I drank myself sick."

"She wouldna." Mr. Kaneh poured Jamie another drink, pushing the glass toward him. "Take this one slow, aye?"

Jamie nodded, taking a small sip this time.

After a few more sips, they heard footfalls thundering down the stairs. Jamie stood, his face losing all its color. "What's happenin', Ma?" he asked when Gretta appeared.

Gretta shook her head, cheeks red. "We need towels and water."

"Is something wrong?" Liam asked, standing as well. Gretta didn't usually fluster easily.

"Eli." Gretta frowned. "He wanted to be a part of the day, but he got too excited and vomited in the corner."

Liam sighed. He'd be lucky if only one of his boys vomited by the end of the day. "Send him down here if you need to."

"He'll no leave now." Gretta rolled her eyes. "He doesna want to miss a thing."

"And Ellie?" Jamie looked crazed, his eyes wide.

"Och, she's fine." She patted him on the shoulder. "Mrs. Danes doesna think it will be difficult fer her." Once she had her supplies, she went back upstairs.

They settled in to wait, drinking and talking among themselves. Hours passed as they listened to Ellie either groan or walk around the top floor.

Once the sun set, Mr. Kaneh stood a little wobbly. "I should get us another bottle."

Liam was feeling a little wobbly himself. "I don't know if—"

"We'll need somethin' to celebrate with when the time comes," Mr. Kaneh said.

"Oh, aye, aye." Jamie nodded. "Da, d'ye no want to toast me bein' a 'Da' too?"

Liam slouched back into his chair, a small smile coming to his face. "More than anything."

"I'll be back presently," Mr. Kaneh said, waddling out of the door.

Moments later, they heard a shrill cry from upstairs. Jamie nearly fell from his seat trying to get up so quickly. Liam followed behind a little more slowly.

"Is that my bairn?" Jamie demanded from the door.

The door opened to Mrs. Danes with a broad smile. "Come in an' meet yer wee one."

Jamie nearly pushed her aside to get to Ellie. Mrs. Kaneh stepped out of his way to give him plenty of room.

Liam went to Gretta's side, wrapping an arm around her. He watched Jamie's eyes well, kneeling next to the bed where Ellie lay with their child in her arms. He gently stroked her hair, kissing her temple.

"Meet yer wee lass." Ellie smiled at him sleepily, offering the child for him to hold. "What should we call her?"

Jamie looked at Liam, holding the baby like he would break her if he held her too tightly. "Da, what was yer Ma's name?"

"Maria," Liam said.

Jamie looked at Ellie, eyes searching her face. "What d'ye think?"

"Maria's a fine name," Ellie said. "Maria Louise McWard."

Liam grinned, pulling Gretta closer to him, as he spoke to the new parents: "That's a fine thing you've done for me, both of you. She would have loved all of you had she had the chance to meet you."

Jamie stood, going to Gretta and Liam. "Would ye like to hold yer granddaughter?"

Gretta grinned up at Liam. "Mrs. Kaneh and I've already had our chance. Grandda's turn."

Excitement went through him when Jamie placed Maria in his arms. Him, a grandfather? He never thought he'd be one.

11

Margaret came to Rowan's room in a simple cotton dress. It would be a warm day, and they would be out in the sun for a few hours. She knocked lightly on the door, surprised when it was answered by Rowan's valet. She thought Rowan would have been ready by now.

"Can I help you, Lady Dorcia?"

"Are His Grace and Samuel prepared for the day?" Margaret asked.

"Let her in," Rowan called from the background.

The valet moved aside to let Margaret in.

She stepped past him and went into the large room, brightened by a wall of large windows overlooking her property. She saw that Rowan was dressed in brown cotton pants and a nearly translucent white cotton shirt. "How did you sleep?"

"Like a king," Rowan jested.

Margaret smiled. "Is Samuel still in his room?" She pointed to the adjoining room to the right.

"Yes, he is. I'm sure he'd love for you to go and get him."

"I'll meet you in the drawing room with him." Margaret went into his son's room. It was meant for the king's servants to never be far away, but it was well large enough for a child to stay close to his father. "Samuel?"

"Maggie!" he yelled excitedly, running to hug her around the waist.

Margaret straightened his hair with her fingers. "How do you like your room, my darling?"

"It's big," Samuel commented.

Margaret smiled at the young boy. "Would you like to wait with me in the drawing room for your father?"

Samuel put his hand in hers, nodding his head.

Margaret gave him a small tour of the house on the way to the drawing room, showing him the portraits of her and her family, and some of the sculptures they had purchased over the years. She didn't want to inundate him with too much, knowing he would tire of anything more.

When they reached the drawing room, Margaret got him situated on one of the couches. "Would you like something to drink?"

Samuel shook his head no, swinging his feet against the couch while he waited patiently.

"Do you want to know what we're doing today?" Margaret sat next to him.

Samuel stuck his hand in hers once again. "Father said you were showing us what your people do."

"That's right," Margaret said. "We'll be outside visiting people and helping pick some of the tobacco so you can see how it's done."

Rowan walked into the drawing room. "I've ordered some breakfast on the terrace for us before we take Sam on his adventure."

Margaret looked over Rowan. He looked very much at ease here in her home. "Thank you, Rowan. That was thoughtful."

Rowan offered her his arm to take her to breakfast outside. "It's a perfect day for this."

"This is wonderful!" Margaret said, looking at the table that was set up for them. A small tent was set up to keep them from squinting in the sun.

Rowan pulled out a chair for Margaret and pushed it in as she sat. He pulled his chair closer to Margaret and sat close enough where he could touch her if he wanted. "I don't know how you stayed at court with this waiting for you every morning." He gestured to the manicured lawn that still had dew on the freshly cut blades of grass.

"Who am I to defy the king?" Margaret said with a hint of bitterness.

Rowan said nothing but looked her over with a light in his eyes she hadn't seen before.

Once they finished their breakfast, Margaret guided them to the fields closest to the house to watch the workers cultivate the tobacco. By this time, the workers had already been in the fields for several hours. There were women walking toward wagons with bundles of tobacco leaves, the largest ones on the bottom of the plants that were already matured for harvest.

"The bottom leaves get harvested first because they mature the quickest," Margaret told them as she pointed at the plants. "See how they're starting to yellow from the tip inward? That means they're ready."

Samuel ran between the large plants, some of the fully grown crops towered over him by a foot or more. "Can I pick one?"

"Of course, you can, my dear," Margaret said with a smile, finding a plant that still had the bottom leaves attached. She knelt next to the plant, grabbing the knife she had tucked in the waist of her apron. She held Samuel's hand and helped him cut the leaf off, leaving a dark sap on both of their hands.

"Ew," Samuel cried, holding his hands up so he could look at them in the light.

Margaret smeared some on his nose with a grin. "You'll be bug-free for the rest of the day with that on you. They hate the smell of it." Her smile partially fell. The scene was reminiscent of her father teaching her the same way. She looked back to the house, missing the sight of him. She wouldn't be able to avoid going to his grave much longer, even if it filled her with dread.

Samuel stood and went to show his father. "Look, Father!"

"Do you want to bring the leaves to the workers?" Margaret asked, taking off the rest of the bottom leaves and stacking them. "They're a little heavy."

Samuel ran back to her. "I'll take them, Maggie!"

Margaret handed them to Samuel, who immediately held them above his head, the bottom of the stack slapping his back. Rowan helped Margaret stand, walking behind his son who ran blindly ahead. Margaret called out directions for Samuel to take him to one of the women bundling the large leaves.

"Why not take the plant as a whole?" Rowan gestured to Samuel with his leaves. "This seems like more work."

"Papa thought it ensured better quality to harvest the leaves as they mature instead of taking leaves that are too young." Margaret shrugged. "No one has complained about our quality, so I don't see a need to change it for efficiency."

The workers were delighted that Samuel was so excited about helping in the fields. They fawned over him while Margaret and Rowan took their time following.

Margaret was excited—this would be her first time speaking to them out in the fields where they were the most knowledgeable. She raised her hand in greeting and repeated what she'd heard Papa say through her childhood following him around, "How goes it?"

They bowed or curtsied to her and Rowan, tipping their hats upward so she could easily see their faces. "Good, Your Ladyship," one of the women answered. "We should have this field done by the end of the week and move on to the next when it's ready."

Margaret smiled, clasping her hands in front of her to stop her from any nervous habits. "Is there anything I can be doing to make sure your needs are being met?" She looked around at the gathered crowd. "Anything that Mr. Amali may have neglected in my absence?"

"Mr. Tevna has already been 'round to ask us, ma'am," one of the men said. He wiped his forehead free of sweat with a dirty cloth before continuing, "He said he would take care of everythin' that'd been mismanaged."

Her eyebrows shot toward her hairline. "Has he really?" He was well ahead of her in planning—she had intended to talk to the workers first so she could have an idea of what they would need and confer with Mr. Tevna, but she was glad he would not let things linger.

"He has, ma'am," another man answered. "A very kind man indeed."

Margaret and Rowan chatted with the workers as they brought in new leaves and bundled them. It was like being in Marbon again, talking with the villagers while she stayed with the Gollacks. Inhaling deeply, she sighed.

It was good to be home.

When Samuel's eyelids started to droop, the couple decided it was time to go back to the house. They'd already been in the field a few hours, and Margaret was starting to feel the heat herself.

As requested, Margaret tucked Samuel into bed for a nap. She ran her fingers through his hair as she told him a story. She told him a story that her father had told her as a little girl about the sea people who worked in tandem with the Tyradrican people. Before Aratia was civilized, the people who lived under the sea helped the Tyradricans defeat a great evil that laid siege on their country. Margaret spoke softly until Samuel was asleep and rejoined Rowan for tea out on the terrace.

"Samuel finally went to sleep. He was struggling to hear the end of the story," Margaret told him as she sat down.

Rowan poured tea for her. "He'll do that when he's really enjoying it."

"I guess I did a good job then." Margaret grinned.

"I'm sure he loved having you put him to bed," Rowan said as he looked out at the fields.

Margaret sighed contentedly as she sipped her tea. She was happy to be back in Dorcia and around the smell of freshly tilled dirt. Margaret's contented look fell to a thoughtful one.

Rowan noticed the change of expression on her face. "What's the matter, my dear?"

"I'm just thinking about visiting my father after dinner," Margaret said softly. She couldn't avoid it any longer. They'd been there two months now, and she hadn't gone yet.

"Would you like me to go with you?" Rowan asked her.

"No." Margaret shook her head. "This is something I should do alone." There were things she wanted to say that she did not want Rowan to hear.

"As you wish." Rowan grabbed her hand and squeezed it.

Margaret blew a slow breath as she walked to the dining room. She didn't want to go. She didn't want to face her father. Some days she was glad he wasn't alive to see what happened to her since she had returned to the capital, and other days she wondered what would have happened to her if he were alive. Would he have gone to the block for her instead? Would they both have? Would he have died for her and her situation ended up the same anyway?

She shook her head, rubbing her first two fingers with her thumbs until they ached. It would do her no good to think about it too much. Margaret would spiral into despair if she did.

Rowan was already in the dining room when she walked in, pouring himself a drink from the serving table.

Margaret smiled at him. "Would you mind pouring me one as well?"

Rowan raised a brow, raising the decanter of whisky. "Are you sure?"

Margaret nodded vigorously. "Please." She would need it to get through dinner.

He poured her a glass, adding in some water. "I think you'll like it better this way."

"Thank you." She took the drink from him, sucking down a large gulp. She let out a hiss once she could breathe again. "Shall we sit?"

Rowan held his arm out toward the table. "After you."

Margaret finished her drink, setting the glass on the serving table before walking past Rowan, his brows furrowed at her. She sat at one of the two place settings.

"Is everything all right, Margaret?"

Of course, it wasn't.

"Yes." She smiled at him. "Is Samuel all right after his day in the sun?"

"He wants to be a farmer now." Rowan chuckled. "He wants to go back into the fields tomorrow."

"He's more than welcome to go back as much as he likes." Margaret fidgeted with her fork on the table, pulling her hands out of the way when a footman came around to serve. "I imagine it will be a while before he's able to come back. He should enjoy it while he can."

"I don't doubt Dianna will regret your invitation."

She didn't either. Dianna was fair skinned and did poorly in the heat. "If you're comfortable, I don't doubt one of the workers would enjoy spending the day looking after him instead of laboring the whole time." Margaret motioned for the footman to continue filling her wine glass when he came around, spinning her hand in circular motions until the red liquid nearly reached the top of the glass.

"I'm sure Samuel would love that."

Margaret took a large drink, emptying half her glass. "I'm sure he would."

Rowan watched her carefully, hesitating before he said, "Have you heard any other news from the palace?"

"No." She shook her head before finishing her glass, motioning for the footman to fill it again. "I suppose that means His Highness is taking his punishment as he should."

"I can't imagine he's really given a choice." Rowan frowned. "He's always been given too lenient treatment. Even when we were younger, my father could never talk him into behaving—even with reminding him we were family."

Margaret doubted very much that family meant anything to Gareth. All he ever thought about was his own personal enjoyment—even if it got people killed, it seemed. "I imagine it was difficult growing up knowing you were the king's cousin."

"It only became a burden when I realized there was only Gareth between me and the throne." Rowan took a drink then. He sighed when he set the glass down. "I've no doubt His Highness will have a multitude of children...it's just a question of whether they're in the line of succession."

Laughing, she took another long drink. "I'm sure His Majesty will find some foreign princess who would love nothing more than to have a whole country's worth of little lords and ladies with the prince."

"No doubt there are plenty willing." He raised his brows, a small smirk on his face. "Before Clairance, there had been a few foreign princesses bandied about for me to marry because I was the heir presumptive."

"And now?" Margaret asked.

"Princesses aren't for second marriages." Rowan shook his head.

Margaret clenched her jaw, reaching for her drink again. He would have to settle in rank then. "I see."

"I'm not the king, and I'll only travel further down the line of succession as His Highness produces more heirs. No princess in their right mind would agree to that marriage, nor would their fathers." He smiled at her. "This is nothing in reference to our courtship."

That was fair. Margaret nodded. "I understand."

"Good." He picked up her hand and kissed it. "I don't want you to ever feel less than."

The longer the dinner went on, the more Margaret drank. Her head was swimming with wine when she motioned again for the footman to fill her glass once more. She knew she wouldn't be able to see her father without liquid courage and took a drink every time she thought about her task.

"Do you think you've had enough?"

Margaret shook her head, wincing when it took a moment for her consciousness to catch up. "I'm all right."

"I don't think—"

Margaret stood, leaning to the side for a brief moment before standing up straight. "I said I was fine." She grabbed her glass, walking toward the door.

Rowan quickly stood as well, his chair scraping against the floor. "Where are you going?"

"To see my father," she slurred over her shoulder.

Margaret stumbled her way outside, headed toward her father's grave. There had been a mausoleum erected shortly after her father was buried in Dorcia, and he was once again moved to reside within. Margaret stumbled onto the steps, splashing her wine as she landed against them. She had drunk too much while at dinner with Rowan, in her preparation to confront the tomb.

"How can this be my life?" Margaret asked the mausoleum, finishing her wine. She dropped her glass, it cracking when it hit the steps. "How can I be left to this?" she drunkenly demanded. "To be trapped by the king with no real hope of escape? He was your friend! You should have known better than to let us be so tied up with that family."

Margaret felt all the emotions she had bottled up since her father's death wash over her as she wept on the steps—heartbreak for what she'd lost of her father and herself; anger that she had made the decisions leading to it all; hopelessness in not knowing if she'd ever be able to return to who she truly was without all the lying and games to try to save herself. Margaret didn't know how long the episode went on for before she heard someone behind her.

"My lady!" Sarah exclaimed, trying to get her up. "My lady, please, let's go inside!"

"Leave me be, Sarah!" Margaret yelled, swatting at her.

Sarah went back inside, Captain Vojvo returning with her. "Margaret," his voice cut sternly through her crying. "Margaret, it's time to come inside."

Margaret shook her head, unable to stop her tears.

Vojvo picked her up, carrying her inside.

Margaret tried to get away from him, continuing to sob. "Please, I don't want you to see me like this," she choked out between her tears.

Vojvo laid her down on the bed, motioning for Sarah to take off her shoes. "Shush," he said, stroking her hair. "We've been with you through worse. Everything will be all right."

"No, it won't." A fresh wave of sobs came over her. Margaret grabbed a pillow, hugging it to her chest. "Nothing will ever be the same again!"

"It will be all right, Margaret," Vojvo countered. "We're right here for you."

"I can't do this on my own," Margaret cried, shaking her head.

Vojvo grabbed her face and made her look at him. "Margaret, you don't need to. We're here for you."

Margaret shook her head, looking at him desperately, though her sobs were subsiding.

"See?" Vojvo smiled. "Things are already getting better. You just need to breathe."

Margaret nodded, trying hard to breathe deeply to calm herself. She was starting to relax, her neck loosening as her shoulders dropped.

Vojvo let go of her as she calmed. "Better?" he asked.

Margaret nodded, her eyes drying. "Yes."

Vojvo grabbed both of her shoulders and squeezed them gently. "I'll let Sarah ready you for bed?"

"Thank you, Marius," Margaret said in a barely audible voice.

Vojvo left her, and Sarah took his place. "Are you feeling better, my lady?"

"Yes," Margaret said, getting off the bed. "I'm sorry for swatting at you."

"Think nothing of it," Sarah said as she unlaced Margaret's dress.

"Did His Grace see any of this?"

Sarah shook her head. "No. His Grace went up to bed when you left to visit your father."

Relief rushed through her. "Good. I would have scared him away with that display."

"His Grace is a good man," Sarah said quickly. "I doubt you could scare him away at all."

Margaret had a heavy head in the morning, her embarrassment weighing more on her than the effects of her excessive drink the night before. Margaret's cheeks colored when Rowan came in. She couldn't remember if she had made a fool of herself at dinner or just at her father's grave. She winced when Samuel called out her name, but she held her arms out to him nonetheless. "My darling, what would you like to do today?"

"Can we go in the fields again?" Samuel asked excitedly.

"As long as your father says it's all right," Margaret said looking at Rowan.

Rowan looked over Margaret, pausing on her weary face. "Why don't we have Dianna take you out to the fields, and Lady Margaret can have a quiet day alone?"

Samuel pouted. "But, Father, I want to go with Maggie!"

"You'll have just as much fun without us." Rowan's tone made clear the conversation was over.

Samuel pouted through breakfast but was excited when Dianna came to take him to the fields. Rowan poured some tea for Margaret. "How are you feeling this morning?"

"In a fog," Margaret said, her face hot with embarrassment. "I'm incredibly sorry about last night."

"I had quite a few nights like that after my wife died, where drink seemed to be the only thing that helped," Rowan told her quietly. "You never had your mourning period, from what I understand."

"No," Margaret quietly confirmed.

"Why don't we go for a walk?" Rowan asked. "Clear your head a little?"

Margaret stood, smoothing her skirts. "That sounds like a wonderful idea."

Rowan pulled her arm through his and took her through the yards. He stopped under a tree to look out at the expanse of her lands. "My lady, has the king said anything to you about marriage since you became his ward?"

"Only that he would find a suitable husband that he approved of," Margaret said, leaving off that the king wanted a husband that would not contradict the king's continuance of his nightly visits.

"I see." Rowan stood in front of her, tucking a lock of hair behind her ear.

Margaret shrugged. "Perhaps now that I've been given my title and lands, I can pick my own husband."

"I certainly hope that I will be a contender when there's a line for your hand in marriage," Rowan told her, pulling her against him.

Margaret looked up at him with wide eyes. Rowan had been affectionate toward her, but he had never been this direct. "Your Grace—"

Rowan cut her off, kissing her for the first time in their courtship. He pulled her tighter against him, cradling the back of her head. He broke the kiss, only to kiss her several more times before resting his forehead against hers.

Margaret wrapped her arms around his waist, her fingers digging into his back. She had felt like she would have fallen over if his grip on her had not been so tight. Margaret had her eyes closed still, her lips tingling with every repeated kiss.

Rowan tipped her chin up to look at him. "Would I be a contender?"

She searched his face, looking for any sign he doubted the lies she had been telling him. "A very strong contender, Your Grace," Margaret said before Rowan kissed her again.

12

"**D**a?"

Liam looked up from his breakfast. "Something on your mind, Simon?"

"What d'ye think of Joanna?"

"The shop girl?" He furrowed his brow. "I think she's lovely."

Simon shifted nervously, pulling on his fingers in front of him. "I'm thinkin' about askin' for her hand. But I willna if you dinna think I should."

Liam frowned at him. Had they even spent any time together aside from visits to the shop? "I didn't think you were so serious about her."

"We've been seein' each other outside of the shop a few months now," Simon said shyly. "Ye were fair busy with buildin' the upstairs fer Jamie an' Ellie, an' then with workin' extra hours to make up for what ye missed."

He supposed it was true—he had been busy the last several months. Liam just didn't think he was that oblivious to what was going on in Simon's life.

"I'm happy for you, son." It seemed him forgetting to have a talk with Simon about making sure not to harass Joanna may have worked in everyone's favor. She was a sweet enough girl, and she would complement Simon well. "If you want to ask her, I think she would make a good match for you."

"D'ye really?" Simon brightened, sitting up slightly.

"I do." Liam leaned back in his chair, taking a sip of his coffee. "Why don't you bring her around some time to meet your Ma? I think she'd like to know who you're planning on marrying."

"Ma's already met her," Simon said.

"Just in the shop, or actually met her?"

Simon furrowed his brows. "In the shop."

"That's not getting to know a person." Liam shook his head. "Why don't you bring her for dinner tonight?"

Simon nodded slowly, rubbing his lips together as he thought. "D'ye think Ma would mind?"

"Of course not." Liam grinned at him. "You know she'll be thrilled, especially if you tell her you want to marry this girl one day."

"All right." Simon gave him a shy smile. "Will ye tell Ma for me?"

"Depends." Liam stood, stretching out from sitting at the table so long. "Do you want to go out with Eli and me?"

"What are ye doin'?" Simon asked.

"I'm taking him hunting."

"I think I'd rather go see Joanna." Simon shook his head. "I'll tell Ma on my way out."

"That's all right." Liam grunted. "I'm sure Eli will be happier with it just being the two of us."

"Oh, aye," Simon agreed. "He's yer little shadow now."

Liam didn't mind—most of the time. He missed his personal space and not being asked fifteen questions every five minutes, but he wouldn't have life any other way now. He even missed the incessant chattering when he was at work.

After Simon left, Liam gathered all the supplies they would need for hunting. He wouldn't take Eli far in—this would mostly be a test to see if Eli could handle going out. He wasn't quite sure Eli was old enough, but he wouldn't stop asking to go.

Little arms wrapped around his hips. "Hey Duck."

"When are we leaving?" Eli asked.

"As soon as I've got all our stuff together," Liam said. "Why don't you go find Ma and ask her to pack us some food?"

The little arms released him, and Eli scampered away.

Liam looked over their supplies, making sure they had everything they needed. He went to check on Eli and found him eating breakfast at the table and Gretta wrapping food at the counter. "Everything coming along?"

"I'm almost done," Gretta said, not turning around. "And then ye two can go."

Liam kissed her cheek. "Thank you."

Once Eli finished his toast, they left for the wilderness.

"Can I carry something?" Eli started reaching for the bow in Liam's hand with a grin.

"You can carry this." Liam quickly handed him their food. "Never grab a weapon from someone unless your life is in danger."

The smile fell from Eli's face. "Aye, Da."

At the forest line, Liam showed Eli where he could see the deer trails. "We just have to follow one of these and settle in to wait for a deer to cross our path."

They followed a trail until they couldn't see the open field any longer. Liam found a small spot for them to settle in and wait. It didn't take long before Eli started fidgeting with the nature surrounding them. "I'm bored, Da."

"We have to make sure we're quiet so that the deer aren't scared away by us," Liam whispered against Eli's ear.

Eli gripped his hands in front of him looking chagrined. "Sorry, Da."

It wasn't long before Eli started fidgeting again. Liam should have listened to his instincts instead of letting Eli's pestering sway him to bring him out. He was too young to have the self-control required for a long day of hunting.

"How long d'ye think until we see somethin'?" Eli sighed heavily. "I'm bored."

"I don't know, Duck." Liam put his finger to his lips. "Now, be quiet."

Eli sighed, throwing his head back in frustration.

Liam would definitely leave him at home next time. He turned his head sharply when he heard a snap in the opposite direction.

"Da?"

"Shh!" Liam held up his hand, listening for another snap.

He drew his bow when he saw the light brown and white hair through the trees. It wouldn't be long before it crossed the opening in front of them.

"Is there a deer, Da?" Eli whispered. He stood, looking around wildly.

"Yes," he said quietly. Liam didn't take his eyes off the opening. "Now, sit down and shush." He waited until he could see the deer clearly. Liam let out a hiss when the string broke, his arrow falling wildly to the ground.

Liam's hand and forearm went numb, and he shook it out. He should have replaced the string sooner, but he was glad a numb hand was all he got from it. He'd heard of people losing fingers—or worse—from their strings breaking.

"Da!" Eli yelled, grabbing onto his arm. "Da!"

Liam looked down to see his forearm was bleeding. The string must have hit him. That was why his hand was numb. "I'm all right, Duck."

"Da, it willna stop bleeding!" Eli started to cry.

He took a closer look, his arm feeling sluggish as he moved it. Yellow fat poked through the gash when he wiped his hand over the cut to clear the blood. It was only a few inches, but it was deep. With the rate it was bleeding, they would need to get home to a healer, and quickly.

"It's all right, Duck. You're going to help me, yeah?" The rest of his arm was starting to go a little numb. Liam pulled out his tucked shirt and handed Eli a knife. He tried to stay as calm as possible for Eli. He must be thinking about his father's hunting accident that killed him—or, at least, what Gretta had told Eli killed his father. "Go ahead and cut all around the bottom—I'll hold out how much you need—and then you can help me tie it on my arm."

Eli snuffled, doing as he was bid.

"All right," Liam said calmly, "now, before you tie it all the way, I want you to find a stick and make another knot."

"Why?"

"It'll help stop the bleeding for now." Liam pointed to the ground. "There's a good one there."

Eli grabbed it and tied it in. "Now what?"

"I'm going to twist it real tight," Liam said as he was twisting, "and then you're going to tie it again in place."

When indicated, Eli finished tying the tourniquet. Liam ruffled Eli's hair when he was done, flexing his fingers. Even with the tourniquet, their makeshift bandage was already soaked through. "You did a great job, Duck. Now let's get back home."

"What about all our stuff?" Eli asked when Liam walked away without grabbing anything.

"We can come back for it later," Liam said, grabbing his hand. "Right now, we need to go home."

Liam walked faster than they did going into the woods. He had to drag Eli a little for him to keep up. He was already starting to feel woozy when The Smiling Fox came into view.

"Why don't you go ahead and get Ma?" Liam slowed, squeezing Eli's hand. "I can make it the rest of the way on my own."

Eli let go of Liam, running to The Smiling Fox, yelling for Gretta.

Liam leaned against the wall at the back, nausea rolling around in his stomach. He'd definitely needed a healer to stitch his arm up.

"What's—" Gretta dropped her rag when she saw him. "Liam!"

Liam gave her a weak smile. "Will you go and get the healer for me?"

"Can ye get yerself inside?" Gretta asked, helping him stand straight.

Liam nodded, his stomach clenching at the motion. "I can." He spotted a tearful Eli in the doorway, holding his hand out to him. "Eli can help me inside."

Eli grabbed his hand tightly, leading him inside while Gretta hurried away in the other direction.

"That's a good lad," Liam said as he sat heavily at the table.

Gretta returned quickly with a healer, pointing him toward Liam.

"What seems—"

Liam held up his arm, blood starting to drip.

"Oh." The healer set down his bag. "Can ye get me some hot water and some towels, Mrs. McWard?"

Gretta hurried to do what she was told.

"I'm gonna give ye a bit o' poppy to dull the pain, Mr. McWard," the healer said, digging it from his bag.

Liam nodded. He was too tired to correct him.

The healer took a wooden board with straps on it from his bag. "I'll need to strap ye onto this," he said as he put it under Liam's arm.

Gretta came back with the water and towels. "What can I do, Healer Crane?"

"That's all." Healer Crane tied the first rope around Liam's wrist, and the second near his elbow.

Liam flinched, growling so he wouldn't curse in front of Eli. It was even tighter than his tourniquet.

"All right," Crane started. "I'm going to release yer bandage and then I'm gonna verra quickly clean and then stitch it, aye?"

Liam nodded. "Ready."

He hissed when the water hit his wound. It was deeper than he had thought it was. When was that poppy going to start working? Crane closed the wound with a curved needle and silk thread, and Liam tried not to flinch away from it. It was almost as painful as his field dressing in the war.

Eli came to his side, hugging Liam's free arm. He sniffled as the healer worked.

When Healer Crane finished his stitching, he released Liam's arm from its constraint. He slathered Liam's wound with a salve that smelled just the same as the one used in the healer's tent on the field. Liam tried not to let it conjure memories he had long tamped down. Healer Crane covered the salve with a clean bandage.

"Ye'll need to keep this clean, an' I want ye to check in with me in a few days," Crane said. "I'm gonna leave ye with some of this poppy if yer pain gets too much to manage."

"Thank you," Liam said, flexing his fingers with some pain.

Once Healer Crane left, Gretta turned to Liam. "What in Olam's name happened?"

"My bowstring broke." Liam took a small sip of the poppy the healer left.

Eli puffed his chest. "I helped Da with the tourniquet."

"Ye must have been so scairt, after yer Da." Gretta pulled Eli against her side, kissing the top of his head.

"He was very brave about it." Liam smoothed back Eli's hair. "I was lucky Eli was out there with me to help."

"Aye, we all were." Gretta squeezed his shoulder. "Will ye still be up for dinner with Simon and Joanna tonight?"

Liam nodded. "As long as I can take a few hours to rest, I think I'll be fine. The poppy should be working by then."

"I'll take ye up to bed," Gretta said, helping him stand up. "I dinna want ye fallin' down the stairs with the poppy an' ye losin' all that blood."

Liam nodded, grateful to have her help.

Liam sleepily came down the stairs when he heard some commotion. The poppy must have put him to sleep—it was dark out now. He tried to rub his face, wincing when he brought up his injured arm. He'd have to get used to one hand for now. Liam stopped when he reached the bottom of the stairs. Dinner was in full swing, the whole family at the dining table.

"Da!" Eli knocked his chair over trying to get to Liam as fast as he could, hugging him around the waist. "Ye're up!"

Liam patted him on the back with his good hand. "I am."

"Let me get ye a plate." Gretta stood, pulling out a chair for him. "We didna want to wake ye since ye needed the sleep after today."

"Thank you." Liam kissed her cheek before sitting down next to Joanna. "It's nice to see you."

Joanna motioned to his arm. "Will ye be all right?"

"Oh, it'll be fine. I've had worse." Liam tried to flex his fingers again, wincing at the pull against his stitches. "I'll just have to take it easy in the shop for a little bit."

Gretta returned, putting a plate full of food in front of Liam and poured him a cup of ale.

"It's startin' to get busy," Joanna said slowly, her brow furrowing.

Liam sighed. "I know. I'll talk to Jossnon in the morning. There will only be so much I can do there."

Joanna pulled in the corner of her mouth, rolling it between her teeth as she furrowed her brow. "We could take on an apprentice for a wee bit. Ye ken, until yer arm isna hurtin'." She looked to Simon briefly before continuing, "Ye could teach 'em and still have work bein' put out so Joss doesna feel the loss of ye."

"There are a few lads in the fields that wouldna be opposed to learnin' to smith." Simon leaned forward to look around Joanna. "I wouldna mind bein' yer apprentice, Da."

A small smile slid onto Joanna's face. "I certainly wouldna mind seein' ye there."

Jamie snorted. "D'ye think Da will put up with ye makin' eyes at each other all day?"

Joanna dropped her smile, her face the model of seriousness. "I can assure ye, sir, I dinna make eyes at anyone but the customer."

"So that's why they keep buying so much!" Liam slapped his good hand down on the table, grin on his face.

Joanna's face finally broke, laughing along with Liam.

Liam patted Simon on his shoulder. "If you two can behave yourself, and Joss says yes, I'd love to have you apprentice in the shop, Simon."

"Really?" Simon grinned.

"Come by at lunch and I'll let you know what Joss said."

Joanna let out a grunt. "Ye ken he was gonna show up then anyway."

Liam watched Simon's eyes crinkle around the edges as he looked at Joanna. They would make a good match for each other. He looked at Gretta and saw the same smile she'd worn when Jamie brought Ellie to meet her.

Clearly, she had the same thought.

13

L illian walked arm and arm with the Dowager Duchess Cecily through the corridors of the palace. She hadn't wanted to spend much time in the hall with the other nobles since Gareth's punishment. It had apparently been too lenient for some, who glared at her and the king whenever they were there.

She didn't know what they expected—for them to imprison Gareth? Banish him? He was the heir to the throne, not a commoner. Even one of the other nobles would have faced lesser punishment because of the fortune of their birth.

Cecily sighed. "I think I might like to return home soon."

"Really?" Lillian looked at her sharply. "You want to leave me for an estate with no one there?"

"This place only reminds me of my husband." Cecily squeezed her arm. "At least at home I can be alone in my grief, no one telling me I should be in white by now."

Lillian looked her over. Cecily was still in the darkest mourning gray, and it had been more than a year since Crompton had died. She really should have been in white by now, but Crompton and Cecily were a love for the ages. They were one of the rare few who had found each other instead of being forced together.

"If you really want to go, I can release you from my ladies." After decades of service, Lillian could hardly deny Cecily the small pleasure of being in her own home to mourn the way she wished.

Cecily nodded. "I wouldn't like to leave you, but I would like that."

"You may leave…" Lillian slowed, her brows furrowing as she noticed the whispers and eyes in her direction. She looked at Cecily. "What is going on?"

Cecily glanced around them, raising her brows at Lillian. "I'm unsure, Your Majesty."

"You always know who has the best gossip." Lillian untangled her arm from Cecily's. "Have someone find out. Meet me in my chambers when you do."

Cecily gave her a small curtsy before walking off.

Lillian kept an even pace as she went to her chambers, despite the continuing whispers.

At this point, it could be about anything—had Sorren taken a new mistress and finally forgotten Margaret? Lillian sighed. If only. There was little hope of that for her. She had tried to get him to denounce Margaret for months.

Had Gareth done something else already? What could he have possibly done that would have caused such a reaction?

A flurry of maids skittered away from their duties to curtsy to Lillian as she walked into the room. "Get back to work," she snapped. The last thing she wanted now was more people staring at her.

Lillian waited until the servants went back to their work before going to the windows in her sitting room. She sighed heavily as she stood in front of the windows. She couldn't stop thinking about what could have happened.

She didn't have long to wait—Cecily returned to Lillian's company hastily. "Your Majesty," she said, giving her a small curtsy.

"Did you get answers?"

Cecily glances back at the servants, motioning toward Lillian's bedchamber.

Lillian looked around the room to see if any of the servants were paying attention to them before going to her bedchamber and closing the door behind them. "Well?"

Cecily cleared her throat. "It seems one of His Royal Highness's mistresses has gotten with child, and she is demanding their child have a place in the succession."

"Surely she can't be so stupid—"

"She's threatening to charge him with assault if he can't." Cecily shook her head. "The girl is determined."

"Which one is it?" Lillian gripped her skirt in her fists. Depending on the status of this girl, this could actually cause trouble for them. "And does His Majesty know?"

"I'm uncertain about His Majesty, but the mistress is the wife of Lord Herbert l'Ander, the Duke of Clemons's oldest son."

Lillian pinched the bridge of her nose, inhaling deeply. "Of course, it would be one of the more powerful mistresses."

"What will you do?"

"I don't know." Shaking her head, Lillian sighed. "I need to speak with His Majesty."

"Would you like me to accompany you?"

"No." Lillian's mouth flattened. "I think it's best done without an audience."

"As you'd like, Majesty." Cecily curtsied to her before leaving.

Lillian covered her face, letting out a groan. Was there nothing her son could do right? She looked at the clock—Sorren should be free now. Making her way to his chambers, she thought of how she would break the news to him, ignoring the whispers following her. Sorren would be incensed. Gareth was already on incredibly thin ice with his father.

She knocked on the door, stepping back with a jolt when Sorren answered it himself. He looked disheveled, tightly gripping a piece of parchment in his fist. "Can I help you?"

"I—"

"Well?" He crossed his arms. "I'm busy."

"It's Gareth again." Lillian licked her suddenly dry lips. "He's causing trouble."

Sorren sighed heavily. "Come in." He stood to the side to let her inside.

Lillian went into his chambers, wrinkling her nose at the mess. "Has no one been in to clean?"

"I told them to go away this morning."

She wanted to ask why, but she couldn't get bogged down with that now. "Gareth has gotten a married woman pregnant, and she is demanding their child be put in the line of succession."

"Of course she is." Sorren laughed. "They all do."

"She's threatening to charge him with assault if it doesn't happen." Lillian rubbed her lips together, inhaling deeply through her nose. "We can't have another public incident with Gareth."

"No, we can't." Sorren shook his head. "What do you propose we do?"

Lillian furrowed her brow. What would she do? He never asked for her opinion. Was he trying to place any blame on her when things didn't go well? "We could send him to my family in Frasisca. It would be a lesson in how other courts work and restrict the access his mistresses have to him."

"Good." Sorren poured himself a drink before flopping into one of his plusher chairs. "We can pay the husband a stipend to not set aside his wife. If they're still married when she gives birth, legally that is his child."

"Unless Gareth claims him."

"Which he won't do." Sorren took a long drink. "He never takes responsibility unless forced, and I won't force him in this."

"Will you send him away?" Lillian asked. "Or shall I?"

"I'll leave it in your capable hands." Sorren pulled back out his piece of parchment. "You may go."

Lillian frowned. "When should I tell him to go?"

"You decide." Sorren waved his hand at her, clearly dismissing her.

Lillian returned to her chambers. She would need to write a letter to her brother to send with Gareth, informing him of the situation. Should she tell Gareth before she sent him away, or should she just surprise him with guards to escort him to Frasisca?

Surprise him. Lillian nodded, getting out a piece of parchment from her writing desk. If she didn't tell him, he wouldn't have any time to wiggle out of it.

Gareth burst in through the doors to her chambers. "What are you doing, Mother?"

Her ladies startled, one of them dropping her book as she gasped.

Lillian calmly put down her needlepoint, raising her brows at him. "Would you like to try again?"

"My things are being removed from my chambers!" Gareth threw his arms wide before crossing them in front of him. "When I asked, I was told it was by *your* order."

"It was by my order." She had to stay calm, or she would lose control of the situation. "And you will be going to Frasisca to visit my brother and learn about how Frasisca rules."

"I will not!"

Clasping her hands together, Lillian said, "You will. And you will not complain, because this will keep you from becoming the topic of even more scandal. Because, for whatever reason, you cannot keep yourself out of trouble."

"You cannot—"

"I can." Lillian stood, inhaling deeply. "I am your mother, and I am your queen. And your king thinks this is a good idea."

"But—"

"Enough!" She pulled her shoulders back. "This is a command from your king and your queen. Now, do what you're told for once in your life and go!"

Gareth glared at her as he bowed. "As *my queen* commands," he spat before backing out of the room.

Lillian sighed, collapsing back into her chair. She closed her eyes, leaning her head back, thankful her ladies remained quiet. She couldn't deal with their whispers too.

14

"**M**y lady, you're beaming," Sarah commented as she looked Margaret over in the mirror.

"I'm happy, Sarah." Margaret spun in her seat to look at Sarah delightedly. "His Grace is making me incredibly happy."

"I believe you." Sarah turned her around to finish her hair. "This is the happiest I've ever seen you."

Margaret grinned at her through the mirror. "And until we return to the capital, you will see me this happy. I'm not even sure the king can douse my spirits then."

Pinning the last of her hair back, Sarah smoothed out the flyaway strands. "I'm glad to hear it."

Margaret stood, looking herself over in the mirror. "How do I look?"

"Beautiful, my lady." Sarah smoothed Margaret's skirts in the back.

"Good." Margaret smiled, practically prancing to the terrace to meet Rowan and Samuel for breakfast. Rowan had continued to drop hints of marriage since he had kissed her. If he meant it, this would finally be her escape. How could the king not approve of one of his own family?

Rowan and his son stood when she approached the table. "Lady Margaret, you look beautiful this morning."

Margaret smiled at him brightly. They had agreed to not kiss openly in front of Samuel to avoid confusion—they didn't talk about the boy's mother much, but Samuel mentioned her lovingly when he did. Still, she itched to greet Rowan with one. "Thank you, Your Grace," she said instead.

Rowan pulled out a chair for her, sitting opposite her with Samuel in the middle. "When would you like to leave today?"

"As soon as we can. I'm looking forward to seeing your lands," Margaret said, putting a few berries on her plate. "I think we should take as long as possible viewing them. I've written the king and told him that I am now subject to your whim…in terms of time, that is."

Rowan raised an eyebrow, sitting forward. "Oh?"

"I'm enjoying spending time with you." Margaret took one of the raspberries on the table and rubbed it lightly along her bottom lip before popping it in her mouth. "And I'm sure that Samuel will enjoy spending time with his playmates in his home province."

"Then I suppose we had better have the rest of your staff help us pack as quickly as possible," Rowan said, staring at her lips. "I'm sure he'll be spending lots of time with his friends."

Margaret gave him a coquettish smile. "And you'll have the time to tell me all the history of the house—every room."

A smirk spread on Rowan's face. "Absolutely, all the time in the world, my dear."

The couple traveled through the rest of Margaret's lands quickly compared to how they started. Margaret did not want to dwell in Silvica long other than to inform its citizens that the former tenant was now their lady. It still brought back too many memories of what had happened there. She refused to visit her cottage where her father had been murdered by Lord Nicholas Oliphant. The only good to come out of the whole ordeal was her relationship with Liam and the Gollacks when they traveled nearly to the Salatian border.

She still thought fondly of them, though Margaret hadn't kept in touch as much as she had promised. She would have to send them a letter once she reached Rowan's home, Craneswile. Margaret wondered if she should name her home in Dorcia—it was certainly grand enough for a name. No, she would leave it nameless. She wanted people to know her father made them something from nothing.

Margaret was greeted warmly upon her arrival, the children of Silvica still gifting her with flowers they had picked. It was like she never left. She promised the people that she would ensure more funds would be invested in the repair of their town.

The party traveled east once they had entered the duke's lands. Rowan wanted to save his lands on the coast as the last stop before they had to travel back to the capital to return to court.

"We'll be right on the border of Salatia when we start the tour. There are a few towns that I have yet to go to," Rowan told her.

"There are places you haven't been in your lands?" Margaret asked, surprised.

"His Majesty split lands from the Dukes Bishop and Bomack to make up for his gifting you my land, so they now touch from the border to the coast," Rowan told her. "They're none too happy with the king for it."

"I'm sorry." Margaret wrapped her arm around Samuel, who was once again sleeping against her in the carriage. "His Majesty surprised us all by extending my lands, I didn't intend to cause trouble."

"I would have happily given you any of my lands without the king feeling he needed to repay me," Rowan told her. "There would have been no hard feelings."

Margaret did not doubt that it was the king's intention to harbor ill will between the two to end their courtship. She was glad to see Rowan did not share the pettiness that wreaked havoc in the Platiri family. "Where is it that we'll be going?"

"Our first stop is a small town called Marbon." Rowan wrinkled his brow. "A very small town from my understanding."

Butterflies erupted in Margaret's stomach. "Marbon?" she asked quietly.

"I'd never heard of it until it became mine," Rowan said with a shrug.

"You might be in for a surprise when you get there," Margaret said mischievously.

"Have you been there before?" Rowan had a surprised look on his face.

Margaret stroked Samuel's hair, a soft smile coming to her face as she watched him sleep. "Do you remember the orphans I told you about?" She had told him nearly her whole life story as they traveled—there wasn't much else to do in a carriage while traveling for days on end.

"They were in Marbon?" Rowan's eyebrows were raised.

"Yes," Margaret said brightly. "And I'd like for you to meet them while we're there."

"It seems like you will once again be the one showing me around."

"I don't mind." Margaret smiled. "There are so many people I want you to meet."

"In such a small town?"

Margaret nodded, telling him more details about everyone she had formed relationships with.

The trip to Marbon from Silvica was much shorter than when Margaret had traveled there with Liam. She saw many familiar spots along the way and couldn't help the memories they brought up. She studied Rowan—there was no comparing the two of them. Liam was so entirely different from the duke. Margaret didn't doubt she would be happy with Liam, but he would never be able to help her and her people the same way Rowan could.

As things grew even more familiar, she could hardly wait for the carriage to stop for them to set up their camp outside of the small town. There were no large houses for them to stay at, nor any inns that would be appropriate for a duke to stay at. Margaret began to fidget in her excitement, looking out the window of the carriage every few seconds.

"Margaret, checking where we are won't make us get there any sooner." Rowan's eyes twinkled with amusement.

Margaret blushed and sat back. "I'm just so excited."

Rowan chuckled, looking out the window himself. "And what are you going to do when we get there?"

"Go see the couple that I stayed with while I was here and then my little monsters," Margaret told him excitedly. She'd heard from Claudette all about how they'd grown and how they were doing in their studies in the years she'd be gone. She couldn't wait to see how true the letters were. "They'll be so happy to see me."

Rowan raised his brows. "I don't think I've ever seen you this excited, even when we went to your home."

"These people were my life while I was here." Margaret lifted her shoulder, still smiling.

"How long do you want to stay?"

Margaret would be happy if they could stay weeks there, but she couldn't hold them up too long. "Just overnight, if you don't mind."

"I don't mind." Rowan picked up her hand, kissing it gently. "I'll supervise setting up camp, and then I'll join you?"

She nodded, a smile slowly sliding across her face. "I think they'll like you."

When the carriage finally stopped, Margaret wasted no time in getting out. She picked up her skirts and hurried to the Gollacks' home, a grin on her face. She knocked hurriedly at the door, impatiently waiting for it to open. She had not received any letters from them while she was on tour, and she was anxious to see how they were.

Aram opened the door, solemnly, his face brightening only slightly when he saw her. "Margaret! What are you doing here?"

Margaret's shoulders fell, the smile dropping from her face. She had expected a warmer greeting. "I'm touring Duke Fradure's lands with him. Where's Elizabeth?"

The brightness that she had brought to his face disappeared. "She's real sick, Margaret."

"What?" Margaret grabbed his arm in shock. "How bad is it?"

Aram shook his head. "It's near the end…I knew it the moment she started talking to you."

"To me?" Margaret furrowed her brow. "But, I wasn't here."

"My mother was the same way." Aram's shoulders drooped even further. "She saw my sister for a full week before she passed."

Margaret hesitated, looking over Aram's face slowly. "And how long has she been talking to me?"

"Two weeks, at least until a few days ago when you said you had to go for a little bit," he said slowly. "She thinks you're stitching in the corner like you used to."

Her breath hitched, tears stinging the back of her eyes. "Where is she?"

"She's in the bedroom," was all Aram was able to say before Margaret pushed past him.

"Elizabeth?" Margaret called out as she went to the bedroom. She fell to her knees when she reached the bed, grabbing Elizabeth's hand. "Elizabeth!"

Elizabeth looked completely different from the way she looked the last time Margaret had been there. Elizabeth's skin was hanging off her, looking almost skeletal. Margaret could see the veins showing through the papery skin on her face and neck.

"Margaret is that you?" Elizabeth asked weakly. "Am I dreaming? Are you back?"

Margaret held her breath to keep her tears at bay as she stroked back Elizabeth's hair. "No, Beth, you're not dreaming." Margaret squeezed her hand. "I'm back"

Elizabeth gripped her hand. "I was hoping I'd see you again before the end."

Margaret put a smile on her face, a few tears escaping. She wiped them away quickly, and they were just as quickly replaced. "I'm here now," she said quietly. "Have you had a healer come?"

Elizabeth shook her head weakly. "You already know a healer can't help what I have."

"Sure he can." Margaret kissed her hand, squeezing it as tight as she dared. "Let me get you a healer."

"No, Margaret," Elizabeth told her. "No healer."

Margaret looked back when Aram entered the room. He was thin—far thinner than she remembered. He didn't look like he'd last much past Elizabeth. She couldn't see him living on his own, if Margaret was being honest. They deserved to be together, always bonded together in life and death.

"She's refused a healer the entire time," Aram said tiredly.

"Why?" Margaret demanded.

"She's ready to go," Aram said sadly. He had obviously had some time to accept her wishes.

"How can you just let her give up?" Margaret demanded, standing up quickly.

"We've lived long lives, Margaret," Aram told her. "We have no children, no money, and we're tired. So very, very tired."

"It's my time, Margaret. I'm ready to go." Elizabeth scooted over and held her hand out to her. "Come tell me more stories about your time in the capital."

She couldn't lose Elizabeth so soon. Not when they had just reunited again. Inhaling shakily, Margaret sat next to the older woman, taking her hand once more. It somehow felt more papery than before. She kept her grip gentle, afraid she would bruise Elizabeth if she held it any firmer.

Margaret told Elizabeth almost every detail of her life at court, leaving out the scandals she and the king had caused. Elizabeth laughed often, coughing harder each time, sinking back into the bed in exhaustion.

Margaret swallowed hard, trying to rid herself of the lump in her throat. It was hard to watch Elizabeth decline in front of her. She tried to keep in her tears, failing on numerous occasions while she spoke at length to the dying woman. When Margaret began telling Elizabeth about her courtship with the duke that resided over the lands that now encased Marbon, she sent Aram to get him so she could introduce Elizabeth.

Rowan entered the room and paused at the sight. "Margaret?"

Margaret wiped her eyes quickly, her bottom lip quivering with the effort to not break down in tears. "Rowan, this is Elizabeth," she said, her voice thick.

Rowan knelt next to the bed so Elizabeth would not have to crane her neck to look at him. "Margaret has spoken of nothing but you and your husband since she learned that we were going to Marbon."

Elizabeth smiled, reaching her hand up and cupping Margaret's cheek in her bony hand. "She's our sweet girl."

Margaret's face heated with her effort to keep in her tears. She kissed Elizabeth's hand before holding it to her cheek. "Oh, Elizabeth, please let me help you."

"You're helping me by being here," Elizabeth told her. "Now, I can die happy."

Rowan grabbed Margaret's free hand and squeezed it. "Margaret tells me she loved staying here, and she wished she had been back much sooner to see you."

The wrinkles at the corners of her eyes deepened as Elizabeth smiled. "We got to see a side of Margaret that no one else did."

Margaret was relieved Rowan was there to offer his support. "And a side that probably only you will see." She wished she could go back to the days of living the simple life with the Gollacks and Liam—a happy little family with no cares but their own, living in peace.

"Unless this handsome man becomes your husband," Elizabeth suggested, eyeing Rowan critically, "then he'll see what we saw in you."

Margaret laughed, wiping away the tears that fell. "Only you would be thinking of my prospects, Beth."

"You're a daughter to me, Margaret," the older woman said before a coughing fit began.

Margaret quickly handed her a handkerchief, grimacing when it came away with blood. Margaret squeezed Rowan's hand until her knuckles were white. She wished they had toured Rowan's lands before her own—she might have been able to convince Elizabeth to have a healer help her in the early stages of her sickness. Now the only thing she could do was make Elizabeth comfortable.

"I'm tired," Elizabeth said once her coughing was done.

Margaret wiped away the blood Elizabeth missed on her lips and stroked back her hair. "Would you like us to leave while you try to rest?"

"Will you stay with me until I fall asleep?" Elizabeth asked Margaret.

"Yes," Margaret said quickly. "Yes, of course I will, Elizabeth."

Elizabeth smiled at Margaret. "Tell Liam that I love him."

Margaret nodded emphatically, unable to speak as tears flooded her eyes once more.

Rowan quietly left the room to give them some privacy.

Margaret gently stroked the back of Elizabeth's hand while she fell asleep, quietly telling the older woman the couple's traveling plans. It did not take Elizabeth long to fall asleep, a tight grip on Margaret's hand. Margaret watched as Elizabeth's face relaxed and the grip on her hand slackened, a whispery breath let out.

Dread oozed down her shoulders as her stomach sank. "Elizabeth?" she asked, tightening her grip on her hand.

She did not wake as Margaret expected her to. Margaret immediately stood and put her cheek close to Elizabeth's. There was no breath fanning her face.

"Elizabeth!" Margaret let out a mournful cry. "Elizabeth, wake up!" she yelled in Elizabeth's face, shaking her.

Rowan was suddenly there, wrapping his arms around her, pulling her away from Elizabeth. "Margaret, she's gone," he said, pulling her out of the room.

Aram took Margaret's place, sitting on the bed resigned. There were no tears on his face as he stroked Elizabeth's cheek.

Margaret buried her face in Rowan's chest, sobbing as he rubbed her back. He held her close to him as she cried.

There was an odd silence in the home, interrupted only by Margaret's hiccupping.

The funeral was two days later, with only Margaret's group and Aram in attendance. Margaret stood with Aram next to the grave as the priest blessed the ground and the family. She wished Liam could have been there with her to see Elizabeth one last time. Margaret reached her hand back to Rowan for him to take. She did not think she could stand there much longer by herself.

Rowan wrapped her in his arms when the funeral was done, holding her close to him. He stroked her hair while she leaned against him. "Can we see my orphans, please?" Margaret asked in a child-like voice. "I need to see them right now."

"Anything you need." Rowan kissed the top of her head.

Aram was already gone by the time she turned around to say her goodbyes. She had tried to convince him to come with them on the rest of their tour and see more of Anatalia, and then settle on her lands with a yearly stipend, but he refused. He wouldn't leave where Beth and his son were buried. Margaret couldn't fault him for that, though she wished he would let her help him.

The few days that she had convinced Rowan to stay in Marbon were condensed after Elizabeth's death. They would stay one more night before they left for Rowan's ancestral home of Craneswile. Margaret picked up Samuel and held him tightly as she led Rowan to the home she had established for the orphans.

Margaret set Samuel down when they reached the front of the house. She knocked on the door lightly.

The governess, Claudette, answered the door, a surprised look on her face when she saw Margaret. "My lady! What are you doing here?"

Margaret smiled at her. "Claudette, may we come in?"

"Of course, my lady," Claudette said, opening the door wider.

Margaret took Samuel's hand, walking in. "Claudette, this is the Duke of Fradure," she said when Rowan entered the home. "He is now the owner of these lands."

Claudette curtsied low to him. "Your Grace, it's an honor to meet you."

Rowan nodded politely, looking around.

"Little monsters?" Margaret called out with a smile on her face.

There were some confused voices calling out to each other before the sound of pattering feet came down the stairs. Several little voices called out, "Maggie!"

Margaret knelt with open arms as children washed over her. She let out a joyful cry as she was knocked over by the horde of children coming to see her. She smiled brightly as she stroked cheeks and got hugs from those closest.

"That's enough!" Jonathan commanded, entering the room. "What's this all about?"

Margaret sat up when the children got off of her. "Jonathan," she said with a smile.

Jonathan immediately went to help her up. "Miss Maggie, what are you doing back? We didn't get a letter, did we, Claudette?"

Claudette shook her head no.

"I'm touring His Grace's lands." Margaret motioned to Rowan.

The children bowed or curtsied in unison and Jonathan raised his eyebrows. "A duke this time? What happened to the last one?"

"He felt the need to travel." Margaret pursed her lips. "I see Claudette hasn't quite gotten you to master your manners yet, Jonathan."

Jonathan gave her a mocking bow. "Lady Margaret, Claudette certainly has done a proper job in teaching me things."

Margaret raised her eyebrows high as Claudette blushed brightly. It would seem that Jonathan had moved on from her. "Has she now?"

"She has," Jonathan said, wrapping an arm around Claudette. "And while you're at it, you can start calling Claudette Mrs. Lerosen."

"You're married?" Margaret asked incredulously.

"Yes, we are," Jonathan said. "She wanted to be the mother of my babies unlike you. You abandoned all of us to go live out your fantasy in the capital."

"Jon, please don't do this. Not today," Margaret said, her shoulders sagging with the weight of her grief. "We buried Beth today."

"Maybe if you hadn't abandoned us all you could have helped her before she died," Jonathan said tartly. "Instead you came back to watch her die."

Rowan grabbed Jonathan's face in one hand while his mouth was open, backing him up to the wall. "You keep talking to Lady Margaret that way, boy, and your *widow* will have to take care of your babies all by herself."

Margaret gasped. "Your Grace!"

Rowan let go and went back to Margaret's side. "We're leaving. I will not tolerate staying around a child who chooses to disrespect you so." He picked up Samuel and took Margaret's hand, leading her out of the house.

Margaret looked at Rowan surprised. "Rowan, I didn't get to visit with the children."

"It didn't seem like the boy wanted you to visit with the children," Rowan told her.

"He was like that when I first met him too," Margaret said defensively. "He isn't used to me anymore."

"He's not a feral dog that needs to be reintroduced to you, Margaret. He's a grown man who should not talk to you that way," Rowan said angrily. "You can send them extra money to make up for your lack of visits. He should just be content that you put a roof over their heads."

"Your Grace, I'm not sure I like this side of you," Margaret told him.

"You don't like that I'm protective of you?" Rowan asked her incredulously. "Or that I demand people respect you?"

"I don't like the way you went about it, Rowan," Margaret said, trying to placate him. "That your first reaction was to threaten someone for lack of respect is not something Samuel should learn."

Rowan whirled around to face her. "Lady Margaret, I couldn't bear to hear him disrespecting you a moment further. I defended your honor as I should!"

Margaret was obviously getting nowhere with him. "Yes, Your Grace."

The duke continued back to their camp, Margaret still in tow. He let the servants know they would leave first thing in the morning. Rowan deposited Margaret at her tent to prepare for the evening meal.

"That didn't take long," Sarah commented. "Is something wrong, my lady?"

"His Grace refused to let us stay for me to visit because Jonathan was rude to me," Margaret complained. "He was 'defending my honor,' as he put it."

Sarah raised her eyebrows. "And you're upset over this?"

"No," Margaret said quickly. "I'm not upset he defended me. I'm upset that he acted like...like the king."

Sarah waited for her to continue, her eyebrows still raised.

"I'm upset because Elizabeth is gone, and I can't even see my children," Margaret said, sitting down on her bed.

"There will be other opportunities, my lady," Sarah said, retrieving a dress for her to wear to dinner. "You won't always be with His Grace."

Margaret sighed, looking at her hands. "You're right, Sarah."

15

"**B**ut I wanna go!" Eli whined as he followed Liam around.

"I'm sorry, but I've said no." Liam gathered his rations for the day. "It's going to be a long day, and I can't take you back when you get bored. Your Ma needs me to get a deer for her."

"Listen to yer Da, Eli," Gretta cut in. "Ye can stay here with me today."

Liam kissed her cheek. "I'll be back this afternoon."

Eli started to sniffle. "But what if ye have another accident?"

Liam paused, letting out a sigh. He set his supplies down and squatted in front of Eli. "I have a brand-new bow, and it won't break like my old one." He pulled Eli into a tight hug. "I promise I will be very careful."

Eli's lip quivered. "Are ye sure?"

"I am." Liam held Eli at arm's length. "You'll be the first person I come to see when I come back so you can see I'm all right."

"D'ye promise?" Eli wiped his nose on his sleeve.

"I promise." Liam stood, kissing Eli on top of his head. "Now you be good for Ma, all right?"

Eli nodded.

"Good." Liam kissed Gretta again. "I'll see you when I get home, Duck," he said before leaving.

It didn't take long for Liam to find a spot he could settle in. There was a natural nook in the tree he could sit in while he kept watch. He hoped he'd find something quickly—he'd heard a fair amount of rustling in the forest on his way there.

Liam leaned back and closed his eyes to listen for anything coming. Wings flapped close to his head. He looked up to see a nest close to his head. He'd just need to be careful of that when he needed to take a shot.

He let out a sigh, closing his eyes again. It was peaceful enough that he could fall asleep. Liam forced his eyes open. Gretta would throttle him if he didn't come back with a deer today. They'd run out of venison the week before, and this was the first chance he'd had to get to the woods. Once his arm had healed enough, Liam had taken extra shifts at the forge to make up for the lack of product Simon was making under his tutelage, preventing a hunt.

Liam sat up straight when he heard a snap in front of him. He scanned the treeline, catching sight of antlers through the leaves. It was coming toward him. Liam took slow aim for the buck. He heard a splat when his elbow went all the way back. He looked down and saw a cracked egg on the trunk of the tree. He hadn't realized there were any eggs in the nest behind him.

Squawking sounded before he was pecked on his ear. Liam let out a curse, his hand loosening on the bow as he swatted away the bird. His arrow flew wildly to the side.

A scream pierced through the trees before an eerie silence settled over the wood.

Liam froze. There shouldn't be anyone else around.

Branches crashed and rattled somewhere in the distance, shaking Liam from his stupor. He had to find whoever made the scream. He abandoned his bow, sliding off the trunk of his nook.

Liam scanned the area. Whoever it was couldn't be far. He tried to remember which way his arrow went, but it was a blur. He thought it went to the left. Traveling that way, he found a small form on the ground with an arrow protruding from it.

Fuck.

Liam rushed forward.

He stopped short, reeling backward. He took in a sharp breath, but it felt like it was going to choke him.

Eli.

It was Eli.

Liam let out a shuddering breath. Eli had followed him.

"Duck?"

Liam took a few tentative steps forward. Eli wasn't moving when he got there.

"Duck?" he asked again.

The silence was deafening.

Liam dropped to his knees beside Eli. He reached out to check, curling his fingers, but fear pulled back his hand. He didn't want to do it. He had to. Bile rose in his throat.

Liam swallowed hard. He had to.

He reached out again. His hand connected with Eli's arm. Liam closed his eyes tightly, turning Eli toward him. He had to.

Liam didn't want to open his eyes. He didn't want to look at what he'd done. But he had to.

Opening his eyes, Liam let out a cry. Blood covered the front of Eli's shirt. It didn't even look like him. He didn't even look like a real person anymore, his eyes glassy and face pale.

"Oh, Duck." Liam's bottom lip wobbled. He looked around helplessly. There was no one else around. No one else who could maybe be responsible and not him.

Liam would have to bring him back to his mother—but he couldn't bring him to Gretta like this. When Liam removed the arrow, he turned to the side and vomited.

His fingers shook when he brushed the hair from Eli's face. He'd just kissed him goodbye a few hours ago. He should still be pestering Gretta about wanting to go hunting.

Liam wiped his eyes before he stood. He had to get Eli home to his mother. He picked him up, cradling him against his shoulder. Hadn't he just done this, when they had gone fishing and he carried Eli home? Only this time, there were no arms tightening around his neck.

No questions in his ear.

Just silence.

He cradled Eli's head to his shoulder, starting the long walk home. Each step brought more numbness.

More dread.

More heartbreak.

How was he going to tell Gretta? Jamie and Simon?

Liam held Eli tighter to him, wishing he'd just said yes to Eli's pestering. What harm would his chattering really have done?

He paused when he saw the town. He didn't want to make his feet keep going. He didn't even want to believe that day had really happened. But he had to.

He looked down to Eli. It was almost as though he could have been sleeping. "We're almost home, Duck. And then we can see your Ma."

Liam ignored the people who stopped to watch him pass. He was sure they were a sight, but he had to get to Gretta. Had to bring his boy home. He needed to be with his family—they both did.

Liam stopped at the door to their home, closing his eyes tightly.

He had to.

Liam opened the door, stepping inside. Its warmth seemed diminished, knowing he'd never hear Eli call for him again. Knowing the grief he'd cause.

"Gretta?"

"Did ye get one so soon?" She turned, the smile disappearing from her face when she saw him. The plate in her hand shattered when it hit the floor. "Liam?"

"There was an accident." His face contorted as his eyes filled. "Eli's dead."

"Dead?" Her hands shook as she brought them to her mouth. "How?

"He followed me, and—"

"You killed my boy?" Gretta swallowed hard, going paler than Liam had ever seen her. "*You* did this?

"I didn't mean— It was an accident." Liam held Eli protectively against him, as though he needed to protect his memory from the events of the day. "I didn't know he was there. My arrow flew off, and then..." Liam slowly backed up against the wall, sliding down it as he sobbed.

"I'm sorry, Liam." Gretta rushed forward, kneeling in front of him and grabbing onto his shoulders. "I ken ye'd never do this on purpose."

Liam nodded, unable to speak as he held onto Eli tighter.

He couldn't look.

He couldn't look at the pyre.

At Eli.

At Gretta.

At anything.

Liam flinched away when Gretta put a hand on his back. "Don't," he said quietly.

She pulled away, her face pale. "It wasna yer fault," she whispered. "Ye didna know he was there. He wasna supposed to be there."

It didn't make it any better. He could still hear Eli's scream before the deafening silence. It haunted his every waking moment.

A priest of Olam circled the pyre, his wooden mask charred to resemble the burning wood under Eli. He held a bundle of burning herbs meant to help Eli pass into Olam's arms unencumbered.

Liam didn't adhere much to religion, but he hoped the realms of the gods lie undivided so he'd one day see Eli again.

Gretta slipped her hand into Liam's when the pyre grew taller. Liam squeezed it. The funeral was almost done. Once they could no longer see the body, everyone was to disperse to let the priest say prayers only the dead were allowed to hear.

Liam lifted Gretta's hand to his mouth, kissing it. It was a miracle only Theotes could grant that she hadn't truly blamed him for what happened. If only he could do that for himself.

Gretta tugged on his hand. "It's time."

Finally looking to the pyre, the flames engulfed everything. Liam closed his eyes tightly as he heard Eli's scream again. He'd hear it for the rest of his life. He clenched tightly to the carved duck he'd made for Eli while they waited the three days of mourning before they could hold the funeral. Liam couldn't bring himself to put it in Eli's hands before the flames were lit.

Liam pulled his eyes away, following Gretta and the family back to The Smiling Fox. Food was waiting for them, prepared by some of the townsfolk who didn't come to the funeral.

Gretta let out a noise from the back of her throat, smiling through her tears. "Thank ye all." She swallowed, taking in a shaky breath. "Thank ye."

Gretta separated herself from Liam to be enveloped by the women gathered. Liam looked around—the men were starting to surround him.

"Let's get ye a drink." Mr. Kaneh wrapped an arm around Liam, leading him to another room away from the women. "Ye'll need it today."

Liam swallowed. He did need one. He clung tightly to the carved duck, holding it to his chest.

Mr. Kaneh sat Liam down, putting a bottle and a glass in front of him. "Drink as much as ye need."

By the end of the night, Liam had several empty bottles in front of him. His head spun, and his stomach started to rebel.

But he no longer heard Eli's scream.

16

I t took the traveling party two weeks to reach Rowan's ancestral home from Marbon. Margaret gasped when they pulled into view of the home. It was enormous—easily two of her homes could fit into it. She watched the gardens pass by quickly in the carriage. She almost wished she could walk the rest of the way so she could see the grounds close up, but there would be time for that later.

It was an intimidating home—it looked like it could have been its own royal palace at some point, with two large wings off the main structure. Each wing and the main building had their own rotunda sitting atop them. Margaret couldn't even imagine the cost of building something like this.

She turned to Rowan with an excited smile, ready to share her wonderment when she remembered they had not been talking. The time between Margaret and Rowan had not been as enjoyable since Rowan's outburst in the orphanage she had established. Samuel tentatively slipped his hand into hers. He could tell that there was something different between her and his father.

Margaret looked around when they got out of the carriage. Just standing at the front carried the weight of history.

Servants waited for them outside, the butler rushing down the steps to greet them. "Welcome back, Your Grace, Master Samuel. My Lady Dorcia, welcome to Craneswile."

"Thank you." Margaret smiled at him before looking down at Samuel. "Will you show me inside, my darling?"

Samuel nodded, rushing up the steps.

Margaret followed him, lifting her skirts to match his pace. Margaret turned to look at the lawn, gasping when she saw that it opened up to a man-made lake. She was tugged inside by Samuel.

There were black-and-white marble floors and a double staircase in the entryway of the home. The railings were made of oak that gleamed in the light. Margaret looked up and saw that the ceiling was painted in a pastoral scene. The family's portraits and busts lined the walls either hanging or on pedestals. Margaret's heels echoed on the floor as she circled the entryway.

Rowan joined them shortly after. "Will you allow me to show you to your rooms, Lady Margaret?"

She tried not to be disappointed. He was still calling her Lady Margaret instead of just her name. It kept her at a distance, and all talks around marriage had ceased. "I would love it if you would, Your Grace," Margaret said.

Rowan offered her his arm to go up the stairs. "Did you know this used to be King Reuben III's home before he became king?"

Margaret shook her head. That would explain the enormity of it. No doubt he had already thought himself king and lived like it before stealing the throne from the Triburn family.

Rowan led her down a long hallway, telling her about each room as they passed. He stopped at her door. "Will you need anything else, my lady?"

Margaret looked up at him. She inhaled deeply, gathering her courage. If she didn't get this fixed now, she would never be able to fix it. "You to make everything better again," she said quietly. "I don't like what's settled between us."

"I don't like it either, Margaret, but I am who I am." Rowan shrugged before crossing his arms and leaning against the door frame. "I won't stand aside and watch while a boy disrespects you just because that's the way he was when he met you."

"And I'm happy that you want to defend my honor, Rowan." Margaret put her hand on his arm, stroking it gently. "I was upset because of Elizabeth."

It was only a partial truth. She had been aggrieved with the death of the only caring mother figure she'd ever had. But she couldn't tell him he was acting like the king. It would have brought up too many questions she didn't want to answer and possibly outed her affair.

Rowan covered her hand, holding it in place. "I just want to protect you from everything," he said. "Even just the threat of disrespect."

Margaret smiled at him tenderly. "And I'm happy that you want to."

Rowan grabbed her face, kissing her. Margaret wrapped her arms around him and tilted in. He opened the door behind her and took her inside. Rowan pressed her against the wall, leaning into her.

Margaret was barely able to breathe, clinging to him. "Your Grace!" she said when she could.

He continued to kiss her, cupping her face in his hands. "What, Margaret?" Rowan asked, sounding frustrated.

"Surely, if you continue, my honor will come into question," Margaret teased.

Rowan pulled away from her reluctantly. "There are two weeks of pent-up emotion to catch up on."

Margaret smiled at him, stroking his cheek. "Perhaps right away is not the best time to release it all."

Rowan lingered on another kiss. "As you wish, my dear."

"Now, let me change," Margaret commanded, her brow furrowing sternly. She couldn't hold it for long, letting out a laugh.

Rowan grinned at her mischievously, giving her a kiss that left her breathless before he went to change himself.

Margaret sat on the bed, letting out a contented sigh and waited for Sarah to come back to help her change clothes for dinner. It wasn't an apology for his behavior, but she supposed that was the best she was going to get. He would be used to behaving as he liked, and if she was fortunate enough to remain with him, Margaret hoped to guide him into a more considerate nature.

Margaret walked in the garden arm-in-arm with Sarah, a parasol held between them. Vojvo walked on the other side of Margaret, hands clasped behind his back. A strong breeze blew around them, dark gray clouds crawling across the sky. Rowan had business to attend to, and she wanted to take a moment to herself, surrounded by the people who knew all her secrets. She hated having to always be cautious, never letting her guard down.

"I don't understand." Margaret sighed. "He hasn't talked any more of marriage since we left Dorcia."

"Is he still interested?" Sarah asked.

Her cheeks heating, Margaret said, "I would say so." Once they had cleared the air, Rowan had been pushing the boundaries of how far they could take their courtship. She was sure the only reason he hadn't pursued it further was because she was still pretending innocence.

"You could bring it up," Vojvo suggested.

Margaret stopped walking, looking at him with her nose scrunched. "Captain."

"What?"

"I can't bring it up." Margaret shook her head. "It's not the way it's done."

"Why not?" Vojvo furrowed his brow. "My wife asked me to marry her."

Margaret looked to Sarah with raised brows before looking back to Vojvo. "That's not the way it's done with the nobility. Papa could have said, or Mother, but neither are here to broker it for me, so I have to wait for His Grace to take the lead."

Thunder peeled as lightning skittered across the sky.

Vojvo looked up, shading his eyes as rain started to pour. He pointed toward the mausoleum at the end of the garden. "We can wait this out there."

Margaret picked up her skirts, sprinting to the covered porch with Sarah. Vojvo followed behind at a slower pace, joining them under the covering. The rain tinged against the copper of the rotunda.

Sarah leaned against the stone walls, letting out a sigh. "What do you think the king will say?"

"To what?" Margaret leaned against the wall next to her, resting her head delicately against the stone.

"To a marriage with the duke?"

"I honestly don't know." Margaret let out a heavy breath, tucking a loose piece of hair behind her ear. "Rowan is close to the throne. He could be controlled with the threat of disinheritance from the line."

"He could just as easily be seen as a threat to the Anatalian throne if he marries a traitor." Vojvo crossed his arms over his chest, leaning his shoulder against one of the pillars holding up the roof.

Margaret looked at him sharply, ready to reprimand him for calling her a traitor. But it was true; she had become one by helping Liam. "Would he not see it as a way to control us both, then?"

"I presume you've not told His Grace about your actions?"

Margaret shook her head, looking down. "How could I? He's my only prospect, and my only hope of getting some semblance of control over my life again."

"And there are no others you'd consider?" Sarah asked slowly. "What about the baron who thought you'd called him to court for you instead of Annabel?"

Margaret laughed harshly. "He'd have no sway with the king. Sorren would take me in the same room just to show that dirt weasel he has no power." Margaret swallowed hard, fighting against the burn in her nose and throat as she held back tears. "That I have no power."

Vojvo cleared his throat. "You have another option." He shifted uncomfortably, not looking at Margaret. "You could join the Church of Theotes as one of his servants."

Margaret's jaw dropped, shocked he would even suggest such a thing. "I haven't suffered this much to get my title and lands in my name just to lose it to the church." She shook her head, brow furrowing. "If the church didn't seize my lands and money first, the king would, and all of this would have been for naught. My people…"

"But you would be safe," Vojvo said, voice verging on desperation. "Safe from him, for all time. Theotes would protect you within the walls of the church."

"He hasn't protected me outside of the walls," Margaret snapped. "And he won't protect me within."

"Then what are you to do?" Sarah asked.

Margaret sighed, her shoulders slumping. "Endure."

Margaret stayed in Craneswile with Rowan and Samuel for a month, enjoying the time that she was able to spend without the prying eye of the king. If she hadn't promised the king to return, she didn't know if she ever would. Perhaps, if she and Rowan married, she would have enough power to say no to the king. As it was now, she received a letter from Sorren requesting—or rather, demanding—they returned to the palace as quickly as they could under threat of revoking her title.

Margaret wished they didn't have to leave this spectacular place so soon. She looked back to Rowan sitting in the shade, watching her and Samuel play. She could never say no to Samuel when he wanted her attention, his pleading always winning her over.

"My dear, why don't you come out of the sun? You'll burn in the harsh light."

Margaret shaded her eyes with her hand. "If you wish."

"Maggie," Samuel droned, tugging on her hand. "Don't leave me."

Margaret smiled, shrugging at Rowan. "It seems the little lord demands my attention."

Rowan smiled, conceding to his son. "Only a short while longer, Sam. We need to leave soon."

Margaret was loath to return, but they had been gone from the palace for almost a year. Sorren had been gracious enough to understand the winter waylaid them for longer than expected, but their time alone was coming to an end. As it was, they would have to race through most of Rowan's lands instead of stopping to obey the king's command of returning within a year of their departure.

"Yes father," Samuel said before excitedly turning his attention back to Margaret.

Margaret returned to Rowan when Samuel began to tire. She sat next to him, and he immediately had her hand in his. She smiled, squeezing it. Even if a true proposal didn't come at the end of this tour, she would be grateful to Rowan for keeping her away from the king.

"It looks like the two of you had fun," Rowan commented.

"I don't know how he has all this energy." Margaret laughed, watching Samuel continue to play by himself. "He's too sweet to say no to."

"He loves you," Rowan told her, his face close to hers. "I love you too."

Butterflies erupted in Margaret's stomach. This was what she had wanted for so long, but fear started creeping in. "Truly?"

"Truly, Margaret, I love you."

Margaret wasn't sure if she should say it back—could say it back. Even with all her hopeful plans, the threat of what the king did to those who took what was his stayed in the back of her mind.

Rowan's brow furrowed as confusion clouded his face. "Do you not feel the same way?"

"I am afraid to love anyone now," Margaret said quietly.

"Why, my dear?"

"Everyone I love seems to be taken away from me," Margaret confided.

"No one will take me from you." Rowan kissed her. "Not ever."

Margaret was still hesitant, but she did want to say it. "I do love you too."

They went to the Hook of Hamuel next in their travels. They stayed at the pointed end of the hook, in Manolt, since it, and not Hamuel, was in Rowan's lands. Margaret was happy to see the city, finally, knowing this was one of the places Liam had stopped during his travels and enjoyed. The carriage took a leisurely pace toward the coast. Manolt was not the prettiest of the duke's cities, but it held the wonders of the coastline that Samuel so enjoyed. Rowan told her whenever they went to the coast, it was hard to pull Samuel away from the sandy beaches and the crashing waves.

"Father," Sam called to him excitedly. "I can hear the ocean!"

"Do you remember which ocean that is?"

"Bragasso," he said.

"Very good, Samuel!" Margaret praised.

His father chuckled when he saw that Margaret's praise had made Samuel puff out his chest. Rowan gently took Margaret's hand in his and kissed the back of it.

She smiled up at him. She was sad their privacy was coming to an end soon.

They arrived at the beachfront manor home Rowan owned. Samuel hardly waited for the carriage to stop before jumping out of the cab to run to the beach. "Sam!" Rowan called out. "Don't go in the water!"

Samuel stopped just short of the waves, looking back at his father with a pleading look.

The couple got out of the carriage and Rowan escorted Margaret to the sandy banks of the ocean. Margaret inhaled deeply and leaned on his arm. Rowan smiled and kissed the top of her head. They watched Samuel take off his shoes and roll his pants up to let the water rush over his toes.

Samuel gasped and jumped back when the cold water hit his feet, giggling loudly.

"It's beautiful here," Margaret breathed.

"Made more so by the company I'm in," Rowan whispered in her ear.

"Thank you." She looked up at him. Margaret would never tire of his compliments.

The couple watched Samuel play in the small waves that came up on the shore until he began to tire. Margaret held Samuel in her arms while he rested his head on her shoulder. He wanted Margaret to put him to bed again, and Rowan led the two to Samuel's room.

She laid him down in the bed, finding that Samuel was already asleep. Margaret gently stroked his cheek. She could see herself being a mother to him— being a mother to her own children with Rowan. It was certainly a nice thought.

Rowan hardly waited until they were out of the room before he kissed her.

Margaret pulled away from him breathless, her lips tingling as they swelled. "What was that for?"

"I can't wait to spend my life with you." Rowan rested his forehead against hers. "I love you."

A thrill went through her. Margaret looked up at him with bright eyes. "I love you too." She waited for him to actually give her a proposal, but it didn't come.

Rowan cupped her cheek in his hand. "That makes me very happy, Margaret. More than you know."

 **17**

iam stumbled as he walked toward the Heated Forge, squinting against the light. He didn't feel drunk in his mind, but his body didn't seem to think the same. His limbs were movable but dull to his senses.

He paused, inhaling deeply before he shook his head. Liam grunted. That was a bad idea. His head spun with the movement.

He needed to go back to work. He hadn't been in a month. Hadn't been since...

Liam shook his head again, hoping to clear it. He couldn't get distracted.

He winced when the hammering reached his ear. Such a disgusting sound.

The hammering paused when Liam walked in.

"What are ye doin' here?" Jossnon asked.

Liam winced, putting the heels of his hands against his eyes. "I'm...coming to work," he said when he finally pulled his hands away from his face.

Jossnon tossed down his hammer against the anvil with a reverberating clang. "Yer doin' no such thing." With his brows raised, he crossed his arms.

"Why?" Liam reached for a bar or steel, shaking out his hand after Jossnon slapped it. "What was that for?"

"Liam, ye cannae be here," Jossnon said. "Yer *drunk*."

"Am I?" Liam grinned at him, chuckling.

"Ye are," Jossnon said, "and it's only fer my love of ye and yer family that I dinna fire ye right here and now."

Liam's face fell. He looked down at his shoes, not being able to bear the disappointment on another loved one's face. "I'm sorry, Joss."

"When was the last time ye were sober?" Jossnon asked gently, putting a hand on Liam's shoulder.

Liam shook his head. He didn't want to answer.

Jossnon grabbed him by the chin, forcing Liam to look at him. "When?"

Liam's brows knitted together, the corners of his mouth turning downward. He really didn't want to answer.

"When, Liam?" Jossnon demanded quietly.

Liam swallowed, looking away as his eyes filled. "The funeral."

Shocked, Jossnon let go of Liam. "That was over a month ago!"

"It's the only thing that keeps me from hearing his scream, Joss." Liam covered his face with his hands. He would do anything to keep from hearing it again. It would drive him to insanity, playing over and over in his mind the moment he was able to think about anything else besides what he'd done.

"Och, Liam." Jossnon grabbed him tightly by the shoulders. "I cannae imagine what ye're goin' through, but ye cannae let yourself continue as ye are. Ye're only gonna hurt ye and yer family more."

Liam shook his head, eyes still covered. "I cannot bear to hear it again."

"Does Gretta ken yer pain?"

"I can't tell her." Liam crumpled further into himself. "She's already burdened enough with her own grief."

Jossnon sighed, turning Liam toward the door. "Ye dinna have to go home, but ye cannae stay here, Liam. Ye'll hurt yerself on something."

Liam stumbled forward, catching himself on the doorway.

"If ye need help, ye can always come to me," Jossnon said. "Ye always have me."

Liam nodded, leaving the smithy. He didn't want to go back home and face Gretta. She was already disappointed in him enough with him making no effort to go to work or stay out of the bottle.

He stumbled down to the Frothing Wench. At least no one there yelled at him.

It was dark by the time Liam returned home. He could barely stand, swallowing hard against his rebelling stomach. He paused just inside the door—everyone was gathered around the table. "Wassit?" he gestured toward them before putting his fist against his mouth.

Gretta stood quickly, ushering Liam to the table. "Where in Olam's name have ye been, Liam?"

He sank into the chair, letting out a burp he was thankful wasn't more. "The Frothin'"—he belched again, patting his chest—"Wench."

"Did ye even try no to drink today?" Gretta said, covering her face with an angry sigh. "Did ye even try to go to work today?" she asked when she pulled her hands away.

"Joss wouldn't let me," Liam said.

"Why?"

Liam reached across the table, grabbing a biscuit.

Gretta slapped his hand, making him drop the bread. "Why, Liam?"

111

He shook his hand, glaring at her. "I'd been drinking."

"Olam above, Liam!" Gretta threw down her rag and leaned back in her chair, crossing her arms. "Ye have to stop."

Liam ignored her, turning to the rest of the table. He started when he saw Joanna. "What are you doing here?"

Simon covered her hand with his, squeezing it. "We just got engaged, Da."

"Engaged?" Liam grinned at him. "I guess I'll get another chance to get my boy a good marriage agreement."

Simon looked over to Gretta, his brows knitting together.

Liam looked between them, his mouth turning downward. "What?"

Simon let out a breath, squeezing Joanna's hand again. "I dinna think so, Da."

"Why not?" Liam demanded.

"I cannae trust ye to no be in the bottle," Simon said quietly.

"Oh." Liam nodded sadly as he slouched back against his chair, looking to his lap.

Gretta slipped her hand into his and gently squeezed it. "Let's get ye upstairs, aye?"

Liam nodded and let her guide him upstairs.

18

Margaret's shoulders drooped as they came into view of the palace. This was it—this was the end of her time alone with Rowan and being away from the king. There would be no more hiding and no more excuses to stay away.

Once they had stopped, Rowan helped her and Samuel out of the carriage. He kissed her before saying, "I'll see you tonight at dinner?"

She nodded. "I can hardly wait."

She paused at the doorway. It loomed over her, a pretty cage that offered her little respite. Margaret looked back at the carriage. She sighed. There was little point in trying to escape her fate now that she was here.

Margaret went to her bed chambers to change. As much as she enjoyed spending the time getting to know Rowan away from the king's prying eyes, she was looking forward to being in her own bed again. It called to her as she started to undress, peeling away her traveling clothes.

She took the pins from her hair, shaking it out. Margaret tossed them onto her dressing table, pausing when she saw a stack of letters. They'd already been opened—likely Sorren prying into her business since she was not there to tell him what was in them.

Picking them up, she saw they were from her investors. They must have sent their replies to the palace to ensure they reached her since she said she was on tour in her letters to them. She'd taken the advice of Mr. Persbrant asking the investors who they would recommend for a new business manager to replace Charles Luther.

Margaret read through them quickly, taking a mental tally of the names offered to her. Mr. Nathaniel Ethum, Mr. Persbrant's suggestion, was the overwhelming choice between her investors.

She would have to send him a summons as soon as she was able.

"My lady?"

"Yes Sarah?" Margaret asked, brushing out her hair.

"His Majesty is here to see you." Sarah almost sounded guilty.

Margaret let out a frustrated noise. She'd been back less than an hour, and he was already there. "Let him in."

When Sarah opened the door, he came in and straight to Margaret. "Lady Margaret, I'm glad to see that you've made it back to me safely."

Margaret curtsied to him. "Your Majesty," she said, turning her attention back to her mirror. She hoped the distance over the last year would hold for at least one more night.

Sorren raised his brows. "Did something happen while you were gone?"

"No, Your Majesty," Margaret said. "Nothing of the sort you're thinking."

"Good," the king said. "I wanted to welcome you back."

"Your Majesty is very gracious to do so," Margaret said with a smile.

"I'll be visiting you tonight," Sorren said as he walked out.

Margaret's face fell into a scowl as he left her chambers. So much for her hopes of distance. "Sarah," she called out to her maid.

"My lady?" Sarah came back into the room.

"Before you leave to go see George, would you please have one of the other maids draw me a bath?" Margaret asked irritably. "It seems the king *can* dampen my spirits."

"Would you like me to stay, my lady?" Sarah started to take off her cloak.

"No, Sarah," Margaret said with a small smile. "You haven't seen George in a year, and I'm sure he's anxious to see you again."

"Thank you, my lady," Sarah said, curtsying to her.

Margaret sighed as she sank into her bath. The tubs at the palace were large enough she could lie on the bottom and still have plenty of room to move. The maids who had filled her bath came to the side of the tub to wash her. Margaret held her hands out for the sponge and soap. "I can handle it ladies, thank you."

They curtsied to her before leaving.

She leaned her head back on the tub, closing her eyes to let the heat soak into her muscles. There was a small noise in the other room that Margaret assumed was Sarah until gentle hands massaged her shoulders. Margaret's eyes flew open, turning back to see the king with his sleeves rolled up to his elbows.

"I thought you weren't coming until tonight," she told him, a small frown on her face.

"I couldn't wait until tonight," Sorren told her, pulling her back to continue massaging her shoulders. "You're very tense."

"It was a long trip back here," Margaret said quietly, "and the carriage was not the most comfortable."

His fingers nimbly dug into her shoulders, massaging out the knots she had developed. "And your trip? How was it?"

"Very enjoyable, Your Majesty." Margaret let out a small smile. "It was wonderful to see my lands and go home again..." She hesitated before adding, "Thank you for letting me be gone so long."

"I'm happy that you're back, Margaret," Sorren said tenderly, standing and removing his clothes to sink in the tub behind her, his arms wrapped firmly around her. "I missed you."

Margaret leaned back against him, cautiously enjoying his affection. Had he treated her like this all the time, she could see herself eventually coming to enjoy being the king's mistress, but she knew that this would only be temporary. He would once again become the irritable sovereign who would leave bruises on her for saying the wrong thing.

"There will come a time when my people need me, and I'll have no choice but to be gone that long again," she told him cautiously.

Sorren tightened his grip around her waist, kissing her shoulder. "Hopefully not for a long time."

He stayed until they had to ready themselves for dinner, leaving Margaret confused. She had never seen him behave so gently. She was happy when Sarah returned, wanting someone to talk to who would understand. Margaret had already chosen her garments for dinner, a simple green dress that should draw no attention to her.

"How was your visit with George?" Margaret asked when Sarah came into her chambers.

Sarah's cheeks flushed as she smiled wide. "It was wonderful, my lady," Sarah told her. "It was better than I anticipated. George has taken on more work to help save for the wedding."

Margaret smiled. "That's wonderful! You know if you need anything, I'm happy to help you."

"I know, my lady," Sarah said, "thank you, but I think we'd like to do this on our own."

Margaret nodded, squeezing her arm lightly, deciding to keep quiet about the king. She didn't want to spoil Sarah's mood. "Do you want to commission a dress with my seamstress?"

"Could I?" Sarah asked with her eyes bright.

"Of course." It was the least Margaret could do if they wouldn't let her do anything else. "It will be my wedding gift to you."

"Oh, my lady!" Sarah exclaimed, hugging her tightly.

"I'll arrange it any time you'd like me to," Margaret said.

Sarah's eyes welled with tears. "You are too good to me, my lady."
Margaret only smiled, turning to dress.

Margaret and Rowan had settled back into a schedule of meeting with all the other nobles publicly so there would be no complaints from Sorren. She knew that it irritated Rowan to not have the privacy they had on their trip. It irritated her as well.

They circled the court arm-in-arm, quietly talking of the goings-on they'd heard from their peers. Margaret had only heard snippets, being on the outs of most of the women in court, thanks to the queen.

Rowan had more information, telling her of what Gareth was doing in Frasisca. He'd been causing even more trouble there without being under the watchful eye of his parents. No doubt it would end with another bastard that would never know their father.

Margaret noticed he was nervous and sweating. "Rowan, are you unwell?"

"I am well." Rowan licked his dry lips, shifting uneasily. He swallowed hard before blurting out what was making him anxious. "Marry me, Margaret."

Margaret's stomach dropped. "Pardon?" This is what she wanted—what she'd worked for over a year to get from him. So why did it feel so horrible?

"Marry me." Rowan picked up both of her hands, giving them a gentle squeeze, sounding more confident.

Margaret looked at him guiltily. Sorren had left her bed only hours ago. Could she really put someone like Rowan through having a wife that was mistress to the king? "You don't want to marry me, Rowan," she said quietly.

Confusion flickered across Rowan's face. "Of course, I do. Samuel loves you—I love you—and I want you to be my wife."

"I can't," was all she could say before taking her hands from his. Margaret quickly left the hall, leaving him behind.

Margaret escaped to her chambers. She did not want Rowan to endure her infidelity until the king tired of her, never knowing if their children would be Rowan's or the king's. She collapsed on her bed with a moan. She wished Sorren would release her from her servitude so she was free to marry if she chose. Though her fellow courtiers no longer openly whispered about her, she could still see their disgust when they looked at her. She didn't know if she could take that kind of reaction from Rowan as well. If they were to marry, she would want only truth between them.

"My lady?" Sarah asked from the doorway. "Is there something the matter?"

"If Duke Fradure comes here, please don't allow him in." Margaret told her, kicking off her shoes. "Tell him I'm not feeling well."

"Yes, my lady."

"And if the king comes, tell him I have a stomach ailment, and I wish him to stay away so that he won't be infected." Margaret laid her head back on her pillow with a sigh.

Sarah quietly left the room, shutting the door behind her.

Margaret heard an agitated knock on the door to her antechamber within minutes. She heard Sarah telling the visitor something, and then suddenly Rowan was standing at her door. Margaret looked at him uncomfortably.

Rowan went to her side. "Why did you leave?"

"I wasn't feeling well."

"So your maid said, but I don't believe her—or you." Rowan sat on the edge of the bed. "Is it because I asked for your hand in marriage?"

Margaret looked away from him.

"I want you to be my wife, Margaret."

"You don't want me, Rowan." Margaret still did not look at him. "I would not be a good wife to you."

He grabbed her hand, kissing her palm. "I think you would be a wonderful wife to me and a loving mother to Samuel. He adores you, and so do I."

Margaret looked at him guiltily. "I can't do that to you or Sam."

"Do what to us, Margaret?" Rowan asked exasperatedly. "What could you have possibly done?"

She swallowed hard against the bile rising in her throat, looking anywhere but him. Her months of denials and lies would have to come to an end. Margaret would have no choice but to tell him now, to ruin her chances of the marriage proposal she'd worked so hard for.

She'd lose him—and Samuel—from this. She'd lose her hope too, but she couldn't lie to him any longer if he genuinely wanted her as a wife.

Margaret looked over at him with a pained look on her face. "The king has made me his mistress."

Rowan pulled his hand from hers, going rigid. His mouth flattened as he stood.

"Rowan—"

His nostrils flared as he glared at her, mouth turning down in a tight frown before he turned and walked out of the room.

THE ANATALIAN KING

Margaret jumped when the door slammed.
This was her worst fear come to fruition.

19

Gretta went to the forge. Her hands were shaking. She couldn't believe she was going to go behind Liam's back and talk to Jossnon, but she couldn't take it anymore. Liam's drinking was getting out of control, and she didn't know how to stop it. No matter what she said or did, he wouldn't stop.

"Can I help ye, Mrs. McWard?" Joanna asked.

Gretta gripped her hands in front of her until her knuckles turned white. She shifted uncomfortably, not wanting to look Joanna in the eye. "I would… I— I'd like to speak to Jossnon, if he has a moment," she finally eked out.

"Let me see if he can take a moment." Joanna looked at her sympathetically before going to the back.

Gretta cringed. No doubt Joanna already knew what she wanted to talk to Joss about. Joanna'd been spending more time with Simon at the house after their engagement. She'd been witness to more than a few drunken occasions where Liam made a fool of himself.

The hammering stopped not long after, and Jossnon came to the front. "Gretta, what can I do fer ye?"

"It's about Liam…" Gretta's face scrunched, and she brought her fingertips to her mouth.

Jossnon looked alarmed. "Has something happened?"

She shook her head. "He's drinkin's nae gettin' better. I dinna ken what to do." Gretta put her hands to her face. She didn't want Jossnon to see the hopelessness she felt. "I dinna ken how to pull him from this."

Jossnon put his hands on her shoulders, squeezing them. "I ken. I see him stumble by on the way to The Frothin' Wench."

"Can ye help me?" Gretta asked. "Can ye talk to him?"

"I've tried. He'll no listen." Jossnon sighed heavily. "He's let his grief consume him."

"What about my grief?" Gretta let out a small sob. Liam acted as though it had only happened to him and not the rest of their family too. "It doesna seem to matter to him."

"It does," Jossnon said, pulling her into a hug. "It matters to all of us."

"Then why will he no stop his drinkin'?" Gretta buried her face into his chest, sobbing against him. "It's as though I lost both of them that day."

Jossnon rubbed her back as she cried. "I can try again if ye like?"

Gretta looked up at him with wet eyes. "Would ye?"

"Aye." Jossnon nodded. "I can come by in a few days to talk to him."

"Thank ye." Gretta wiped her eyes, leaving the forge with a little more hope than she came in with.

20

"**M**y lady, you have to get out of bed."

Margaret looked at Sarah, shaking her head against her pillow. She couldn't. She wouldn't. Not when she'd lost the only thing going right for her.

"Please, my lady. It's been three days." Sarah pulled down the covers to try to rouse her. "You have to get out of bed. You have to eat something."

"What's the point?" Margaret turned her face, smooshing it into the pillow. "I've lost him. I've lost my only chance."

"Lady Margaret, I *will* get the captain to forcibly get you up if I have to."

She couldn't see it, but Margaret knew Sarah had her hands on her hips.

Margaret turned the other way so she wouldn't have to see her maid's face. She took a deep breath, letting it out through her nose. "Pull the covers back up, Sarah."

"No."

Margaret furrowed her brow, whipping her head in the opposite direction to look at Sarah. "No?" Anger started to bubble in her, her shoulders tensing.

Sarah crossed her arms. "No. You will get out of this bed. You will eat something, and you *will* continue on. You have fought too hard to survive here, and we will not let you fail now."

Some of Margaret's resolve dissipated, her shoulders melting into the bed as she turned onto her back. "I can't, Sarah." Margaret covered her face with her hands. "I can't do this anymore. It's too hard."

When there was no response, Margaret took her hands from her face. She was gone. "Sarah?"

No answer came.

Margaret sat up in the bed, looking around the room. Sarah must be making good on her threat. She grabbed the covers, pulling them up with her as she lay back down. If she was going to be dragged from the bed, she would at least be warm first.

Sarah returned with Captain Vojvo in tow. "All right, my lady. You can either get out of bed on your own, or the captain can get you out. But today is the last day you stay in bed moping."

Margaret's mouth pursed defiantly, a single brow raised. "I will not be ordered about by my servants."

"You would make an old man drag you from this bed?" Vojvo crossed his arms, raising his brows at her.

"Captain, you're either calling me so fat that you cannot possibly lift me or telling me you're no longer capable of your duties." Margaret's mouth went flat. "Either direction is a poor choice."

"That's enough," Captain Vojvo snapped. "You'll not take your sadness out on us. Now get out of bed, have something to eat, and leave this room today."

Margaret looked away from him, her lip wobbling. She *was* taking it out on them. She had been for the last several days. "I'm sorry," she said in a small voice.

Sarah pulled back the covers again, and Margaret sat up this time. "I have your breakfast in the other room."

Margaret nodded as she stood, shaking out her chemise. "I don't know if I have the stomach to eat."

Sarah put Margaret in her dressing gown, buttoning it up quickly. "Will you try at least?"

Margaret looked between Sarah and Vojvo before nodding. "I'll try."

"Good." Vojvo led her to her sitting room, putting her in the chair in front of her breakfast. He sat across from her, watching her expectantly.

Her stomach turned at the smell. She was too grief-stricken to find any delight in food. Margaret felt foolish grieving since Rowan was still alive. But it was grief just the same—for the life she would no longer have. For the life she'd condemned herself to.

"I can't—" Margaret shook her head, her face scrunching. "I feel sick smelling it."

Sarah squatted next to her, gripping her hand. "You have to eat, my lady. It's been three days since your last meal."

Vojvo slowly scooted a cup in front of her. "At least try to drink something to start."

Margaret picked up the cup of tea. It had the barest hint of heat, likely sitting while she'd argued getting out of bed. She took a sip and closed her eyes, savoring the feeling of the liquid on her tongue. She finished the cup in two large gulps before setting it down.

Vojvo pushed forward the plate of scrambled eggs as Sarah poured her another cup of tea.

Margaret picked up her fork, spearing a few eggs with the tines before eating them. Her stomach clenched against the food. She set her fork down, shaking her head.

Vojvo picked up the fork and handed it to her. "Just two more bites, and then we'll see how you feel, all right?"

Margaret looked between them. Sarah nodded at her encouragingly, and Vojvo reminded her of a father coercing a child to eat. She sighed, taking the prescribed forkfuls of food, wincing as her stomach cramped viciously.

"Drink some more tea, and then I'll get you ready for the day," Sarah said.

Margaret leaned back in her seat, hand on her stomach as she drank the second cup. She was ready for this to be over. "I don't want anything too nice."

"We'll make sure you're comfortable, my lady."

Standing when her tea was done, Margaret motioned to the food. "Whoever wants extra breakfast can have the rest. I won't be eating any more."

Sarah followed her to her bedchamber, dressing her in one of her more comfortable gowns. It was modest for the court, high necked with only a few embellishments.

When they came back into the sitting room, Vojvo stood. "Would you like me to escort you around today?"

Margaret shook her head. "I'll be all right on my own. I should get used to it after all." She didn't let them argue before she left her chambers, headed toward the grand hall where the court gathered.

Margaret stopped in front of the door to the court and rubbed her fingers together. She didn't know who would be on the other side of that door. She wanted desperately to see Rowan, but at the same time not to. She nodded to the servant at the door to open it, slowly making her way into the room.

Everything was as it was before, courtiers mingling with each other. The room was filled with chattering and laughter. It made her feel insignificant in her grief, no one even looking in her direction.

Life moved on, whether she wanted it to or not.

Margaret ventured further into the room, looking for any familiar face she could spend time with. She searched the room for Rowan as she went—no matter how much it would hurt, she wanted to see him. She locked eyes with Sorren, hating she was relieved he was there despite him being the root of all her problems.

Sorren made his way toward her, parting the crowd as he went. "Lady Margaret, you're here."

"I am, Your Majesty." She curtsied to him. "I haven't been feeling well the last few days."

"So I've been told." Sorren picked up her hand, kissing it before looping his arm with hers. "I've missed seeing you."

Margaret made a noncommittal noise in the back of her throat, walking the room with him at his pace. She let him do the talking as they circled the room. She didn't really care about what he was saying, nodding occasionally to show she was listening.

None of it mattered anyway.

Margaret stopped short when she saw Rowan across the room with Samuel.

Sorren looked down at her, brow furrowed. "Are you all right, my dear?"

Samuel started walking toward her, a grin splitting his face. He'd lost a tooth since she'd seen him last, and she hated that she'd missed it. Rowan grabbed him by the shoulder, pulling Samuel back toward him.

Her knees weakened at the confused look on Samuel's face and the glare in her direction from Rowan. "I...I'm not feeling well." Margaret looked up at Sorren, trying to keep the bile from rising up her throat. "May I please return to my chambers?"

Sorren searched her face before nodding. "I'll check on you later."

Margaret untangled her arm from his, rushing from the hall. She took in a ragged breath when the doors closed behind her. It was too much to see Rowan hating her—to have him keep Samuel from her. All of it would have been so much easier if she had been able to use him instead of falling in love with him.

She couldn't—

Margaret sprinted to a small alcove, letting out what little the captain and Sarah had convinced her to eat into the large vase.

She leaned back on her heels, sucking in a deep breath. Margaret shakily wiped her mouth with the back of her hand. She should have let the captain come with her. Margaret slowly made her way back to her chambers, sticking close to the walls in case she needed another emergency alcove.

Margaret let out a relieved groan when she made it to her room. She flung herself through the door, closing it behind her with a shaky breath.

"My lady?" Sarah stopped her cleaning, alarm widening her eyes.

"Get this dress off of me."

"What happened?"

"Rowan." Margaret shook her head, her face scrunching as hot tears welled in her eyes.

"My lady, His Majesty is here to see you," Sarah said.

Margaret sat up, wiping her face, trying to clear her tears. She had been crying on and off since the morning. She pulled the covers higher up her chest. There wouldn't be any avoiding him, not when he'd specifically said he'd come. "Send him in."

The door closed behind Sarah briefly before it opened to reveal Sorren.

He looked at her with furrowed brow as he came to her bed and sat next to her. "Have you been crying?"

Margaret nodded, wiping fresh tears away.

Sorren tipped up her chin with a crooked finger, searching her face. "What's happened?"

"Rowan has ended our courtship." Margaret stifled a sob with her hand. She wasn't even sure that was true—he hadn't said they were done with his words, but his actions had—especially keeping Samuel from going to her.

Sorren gently stroked her cheek, wiping away each new tear that fell. "Did he give a reason?"

Margaret shook her head. She didn't want to tell the king it was his fault. He would just remind her that she'd agreed to this arrangement to keep from being executed as a traitor.

"You can tell me," Sorren urged. "You can tell me anything, Darling."

"I told him I was your mistress. He proposed when we returned, and I didn't want to lie to him anymore." Margaret took a deep breath, letting it out through her nose. Her chin started to tremble as she held back her tears. "And he walked out. He didn't even say anything…he just left."

"I'm sorry, my sweet." Sorren pulled her in close, stroking her hair. "He always was the most moral of the cousins."

Margaret looked up at him in surprise. He was apologizing to her? It wasn't the reaction she had expected.

"Is that why you've been cooped up in your room the last few days?"

Margaret nodded against his shoulder.

"This is why I told you I would find a husband for you," Sorren said. "So you wouldn't get your heart broken." He cupped her cheek in his hand. "I loathe to see you hurting."

She wasn't sure how true that was, but it was nice to hear in the moment.

Sorren let her go before he stood and removed his outer layer of clothes. He went to the other side of the bed before getting in, pulling her back into his arms.

Margaret sank into him, sighing as she rested her head against his chest. It was comforting to be held, even when she hated that it was Sorren doing it.

"I have someone special in mind for you." Sorren smiled at her. "All will be well, I promise."

Margaret sighed when the curtains opened, letting in the light. Blessedly, Sarah didn't try to force her from her bed this time.

"Would you like me to put you in your dressing gown today, my lady?"

Margaret shook her head, blinking slowly as she sighed. She didn't have the will to dress. To feel like a person again.

"Can I get you to take breakfast, at least?" Sarah came to her bedside, straightening the comforter. "You seemed to do well enough eating dinner with His Majesty last night."

Sorren had spent the last day and a half with her, gently plying her to eat and trying to pull her from her pit of despair. She'd never seen him so caring—not even when it came to the queen.

She should eat, if only to make Sarah feel better. "Just something light. I'd like to take it in here, please." Margaret wasn't interested in leaving her bed any time soon.

"Very good, my lady." Sarah smiled at her. "I'll be right back."

Sighing, Margaret rubbed her face with both hands. Maybe Sorren was right—she should have let him find her a husband and not bothered with love.

The door to her room opened sooner than she expected for Sarah to return. She lifted her head, furrowing her brow. "Sarah? What are you doing back already?"

"My lady, His Grace is here to see you," Sarah said hesitantly at the doorway.

Margaret shot to a seated position, her heart pounding. He was here to see her? "Send him in, Sarah."

"Would you like me to dress you first?" Sarah frowned as she looked Margret over.

Margaret shook her head, getting out of bed. "My dressing gown will be fine." She grabbed it off the chair, pulling her arms through it. "Send him in." She rushed to her mirror, pulling her hair from its braid, running her fingers through it to be somewhat presentable.

Sarah left, Rowan taking her place a few moments later. He was tense, brow furrowed and mouth tight.

Margaret clasped her hands in front of her, rubbing her lips together. Who should speak first? He was the one to walk out on her, but she was the one who lied to him for so long.

"I—" they started at the same time.

Margaret let out a shy chuckle. "I'm sorry, go ahead."

Rowan seemed to relax a little, his mouth softening. "I came here for clarity…to see if maybe we can…" Rowan sighed, running hand through his hair. "I want to talk."

"I'll tell you anything you want to know." Margaret squeezed her hands together, resisting the urge to go to him. She had to keep the space between them while they figured out what was to become of them. "I don't want there to be secrets between us. Not if there is a possibility of an *us* again."

Rowan motioned to a chair near the bed. "May I?"

Margaret nodded, sitting on the edge of the bed when he sat in the chair.

Rowan leaned forward on his elbows, letting out a deep sigh. He looked weary as he asked, "How long have you been his mistress?"

"Two years now—a year if you take out the time we were away. He visited me every night for the year before we toured our lands, and returned to it the moment we came back." Margaret looked down at her hands rubbing her thumb against her forefinger hard enough to hurt the joint. "I am the king's whore."

"The king does not take a mistress without, in his mind, good reason," Rowan chose his words carefully. "What was his reason?"

Margaret looked up, her eyes wide. He really wanted to know. The words came tumbling out of her mouth before she could stop them. "I gave shelter and aid to the traitor Liam Fulton, and I was caught. King Sorren is doing this as payment for not executing me." Margaret explained all that had happened and her convictions that Liam was innocent.

Rowan began pacing in front of her, one arm crossed over his chest with his other hand on his chin, one finger crooked over his mouth. She could see he was having a conversation with himself, his head tilting this way and that. He paused in front of her, pulling his hand away from his face. "So what was the point of this, Margaret?"

"Of what?" she asked slowly.

"Of courting me." He angrily threw his arms out wide, a lock of his hair falling into his face with the brash movement. "Of trying to get me to marry you." He started to pace again, resuming his previous position.

"Protection." There was no point in dancing around it.

He stopped pacing again. "Because I'm the cousin of the king? Is that why you chose me?"

"I chose you because you'd been away from court, and you wouldn't have heard the rumors before I could pique your interest." Margaret looked down at her hands. "And I wanted a powerful husband who could put an end to my suffering. I didn't know you were the king's cousin until later."

"And I'm supposed to believe that? That you didn't know our relation?" Rowan laughed at her, hands on his hips as he bent closer to her face. "You lied to me and manipulated me for over a *year*, Margaret!" He straightened, throwing his hands in the air. "We traveled together for a year, and you lied to my face every single day."

"I'm sorry." Her bottom lip trembled as she pushed her thumb hard into her palm. She deserved that. Margaret had done everything he said. "I wanted to tell you. There were so many times I almost *did* tell you, but I—"

"But you what?" he shouted. "Didn't want to give up your prize?"

Margaret swallowed hard, pushing into her palm until it hurt. "I was scared you would leave. Scared of what would become of me if you did." She looked at him briefly, shaking her head when her eyes started to well. She gestured to the both of them. "Scared of…this."

Rowan fell back into the chair by her bed, a deep sigh escaping him as his shoulders slumped. He looked like every ounce of energy had been taken from him. He looked at her, woeful. "Did you even love me, Margaret?"

"Theotes above, of course I did, Rowan." Margaret slid from the bed, gathering up her skirt as she knelt in front of him. Her face scrunched as she looked at him pleadingly. "I didn't expect to—didn't plan to—but I did. You *and* Samuel. I would be devastated to lose both of you."

"Samuel asks about you every minute of every day." Rowan rubbed his forehead with his fore and middle fingers, his thumb rested on his cheek. "He misses you."

Margaret leaned back on her heels, mouth trembling with her effort not to cry. "I—"

"And I miss you too, Margaret. I tried not to. I tried to hate you for what you did, even, but I couldn't." Rowan leaned forward, grabbing her hands in his. "It's been torture being away from you."

It had been the same for her. "The king…he still has his hold over me," she said slowly. "Can you bear that?"

"And I'll hate him for it." Rowan squeezed her hands tightly. "But I love you more than I hate him. I can't stay parted from you, Margaret. It will kill my spirit."

"Does this mean you still want to marry me?" Excitement fluttered in her stomach for the first time since they returned to the palace.

Rowan nodded. "I do."

Margaret let out a happy sob, wiping her face free of the tears that fell. "What about His Majesty? We would need his permission to marry since he is my *guardian*."

"I will ask, and we'll both offer to pay a large fine," Rowan explained. "The royal coffers are starting to dwindle again, and he won't be able to resist filling them."

Margaret started to feel hopeful for the first time since he had asked her to marry him. "Do you think it will work?" She relished at the thought of being free of Sorren.

"If it doesn't, then we'll get married anyway and escape to Frasisca or Glessic, or even Salatia if we have to." Rowan kissed her hand again. "I will protect you from him, Margaret."

Margaret smiled at him excitedly. "Then I'll marry you."

"Good." He kissed her fiercely before giving her a boyish grin. "I'll go speak with His Majesty on your behalf."

Margaret felt a tingle in her stomach, whether it was from excitement or nervousness, she couldn't tell. She smiled at him brightly, feeling hopeful for the first time in a long while.

Margaret hurried to catch the king before he went to his meetings. "Your Majesty!" she called out.

"You look happy, my dear," Sorren said once she reached him.

"I have something I need to talk to you about." She should let Rowan be the first to tell him, but she wanted to soften the blow to make him more amenable. If the first time their reconciliation and marriage was talked about was by Rowan, it could anger the king and risk him saying no to their request.

"I think I have something more interesting for you to hear first," Sorren told her. "Come—sit and listen."

Margaret was confused but entered the chamber nonetheless. She sat at the side of the room; there were only a few other nobles with her. There was a row of the king's advisors at the front of the chamber. The men rose and bowed when the king entered and sat in the middle of them.

"Bring her in," the king commanded.

The queen was brought into the room by two knights. Lillian looked disheveled as she stood in front of the council.

"Do you know why you've been brought here today?" one of the councilmen asked.

"You should address me as 'Your Majesty,' and no, I do not know why I've been dragged here like this," she fumed.

"You are being charged with treason," another councilman said.

"*Treason!*" Lillian reeled back incredulously. "I've done nothing to warrant a charge of treason!"

"You are being charged with adultery and spreading malicious rumor accusing His Majesty and the Lady Margaret of having an affair to cover up your own indiscretions," the same councilman said.

"You can't believe that I would have an affair, Your Majesty!" Lillian shouted. "Not when you're sleeping with this tart!" She pointed to Margaret with a glare.

"I do," the king said coldly. "You are to be confined to your rooms with only two ladies while you await a trial for your crimes."

"Your Majesty!" Lillian gasped. "Majesty, no!"

Sorren stood, giving the queen a disgusted look. "Take her away!"

Lillian was white as a sheet. "Your Majesty," she said, falling to her knees. "Please, have mercy. I've only ever been a faithful wife to you!"

The king ignored her, walking out. Margaret watched as the queen stared in shock where the king had once stood. She was picked up by the arms, and she turned her gaze on Margaret.

"You!" she snarled. "This is your fault!" The queen screamed and fought as she was taken from the room.

Margaret went to Rowan's chambers, pale and trembling.

"My dear, what's the matter?" Rowan put his hands on her shoulders.

"His Majesty has accused the queen of treason," Margaret said shakily.

"What?" Rowan asked incredulously.

"I know," Margaret said, looking around. "I don't know what His Majesty is thinking."

"I think asking His Majesty's permission to marry will have to wait." Rowan squeezed her hand. "I don't think I'll be able to sway him while he's behaving like this."

"I think you're right," Margaret agreed. Dread started to fill her again. She didn't know what the king had planned, but she didn't feel good about it.

21

illian swallowed hard, looking between the two knights escorting her to the courtroom in a simple blue house dress. She was denied her queenly regalia, her jewels and dresses taken out of her rooms as promptly as she was accused of her imagined crimes. Being denied a maid, her hair was left limp around her shoulders and her face free of any makeup.

Lillian supposed she should be happy she was not brought in with heavy iron manacles like a common criminal; she was being denied enough as it was. It was clearly a trial for show—she didn't even have representation. Lillian wasn't even offered a counselor to help plead her case.

She didn't know what Sorren was thinking. She was a foreign princess—this could bring war onto Salatia. And for what purpose? Setting her aside to marry a woman who didn't even want him?

They stopped at the closed door to the courtroom. It didn't matter that it was closed. She could hear the rumbling of the people inside, all there to witness a queen stand trial for trumped-up charges. It would be the event of a lifetime—royalty very rarely, if ever, went on trial.

"Are you ready, my lady?" one of the knights asked.

My lady? Lillian stared at him dumbfounded. Did they know something that she didn't?

With no answer, the knight opened the door to the courtroom, nudging her forward with a hand on her back.

The queen looked around the room and saw many familiar faces that would not meet her eyes. She walked with her head held high and her back stiff. Lillian would not let their cowardice discourage her. She was a queen, born a Princess of Frasisca. She would not be cowed by her husband's lies, and she knew her people would support her. Lillian had managed to make many alliances among the nobles, despite having come from a foreign country.

Lillian doubted Lady Margaret would ever manage the same if the harlot was to become queen. She curled her lip when she saw the tart sitting next to her trial box. Lady Margaret looked as if she wanted to say something but thought better of it and closed her mouth. She sat next to the king, who looked like the cat who had just eaten a bird.

Lillian looked back to the herald, glaring at him. Why wasn't he announcing her?

"Her Majesty, the queen!" the herald announced belatedly.

Lillian tried not to roll her eyes.

"Your Majesty." The judge for her trial, Duke of Clemont, smiled at her encouragingly. "You have been charged with treason by His Majesty the king. How do you plead?"

"Not guilty," Lillian said emphatically. She had done nothing wrong, and the king's charges were a frivolous way to get rid of her. Lillian was no longer useful to him. It was a terrifying thought, that she could be set aside so easily even when she had made every effort to get back into his good graces while Lady Margaret had been away.

"Then we will proceed with your trial, Your Majesty."

Lillian nodded, waiting to see who the king had scraped up to testify against her.

"The first witness to testify will be Mr. Scott Byrd," the judge said, the witness coming in to stand in front of the court.

Mr. Byrd looked at the queen with guilty eyes before turning his attention to the duke. "Your Grace," he said with a bow.

"Mr. Byrd, can you tell us how you know Her Majesty?"

"I am her chauffeur," Mr. Byrd told the court.

"And how else do you know Her Majesty?" the judge asked, a single eyebrow raised.

"I am Her Majesty's lover," Byrd said, his cheeks reddening as gasps resounded through the ladies of the court.

How dare he! What did the king have to pay him to get that kind of testimony? If there was undoubted proof that she had committed crimes, her country could do nothing to retaliate. Lillian's own cheeks heated with rage, surely making the courtiers think she was blushing at the revelation. Lillian clenched her hands in her skirts. She couldn't cover her face to hide the color. It would make her look guilty.

Duke Clemont held his hands up to quiet the chatter. "And how long have you been her lover?"

"Since I started my job six years ago, Your Grace," Byrd said, shamefaced.

Lillian sat in silent fury at his lies. She had barely noticed him, much less had an improper relationship with the man. She would pray for his soul for the lies that he was telling against a queen ordained by Theotes. He would surely need it.

"How did this come to pass, Mr. Byrd?" Clemont asked, prying further than the queen thought necessary.

"Her Majesty came to me one day and told me that her bed was cold from the king, and she wished for it to be warm again, and it would please her greatly if I were to warm it for her," the servant told the court, looking at the queen directly now. "I could not deny the queen her request, her being the queen and all."

Lillian frowned at his words. It was believable, no doubt. He was handsome enough, and she saw him nearly every day. Besides which, everyone knew that the king did not frequent her bed after begetting his heir.

"Thank you, Mr. Byrd." Duke Clemont nodded to him. "You may go now."

Byrd bowed, casting a regretful look to Lillian before he left.

"Our next witness, please," the judge called.

Lillian was shocked to see one of her maids coming forward. Marjorie Vionet was the one who had been with her the longest. "Marjorie..." she said quietly, leaning forward in her seat as if to touch her.

Marjorie walked slowly to her appointed spot at the front of the court, her hands trembling and face ashen. She jumped when Duke Clemont addressed her.

"Miss Vionet, how do you know Her Majesty?"

"I... I have known H-Her Maj-jesty for f-f-f-fifteen years..." came the mousy response.

Lillian felt sorry for her. Marjorie was timid on her own. Being in front of the large group of people, she must have been terrified out of her mind. Lillian wanted nothing more than to comfort poor Marjorie; the maid was certainly one that she had coddled in her service.

"And is it true that you have heard Her Majesty plot against His Majesty?"

Marjorie shot a panicked look toward Lillian before answering quietly. "Yes."

"I'm sorry, Miss Vionet," the duke said, looking at her encouragingly. "A little louder please."

"Y-yes," Marjorie answered louder, tears starting to flow down her cheeks rapidly. "She f-frequently spoke of her d-d-desire for H-His Majesty to be d-deposed by His R-Royal H-H-Highness..."

The crowd gasped as shock ran through Lillian. She would never depose Sorren with Gareth...he was far from ready to be king. She was the one who had sent him away to keep him from getting himself into more trouble!

"You lying little beast!" Lillian shot up from her seat.

Marjorie backed away as though the queen's words could harm her, looking at her wide-eyed.

"Your Majesty, if you cannot keep quiet, we have to remove you until the verdict is reached," Duke Clemont scolded her.

Lillian glared daggers at him but sat silently nonetheless.

The day was spent with witness after witness being called, some claiming to be her lovers and others claiming that she had coerced them to help with her plot to murder the king and take the throne for herself. Sometimes, she would be taking the throne for her son. Lillian had to admit that many of the ideas were rather good, and had she actually wanted to murder Sorren, she could have easily gotten away with the crime.

Lillian smirked. Maybe someone would use one of those fake plots to actually kill the king. She wouldn't weep for him if they did.

Duke Clemont stood and cleared his throat before addressing the court. "Your Majesty, if you would please stand to hear the verdict."

Lillian stood, casting an imperious look Sorren's way. He could have at least had one witness in her favor, but he was so desperate for her to be gone that he'd stacked the whole court against her.

"Your Majesty, you are hereby found guilty and stripped of all your titles and lands, and sentenced to death by any method His Majesty sees fit." The duke's ruling was soon met by outcries of the women in the court who knew Lillian.

Lillian closed her eyes tightly, swallowing hard. She could at least be assured of Gareth's safety—he had been with her family in Frasisca the last few months to learn what he could from their court. Sorren would not think to rid of him too, if Gareth wasn't present.

Sorren stood and stared Lillian down with more hatred than she thought possible. "You are to be burned at the stake in three days' time in a public execution."

Lillian heard Margaret gasp behind her and turned to see the little whore was pale as a ghost, her hands over her mouth. She quirked her eyebrow at the reaction.

Perhaps Margaret had not wanted her out of the picture.

22

Margaret paced outside the queen's chambers. The king had allowed the queen to have people come to Lillian to say goodbye, and Lillian had one of her ladies summon Margaret prior.

Margaret looked to Captain Vojvo, anxiously peeling the skin from her bottom lip with her teeth. "What do you think she wants?" She didn't know why the queen would want to see her. Lillian hated Margaret.

Vojvo shrugged. "I couldn't say, my lady."

A knight exited the room, closing the door behind him. "She's ready for you, my lady."

Margaret was announced, and she warily stepped in, her stomach turning as the door locked behind her. She still didn't know if she had made the right decision to accept Lillian's invitation.

"Lady Margaret," Lillian said quietly. She remained seated, hands in her lap. "I'm pleased you came."

Lillian was far calmer than Margaret expected, like nothing out of the ordinary was happening. Margaret curtsied to her. "Your Majesty."

"Didn't you hear? I'm not the queen anymore." Lillian scoffed, a smirk coming to her face as she waved her hand nonchalantly to the side. She shook her head, her expression dropping as her shoulders slumped forward.

Margaret frowned at her. Maybe Lillian wasn't as nonchalant as Margaret first thought—she seemed to flit from one emotion to the next, never settling on one for long. "Why is it you brought me here?"

"I wanted to make sure you saw this as a cautionary tale for what can happen when you get involved with my husband," Lillian told her plainly. She smiled, extending her hands to show the bare room. "If you marry him to become the next queen, then this can be your fate too."

The thought made Margaret wish she had let the king execute her. "I didn't choose to be involved with your husband." Margaret shook her head, stepping toward the queen. "I—"

"It doesn't matter, Lady Margaret," Lillian snapped. "He has his eye on you, and there is nothing you can do now to keep it off you."

Margaret feared that was the case. "Surely there is a way."

"None, Lady Margaret." Lillian looked to the slit window when it momentarily darkened. "That's how *I* ended up as his wife. I was engaged to be married to another, and he would have none of it and pursued me until my father relented."

"Your Majesty, I would be happy if His Majesty never wanted to see me again." Margaret would be happy if she never saw him again as well. She tried not to sigh as she was brought back to thoughts of having left with Liam and how much happier she would have been had she stayed with him.

Lillian pursed her lips, a brow arching. "I'm sure."

"Really, Your Majesty." Margaret clasped her hands in front of her, leaning in to say quietly, "I hate Sorren with a passion."

Lillian held her hand up. "Enough, Lady Margaret."

Margaret fell silent, waiting for her to say more.

"I would like for you to attend my execution tomorrow. I have a very special message for you."

"Your Majesty…" Margaret hesitated, her mouth turning downward. What could Lillian possibly want from her being there? "I don't think it would be appropriate."

"I want you there, Lady Margaret," Lillian told her firmly.

Margaret nodded slowly, sighing in resignation. "If you wish for me to be there, I will attend, although I wish you would change your mind."

Lillian smiled, her eyes bright. "Oh, I don't think I will, Lady Margaret."

Margaret frowned again. She knocked on the door, waiting for it to unlock and open before stepping forward. She let out a relieved breath when she saw Vojvo waiting there.

He waited until the door closed again before speaking. "What did she want?"

"She has invited me to her execution." Margaret clenched her hands in front of her, wincing when her knuckles popped. "I don't have a good feeling about it."

Dread weighed heavy on her shoulders as Rowan brought her back to her chambers after dinner. "And you'll be there with me tomorrow?"

He nodded solemnly. "I can't say I'm particularly excited to go, but I'll stand by your side whatever may come."

They stopped at the doors, she wrapped her arms around his waist, leaning her forehead against his chest. "I wish this was all over. Did you see him at dinner?" Margaret swallowed against the rising bile. The king had been positively gleeful tonight.

"It was sickening."

Margaret looked up at Rowan. His face was paler than usual. "We should get some sleep if we can…tomorrow is going to be a hard day."

He nodded slowly, giving her shoulders a light squeeze. "Will you be all right?"

"I don't think I'll get much sleep." Margaret didn't want to tell him the king would likely see her tonight, especially with how happy he had been at dinner. "I'm worried about what the queen has in store for me tomorrow."

"We'll face it together." He kissed her forehead. "I'll see you tomorrow?"

Margaret nodded silently, giving him a small smile before he walked away. When he turned a corner, she let out a sigh, going into her chambers.

Sarah was already waiting for her, hands clasped in front of her. "How shall I prepare you tonight, my lady?"

"I don't think you have to." Margaret unceremoniously dropped onto one of the sofas, taking the crystal topper of the decanter of whisky she kept for the king. She poured two glasses, taking a sip from one of them. "I don't think it will take long for him to arrive."

"Would you like me to stay in case you need me?" Sarah asked hesitantly.

"No." Margaret took another sip, leaning back against the high back of the sofa. "I'll call for you if I need you, but I don't think I will."

Sarah gave her a small curtsey. "As you like, my lady," she said before leaving.

Margaret let out a heavy sigh through her nose, leaning her head back against the sofa. She closed her eyes. Maybe after tomorrow she and Rowan could finally ask the king for his permission to marry her. She hated the delay, but she didn't want to anger the king in the midst of him executing his wife on made-up charges. Had their laws been equal, he would have faced the same charges.

But he was a king, and he did what he wanted. As he had told her many, many times before.

When the door creaked, Margaret opened her eyes. She briefly smiled wide, trying to bring forward feelings she didn't have before dropping it. She stood, turning to Sorren, curtsying to him. "Your Majesty."

Sorren took the drink from her hand, setting it on the table next to his before sweeping her into his arms. He rested his forehead against hers, a wide grin on his face. "You look lovely this evening."

She couldn't help but be swept up by his exuberance, smiling back at him even though it felt wrong. "Thank you."

He took her hand, leading her away from the sofa before kissing her knuckles. "Dance with me?"

Margaret furrowed her brows. He was having his wife killed tomorrow, and he wanted to dance with her? "I—"

"It's my last night before I'm a free man again," he said, swaying her to imagined music. "I want to celebrate."

Her stomach clenched. She knew he was cruel, but this was truly insane. How could he not care at all? To think of the queen's death as something to celebrate when she was innocent? It was pathological.

Sorren spun her out before pulling her close to him, resting his forehead on hers again.

"Why are you doing this?" She didn't want to, but she looked up into his eyes. It raised her hackles when she did. "Executing her, I mean."

"She was found to be a traitor." He pulled away from her face, shrugging. "I couldn't very well allow her the same deal we have. After all, she's already my wife."

Margaret tried not to react, but her grip tightened on his hands. "But you know she's not guilty."

"She's impeding something very important that I'd like to do." He pulled her flush against him, holding her tightly.

"What would that be?" She was almost scared to ask, but she had to know. Had to hear it from his lips.

He grinned before kissing her with an excitement she hadn't experienced from him. "You'll see."

Margaret stumbled back when he let her go, putting her fingers to her lips. She hadn't realized he'd been holding onto her so tightly.

Sorren went to the table, picking up his drink and tossing it back in a single gulp. He held out a hand to her, eyes crinkling as they softened. "Shall we?"

Swallowing hard, she slowly nodded and took his hand.

The courtyard was filled with people as the executioner piled wood and hay against the stake the queen would be burned upon. Margaret stood close to Rowan as she looked on with the rest of the crowd. Margaret was still apprehensive at the request she be in attendance for the execution.

"The queen!" the herald shouted. It was an incorrect announcement now that Lillian had her titles stripped, but everyone, including Margaret, still thought of her as the queen.

Margaret doubted it mattered what he said anyway. She could barely hear him over the crowd.

Lillian walked through the parted crowd, her head held high. Sorren, in his disgusting form of justice, had forced the queen to wear her wedding dress to her execution. Lillian was in an all-white gown that had a high neck and tightly fitted sleeves all the way to her wrists. The front of the dress was simple while the back held most of the elegance. There were pearl buttons sewn down the back of the gown all the way to the end of her small train.

The closer the queen got to the recently constructed platform, the quieter the crowd grew until it fell silent. Margaret's stomach clenched when all that could be heard were the birds. Everyone wanted to hear what Lillian had to say.

Margaret tightened her grip on Rowan's arm. Only Margaret knew it would be a special message for her.

Lillian was brought onto the platform to face the crowd. She stared down at the gathered people intently as though daring someone to call out a slanderous word.

"Is there anything you would like to say, my lady?" the executioner asked her.

Lillian set her shoulders straight before addressing the people. "My lords and ladies, it has come time for me to journey into Theotes's hands." She looked over the crowd, her voice clear and strong even while her hands shook in front of her. "I will happily go as your good king commands."

Margaret paled as she listened, worried what Lillian would say. She was still in shock that Sorren was so callously executing his wife.

Lillian leveled Margaret with a cold stare before continuing on, "But know, good people, that I am not put to death for my own sins. I am being executed today by the will of my husband's mistress, Lady Margaret Doremis, Countess of Dorcia, who wishes to marry my husband when I am gone."

Now Margaret understood why she was invited to her execution. It was the queen's last revenge on her.

Cries of outrage erupted from the crowd and many heated stares were shot in Margaret's direction. She pulled in closer to Rowan. She didn't know if they would make any sort of move toward her.

Lillian smirked as the crowd was hushed. "I pray that you will forgive Lady Margaret for causing my early death to come to pass." Lillian looked at the executioner, nodding. "I am ready to die."

Margaret gripped Rowan's arm tightly, her face numb, as servants laid bundles of hay at her feet and against her legs. Margaret could hear Lillian quietly repeat a small prayer as the servants worked.

"Do you forgive me?" the executioner asked the queen.

"With all my heart do I forgive you, sir, and will beg Theotes' mercy on you when I reach him." Lillian handed him a bag of coins to pay him for his trouble, as was tradition in public executions.

Lillian was willingly bound to the stake before the executioner was given a burning torch. Margaret did not want to see the queen burn, but she could not look away from the horror unfolding before her.

"Theotes have mercy on me, and to the Allcaring, I commend my soul," Lillian said one last time before the pyre was lit and her screams overtook her words.

Margaret gasped at the sound, the shrieks grating down her spine. She swallowed hard, looking around the crowd. Some gleefully watched, others looked as repulsed as she felt.

Margaret fled, unable to hear any more of her screams. She pushed her way through the crowd, squeezing through any suffocating opening she could find. Her breath hitched as she was pushed into several other people, trapped in a constricting circle until she was able to break free of them.

She nearly fell to the ground when she escaped the packed crowd, taking in a gasping breath. Margaret flinched when Lillian let out another scream, then picked up her skirts and ran until she came to her chambers. She slammed her door behind her, her face pale. She could still hear the crowd in her chambers.

"My lady," Sarah said, her own face pale. "The king wishes you come to his chambers whenever you are done with....with the *fanfare*, as he called it."

"He isn't coming here?" Margaret asked, surprised.

"His Majesty requested that you come to his chambers," Sarah told her again.

Margaret went to Sorren's chambers, anxiety gnawing at her stomach. She had never been to his private rooms. She had never been invited to anywhere but a room that would not bring on suspicion. Margaret was let in by a manservant.

The entire floor was covered with a behemoth Radovian rug, filled with blues and golds, creams and reds. Margaret was amazed that it was even possible to make a rug that large. The walls were a dark, dusky blue with white molding accents. The room was topped with a rotunda painted with portraits of past rulers in various epic scenes.

The squinches were lined with white molding with gold scrolling in the center. All the arched structures were divided into two panels, each with matching floral designs. The surrounding pendentives had a larger version of the floral arrangement in the squinches. From the ceiling came a massive chandelier of gold plated metal. Margaret instinctively went to the wall sized windows to look at the view. The king could see nearly the entire city from that view.

Margaret started to back away from the windows when she caught sight of dark gray smoke wafting past the upper corner, her stomach curling.

"Are you enjoying the view?" Sorren asked from behind her.

Margaret jumped and turned around quickly, curtsying to him. She wasn't, but she wouldn't tell him that. "Yes, Your Majesty."

"Did you see the execution?" Sorren asked.

"The queen looked beautiful in her wedding gown, Your Majesty," Margaret said slowly, omitting that Lillian had blamed Margaret for her death. "But I could not stay past the first scream."

"Shame, really," Sorren said nonchalantly. "It's over by now, nothing left to see, I'm sure."

"Yes, Your Majesty." Margaret's stomach seized at the thought.

"Lady Margaret, I called you here to ask you something quite personal."

She looked at him sharply, fear creeping down her neck. Was this what he had hinted at last night? "What is it?"

"I would like for you to marry me and become my next queen," Sorren proposed, looking at her as if he had just handed her the world on a golden platter.

"Your Majesty, I cannot," Margaret told him fervidly, backing away from him. "Your wife is barely deceased and Duke Fradure and I have reconciled—he has already proposed marriage to me."

Sorren grabbed her arms tightly, pulling her back until his face was close to hers. "I burned my wife at the stake to marry you, you *stupid* girl!" A vein popped out in his forehead, his cheeks red. "I could have you executed right along with her!"

This is what Lillian had warned her of. Margaret tried to back away from him again, only to have his grip tighten on her arms. Fear exploded in her chest. If he did, this would have all been for nothing. She'd have been tortured for absolutely nothing. "Your Majesty, you must see the error in this," Margaret begged. "You would have to make me an ordained queen to quench any rebellion, and then Gareth would never be able to inherit the throne."

Sorren rolled his eyes at her. "Gareth is not fit to be king."

Margaret knew this already but was shocked by Sorren's admission. "Your Majesty, he is the rightful heir."

"And he is a bumbling idiot that will sell my kingdom to the highest bidder. He can't even be bothered to learn how to rule when there are beds to fill," Sorren snapped. "Lillian could give me no more children and Gareth cannot be allowed to take the throne. I need you to give me a new heir."

"Your Majesty, I am certainly not suitable to produce your heir—you gave my family our titles barely twenty years ago," Margaret tried to reason with Sorren.

Anything to get him off this train of thought. "And Duke Fradure would surely support Gareth over you—or even put himself as an option—if you took me away from him, and he would no doubt convince other noblemen to follow his example."

"The duke would never have the gall to turn against me." Sorren laughed, looking at her as though she was a naive child. "He has his power only because he is a part of my family."

"Love can make you turn against your own flesh," Margaret told him.

"Enough talk about that." Sorren let go of her arms, going to a table behind her. "I've had something made for you."

Margaret was wary, rubbing her sore arms. Was this Sorren's first step in trying to court her? "What is it, Your Majesty?"

"Come, see it for yourself." He held his hand out to her.

Margaret hesitantly took it, looking at the chest he opened. Inside was a string of pearls surrounded by diamonds. "Your Majesty, this is too much for me." Margaret shook her head, stepping away from the chest.

Sorren grabbed her wrist. "Let me put it on you, Lady Margaret."

It was an order formed as a request. "As you wish," she said meekly.

Sorren let go of her, grabbing the pearl chain, placing it atop her head as a circlet. "To my future queen."

Margaret started at his words. "Your Majesty, I cannot accept this," she told him, reaching up to take off the circlet. "The Duke of Fradure intends to ask you, as my guardian, for my hand in marriage."

Sorren grabbed her hands quickly to keep her from removing his gift. "You will wear it, and I expect you to stay close to me today at court."

Margaret's stomach sank. The king *was* trying to court her. "As my king commands." Her shoulders slumped. What would this mean for her and Rowan?

Margaret entered the hall on Sorren's arm, the pearl circlet still on her head. She saw the whispers between couples and friends as she was brought to the front of the room and seated in what was previously the queen's seat to observe the court. Margaret's stomach curled at the distressed look on Rowan's face. Sorren was putting her on an obvious display. She was forced to follow him around in his mingling and listen attentively in his meetings.

Margaret was only able to escape when she was to change for dinner. She called for Rowan to come to her chambers immediately.

It was not long before Sarah returned with the duke and Margaret immediately went into his arms. Margaret looked at Rowan desperately. "Rowan, he refuses to allow us to marry. He wants me as his bride instead." She wiped a tear from her cheek. "What are we going to do? We can't marry in secret."

"Let me speak with the king, my love." Rowan cupped her face in his hands. "Our relationship might give me an upper hand in convincing him to allow us to marry."

"What if he won't leave my bed?" Margaret asked with a crestfallen look.

Rowan's face darkened at the mention of the king's visits. "I will make that a strong point in our agreement." He kissed her forehead. "I will do anything to make you my wife."

23

Rowan waited in silent fury for the king to see him. How dare the ruler of his nation use his authority to violate any woman he pleased? Especially the woman Rowan intended to marry. He clenched his hands together to keep them from shaking. He had not allowed Margaret to see his anger after her reaction in Marbon, nor after finding out she was the king's mistress. He didn't want her to change her mind about being his wife. Rowan looked at the door of the king's private audience chamber when it opened.

"Your Grace, the king will see you now," the servant told him.

Rowan stood and pushed his way past the servant to see the king. "We need to speak, Your Majesty."

The king didn't bother looking at him, papers in hand. "I've already told Margaret she will marry a man of my choosing, and that man is me."

"Damn it, Sorren!" Rowan slammed his hand down on the table next to him. He was not a lowly subject begging for a wife. He was the king's cousin, trying to keep his bride-to-be out of harm's way. "Margaret will be my wife one way or another."

Sorren raised his brows, calmly setting down his papers. "I have given my answer to you and Margaret both, and my answer is no."

"Your Majesty, I will do anything to make her my wife. She's Samuel's world," Rowan confided, his anger deflating to desperation at the thought of not having Margaret as his wife—as Sam's new mother.

"She helped Liam Fulton, and she is being punished accordingly." Sorren looked over Rowan, a calculating look coming to his face. "Has Lady Margaret spoken to you about him?"

Rowan tried to keep his face slack in his reservation. "I know she helped him, but I won't incriminate her further."

"You said you would do anything, Rowan," the king reminded him. "I would be willing to consider letting you marry Margaret if you can give me the information I want to know."

Rowan rubbed his thumb against his first two fingers as he debated if he should betray Margaret's trust for her own benefit. He could risk her hating him if she found out he was telling the king her secrets, but he couldn't let her stay in this situation. "She sends letters to him through a mutual acquaintance of theirs," he said reluctantly.

"And does she get any back?" Sorren leaned closer, his face intent.

Rowan frowned. "Will you stop visiting her bed?"

"Answer my question, and I'll think about it," the king said.

Rowan sighed, closing his eyes. "Yes." Guilt shot through him. It was for the best. For him. For her...for Samuel.

"If you can get me those letters, I will allow you to marry." Sorren extended his arms in an open gesture. "I will even throw Lady Margaret the wedding of her dreams and give you her father's lands and title as an added gift if you give me those letters and any future letters she receives from the traitor." The king held his hand out to Rowan. "Do we have an agreement?"

Rowan looked at the king's hand, swallowing hard. "Will you stop your defilement of Margaret?"

"Yes," Sorren said, his hand still extended.

Rowan grasped the king's hand firmly. "We have an agreement, Your Majesty."

The king smiled boyishly at him. "I'm happy to congratulate you on your engagement, then, dear cousin."

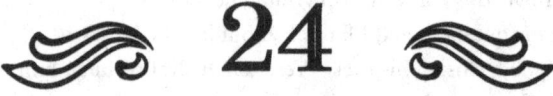

24

Sorren's smile slipped off his face when Rowan left the room. He threw the vase of flowers on one of the numerous tables in his chambers. He groaned in frustration, hands clenched at his sides as he paced. He did not want to let her marry Rowan. Margaret was *his* and no one else's.

Sorren ran both of his hands over his face. He couldn't believe he had agreed to stay away from Lady Margaret's bed, even. Sorren wanted no one but her, and now he could not have her either in marriage or intimacy.

The only pay off would be finally getting rid of the last threat to his throne. With Crompton dead and no longer able to push him out, Liam Fulton was the only one left who had a chance to unseat him. It had been startling when Sorren had first seen Liam in the courtroom for his trial—he was the spitting image of his however-many-times great-grandfather, the last Triburn king, King Ettien Triburn. Sorren had seen that portrait many times when he was a boy, his father taking him to the Triburn Room to remind him of their power and what kind of kings they were.

It had just been dumb luck that Crompton selected Liam to take the blame for his own treasonous behavior.

Sorren sighed, standing in front of the window. There would be good things that would come out of letting her marry someone else. It was too soon to marry after executing his wife, as Margaret had pointed out. Sorren put his hand on the window and looked down at the view below. Her marrying Rowan would certainly keep the courtiers from gossiping that Sorren had executed Lillian in order to marry Lady Margaret.

He rested his forehead against the window, sighing again. Sorren had been so excited at the thought of marrying Margaret and restarting his line that he hadn't thought the consequences through. Now, he would have to figure out a new plan.

Scowling at the view of his people bustling on the streets, he went to the table with a physical map laid across it that showed the land barriers of the nobility. Sorren looked at the barriers of Margaret and Rowan's lands. The king raised his brows when he noticed that the deal he had arranged with Rowan would allow the couple to own almost half of the country. A smile started to form on his face. If Lady Margaret married Rowan, then she would be in possession of those lands if Rowan were ever to be out of the way.

There was a wide grin on Sorren's face now. He would happily let Lady Margaret marry Rowan and have wedded bliss for a short while. He would use

Rowan to find Liam and execute his last threat to the throne. Then, he would find a way to rid himself of Rowan and marry Lady Margaret to acquire the lands for himself without turning his people against him. Sorren would easily be the richest man in Anatalia once Lady Margaret was his wife, and he would have everything he wanted and still look honorable in the eyes of his people.

The day was looking much better after the revelation. Sorren would be a very happy, and a very rich, man soon enough. The king summoned one of his servants to inform the cook that they would be having a feast that night and requested that Lady Margaret and Rowan sit with him at the head table.

Sorren walked into the dining hall and saw Margaret and Rowan were already in their places next to his chair at the center of the long head table. Everyone stood when he entered the room and bowed or curtsied to him in turn as he walked to the table. Sorren watched the wary look that settled on Margaret's face as he approached. He noted that Rowan had made sure to sit between them.

"My lady, Your Grace, congratulations on your engagement," Sorren said when he sat.

"Thank you, Your Majesty," Rowan responded for the both of them.

When the wine had been poured for all in the room, Sorren stood with his glass raised. "I would like to make a toast to Lady Dorcia and His Grace the Duke of Fradure on their engagement today. May they have a long and happy marriage!"

The rest of the dining hall called out toasts to the engaged couple before taking a drink from their cups. It didn't take long for whispers to start between the nobles as they looked up to the head table. Some looked suspicious of the news, while others looked pleased. No doubt, the latter would be shoving their daughter at him for the chance to be the next queen, willing to run over the ashes of his wife as quickly as he was in trying to marry Margaret.

Sorren's smile temporarily fell from his face when he saw Lady Margaret smile tenderly at Rowan the way Margaret's mother, Catherine, used to smile at him. The way he wanted Margaret to smile at him for so long. The happy smile returned to his face when he turned back to his nobles and sat down at the table.

Rowan leaned over to the king to whisper to him. "I want to make sure you know, cousin, that your defilement of Margaret stops tonight, not when we marry."

Sorren scowled at him. "Fine," he growled shortly.

"I'm glad we have an understanding." Rowan grabbed Lady Margaret's hand and kissed it, whispering to her something Sorren could not hear.

There was a look of relief on her face that made him sick to his stomach. It didn't matter—not for long, anyway. Sorren would be able to get everything he wanted soon enough.

A knock sounded on Sorren's door, and he sighed as he tossed his parchment down on his desk. "Come in."

Christian timidly entered the room. "Your Majesty, there is a Mister Cain Ellis here to see you. He says you're expecting him."

Sorren stood. "Send him in, Christian." He had gotten a letter last week that Ellis had some information that Sorren would be very interested in hearing.

The servant bowed deeply and disappeared from the room, quickly replaced by Cain Ellis. "Your Majesty," he said with a deep bow. "Thank you for seeing me."

"What do you have for me?" Sorren demanded.

"I have heard news of the traitor, Liam Fulton."

"Oh?" Sorren's forehead wrinkled deeply as his brows raised high.

"He's in Salatia, Your Majesty," Cain told him, "in a town called Numetra. They're calling him the 'Hero of Chenalieu.'"

Sorren rolled his eyes. *Hero of Chenalieu.* The man was no more a hero than he was a traitor.

Sorren paced his chambers as he heard the news. In a town called Numetra, the traitor had come out of hiding. There would be no way for the king to extract him for execution—not when he had alienated King Peralta after sleeping with the other monarch's wife.

It disgusted him, seeing Liam heralded so.

With a curled lip, the king commanded the messenger out. He could not stand the sight of him any longer. There was nothing the king could do now except to wait for the traitor to come back into his lands, and who knew how long that would take. Worse yet, he'd traded Margaret for an impossible goal.

Sorren threw his glass of amber liquor against the wall and let out a curse.

25

Margaret looked out the window, arms crossed tightly in front of her, holding her shawl close. It was snowing out, slowly piling against the walls of the palace. She'd finally be meeting with Mr. Nathaniel Ethum, her investors' overwhelming choice for who would make a good business manager for her—that morning, Margaret had received news he would be in to see her before the evening. In all of the wildness of the past month, she had forgotten she'd invited him.

He'd made good time. She'd sent him a summons the day after she returned from her tour with Rowan, and he arrived only a month later. Margaret hoped he would be amenable to becoming her business manager. She needed to replace Charles Luther, quickly.

Sarah set down a tray of tea, coming to stand by Margaret. "Would you like one of us to stay with you, my lady?"

"You're welcome to stay if you'd like, but I'll only require Captain Vojvo for now." Margaret turned to Sarah, a small smile on her face. "You're more than welcome to get one of the maids for tea service if you'd like to go see George."

Sarah hesitated, rubbing her lips together. "Are you sure, my lady?"

Margaret nodded. "Of course. You have wedding planning to do, which I'm sure you aren't left much time to do here."

"Not a lot, no." Sarah gave her a shy smile. "Thank you, my lady. I'll be back for dinner to dress you."

"Would you send Vojvo in on your way out?"

"Of course." Sarah gave her a small curtsy before she left.

Margaret sighed, turning back to the window. The day reminded her of the first time she had summoned Charles to the palace to give her lessons about her business two years ago. She'd not make the same mistakes she had with Charles—trusting him to operate unchecked as he had while she and Papa lived in Silvica for his health. If Mr. Ethum agreed to work for her, she would need monthly reports and quarterly meetings with him.

She wouldn't let anyone keep her from knowing her own business. Not ever again.

"My lady, where would you like me?" Vojvo asked when he came into the room.

"Wherever you're comfortable, Captain." She turned around to look at him. "And when Mr. Ethum arrives, wherever you can get the best read on him."

"Very good." Vojvo settled on the couch closest to the door, interlacing his fingers over his stomach. "Do you know anything about this man?"

"Only that he comes highly recommended by my investors." Margaret still regretted not being able to see any but Mr. Persbrant while she was on her tour. Maybe next year she could try again just to see them, or she could summon them to the palace. She needed them to be comfortable speaking directly with her if anything went amiss, getting them unused to going only to the business manager.

They remained quiet until a knock sounded on the door.

Vojvo pushed himself up from the couch as the door opened, a servant announcing Mr. Ethum.

He shyly stepped inside, looking around with wide eyes. "Lady Dorcia, it's an honor to meet you," Mr. Ethum said as he bowed.

"The honor is mine, Mr. Ethum." Margaret looked him over—Mr. Persbrant was right. Mr. Ethum was younger than most to be considered for such a position. But she wasn't going to let that stop her from having the best candidate work for her. "Would you like to sit?" She motioned toward the plush chairs by the fireplace.

"Yes, of course." Mr. Ethum waited to sit in the chair opposite her until she was seated.

Margaret scanned the room until she saw Vojvo. He'd settled himself opposite them where she could still see him if she had any need of him. She turned her attention back to her potential hire. "Mr. Eth—"

"Nathaniel, please, my lady," he said, color coming to his cheeks. "Mr. Ethum sounds like my father conducting a meeting."

Margaret stole a quick glance at Vojvo. He only shrugged. "If that's what you'd like, Nathaniel." She cleared her throat, giving her a moment to regain her momentum. "I can assume you know why I've summoned you here?"

"I wouldn't like to presume anything, ma'am." He shifted uncomfortably, looking around the grand room as he pressed his lips together. "But I have a few inklings of how this will go."

With no maid having come in Sarah's place, she poured herself and Nathaniel steaming cups of tea, gently pushing his cup toward him to flavor however he liked. She dropped a spoonful of sugar into hers before stirring. Nathaniel left his untouched.

"Good." She gave him a small smile, leaning back into her chair, the hot tea warming her hands. "I reached out to all of my investors, and your name was the most frequently named as a viable replacement for my current business manager."

"My lady, if I may…" Nathaniel leaned in before continuing, "What is so wrong with your current manager? He's been doing the job for over twenty years now."

"Mr. Luther and I have had a falling out in the last couple of years." Margaret didn't want to give him all of the details, but she supposed she did owe him some sort of explanation if she wanted him to feel wanted in this job. "And I need a business manager who will not cut me out of knowing my business simply because he doesn't like me."

"I see." Nathaniel steepled his fingers, tapping them against his chin as his brow furrowed.

"Is that a problem?" She raised her brow at him. Margaret didn't know how to interpret his reaction. Was he judging her for her non-detailed truth, or had he already heard another version himself?

"No, my lady." He pulled his hands away from his face, brow still wrinkled. "How long has it been since you received a report from Mr. Luther?"

"A year, at least?" Margaret's shoulders dropped as she looked at Vojvo, her brows raised. When he nodded, she said, "Over a year. I haven't received one since before I went on tour of my expanded lands."

"I heard news that it was quite a successful trip for you, my lady." Nathaniel smiled briefly before turning serious. "I suspect that would mean you'd like me to do a thorough going over your ledgers to make sure everything is in order?"

"If you accept the job as business manager, I think that would be a wise choice," Margaret said. "I don't suspect Mr. Luther of anything untoward, but I think you and I would like to know the state of things." She doubted she would have two people like Mr. Amali in her service, stealing from her and her people.

Nathaniel nodded, remaining silent.

"Will that be an issue?" Margaret asked slowly. Nathaniel seemed to be an odd one. But as long as he did the job well and kept her informed, she didn't really care if he was odd.

"No, ma'am."

"Then will you accept the job?" Margaret rubbed her lips together before saying, "I'll match whatever your current salary is and give you a three percent raise for every year that you work for me." It was the same deal Charles had gotten from her father. It worked well enough for him, so Margaret was sure it would work well enough for Nathaniel.

"It would be my pleasure to, my lady," he said. "I only have one question."

Margaret leaned forward. "And what is that?"

"What if Mr. Luther refuses to hand over all the ledgers and paperwork pertinent to running your business?"

The thought had never crossed her mind. Margaret gestured to Vojvo on the other side of the room, with a sly smile. "The captain here can be very persuasive."

Vojvo stepped forward, standing up straighter. "Whatever Your Ladyship requires of me."

"There you have it." Margaret let out a small laugh. "I'm sure Mr. Luther will be more than happy to be rid of me at this point. I don't doubt he'll bring what we ask of him."

"Have you already let Mr. Luther go?"

Margaret shook her head. "I wanted to ensure there were no gaps. Now that you've accepted, I'll send for him and inform him of the need to surrender any business material he has."

Nathaniel hesitated before saying, "Would you like me to be with you for that meeting, ma'am?"

"If you think you can be of use, I certainly won't bar you from it." Margaret shook her head. "I'll only caution you that it could become explosive."

"I think not, then." Nathaniel furrowed his brow. "How long do you think it will take to call the meeting and receive the required paperwork?

"I'll be summoning Mr. Luther for a meeting tomorrow," Margaret said, "and I don't suspect it will take him longer than a week to have everything returned to my possession. Why?"

Nathaniel blushed, sinking into his chair. "Might I ask for an advance on my first month's salary?"

"May I ask why?" Margaret saw Vojvo shift forward out of the corner of her eye. She hoped he hadn't somehow gotten into trouble that would take his concentration away from her business.

"I would like to leave with all of the ledgers in my possession—things can get lost when other people carry them, you see." His cheeks grew darker in color. "If I'm to stay that long, I don't think I'll have the money for the hotel."

"Ah." Margaret let out a relieved breath. "Have them send the bill directly to me then. I'll have a contract with our agreed-upon terms sent to you at...?"

"Thank you, ma'am. I'll be at the Dame Spaglion." Nathaniel stood abruptly. "I wouldn't like to take up any more of your time for today."

Margaret was startled at the suddenness. She stood slowly, holding out her hand. "I hope that we will have a long business relationship, Mr. Ethum."

"As do I, my lady." Nathaniel took her hand, shaking it firmly. "You'll let me know when all the papers are in?"

"The moment I have them."

Once he left the room, Margaret turned to Vojvo. "What'd you think of him?"

Vojvo came to sit on the chair Mr. Ethan had vacated, shaking his head. "I'm not really sure. He seems harmless enough, at least."

152

"I suppose he wouldn't come so highly recommended if he weren't good at what he does." Margaret shook her head. "Maybe he's just shy?"

Vojvo nodded. "Perhaps. Would you like me to deliver a summons to Mr. Luther myself to ensure he receives it?"

"I think that would be wise." Margaret sighed. It wouldn't be the first summons that went unanswered if he didn't come tomorrow. "And let him know you're happy to escort him if he's having trouble making the walk to the palace."

"That will get him here." Vojvo grinned. "I'll report back to you if I have any trouble, my lady."

"Thank you, Captain." Margaret wrote a quick note and handed it to Vojvo before he left.

Margaret waited impatiently for Charles to arrive, pacing in front of the fireplace. She was nervous about how this meeting would go, especially since the last one had ended poorly. And he hadn't listened to her demands anyway. Maybe she should have had Mr. Ethum along for this meeting. He would know more than she what was needed.

She paused looking at the door when it opened. Her shoulders dropped. It was only Captain Vojvo. "Any sign of him?"

"Not yet." Vojvo shook his head. "Would you like me to retrieve him?"

Sighing, Margaret looked at the clock on the mantle. "If he isn't here in the next ten minutes, I think that would be wise." It would give Charles thirty minutes' leeway. It was more than he deserved, but she wasn't looking for a fight. It was going to be heated enough as it was.

They waited quietly, the only sounds were the crackling of the fire and Margaret's pacing. Margaret continually glanced at the clock while Vojvo waited patiently, hands clasped behind his back.

When the ten minutes were nearly up, Margaret stopped pacing, turning to Vojvo. "Maybe—" A heavy knock sounded on the door before it opened, making her jump. It couldn't have been a servant—none of them would knock so crassly.

Charles walked into the room. "May I come in?"

Margaret tugged on the inside of her lip with her teeth for a moment before extending her arm toward the rest of the room. "Please, sit wherever you'd like."

Charles went to the sofas, plopping down before Margaret could even move. The gall of him. She frowned, taking a quick glance at Vojvo with her brows raised.

Vojvo returned the look, shaking his head.

She sat on the sofa opposite Charles, smoothing out her skirts. "Is there anything I can get for you to drink?" Really, she wanted to ask why he was half an hour late when he was under strict instruction to arrive on time.

"No."

Vojvo cleared his throat, coming to stand behind Margaret.

Margaret balled her fists in her skirts, digging her nails into her palms. Charles was not going to make this day easy for her. She would have to make sure to keep her temper even. It would do no one any good to start a screaming match. "That's probably for the best. It would likely arrive by the time we've finished here anyway." Margaret waved her hand nonchalantly. "You know how long the halls are here."

"Why is it I was summoned here?" Charles leaned back against the couch, crossing his arms.

Margaret took in a slow deep breath and let it out just as slowly. "As you'll know, I returned from my tour not too long ago—"

"And?"

"Hold your tongue!" Vojvo barked.

Margaret jumped at Vojvo's harsh tone. No doubt it was the same one he used on unruly soldiers in his day. "*And* I had a chance to confer with some of my investors. You have become a problem for me, Mr. Luther."

Charles frowned, leaning forward onto his elbows. "What do you mean?"

"Your dislike of me has bled into how you treat me as a business owner." Margaret leaned back, shaking her head. "I will not allow you to keep me from knowing what is going on."

"What are you saying?" Charles furrowed his brow. "Margaret?"

"It's Lady Margaret or Lady Dorcia to you, Mr. Luther," Vojvo growled.

Margaret took in a breath to bolster herself. "It means that I have conferred with my investors, and they have all suggested a name as your replacement, and I have found him an acceptable choice. He's waiting the week to receive all of the books and paperwork pertaining to my business."

Charles stood, the color draining from his face. "You're *firing* me?"

"What did you expect?" She looked up at him, eyebrows raised. "You have all but frozen me out of my business. This should have been done a long time ago."

"Your father trusted me enough to run your business," Charles said, throwing out his hands as he leaned toward her. "What would he think of you firing me?"

White-hot anger flashed through her chest as she stood. How dare he try to use her father against her. "He can't think anything. He's dead, Mr. Luther."

"Because *you* got him killed!" Charles leaned in close to her, eyes narrowed. "He would be ashamed of you."

Margaret stood frozen, her eyes wide. Bile crept up her throat. Besides her and the king, Charles was the only one left who knew her father well. Would he have been ashamed of her? She'd thought it but never voiced the words. Having someone close to Papa say that…it was a stab to her heart.

Vojvo came from behind the couch, pushing Charles back a few steps. "It's time for you to go."

Margret barely heard what Charles said back as Vojvo escorted him to the door. She turned to Charles. "If I don't have every bit of my business's property returned to me in two days, I will have Captain Vojvo accompany Mr. Ethum to your home and help him retrieve it."

"I—"

"And if you try to deny them entry, I will have you arrested for theft." Margaret swallowed hard. "I will not allow you to besmirch me in my father's name without consequence, Mr. Luther."

When Vojvo pushed Charles from the room, Margaret collapsed on the couch, her face in her hands. She heard heavy footsteps rush toward her.

"My lady, are you all right?"

Margaret pulled her hands away from her face, looking up at Vojvo. "How could he say something like that to me?"

"To take away your peace." Vojvo squatted in front of her, taking her hands in his. "If it is any consolation, I think your father would be very proud of you. I know that I am."

It was. She smiled at him through the tears forming. "Thank you, Captain.

Margaret watched as several chests were brought into her chambers. Charles had sent the material by messenger instead of bringing it himself. Each one was labeled by a set number of years. She couldn't believe he had kept all of that stored in his city home.

"Is this all of them?" she asked the messenger.

He nodded, wiping the sweat from his brow with the back of his hand. He quickly counted the trunks, pointing to each one in turn. "Yes, my lady. There are ten trunks here."

"And has Mr. Luther paid you?"

The messenger shook his head.

Margaret sighed. Of course, he would stick her with the bill after all of this. "Let me—"

"I have it," Rowan said, pulling a gold tal from his pocket. He handed it to the messenger before thanking him.

She smiled. "You didn't have to do that, you know."

"I don't mind." Rowan gestured to the trunks. "In a few short months, this will also be my business."

She supposed that was true. Once they were wed, everything of hers became his and vice versa. "Mr. Ethum will be here to retrieve these this afternoon before returning to Dorcia if you'd like to meet him."

"Would you like me to come back this afternoon, then?" Rowan grinned, pulling her toward him. "I know you're to be my wife, but I don't want to give anyone the wrong impression of you."

As though that were possible. They already had the wrong impression of her—the queen had made sure of that, along with several other peers. "You don't have to worry about that. Captain Vojvo should be here shortly."

"Then I suppose I should take advantage of the time." He wriggled his eyebrows mischievously before kissing her.

Margaret laughed against his mouth, wrapping her arms around him and resting her hands on his upper back.

Rowan snaked his hand behind her neck as he deepened the kiss. He pulled away, grinning at her. "Before I forget, I have something for you." He reached into his pocket, pulling out a small velvet pouch with a button buckle on it.

Margaret looked at him expectantly. "What is it?"

He opened the pouch, pulling a ring from it. It was a pearl, surrounded by diamonds to look like a flower. "It was my grandmother's. I sent for it as soon as you agreed you'd be my wife."

"It's beautiful!"

Rowan slipped it onto her finger, kissing her knuckles. "It was gifted to her from the royal collection by Reuben III not long into his reign."

She squeezed his hand, holding a smile on her face. That meant it was possibly from Liam's family jewels from when his line was in power. What a cruel twist of fate, wearing a ring that could have been hers no matter how the tides of history had turned.

"Do you like it?"

"I love it." Margaret pulled him to her, kissing him.

Rowan cupped her face in his hands, walking her back toward the wall.

Margaret jumped, pulling away from Rowan when someone behind them cleared their throat. She put a finger to her lip, wincing. She'd bitten the inside of it when she'd started.

Rowan threw an annoyed look over Margret's shoulder. "I see you've wasted no time in arriving, Captain."

Margaret turned to see Captain Vojvo standing up straighter.

"I take my service to Lady Margaret very seriously, Your Grace." He bowed his head slightly to both of them.

Smiling, she said, "And I always feel very safe while you're around."

Vojvo only gave her a small nod, but she could tell he was pleased.

"Shall we sit?" Margaret turned to Rowan, motioning toward the sofas.

"I think I'll take a turn about the room." Rowan looked around before continuing, "I've never been in here long enough to really appreciate the decoration."

Margaret frowned. "If you'd like."

"I would." He kissed her hand before going to the furthest corner where an ornate painting hung.

Margaret shrugged at Vojvo, grabbing a book from one of the tables and settled on a sofa to read, quickly becoming engrossed.

Margaret turned when she heard Vojvo clear his throat. He and Rowan were standing at her writing desk, a letter in Rowan's hand.

"Is there something I can help you with, Your Grace?" Vojvo asked.

"No." Rowan quickly put the letter down, straightening himself. "I was looking for a piece of parchment to send some correspondence while we waited. I thought some might be under the pile."

"It's in the third drawer down, if you'd like some." Vojvo straightened, clasping his hands behind his back. "Or if you'd like, I can bring it to you while you sit with Her Ladyship."

Margaret furrowed her brow. Vojvo was behaving oddly toward Rowan. She only had one secret she kept from him, and that was proof of Liam's heritage. Any information about that was locked away in her bedroom. She wouldn't leave anything so precious out in the open like that. There was no reason for the captain to be protective of her writing desk.

"I can find it, thank you," Rowan said, pulling out the drawer and taking several pieces of parchment before sitting down with Margaret.

Margaret was relieved when her door opened, and a servant entered. "Yes?"

He bowed to her quickly. "My lady, I've been sent to start collecting these."

"Did Mr. Ethum send you?"

"Yes, my lady," he said. "He's preparing the wagon now."

Margaret turned to Vojvo, smiling. "Would you please collect Mr. Ethum so he can meet His Grace?"

Rowan waited until Vojvo had left the room before turning to Margaret. "He's too protective of you."

"It's his job," Margaret reminded him. "He's been with me through thick and thin."

"I'm to be your husband. It's now my job to protect you." Rowan picked up her hand, cupping it between his. "Something I've already been doing with the king."

"And you're doing a fine job of it." It had been nice not to be visited by the king again. "What are you getting at?"

Rowan frowned. "I don't know if you need both of us looking out for your safety."

"Are you asking me to release the captain from my service?" Panic started to rise in her chest.

"No," he said slowly. "No, I just don't know if he needs to be here, with you, all the time."

"Where else would he go?" Margaret asked.

Rowan opened his mouth to say something, closing it when the door opened. Vojvo walked in with Nathaniel. "Mr. Ethum, my lady."

"We can talk about this later," Rowan said quietly to Margaret before standing and extending his hand to Mr. Ethum.

Margaret frowned as she stood. She didn't like the thought of Rowan pushing Vojvo out, but she also didn't want to make any waves with Rowan before they married.

 **26**

Vojvo furrowed his brow when he opened the note left for him. He had been called to the Duke of Fradure's chambers. What could the duke possibly want with him? He went to his chambers promptly—people like him didn't get to keep peers waiting.

He was admitted as soon as he knocked on the door. Lady Margaret sat in the drawing room while the duke was standing at the window. Vojvo bowed to his mistress and then to her fiancé when he turned toward him.

"Your Grace, Lady Margaret," Vojvo said respectfully. "What is it I can do for you?"

Duke Fradure came to stand behind Lady Margaret, resting a hand over her shoulder. It was very picturesque. The only thing missing was a painter to draw their portrait.

"I have arranged for you to take a position as a palace guardsman at the start of next week until we leave the capital after we are married." The duke gave Lady Margaret's shoulder a gentle squeeze. "You will not be needed in Her Ladyship's service until that time."

Vojvo raised his brows, looking between the two nobles. "With all due respect, Your Grace, that is Lady Margaret's decision to make."

"Lady Margaret is behind my decision, Captain," the duke said, cutting off Margaret's rebuttal. "I will be taking over your role of advisor."

Vojvo's hackles rose, but he tried not to let his irritation show. He didn't like how the duke was speaking for Lady Margaret now that they were engaged. "I would like to hear that from Lady Margaret, Your Grace."

Margaret cleared her throat delicately. She smiled at him reassuringly. "Captain, it's all right. We can try this temporarily and if it does not work, then we can reevaluate the situation and change accordingly," she said despite the stern look Duke Fradure was giving her.

Marius bowed to her, his eyebrows still raised. "As you wish, my lady."

"You may go now," the duke dismissed.

Captain Vojvo reluctantly bowed to the duke before he left. So, the duke was the one who wanted him gone from Lady Margaret's company. It made Vojvo suspicious of the duke's intentions. He would need to keep a careful eye on Lady Margaret's future husband.

Vojvo entered Lady Margaret's chambers quietly as she ate her breakfast. She sat by the windows, sleepily sipping her teacup.

"My lady," he greeted.

She smiled at him. "Come join me." She extended her hand toward the chair across from her. "You know they always load these trays down with too much food for one person."

He wouldn't say no. The food in the servant's hall was considerably subpar compared to the food they served the nobles. Vojvo sat across from her, grabbing a biscuit and slathered it in butter before shoving two slices of bacon between it.

"I'm sorry about His Grace," Lady Margaret said quietly, not looking at him.

Vojvo set down his makeshift sandwich before he could take a bite. He didn't think it would be brought up this soon. "Why did you let him do it?"

"I want to ensure this marriage goes through." She pulled in her bottom lip, rubbing her teeth along it. "I didn't want to upset him. He seemed so insistent."

Likely because Vojvo caught him snooping in her writing desk. There had to be something he was looking for behind Lady Margaret's back, but there was no proof of his suspicion. Not yet, at least.

"I'm concerned if you concede to him on this, you'll concede to him on a lot more."

"No." Lady Margaret shook her head. "I won't be a wife controlled."

Vojvo swallowed. He knew they had a close relationship, but he didn't know how far he could push it. "Are you sure?"

Lady Margaret looked at him, more fire in her eyes than he'd seen in some time. "His Grace arranged it so the king would no longer visit me, even before our marriage. If this doesn't go through, that arrangement is over."

Vojvo sat back. So that was it. He couldn't say he blamed her for his change of service then. For all he had tried to get her to run away to keep the king from her bed, the duke succeeded in making it happen. "I understand, my lady."

"I would rather fling myself from the balcony than go back to the king." Lady Margaret swallowed hard. "With the queen gone, we know I would be forced to wed him."

Vojvo grabbed her hand across the table, squeezing it firmly. "My lady, as long as I'm by your side, I will never let that happen."

"I know, Captain." She squeezed his hand back. "I know."

Vojvo pulled the strings taut on his boot, tying them tightly before tucking the excess in the inside. It had been some time since he had to wear a uniform, never one of a palace guard. He stood, looking himself over in the mirror.

He shook his head. Ridiculous. He looked like a drawn character in a fairy tale with his tight-fitting white pants and heavily decorated short coat. Why didn't the palace guard have similar uniforms to the one he wore as a soldier?

Vojvo made his way to the palace's quartermaster for his assignment. The duke hadn't seen fit to do more than get him assigned the palace guard, so he had to find out where he would be on his own. He reached the small office, knocking sharply on the door.

"Enter."

Vojvo opened the door, standing at attention once he was inside. "Captain Vojvo reporting for assignment, sir."

The quartermaster raised his brow, pulling his glasses down his nose. "Captain?"

"Yes sir."

"And you're here?"

Vojvo splayed his fingers behind his back for a moment, releasing any irritation building. It was already humiliating enough being in this position, and he didn't want to make it worse by getting punished his first day on the job. "I have been told by the Duke of Fradure he arranged a temporary position on the palace guard for me."

"Oh, yes. You." The quartermaster pushed his glass back up his nose before rifling through the papers on his desk until he picked one up. "You'll be assigned to duty in the dungeons."

Vojvo furrowed his brow. "Wouldn't my skill be of better use in the halls of the palace?"

"No." The quartermaster shook his head. "You're too old to serve on the palace floor. We don't want the nobles thinking they won't be protected if you're around."

Vojvo inhaled deeply, pulling his mouth flat. "I see."

"Besides" —the quartermaster shrugged— "no one leaves their cells until they die or their term is up after the unfortunate escape."

"Really?" Vojvo's brows flew toward his hair. "How do they get their exercise?"

"Not our problem." He shook his head. "If they wanted freedom, they shouldn't have committed a crime."

Vojvo tried not to make a disgusted face. "What will my shift assignment be?"

The quartermaster handed him a piece of parchment. "You'll start your first shift now, but these will be the rest of your shifts for the month. You'll find your reporting officer at the entrance to the dungeon. At the start of each month, you'll come here for the hours you'll work."

Vojvo nodded. "Sir." He saluted before leaving.

He opened the parchment as he walked the halls toward the dungeon entrance. It seemed a standard assignment schedule—half the month would be serving in the day and the other half would be overnight with every third day off and a day to adjust to from day to night shift.

True to his word, Vojvo found the reporting officer at the entrance to the dungeon. "Reporting for duty, sir." Vojvo nearly choked on the sir. The officer was young enough to be Vojvo's grandson if his son had lived to sire one.

He stuck his hand out. "Corporal Cane."

Vojvo shook it firmly. "Captain Vojvo."

Cane paled slightly. "Captain?"

Vojvo nodded. "That's right."

"If you don't mind my asking, sir, what's a captain doing under my watch?" He shifted nervously. "You outrank me...considerably."

A suspicious noble who wanted him out of the way for some reason, but Vojvo couldn't say that. "It's only a temporary assignment before my lady marries and we move to her husband's home. There was no point in a leadership position."

Cane's brows knitted together but said nothing more about it. "I have you on the fourth level down, block C."

"Sir." Vojvo nodded to him before heading to his post.

Each cell he passed was empty. What was the point of anyone guarding this area?

He turned the corner to block C, stopping short. The only other officer on the block looked familiar—older, but familiar.

"Marius Vojvo?" the man questioned.

"Theordore Allen?" He laughed. Vojvo hadn't seen him since the war. "You rank bastard, your wife hasn't killed you yet?"

"Nah." Theo shook his head, grinning. "Who else would she get to put up with her?"

Vojvo laughed again. It was fair. His wife wasn't the most pleasant to be around. "Who else is here?"

"Just a few you'd know. Flory, Smure, Townsen." Theo slapped him on the shoulder. "I'm surprised to see you here. I thought you retired."

"I did, until a stubborn lady convinced me to come out of it." Vojvo smiled fondly remembering the day. Honestly, she only gave him the push to come back into service. Retirement had been lonely.

"You were workin' for the Lady Margaret, yeah?"

"I still am," Vojvo confirmed warily. "This is only for a few months."

"Is it true, then? That she is the king's mistress?" Theo asked.

Vojvo supposed he should have expected these types of questions. "Her Ladyship is very happily engaged to Duke Fradure."

"That doesn't mean anything." Theo snorted. "All these nobles sleep with whomever they please."

Vojvo puckered his mouth as he contemplated his reply.

"That's answer enough," Theodore said, the confirmation clear on his face.

"I'll not have you speaking ill of Lady Margaret while in my presence," Vojvo threatened.

"I wouldn't dream of it, Captain."

 **27**

L iam blinked hard before squinting against the light.

Fuck.

Why was it so bright?

He leaned his head back against the wall, his head swimming with the motion. Something was supposed to be happening today...but he couldn't...didn't...

Fuck. Liam closed his eyes tightly, putting the heels of his hands against his eyes. What was it?

"Liam?"

He turned sluggishly toward Gretta, pulling his hands away from his eyes. If he didn't move fast, his head wouldn't need to catch up. "Yeah?"

"Are...are ye goin' to get ready?" She looked deflated, her shoulders slumped forward and her eyes sad.

Running his hands over his face, Liam inhaled deeply. He still couldn't remember what he was supposed to do today. "What is this for again?"

"Olam above, Liam!" Gretta covered her face. "Can ye no be drunk for yer own son's weddin'?"

Liam let out a deep sigh, his teeth clenched. How could he forget Simon's wedding was today? He had promised himself last night that he wouldn't drink too much and embarrass Simon, but here he was still failing his boys. He couldn't stop being a failure.

"I'm sorry, Gretta." Liam stood, but his world spun. He put his hand to the wall to steady himself and paused until his head caught up with his body. "I'll get ready now."

"Dinna bother," Gretta spat. "Ye'll no be able to get past the door wi'out blowin' yer stomach out."

"But—"

Greta slammed the door behind her, and Liam winced as the sound reverberated in his skull. He tried to walk to the door to follow her but had to stop when his stomach seized. He put his hand to his mouth.

She was right. He wouldn't make it to the door.

Liam slumped against the wall, sliding down until he sat on the floor. His hands grabbed at the floor. There had to be a bottle around here somewhere.

He let out a triumphant grunt when his hand hit glass. Swallowing hard when his stomach turned, Liam brought the bottle to his mouth, taking a deep swig.

He let his head drop back against the wall. His head pounded, but it was no less than he deserved. He couldn't do anything right these days. Not for Gretta. Not for his boy. Not for himself.

Liam closed his eyes tightly when the door opened, the sharp sound of the hinges grating against his ears.

"Ye cannae even go ten minutes wi'out drinking', can ye?" Gretta demanded. "Ye're a disgrace to ye're family, Liam."

"Gretta, I—"

"A disgrace," she spat, slamming the door again.

A wave of nausea crashed through him as the rattling of the wall resounded in his head.

Liam could hold it no longer, letting loose the contents of his stomach.

He was a disgrace.

Liam startled awake, groaning at the music coming from downstairs. Everyone must be back for the reception. He put the heels of his palms into his eyes to try to stop the pounding, to no avail.

He swallowed, his throat scratchy from his earlier vomiting. He needed another drink to soothe it.

Liam stumbled down the stairs, pushing his way through the doors to the main dining room. He paused when people slowly started to look at him. He looked around confused. He was disheveled, but it was hardly enough to stop a party.

Jamie came to his side first. "Da, what are ye doin' down here?" he asked quietly.

"I came for a drink." Liam swallowed hard against his rising stomach.

"I dinna think ye should have annithin' more to drink." Jamie patted his shoulder, trying to turn Liam back to the door. "Ma's already right mad at ye."

Liam shook him off, heading toward the table with the drinks and food. He grabbed a plate, piling it high before he grabbed a flagon for himself. He sat himself in the corner, drinking directly from the pitcher.

When he set it down, Gretta was standing in front of him, hands on her hips. "What in Olam's name are ye doin' down here?"

Liam looked around confused. "Eating...?"

"Ye're no eating." Gretta rolled her eyes. "Ye're drinkin', and ye shouldna come down."

"Why not?" Liam raised the flagon again.

Gretta took it from him, setting it heavily on the table. She glared at him. "Ye couldna drag yerself to yer son's weddin, so ye dinna get to come to his reception."

"But—"

"Nae buts, Liam." Gretta pulled the plate out of his reach. "Ye're upsettin' Simon and Joanna."

Liam searched the room for the two of them. They were occasionally looking his way while talking to other guests. Simon, in particular, looked like he'd sat on a thistle each time he looked at Liam.

Liam's head dropped, staring at the table in front of him. He never wanted them to look at him that way, but it was now all too common an occurrence. But he couldn't go back to hearing Eli's screams. The drink kept them from haunting his soul.

"Go on now," Gretta said, waving toward the door. "Before ye make us look more the fool."

Shoulders drooping, Liam went back upstairs. He couldn't do anything now without upsetting someone. He was the disgrace she said.

Liam slumped in his chair at the bar where he sat at The Frothing Wench. He hadn't been out of the house for a few days because of the Jamonat snow, and his fingers itched to hold a pint in his hand. He looked around, his brow furrowed. The bar was buzzing in a way he had never seen.

Was it the drink or the general excitement? He wasn't quite sure.

Liam tapped his palm on the bar twice to indicate he wanted an ale, wilting in relief once the cold glass was in his hand again. He took a long drink, letting out a gasp as he came up for air. "What's going on?" he asked, wiping the foam from his lips.

"Have ye no heard the news?" Elias asked.

"What news?" Liam took another sip, savoring the hoppy taste.

"The Queen of Anatalia has been executed."

Liam nearly spit out his drink. "Queen Lillian? What for?"

Elias grinned, his eyes alight with his eagerness to spread the latest gossip. "Apparently, she was burned at the stake in her wedding dress for charges of adultery, with his mistress lighting the fire. People are saying that King Sorren was trying to get rid of the queen to marry his mistress."

Liam scowled. "Who is his mistress this time?" No doubt it was a social climbing harlot with no scruples.

"The Countess of Dorcia, according to the rumor," Elias said. "Whoever that is."

Liam dropped his ale, standing up quickly to avoid the drink spilling on him. It didn't matter. He'd lost his appetite for it. "Sorry, I'll clean this up."

Elias already had a cloth to clean up the spilled drink. "What's the matter, Liam?"

"Nothing." Liam shook his head. "I've got to go."

"Liam," Elias started, but Liam had already put money down on the counter and walked out of the Frothing Wench.

Why hadn't Margaret told him this was happening to her? Nothing in any of her letters over the years had indicated she was anything but happy. Granted, he hadn't heard from her in some time, nor the Gollacks, who had been passing along her letters.

He ran his hand quickly through his hair. He knew she would never become the king's mistress if she had a choice. She'd nearly let him freeze to death for the sake of propriety when they traveled together before he had convinced her to share their cloaks while they slept.

He had to go to her.

He—

Liam let loose the contents of his stomach on the cold ground, his hand resting against one of the buildings. He spat, lifting a shaking hand to his mouth to wipe it clean.

He had to sober up.

28

Gretta watched as Liam groaned, his face slick with sweat even in the cool of Femonat. It'd been a week since he'd had his last drink. She felt sorry that he was suffering, but at the same time, she wished the suffering on him.

All of Gretta's begging, all of her nurturing and pleading for Liam to come back to their family, and he committed to becoming sober for *her*.

He had said he would always be in love with Margaret, but she'd thought Liam loved her more. Loved their family more.

Gretta wiped his forehead clean of the sweat. She didn't want to be here taking care of him. She almost couldn't look at him, but she had made a commitment to them being a family when he moved in with her. She had wanted to marry him—still did, despite this, if she was being honest.

"I'll check on ye in the mornin'," Gretta said quietly.

She went downstairs to her children. Gretta halfway expected Eli to jump up from the table to hug her around the waist.

She inhaled deeply through her nose, breathing out through her mouth. It had been months, but it felt like hours. Gretta couldn't help herself; she broke into sobs, covering her face. Arms wrapped around her as she bent in two.

"Ma?" Jamie asked.

"I cannae do it," Gretta said thickly into his stomach. "I cannae lose him too."

"Ye'll no lose Da," Jamie said, pulling her tightly to him.

Gretta shook her head. "I can feel it," she sobbed. "After all this time, we're still no enough fer him."

"Let's get ye to bed." Ellie smoothed the hair out of Gretta's face, tucking it behind her ears. "Ye'll feel better in the mornin' when there's light on yer face."

Gretta nodded. Her breath still came hard, but she had stopped crying. For now, at least. It seemed she never stopped crying now—first for Eli and then for Liam.

Ellie took her from Jamie, wrapping an arm around her middle. "I'll take ye up, Ma."

Turning to Ellie, Gretta cupped her cheek. She smiled, but her mouth struggled to keep upturned. "What would I do wi'out ye two?"

Ellie smiled at her sadly. "We'll always be here fer ye."

Gretta stopped at the bottom of the stairs with a start. She did a double take—Liam was sitting at the table with Jamie and Ellie. He was pale, but he was upright, and there was no longer any sweat on his brow. The way he looked the night before, she wasn't sure if he'd ever make it out of bed.

"Liam?"

He looked at her guiltily. Next to him on the floor was a full pack—she could see one of his shirts peaking out. He was leaving, going to her. "Good morning, Gretta."

It was the first time in months she hadn't heard him slurring. Happiness and grief tore through her. She wished he had done it for her. For the children. Even just for himself.

But he did it for Margaret. So he could go save her from whatever trouble she got herself into. If it was even any trouble—she didn't ask Liam for help. She hadn't even sent any letters to Liam in a year.

"Mornin'," Gretta said slowly.

"Thank you for taking care of me last night." Liam took a small bite of plain toast, grimacing when it crunched.

"I'm surprised ye remember annithin', ye were so out of it," Gretta said.

Liam looked ashamed, turning his eyes to the table. "I'm sorry I put you through that."

"Ye should be," Jamie said from his side. "Ye had all of us worrit."

Liam nodded, his eyes still on the table. "I hope when I come back we can all start fresh."

"When ye come back?" Gretta raised her brows.

"Yes," Liam said, finally looking up at her. "I have to go to her. I made a promise to protect her, to help her when she needed me because of all the pain I caused her."

"And what o' the promise ye made to me?" Gretta demanded. "To us?"

Liam slowly stood, pushing his pack out of the way. "I want to keep that promise too…but I have to go to her, Gretta. She needs my help."

"We need ye!" Her eyes welled with tears. It felt like her chest was ripping in two. "We've needed ye this whole time, and ye couldna even keep the bottle from yer hand. And now? Ye dinna even ken if she *is* in trouble!"

"I know she'd never be in the position she's in now if she had any choice in it," Liam said quietly. "If it wasn't for me."

"A lot of us would never be in the position we're in if were no for ye!" Gretta yelled at him. She deflated slightly when she saw his guilty face. She knew Eli wasn't his fault. He had shot him, but he didn't know he was there, and he didn't mean to do it.

"Gretta…I love you," Liam said. "I want to fix what's broken between us when I come back. I want us to be happy again."

"Liam, if ye leave, ye cannae come back." Gretta swallowed hard, her hands gripped tightly at her sides so they wouldn't shake. "Ye'll no be welcome."

He looked around the room. No one would make eye contact with him. "Gretta…"

"It's her or us, Liam." She inhaled sharply, shaking her head. "Ye have to choose."

"Gretta, please," Liam said softly.

"No, Liam. Choose."

Liam picked up his pack, looking around the room once more like he was trying to memorize it. He came to her side, looking down at her with glistening eyes. "I love you, but I cannot break my vow." He kissed her before he walked from their home.

Gretta inhaled shakily, looking to her children. They looked as shocked and heartbroken as she felt.

"We'll be all right, Ma," Jamie said.

She shook her head, unbelieving. Gretta couldn't stop her quick breaths before she burst into tears, crumpling to her knees.

29

iam patted his horse, Ashka, on the neck as they rode across the bridge over the Frasisca River separating Salatia from Anatalia. He inhaled deeply, the fresh smell of the water wafted toward him, lifting his spirits. It had been a long time since he had made any sort of journey, and it had not been easy on him. Especially not after stopping his drinking habits so abruptly.

He was looking forward to seeing the Gollacks again and spending a brief respite in Marbon with them. It would be nice to feel like his old self…what little of Liam he could pretend he still was. He knew he could never go back to that, not really. Not with the burden he carried in his chest.

Liam reached into his pocket, gently stroking the wooden duck he had carved for Eli's pyre. It had brought him comfort on his journey, having more than just his memories with him. He wished he'd been able to take more than just memories of the rest of his family. He certainly needed it. He hated rejecting Gretta's ultimatum, but he'd lost his way. Liam had never broken a vow, and he intended to keep it that way.

The sight of the familiar town brought him out of his spiral. He couldn't wait to sit down with one of Elizabeth's sweets in hand as he basked in their soothing presence. Liam urged Ashka faster as he went through the main thoroughfare. Even Ashka had a spring in his step, surely remembering the surroundings he'd spent quite some time in.

Liam went to the stable he'd helped build for Ashka and Duchess while he lived there, finding it locked. He supposed there was no need to use it if there was no horse in it anyway. He went to the front and tied Ashka to the railing before knocking on the door. He waited patiently for someone to answer.

When no one did, he opened it himself. Dread trickled down his shoulders. Dust had settled into the corners, the air stale. He slowly stepped inside, looking around. Several fat letters sat on the floor, only the top one holding no dust. When he caught sight of Margaret's swooping letters, he carefully picked them up so he wouldn't bring up clouds of dust.

He walked through the rest of the house. It looked like it hadn't been lived in for months. There were plates set on the table but no food. Liam looked around the kitchen before going to explore each room. He stopped short, dropping the letters when he saw Aram.

He was lying on the bed, a withered husk of his former self. The skin clung tightly to Aram's body, his chest barely rising and falling.

"Aram!" Liam called out, when he was finally released from his stupor, going to his side.

Aram barely cracked open his eyes. His lips were dry and cracked to the point of bleeding. "Liam," he croaked out, weakly holding his hand out. "Water."

Liam knelt and pulled out his water skin and put it to Aram's lips, slowly lifting it so he would not be overwhelmed. Liam pulled back when the old man coughed violently. It was probably the first time he had any water in days. "Aram, what happened? Where's Elizabeth?"

Aram's face scrunched up as if he was in incredible pain. "Dead."

Liam's breath was knocked out of him as easily as if he had taken a blow to his stomach. "*What?* For how long?" He could still picture her there in the tiny little house with barely the room to fit the four of them in there together. She couldn't be gone.

"Eight months now." Aram shook his head almost as if in disbelief himself, his face scrunching tightly. Liam was sure Aram would have tears running down his face if had any water left in his body.

Eight months? That had been around the time Eli had... He'd been so wrapped up in his own grief he hadn't even noticed the letters had stopped. That he stopped reaching out—to anyone.

"We have to get you some help, Aram." He tried to sit Aram up.

Aram struggled against him with more strength than his condition should have allowed. "No!" he yelled out hoarsely. "No."

Liam furrowed his brow, taking his hands off Aram. "You need to get help."

"Just let me die." He groaned, closing his eyes. "I don't want to live any more. Not without my Beth."

Liam stood, running his hands over his face. He didn't know what to do. There was no winning here—Aram could maybe be helped if he would take it, but he was clearly opposed to any. He opened and closed his fists in front of him as he thought.

"I'll be back," he said quietly before leaving for the apothecary. He wasn't sure what he would get there yet, but he couldn't let his friend suffer.

Liam left Ashka tied to the rail, walking to the town center. He needed the time to think. About what he could have done differently leading up to this moment. About what he could do now. About what he *couldn't* do.

His shoulders felt lower than they'd even been by the time he reached the apothecary, the bell dinging when he opened the door.

"Can I help you?" one of the healers asked when he walked in.

"I'm looking for something to help...sleep," Liam hesitated. "I have been traveling and the ground does not agree with me."

"Poppy's milk then." The healer grabbed a bottle from under the counter. "You do not want to take more than two drops if you want to stay alert enough in case any rebels happen upon you."

Liam nodded. "I'll take it."

The healer set it on the counter and told him the price that Liam easily paid.

He went back to Aram and sat by his side. He was weakly sleeping and Liam gently laid his hand on Aram's shoulder to wake him. "Aram…"

The old man moaned, barely opening his eyes. "You're back."

Liam nodded. "I have something to help you sleep peacefully for a little while."

"Really?" Aram looked hopeful at the news.

"Yes," Liam said quietly. "Would you like to sleep now?"

Aram nodded eagerly, licking his cracked lips.

Liam grabbed the poppy's milk out of his satchel and squeezed some into the beaker. His hands shook as he held it up to Aram's lips that opened enough to take the liquid. Liam squeezed the entire contents into the older man's mouth before he screwed the top back on the bottle.

"I'll be right here for you when you wake." He squeezed Aram's hand. "And then we can talk about Beth."

A smile came to Aram's face at the mention of Elizabeth. "I'll be dreaming of my sweet Beth."

Liam smiled encouragingly at him as his eyes started to droop. "I love you, Aram," Liam choked out, squeezing his hand tightly.

"I love you too, son," Aram sighed out before he went to sleep.

Liam pulled the duck he carved for Eli's funeral pyre from his pocket, gripping it tightly. He told Aram of his family in Salatia, what happened to Eli. He didn't know how Aram and Elizabeth bore it all these years without their son, when he felt he could hardly breathe after Eli's death.

He put the duck in Aram's age-gnarled hands, cupping them with his own. "Will you look out for my boy if you can find him?" Liam inhaled deeply, resting his forehead against Aram's arm. "I would like someone good to look after him until I can be with him again."

Aram's hand tightened under his, letting out a heavy breath.

He'd take that as a yes.

Liam's eyes burned and his throat tightened as he watched Aram sleep, waiting for the poppy's milk to carry his friend to his beloved Beth. He let go of his hand when he heard his final breath let out. This was it. The last of his family that accepted him was gone.

He was all alone in the world again, except for Margaret.

Liam returned to the apothecary, happy to see it was a different healer than who sold him the poppy's milk. "When is the last time anyone has seen the Gollacks?" Liam demanded when he entered the shop.

"At Elizabeth's funeral when Lady Margaret was here," the healer answered, unfazed by the demanding tone.

"Aram is dead and needs a burial," Liam informed the healer, his voice shaking.

"We'll give him a burial tomorrow." The healer was unfazed by the news. "And we'll collect the body this afternoon."

Liam nodded and left the shop to wait outside the Gollacks' home. While he waited Liam opened the letters from Margaret. He had found more on the table when he was exploring and noted many were dated from more than a year before, some still addressed to Elizabeth. That would explain why he had not heard from Margaret in so long. He read the ones to the Gollacks first, most of them turning to telling Aram how sorry she was about Elizabeth and that once she was done with her pilgrimage, she would send money to him for him to come to the capital to visit her.

He wished she had done that. Liam turned to the letters addressed to him.

They told him all about her adventures with a duke as they traveled her lands and his. He was glad for her that she had finally achieved her goal of having her lands and people under her purview. He knew she would have never stopped until she'd gotten it.

On a letter that matched the harsher quality parchment the Gollacks used was a letter she wrote to inform him of Elizabeth's death. She had tried to tell him at least. Aram must have been too grief-stricken to forward it—any of them, really. Liam couldn't be upset at him. Grief of this magnitude was all-consuming.

Liam blanched when he read her last letter to him.

Dear Liam,

We have finished our pilgrimage and have returned to the capital. It was nice to get away from the capital for that long of a time. I was able to see the rest of His Grace's lands without incident, other than my skin darkening slightly like it had while you and I were traveling.

There is some news that I am slightly anxious to tell you. Not long after we arrived back, His Grace proposed marriage to me, and I have accepted. The wedding planning has already started, and it will be the event of the season according to His Majesty, who is gifting me with the wedding. After the wedding, we'll be going to His Grace's lands for our honeymoon.

I wish that I could see you before the wedding. I'll be gaining a son with this marriage, and if the pilgrimage has been any indication of what my time will be with Samuel, Rowan's son, then I will be incredibly busy.
With all my love,
Margaret

Liam set down the letter. Margaret was getting married. She was getting married to a duke whom he knew nothing about. What if he would be an abusive husband to Margaret? What if this duke was only using her for her wealth? It wasn't as if she were tied to Liam, but he still felt a stab of betrayal that she was getting married. Liam would leave after Aram was buried and make his way to the capital in hopes of reaching her before she did marry the man. Liam felt a need to be with her fiercer than he had ever had before.

Liam left after the healers picked up Aram's body for burial and went to spend the night next to the river as he had before he had met the Gollacks. They had treated him like a son once they had gotten to know him, and he had felt almost as if they could have been his parents whenever he visited. Liam leaned back against the tree he sat under and sighed.

The funeral the next day was short, and Liam was the only one in attendance. The funeral was to the point, the priest blessing the land and the burial, saying a few words about Aram himself. Liam watched, feeling distracted as Aram was covered with dirt. It was sad that there was no one there to mourn the man but him, and even he couldn't fully keep his attention on him. He wished that Margaret could have been there with him to bury their friend. All he could think of was making sure Margaret was not in danger from her surroundings.

Liam left the small town of Marbon, knowing it would more than likely be the last time he would ever be there. Liam turned around on Ashka when he reached the outer limits and took one last look. He would miss this town and the Gollacks, but his life path had changed, and there would be things he would lose that he did not want to. Liam hoped that Margaret would not be one of those things he'd lose.

Once Liam reached a well-used road, he hesitated. He had no idea how long ago Margaret tried to tell him of her upcoming marriage. There wasn't time to waste, but he was still a wanted man. He'd be a wanted man until he or the king died.

Ashka shook his head, letting out a snort.

Inhaling deeply, Liam patted his neck. He didn't have much choice. He would have to travel the main roads to reach the capital faster. He couldn't make his way through the forests and odd tracks here and there to keep himself safe.

Liam couldn't risk having lost the family he built to save Margaret and fail before he even reached her. He urged Ashka onto the road. He'd just have to keep his head down any time someone came along his path.

Even taking a more straightforward route, it took him almost a month to reach Jalmar. Liam stopped to look at the city walls. The city had once held pride for him as he protected the streets there. Now they only held dread for him as he'd have to slink about hiding his face. It would be easier with all the people bustling through the gates—more than he'd ever seen there before.

He shook out his shoulders, letting out a long breath from his nose. For Margaret.

Liam approached the city gates, slipping in with the multitude of people. There were too many of them for the guards to check each face and purpose of their visit. It was a blessing for Liam not having to sneak over the walls in the night like a criminal.

He chuckled to himself. Like the criminal he was *accused* of being.

Once he crossed the threshold, he saw flowers everywhere, the streets abuzz with excitement. Liam brought up his hood to shield his face. He doubted anyone but the soldiers would recognize him, but he did not want to take the chance. All the soldiers were required to memorize his face and actively search the crowd for Liam. He wondered if it was still a rule, even though it had now been twelve years since his escape. Liam stopped a woman who was carrying a bundle of cloth in her arms.

"Madam, what is going on here in the city?"

"Where have you been, man? The king's ward is marrying today, and His Majesty has made sure everyone is celebrating," the woman said, a look of derision at his lack of knowledge.

Liam watched her walk away, his stomach sinking.

Was he too late? Was all this for nothing?

He had to get into the palace—quickly.

30

Margaret let out a slow, shaky breath as she was prepared for her wedding ceremony. The planning for the day had been a whirlwind of emotions for her. She was going to be a duchess and marry into the Platiri family—if her mother could see her now, she might actually be proud of Margaret. She sighed. Thinking of her parents today would do her no favors; it would either make her sad or angry, neither of which she wanted to be on her wedding day. Her father couldn't be there because of Margaret's actions, and her mother because she'd abandoned them.

Margaret sat as her hair and makeup was done. The hair on the sides of her head was braided and pulled slightly loose to make them look thicker before the rest of her hair curled in thick loops. The braids were woven into the curls in crisscrosses, looking as if it were caging the curls down the length of her back. The hair at her temples was spun into thick bands before it was pinned at the back of her head just above where the braids were first crossed to cushion a strand of diamond flowers with pearl centers. Throughout the rest of her hair were pinned single pearls and diamonds making her hair glitter in the light.

"My lady," Sarah breathed. "You look beautiful!"

Margaret smiled at her. "Thank you, Sarah."

"Are you ready for your dress?"

"I think so." Margaret eyed it warily. The dress was a behemoth, barely allowing her to stand under the weight of it.

Margaret was dressed in her gown, nonetheless. Her under corset was cinched in tightly, blessedly giving her the support she would need to stand up straight in the dress. The skirt was hoisted up above her head to lay over the small hoop skirt at her hips. The skirt took three women to lift and rest it on her hips, the train gathering on the floor behind her. She was told that it was half the length of the throne room. Edging the bottom of the gown and the length of the train was a floral pattern in small diamonds and pearls sewn into the center of them to match her ring and bejeweled hair.

"I hope you have someone helping you drag this through the throne room, my lady." One of the women clucked as she looked at the gathered fabric. "You'll be falling asleep at the feast dragging this around by yourself."

Margaret looked down at her dress. She hadn't thought of that, and even if she did, she hadn't anyone to ask. "I don't." Even with her engagement to Rowan, the women of the court still rebuffed her for her scandalous past. Perhaps once she was a duchess and could form a household of her own, she would have some ladies she could call friends once more.

A few of the others shook their heads, grabbing the top of her dress form, putting it on her. The bodice was shaped in a sweetheart neckline and encrusted with the same diamond and pearl flowers. Her sleeves were a gossamer fabric that stopped at her wrist in diamond cuffs, the fabric blousing over them.

Margaret looked at her wrists, swallowing. She had never seen so much wealth in one place, much less draped over her. She hardly felt like she deserved it all.

Around her neck, Margaret was given a diamond necklace from the king that looked like it cost as much as the former queen's royal diadem. It started off as two strands of tear drop diamonds made to look like petals, joining together at her collar bones to form a pure diamond flower on each side. Blooming from those were four strands of diamonds, at the center of each were diamond flowers, a larger flower on each strand of diamonds as it trailed downward. At the center of each diamond flower was a pearl that grew in size according to the size of the flower. Hanging off the bottom flower was a large pearl that rested just above Margaret's cleavage.

Margaret was brought in front of a looking glass. She gasped when she saw herself. "His Grace won't even recognize me!"

"You look like a queen, my lady!" one of the women helping her praised.

Margaret kept her composure at the comment, only smiling and thanking her. No doubt that was Sorren's intended reaction. The outfit she was wearing alone must have cost at least a year's income. "Where is His Majesty?" Sorren had told her he would be giving her away to Rowan. Rather fitting, she thought.

"His Majesty is waiting for you outside in the drawing room," Sarah told her. "Would you like for me to get him?"

"Is it almost time?" Margaret's stomach erupted in butterflies. Her parents snuck back into her mind. If they could see her now, her mother would be enamored with all the wealth that she was wearing, and her father would have been the one to give her away.

"Almost, my lady." Sarah gave her a bright smile.

"Bring him in then," Margaret said before she lost the confidence that her dress was giving her.

Sarah returned with the king behind her. "My lady, His Majesty has arrived."

Margaret bowed her head to the king "I would curtsy, but I fear I would not be able to rise afterward."

Sorren stopped short as he took her in, scanning her several times. "My dear, you look stunning."

Margaret smiled coyly. "I should. All of this looks as though it cost an entire years' worth of taxes."

Sorren finally went to her, raising her hands to his lips. "It suits you, my dear." "Shall we go?"

"Your veil, my lady!" one of the women called.

She placed the veil on Margaret's head and secured it in place. It came past Margaret's fingertips, decorated with embroidered flowers in the same shape as the jeweled ones on her gown, small pearls in the center.

"Now you may go," the woman said, a satisfied look on her face.

Sorren linked Margaret's arm through his, taking her slowly through the halls to the throne room. He whispered in her ear while her train and veil were properly adjusted to flow behind her, "You are lucky my dear cousin has made me agree to stop bedding you." Sorren inhaled deeply, smelling her hair as he put his hands on her one last time.

Margaret tried to resist curling her lip in revulsion. Instead, she only gave him a tight smile.

As a horde of trumpeters announced her presence, the doors to the throne room opened. As Sorren led her forward, a choir of castrati erupted in a song that Margaret had never heard before, bringing chills down her spine and raising goose bumps on her arms.

"Composed just for you," Sorren whispered to her.

The nobles gathered were enough to fill the room on either side. They were in their finest, dripping in jewels the same as she. It must have been the whole court in attendance. Margaret tried not to look surprised when they walked further into the room. She supposed this would have been akin to a royal wedding—just not *the* royals. Margaret wouldn't have missed being seen there either if she were in their shoes.

They bowed or curtsied as she and Sorren passed. Margaret knew it was in deference to the king, but it was nice to pretend it was actually for her. Today, there were no whispers behind hands and sly looks in her direction. Today, it was only quiet admiration.

The throne room had been decorated in honor of her wedding, the center aisle marked by a pure white runner. Set in equal spaces were tall bouquets of white roses that had depleted the garden of its supply, as well as some being imported from several other provinces to fill the large bouquets placed on each side of the aisle. The king had spared absolutely no expense as he had promised. Walking in front of them was the king's youngest cousin, Abriella, in a subdued version of Margaret's dress, throwing rose petals for her to walk on.

Margaret inhaled deeply, her stomach tightening in her excitement. Rowan had not yet turned around, and she was anxious to see his reaction to her appearance. They were halfway down the aisle before her future husband turned to look at her, his face going slack.

When Margaret and the king came to a stop next to Rowan, she held her hand out to him.

Rowan took her hand, inhaling deeply, smiling at her. He brought it to his lips and kissed her fingers.

The prelate waited for the castrati to end their song and the courtiers who had gathered to quiet. "We have come here today to witness the marriage of His Grace, Duke of Fradure, and Lady Dorcia, Countess of Dorcia. Are there any objectors?"

Margaret snuck an apprehensive look at Sorren to see if he would say anything.

Sorren was stony faced as the silence rang out loudly.

"Since there are no objectors, we may begin. Your Grace, will you have this woman to be yours, blessed by Theotes, to keep only unto her so long as you both shall live?"

Rowan smiled at Margaret, his face almost glowing. "I will."

"And Your Ladyship, will you have this man to be yours, blessed by Theotes, to keep only unto him so long as you both shall live?"

Margaret smiled jovially. She was finally escaping the king for good. "I will."

"Your Grace, please repeat after me," the prelate said, telling him the words he should say.

"I, Rowan Matthew George Fradure, fourth Duke of Fradure, take you Margaret to be my wedded wife, and pledge my vow before Theotes that from this day forward, I will bring only honor to you and to our families."

Margaret repeated the words in turn, substituting the appropriate words, her excitement growing.

"My lord." The prelate motioned to Samuel to bring the rings on the velvet pillow that he was holding. Rowan and Margaret placed the rings on each other's hand in turn.

Margaret gave Samuel a reassuring smile when he stepped back. He was nervous to be in front of the entire court, his eyes wide as he looked at everyone.

The prelate then had them kneel at the altar and prayed over them, blessing their marriage. Margaret was helped to stand by both the prelate and Rowan. "You may kiss your bride, Your Grace."

Rowan gave Margaret a grin, grabbing her face and kissing her fiercely to the delicate applause that erupted from the nobles.

"Their Graces, the Duke and Duchess of Fradure," the prelate announced as they turned to the crowd.

They exited the throne room, several ladies moving Margaret's massive train and veil out of the way. "Well, my beloved," Rowan started. "What happens now?"

"Now," Margaret said, resting her hands on his chest as she looked up at him, "I must change for the feast, and you must greet our guests."

Sarah came to Margaret with a smile but worry tugging on her eyes. "Your Grace, you must come and change quickly so that you can rejoin your husband."

'Your Grace' sent a thrill through her, only slightly dampened by Sarah's distressed look. Margaret tried not to let her own worry show. "I am being summoned, my love." She gave him a kiss before she left with Sarah.

"My lady, please hurry before the other ladies join us." Sarah was almost running back to Margaret's chambers.

"What has gotten into you, Sarah?" Margaret asked, trying to hurry behind her, but her dress made it difficult.

"There is someone in your chambers that you have to see...alone."

Margaret's face paled. "It's not His Majesty, is it?" There was a panic in her voice.

"No," Sarah reassured. She handed Margaret the letter that must have arrived after she left for the ceremony. "Please, my lady, hurry!"

Margaret read the note and went into her chambers as quickly as the weight of her dress allowed. "Out!" She ordered at the other women that had started to gather in the parlor.

The women paled and left the room quickly.

Sarah whispered to Margaret. "He's in your bedchambers."

Margaret rushed into her private bedroom. Standing at her windows was a familiar figure that she had not seen in almost four years. Her breath caught in her throat when he turned around to look at her.

"Liam..."

31

iam's breath left him when he saw Margaret in her wedding gown. "Margaret," he breathed, closing the distance between them. He reached his hands up to cup her face, but Margaret shied away from him, bringing a stabbing pain to his stomach. "You look beautiful, Maggie." Liam let his hands fall awkwardly to his sides.

He didn't know what he was thinking would happen—she was committed to someone and hadn't seen him in years. He probably would have done the same had she tried that in front of Gretta.

"Thank you." Margaret smiled shyly. "What are you doing here?"

Liam swallowed. It seemed foolish now seeing that she was well, at least physically. "I heard about the queen's death, and you being the king's mistress. I wanted to see that you were all right," Liam admitted. "I couldn't break my vow to you."

Her face softened, holding a hand out to him. "You put yourself in danger for me?"

He took it, squeezing her hand tightly. It grounded him, assuring him he had done right in coming to her. He just wished he'd made it sooner so he could…he didn't know. He wouldn't have talked her out of her marriage if she truly loved the man she married. "Yes," Liam told her. "I had to make sure that you were all right."

"Why wouldn't I be all right?" Margaret took a step back, motioning to her dress with her free hand. "I just married."

"I can see that." Liam looked her over slowly. He'd never seen a more jewel-encrusted gown. It suited her and didn't at the same time. He liked her better as the simple woman in Marbon he'd grown to love, but he couldn't deny she looked like she belonged in the finery. "It must have been a sight to behold."

Margaret smiled at him. "It was," she said. "His Majesty spared no expense in throwing this wedding."

Anger ignited in Liam's chest at the mention of the king. "Is it true?" He prayed to Theotes it was only malicious gossip, but he had to be sure. "That you were his mistress?"

Margaret's face fell as she dropped his hand, severing their connection. "Yes," she said quietly.

Liam closed his fist tightly, feeling the loss keenly. "Of your own volition?"

"No," Margaret said even quieter than before.

His chest panged. "Theotes, Margaret. Why did he do this to you?" Liam demanded.

Margaret looked away from him, her lips pulled in between her teeth.

"Maggie."

"Yes?" she asked innocently.

"Tell me." Liam crossed his arms, narrowing his eyes at her. It wasn't like her to keep secrets.

Margaret inhaled deeply. Liam could tell that there was an internal battle going on in her head. She could tell him anything, and he would be there for her.

"Now," he urged.

"Because I helped you, because I gave you food and shelter." Margaret wouldn't look at him. "And the choices the king gave me were to either become his mistress or live a very, very short life."

Liam staggered back, her words hitting him like physical blows. All of this because of him. "You were raped by the king on my account?"

Margaret looked at him guiltily, her lips pursing slightly, remaining silent.

"Is this still going on?" Liam asked.

"No." Margaret relaxed, her shoulders drooping slightly. "My husband negotiated as part of our marriage contract that His Majesty would no longer come to my bed, starting at our engagement several months ago."

Liam could thank her husband for that, at least. He sat on her bed, running his hands over his face. He could barely contain his sorrow. There he went, fucking everything up again. "Theotes, Maggie," he groaned. "I've ruined your life. Again." He was the disgrace Gretta had said he was.

"You didn't ruin my life, Liam."

"Maggie—"

Sarah entered the room. "Your Grace," she said anxiously, casting a pitying look to Liam, "you need to change now, and he needs to leave."

Margaret looked at Liam, worry tugging at her eyes. "I have to go to my feast," she said hurriedly. "Can you sneak out?"

Liam nodded. "I can," he said. "I'm staying in The Whistling Squire under Aram's name." It was a risk staying at so popular an inn, but he hoped he could blend in with the large crowd.

"I'll send you a letter when it's safe for me to come," Margaret told him, touching his arm. "You shouldn't come to the palace again. It's too risky."

Liam picked her hand up and kissed it. He gave her one last look before cloaking himself. He snuck out of the palace the same way that he had snuck in. Liam felt sick to his stomach seeing Margaret in her wedding gown. It had stabbed him in the gut knowing that she was tied to another and that he had lost whatever chance that he had.

Liam went to his rented room, lying on the bed with a heaving sigh. He covered his face with his hands with a groan. He was a fool for coming. Her husband would keep her safe now, and in leaving, Liam had lost Gretta and the boys.

32

Sarah quickly changed Margaret for her wedding feast. Her bodice remained the same, but she was changed into a skirt that was similar to the one she had for the wedding, holding only a small train instead. She inhaled deeply, smoothing her skirts.

Her stomach was uneasy after seeing Liam. It had been good to see him, but it flooded her with feelings she shouldn't have on her wedding day. At least, not for a man who wasn't her husband.

She couldn't believe he had snuck all the way into the palace and risked everything to check on her welfare. He looked weary, the world weighing heavily on him. She wanted to ask, but she couldn't risk him staying longer and her being caught with him again. Margaret didn't know what she would have done had he come before her wedding ceremony.

"Your Grace," Sarah said quietly. "It's time to go."

Margaret nodded, torn from her thoughts. 'Your Grace' was far less thrilling after seeing Liam again. She went to the ballroom where the feast would be held instead of the dining hall as many of the other great feasts were. Rowan waited for her outside the doors. A grin erupted on his face when he saw her. Margaret smiled at him, all thoughts of Liam fleeing from her mind.

"You look even more stunning if that's possible, beloved." Rowan pulled her into his arms, giving her a gentle kiss.

Margaret smiled brightly at him, cupping his cheek in her hand. "Thank you," she said tenderly. "Shall we go start our feast?"

They entered the ballroom together to the applause of the nobility. Margaret noticed more of the faces now that she wasn't focused solely on getting to Rowan. Some of the nobles looked happy for them, while some whispered to each other as they passed. Most looked indifferent to them.

They smiled as they went to the head table. In a great display of humility, Sorren had allowed them to sit at the head table while he sat with other nobility. She knew it was all for show—he could never be that humble without some benefit to him.

Margaret looked around the room in awe. It was unlike any other feast she had ever seen. Each table had a dark tablecloth accented with a red silk square—the Platiri colors. There were bouquets of flowers at the center of each table of Margaret's favorite blooms. There were red, white, and pink roses mixed with dragon flowers, and white lilies along with white-and-green hydrangea.

In front of each seat was a small vase of white and green hydrangea and pink and red dragon flowers. Margaret thought it was quite remarkable that there had been that many flowers in bloom to put in all the bouquets.

It was a feast fit more for a queen than for herself. No doubt the king was showing her what he could have given her had she agreed to be his wife. There were fifty courses served, each more decadent than the last. The king had ordered almost triple the amount of wine as there were courses in the dinner to make sure there was always drink to be had.

Margaret herself watched the king drink double what she and Rowan had combined. With each drink, she worried more that he would say or do something to ruin the day.

Rowan decided to start the dancing, with Margaret, not wanting to sit idly any longer.

The music was lively as he twirled her around the floor. A thrum of excitement came from their gathered peers as several joined them. She hadn't seen the court this happy since before the queen's execution.

Margaret smiled brightly at her husband and easily danced with him. "This is amazing," she breathed.

"It is no less than what you deserve, my dear," Rowan told her.

Margaret looked at the other nobles as even more joined their dance, thinking of all the rumors they had started at her expense after news of her affair with the king surfaced. She wondered briefly how they would gossip had they known that she had just had a known criminal in her bedchambers. "How long until we are able to travel to Fradure?"

"We must stay here at least a week before we'll make our way home with Samuel," Rowan informed her.

"Is there any way that we can leave sooner than that?" Margaret asked desperately. "I wish to be as far away from the capital as possible."

Worry clouded Rowan's face as he looked in the direction of the king. "Why, has something happened?"

"Something has," Margaret said. "Not of the nature that you're thinking," she added quickly at the look that Rowan gave her.

"What has happened?" Rowan demanded.

"Not here." Margaret looked around at all the people who could be listening. "After the feast is over."

Rowan did not look happy that he could not know now, starting off their marriage with another secret. He danced the night away before the king stood and all were quieted. "And now the favorite part of all weddings!"

Margaret was confused, looking at Rowan.

"Time for the bedding ceremony!" the king bellowed. "My lords and ladies, take hold of the bride and groom!"

The bedding ceremony? Margaret looked around frantically as the court started to descend on them. Did that mean people were going to watch her and Rowan? That Sorren...that he would be able to see her one last time?

Margaret was ripped away from Rowan by the gentlemen of the court and the women swarmed over Rowan. Margaret looked at Rowan desperately, panic building as more hands were on her.

Rowan did not look worried at the women dragging him from the room.

Margaret looked at Sorren with wide eyes when he joined the group of men dragging her the opposite way the women took Rowan. "Are you ready?" His eyes glinted.

"For what?" Margaret backed away, letting out a yelp when she ran into someone.

Her clothes were grabbed at, and fear struck her at the thought that she would be stripped by the men as she was pushed out of the ballroom.

"Shall we have a look?" one of the men asked once they were in the corridor, grabbing her skirt.

The king smacked his hand. "Absolutely not."

Margaret looked at him desperately, grabbing onto Sorren's arm. As much as she hated it, he was a lifeline to her now. He would be too jealous to let anyone try another time.

Sorren grabbed her hand in one of his, clasping her elbow tightly with the other as he walked her forward. A man on the other side did the same as the others started to grab at her again. There would be no escaping, not that she could with how heavy her dress was. She would make it mere feet before being caught.

Margaret was deposited in the massive bedchamber that her marriage would be consummated in. Her clothes were loosened during the journey, but none had actually been taken off, thankfully.

Sorren kissed her knuckles before letting go of her. "I'll be thinking of you."

She was given over to the women who were to prepare her for bed after Sorren had pinched and prodded to get her in the appropriate place.

Once the men left, she let out a sigh of relief. She was finally free of any prying eyes or tempted hands.

"Let's get you proper ready, Your Grace," one of the ladies said as she pulled pins out of her dress, handing them to another woman. "I'm sure you're ready to be in something simple."

"Oh, I am." Margaret laughed. "I'm amazed I'm still standing."

The women already in the chamber undressed Margaret and put her in a floor length shift. She was almost giddy with how light she felt without her dress on. Gorgeous as it was, it weighed nearly the same as a small child.

Her hair was taken down, releasing the heavy weight of it. Margaret marveled at the growing pile of jewels that came out of her hair. The tresses were then plaited into a single long braid that flowed down the length of her back, rather than the jumbled one she already had.

One of the women pulled down the covers on one side of the bed. "You'll want to be in bed before His Grace arrives, Your Grace."

Margaret got into the bed, furrowing her brow. "Why?"

The woman only raised her brows, a small smirk on her face. She motioned for the other women to leave the chambers. "Goodnight, Your Grace."

Margaret pulled the covers up to her neck when she saw a group of men following Rowan into the room. She looked at Rowan in confusion. No one had explained how the bedding ceremony would work, not even Rowan in his experience had told her what to expect. He shrugged at her and was undressed by the men that had joined him.

Rowan was soon in the bed with Margaret and the men retreated from the room. He grinned at her. "I have requested that there be no audience."

Margaret was relieved. "Thank Theotes," she breathed out. "I don't know if I could have done anything with them in the room, especially not the king."

Rowan chuckled. "It's not pleasant."

Margaret smiled, a blush growing on her cheeks. "Well…" she started awkwardly. "Shall we?"

Rowan kissed her gently. "We shall."

Margaret lay next to her husband contentedly. The evening had been much more pleasant than the ones that she had spent with the king. She smiled as she turned on her side, wrapping her arm around Rowan's waist.

He wrapped his arm around her, holding her tightly against him. "What is it that you wanted to speak with me about, my love?" Rowan asked.

"Hmm?" Margaret snuggled closer to him sleepily.

"What you brought up at the feast," her husband reminded.

"Right." Margaret yawned, stretching against him, laying her head on his chest. "I had a guest before I went to the feast."

"Don't be cryptic," Rowan chided.

"Liam was in my room when I came back to change for the feast." She looked up at Rowan. "He heard the rumors of my affair and wanted to ensure that I was safe."

"He's here in the capital?" Rowan sat up, looking at her sharply. "What the hell is he doing here?"

Margaret was confused by his anger. "Yes," she said quietly. "He came because he was concerned about me."

"He put you in danger!" Rowan growled. "Had anyone else seen him, the king wouldn't have been able to just privately punish you, he would have had to execute you."

"But no one saw us," Margaret reminded him. "And he was being protective."

"I'm here to protect you now," Rowan said. "*I* am your protector, not him."

"Rowan, there's no need to be upset." Margaret sat up, grabbed his hand and held it in both of hers. She gently kissed his knuckles as she looked up at him. "He was just concerned."

"I understand, Margaret," he said, still irritated, "but he put you in more danger than he was protecting you from."

Margaret's shoulders drooped as she let go of his hand. "I'm sorry."

Rowan sighed, cupping her face in his hands. "You're too tenderhearted to see that he could have put everyone in danger because he was concerned about you."

Margaret only frowned.

"Dearest," Rowan said, trying to appease her. "We can talk about what to do in the morning."

"I told him I would see him when it was safe for me to come," Margaret told him stubbornly—almost defiantly.

"Margaret," Rowan groaned. "You can't see him."

"Why not?" Margaret demanded.

"Because, my dear, he'll end up imperiling you more than you've ever been before," Rowan told her gently. "I don't feel comfortable with you seeing him."

Margaret frowned. "Rowan…"

"I don't want you to see him," Rowan said firmly.

Margaret pursed her lips, lying down with some distance between them. "I can't not see him."

"Do you have a relationship with him?" His voice was hesitant, unsure.

"No!" Margaret burst out. "There isn't anything between us other than friendship."

Rowan furrowed his brows. "Are you sure?"

"Yes." Margaret sighed exasperatedly. "He was my protector and friend while we traveled, and now he's just my friend."

"He seems to think he's still your protector," Rowan mumbled.

Margaret's frown deepened. "Are you jealous of Liam?"

"No," he said defensively.

"He asked several times for me to go with him," Margaret told him, "but I've always refused. And now I've married you, and I am devoted wholly to you."

Rowan's face softened at her words, "I know you are, my love."

Margaret kissed him, melting against his side.

33

Though he liked watching her sleep peacefully, Rowan disentangled himself from his new wife. She was sleeping soundly in his arms and did not awaken when he moved away from her. He was unnerved by the news she had shared.

Rowan dressed before pouring himself a drink. He sat with a sigh in a chair near the fireplace. Part of the deal to even have Margaret as a wife was that he would tell his cousin when there was news of the traitor she'd helped. He had resigned himself to give the king only snippets and non-incriminating messages that the two sent to each other.

But now…the information she had just given him made him want to reveal everything he had to the king. Rowan didn't want any competition for Margaret's affections. He did not trust a man who was so reckless to continue contact with his wife. With his family. Liam's coming to see her had not only put Margaret in danger, but Samuel and himself as well.

Rowan knocked back his drink and rose before he changed his mind. He went to the king's chambers, knocking lightly on the door.

A servant sleepily opened the door. "Your Grace, how can I help you?"

"I must see His Majesty," Rowan told him.

"His Majesty is sleeping right now."

"Then wake him up," Rowan snapped.

"Yes, Your Grace." The servant retreated into the room, coming back moments later. "Your Grace, His Majesty is ready to see you."

Rowan barged in past the servant and went to the king in his chambers.

"What do you want, Rowan?" Sorren asked as he sat up in his plush bed. "Aren't you supposed to be enjoying your new wife?"

"Margaret's asleep," Rowan flippantly responded. "She told me something very interesting before she went to sleep."

"Oh?" The king was more awake now, his interest piqued.

"Liam Fulton is in the capital," Rowan said. "He was in the palace today to see Margaret."

The king's anger was slowly growing on his face. "The traitor was here?" Sorren demanded quietly. "Here in my palace, conversing with my—*your* Margaret?"

Rowan did not miss the slip. It was obvious that Sorren still was not happy about losing Margaret to him. "And it turns out that he had asked her to travel with him instead of returning here to Jalmar."

Sorren's face was red with anger. "Is there something between them?"

"She speaks of him fondly, but revealed no details other than that," Rowan said, a wave of jealousy flaring within him. "He obviously came here because he cares for her. He heard rumors of her being raped by you, and that is why he came. To ensure her safety."

Sorren curled his lip. "She was not being raped. She willingly accepted my affections."

"Who can say no to a king?" Rowan demanded in a fit of anger, the outburst taking the king by surprise.

"She had a choice: keep her innocence and have it publicly known that she is a traitor to Anatalia or lose her innocence and no one knows that she betrayed her country for its greatest traitor," Sorren told him plainly. "And she willingly made the choice to become my mistress."

Rowan ran a hand through his hair. It didn't matter that Sorren had given her a choice, it was plainly the answer that Sorren had wanted, and Margaret would have had no other choice but to become his mistress.

"Your Majesty," he said quietly. "It does not matter the reasons for her predicament. It matters that she is his weakness, and he is hers."

"Find out from her where the traitor is, and he'll no longer be something to take away Margaret's affection for you," the king said finally after a long period of silence.

It irked him almost as much as Sorren that she could have any sort of feelings other than pity for the traitor that tried to ensure that Anatalia lost the war.

"I'll have a location by tomorrow night," Rowan told him before leaving to rejoin his new wife.

Margaret stirred when he got into the bed again. "Where were you?" she asked sleepily.

Rowan kissed her lightly. "Nowhere of import, my darling."

Margaret moved to snuggle in his arms. "Come, sleep. We have a long day tomorrow."

When Rowan awoke in the morning, Margaret had already been dressed for the day. Her face glowed when she looked at him. He went to her, wrapping his arm around her tightly. "You look more radiant than the sun, wife."

Margaret turned in his arms and smiled up at him. "And you, husband, need to dress quickly. We have much to do today."

"And what is it that we must do?"

"There are gifts to be opened and appearances to make, and I will see Liam today," Margaret told him.

"You are not to see the traitor," Rowan commanded. "You are too recognizable and will only put yourself in danger."

Margaret looked shocked at his firm tone. "What happened to your support of me helping him? What about me doing only what I thought was right?" Margaret demanded.

"Now, I am responsible for your safety, and I do not wish to be a widower twice over," Rowan pleaded with her. "Surely, you must understand, my love. I cannot bear to lose you too."

Margaret sighed. "Rowan, I gave him my word."

He rolled his lips between his teeth. He didn't want her to go, but he did tell the king he would have a location for him today. "Let me go with you."

"Go with me?" She blinked rapidly, as though trying to keep up with his rapid change of conviction.

"If I go with you, I can keep you safe." And Rowan could tell the king she only saw Liam because Rowan needed to find where he was. It was the only thing he could think of to save her from herself. "I can make sure no one suspects you of anything."

"I…" She hesitated before starting again, "I don't know if he would see me with you there."

"I can wait outside of the room." Whatever it took to get his location and keep Margaret safe.

"All right." She nodded slowly. "We'll go this afternoon."

The couple continued preparing for the day with the silence that fell between them.

"Will Samuel be joining us for breakfast?" Margaret asked finally.

"If you wish him to." Rowan tucked a lock of hair behind her ear.

"I think he'll feel left out," she said. "This is an adjustment for him too."

"My wife," Rowan said, tenderly touching her cheek, "the ever-loving woman."

Margaret smiled. "Let's go to our son."

Rowan grinned boyishly when she claimed his son for her own. "He will be pleased to see you this morning."

Rowan led her to their son's room, entering without knocking. "Sam?"

Samuel poked his head out of his room. "Father!" He called out excitedly, running to him.

Margaret smiled at him and Samuel reacted almost shyly to her attentions.

"Sam, what's wrong?" Rowan asked.

Samuel looked between the two before finally speaking. "May I call you mother?"

Margaret knelt to his level. "I quite prefer it."

Samuel threw himself at her, tightly hugging her around her neck. "Mother!"

Rowan sighed happily, the guilt of betraying her to the king sliding away at the happiness he saw on Samuel's face.

Rowan and Margaret walked hand in hand through the city in simple clothes to not draw attention to themselves. He didn't know why he was anxious—he was doing this for the king. He wouldn't get in trouble, and Margaret wouldn't by proxy since she was only a pawn in this game.

She smiled up at him when he squeezed her hand. "We're almost there."

He didn't know how she was acquainted with such a tavern, and he wasn't going to ask. It seemed a seedy place to him, unworthy for a duchess to step foot into. But he supposed it was fitting for a criminal to hide in.

"There." Margaret pulled on his hand, eagerly walking ahead of him inside.

His stomach growled at the smell of the food. It smelled like it could redeem the quality of the establishment, but he still didn't like being here. Or Margaret being here.

She dragged him to the bar. "We're looking for Aram Gollack," she said loud enough to be heard over the crowd.

"Room eight," the man said. "On the third floor."

Margaret called a thank you over her shoulder as she dragged Rowan behind her. He wasn't going to let go of her hand and let something happen to her here.

When they reached the third floor, they walked to the end of the hall to room eight. The number was partially worn away, a shadow of itself. Much like this tavern, Rowan assumed.

"Rowan…" Margaret turned to him, rubbing her lips together as her brow knitted. "Would you mind waiting at the end of the hall? I promise it will be a very short talk."

Anger flashed through his chest. The end of the hall? "All right…" It didn't sit well with him, but he did as she asked. He had all the information he needed to give to the king, even if he didn't hear what they were saying.

And he would be sure to give it.

 **34**

"**Y**our Majesty?"

"What is it, Christian?" Sorren slammed down his knife next to his plate. "I've asked not to be disturbed during my dinners."

Christian took a step back, eyeing him hesitantly. "I'm sorry, Your Majesty...but His Grace, the Duke of Fradure is here to see you."

Sorren stood, excitement bubbling in his stomach. Rowan had promised the location of Liam Fulton today. He hoped this meant Rowan would deliver Liam straight into his hands. "Send him in."

Christian retreated before returning with Rowan, bowing out of the room shortly after.

"Have you found out the location of the traitor?" Sorren tried not to let his eagerness show.

Rowan poured himself a drink without invitation, throwing it back quickly. "He's staying in The Whistling Squire, room eight."

A slow smile formed on Sorren's stubbled face. Things were coming together much more quickly than he'd expected. "How did you find out the room number?" Sorren held up his hands. "No, wait. I don't want to know. I'll just be content the traitor will be in my dungeon by the day's end."

Pouring himself another drink, Rowan shook his head. "I don't care what happens to him as long as he's gone and away from Margaret."

Sorren could say the same for Rowan. If all went well, he could have Margaret as his wife by the end of the year. He would send his soldiers to collect Liam and put him in a cell until a proper executioner could be brought it. He wanted to make the execution as painful as possible.

It didn't matter that Liam was not an actual traitor; he was a threat to Sorren's throne. The whole country saw him as a traitor, and Sorren would not give Liam a chance to correct them. No one would know that Lord General Crompton had truly been the one to try to steal Sorren's throne. This would give him an opportunity to show all Aratia what happened to the people who crossed him.

Sorren grinned at the thought. He knew exactly the way the traitor would be executed. Liam would be executed by becoming a Blood Eagle—it was a particularly gruesome way to go. Sorren had heard of it as punishment when his grandfather ruled Anatalia. It had been very common among the traitors when the

Platiri line had taken the throne in order to show their supplicants they were indeed the ruling family.

"You've done well," Sorren told Rowan in a dismissive tone. "You may go."

"What will happen now?" Rowan asked by the door to the king's chambers.

"That is none of your concern." Sorren was annoyed that Rowan was still in the room. He wanted to start executing his plan.

Sorren waited until his cousin left before he let out a grunt of excitement. He would be the most powerful man in the country once more. Rowan didn't realize that with the combined wealth of his wife and land, he could easily take the capital for his own. That alone was a reason to have Rowan eradicated from Margaret's life and take her to wife—she'd inherit her husband's lands and money until the duke's son was old enough to take control. But by then, it wouldn't matter. Sorren would already have what he wanted.

He pulled the cord in the corner of the room to summon Christian. When he entered, Sorren said, "Get me the captain of the city guard."

35

L iam lay on his hard straw mat at The Whistling Squire, his face covered with his hands. He couldn't stop reliving the conversation he'd had with Margaret earlier. He didn't know what he'd hoped for when she sent word she'd see him today, but it wasn't that.

"You need to leave. Go home, or wherever it is you want to go, but you cannot stay here," she said. *"It isn't safe for you to stay.*

"I promised you—"

"I release you from your vow, Liam." Her face scrunched painfully before she turned from him. *"My husband will keep me safe now. You don't have to worry about me anymore."*

He put a hand to his chest, feeling like he'd taken a blow. *"I'll leave in the morning, Margaret."* Liam let out a heavy breath. *"But I will not let you release my bond. It's there forever."*

Margaret grabbed his hands, squeezing them tightly. "Go, Liam. Please. For your safety— and for mine." She kissed his cheek before leaving.

He knew she was right. It was reckless for him to be there. If he was found, he would be executed. Even worse, if the king found out who he was there for, they would execute Margaret right along with him. She would not get a second chance.

The thought kept him wide awake. Liam couldn't be caught unawares. He would wait until it was full dark before he left the city.

Liam nearly jumped out of his skin when his door crashed open, and soldiers poured through the splintered door frame.

"Grab the traitor!" one of the soldiers yelled as they flooded the room, blocking off any escape route through the door they had just entered.

"No!" Liam yelled as he clambered out of the bed toward the window. He had just gotten it open when he was grabbed from behind. Liam yelled in frustration as his fingers slipped off the windowsill.

"You are under arrest by order of His Majesty," the soldier that grabbed Liam yelled as he struggled to hold on to Liam by the back of his shirt.

Liam whirled on the soldier and punched him in the jaw. When the soldier stumbled back, Liam tried to get out the window again. Several hands grabbed anywhere they could reach on him, dragging him from the window. Panic squeezed his throat as he fell to the floor.

He couldn't be caught—not again. There wouldn't be any escape from the dungeons for him this time. Pushing himself from the floor, Liam held up his fists.

He didn't want to kill anyone like he had in his first escape, but he would if he had to.

Several soldiers advanced at once. Liam swung at the closest, letting out a growl when he was grabbed on the other side. He was knocked back, his other hand and feet grabbed by three other soldiers. Liam struggled, trying to pull his limbs from their grips to no avail.

"Make a path," one of the soldiers ordered another before he was taken from his room and through the tavern.

Liam struggled harder when they reached the tavern floor. If he could escape in the crowd and through the city, he might have a chance. He kicked his feet out as hard as he could, nearly toppling one of the soldiers holding him.

The soldier holding his right arm briefly let go with one hand to hit Liam. "Keep at it, and you won't make it to the dungeons," he spat.

Closing his eyes tightly, Liam shook his head. The ringing in his ears grew louder by the second. He tried to pull his arm free, but the soldier had retaken his grip firmer than before.

Liam struggled until he wore himself down, muscles burning throughout his body. The soldiers escorted him through the streets, his exhausted body hanging between them, barely keeping him high enough off the ground to keep his head from banging on the cobblestones. It reminded him of the first time he was taken to the dungeons, but this time Nicholas Oliphant wasn't around to whip him.

They made quick work of getting him to the dungeons, putting him in a cell further in than he had ever been before. Most likely they did not want him to inspire any sort of riots. There was no shortage of people who hated King Sorren in the dungeons, and he could easily be a figurehead for their frustrations.

Liam slammed his fist into the wall when he was thrown into the cell, letting out a roar of frustration. He should never have stayed in such a popular inn. Liam leaned against the wall, sliding down it and putting his face in his hands. He hoped the king would not find out his intention for his trip to the capital. He couldn't bear knowing he had caused any more harm to Margaret.

Liam paced his cell—he didn't know how long it had been since he'd been thrown into the cell. Was it mere hours, or the whole night long? Time meant nothing in the dungeons. He learned that too well the last time he was there.

He paused when he saw a shadow against the back wall of his cell. When he looked back, he saw the king standing there with a smirk on his face. "You!" he growled, going to the bars.

"Me." Sorren grinned widely, stepping closer to the cell.

Liam was barely able to stop himself from trying to grab the king through the bars. "You're the sick bastard who defiled my Margaret."

"*Your* Margaret?" Sorren laughed at him. "Oh, my dear man. She was never 'your' Margaret. The duchess belongs to the nobility, and she could never have left to be with a commoner such as you, no matter how much you asked her to run away with you."

Liam's face paled slightly. "How do you know I asked her to go with me?"

"She tells her husband everything." The king shrugged, crossing his arms over his chest. "And he in turn tells me so that he can have *my* Margaret."

"She's not yours. You took her against her will!" Liam spat, charging toward him despite the bars separating them.

Sorren stepped back, his arrogance losing its edge slightly. "That may have been true on many occasions, but I was the one who had her first, and you will never have her." There was a sickening gleam of glee in the king's eyes as he taunted Liam. "And I'll tell you, Liam, what a fine woman she is. A shame you'll never hear the noises I got out of her. Oh, her noises, Liam!" The king growled in appreciation.

Liam's battered hands shot through the bars of his cell to grab at the king, letting out an angry roar. Sorren laughed at his efforts, backing out of Liam's reach. "As soon as the executioner arrives, your miserable life will finally be ended, and you'll be out of my hair forever."

Liam slammed his hands against the bars. "I will find another way to escape, and I *will* kill you if I ever see you again."

Sorren laughed again. "I'm sure you will," he said before he walked away.

Liam let out another yell, shaking the bars. By Theotes, he'd get out of there again, and he'd see that man dead.

36

Vojvo sighed as he tucked his laces into his boots. There wasn't much longer left for him on dungeon duty now that Duchess Margaret had married, just a few more days before he would oversee their transport. He couldn't wait—nice as it had been to reunite with men he'd served with before, they weren't the same. Age had mellowed them to lack ambition or effort in their work.

Sometimes they barely bothered to make their rounds knowing there weren't any prisoners on their block. Even so, it was their duty. Vojvo couldn't stand it.

He made his way to his post, frowning when he didn't see any of the other men on the level. Were they sleeping in the cells again?

Vojvo opened his mouth to yell for his other guards to get off their lazy asses as he turned a corner, but quickly backed up and put himself against the wall.

It was the king standing in front of a cell talking to someone.

No—taunting someone.

Vojvo scooted as close to the edge of the wall as possible without being seen around its corner.

"How do you know I asked her to go with me?" Liam said.

"She tells her husband everything. And he in turn tells me so that he can have *my* Margaret."

Vojvo let out a slow breath from his barely parted lips as he tried not to let his rage bubble over. His fists shook at his side as he clenched them tight.

So, this was the reason the duke had pushed him out of Lady Margaret's service. He had intended on betraying her and couldn't with Vojvo around. The king had just confirmed Vojvo's suspicions about Rowan were correct.

He had to warn her of her husband's betrayal as soon as he was able. Vojvo couldn't let this stand, even if a partial good had come out of it. It was still a lie and a betrayal of her trust.

Vojvo peeked his head around the corner and quickly bowed his head as deeply as he could to obscure his face as King Sorren passed him. He doubted the king would bother remembering him, but he didn't want to take any chances.

When he raised his head, Vojvo looked at the cell. Liam leaned against the bars with one arm, his head resting against it.

Should he talk to Liam? Lady Margaret—he shook his head, it was Duchess Margaret now; he wasn't used to her new title—was sure of his innocence, but he couldn't bring himself to agree. Or bring himself to forgive Liam for the death of his son Jorren.

Shaking his head, Vojvo went back to his route of the dungeon. He couldn't. He'd tell Duchess Margaret when the guard was changed, and he was off duty and let her do with the information as she would. He went through the rest of his shift, his thoughts on Jorren. He would have certainly had some things to say about Liam's predicament and his views on whether Vojvo should help or not.

Vojvo regretted helping Jorren switch into Liam's regiment, before the war started, so they could be together. He knew they were close friends, and he wanted his son to have someone looking out for his back. But that someone had gotten Jorren killed, along with most of the rest of their group, for some coin.

Vojvo pressed his hand against his breast pocket where he kept his last letter from Jorren safely tucked away. It was the only thing he had left of his son now.

For the rest of his shift, he completely ignored the row of cells Liam was on. He could be someone else's problem for now. Once the relief guard had come, Vojvo went to Duchess Margaret's new chambers.

He knocked on the door lightly, relieved that Sarah answered the door quickly.

"Captain, can I help you?"

"I need to speak to Her Grace—urgently," Vojvo said.

"Please come in." Sarah opened the door wider, gesturing toward one of the many chairs. "Have a seat."

Vojvo paused when he entered the room. It was more extravagant than her room as a countess. The floors were a light hardwood, mostly covered by a massive Radovian rug that held reds, golds, creams, and splashes of blues. The center of the ceiling mirrored the center of the rug with the large flowers surrounded by laurels. From the center of the largest flower hung a chandelier that gradually tapered down in size, smaller replicas in each of the four corners of the room.

All of the furniture in the room was upholstered with golden cloth and the wood had been painted with a golden paint. Seated just past the largest flower on the rug were two couches facing each other next to a massive fireplace. There was a small table between them. Above the fireplace there was a large mirror with a gilded frame. Throughout the room, there were several chairs and tables, all with gold painted wood and upholstery.

Vojvo shook his head. It looked like a room designed by whoever decorated the throne room, stuffing it to the gills with gilding and taking no consideration that it could appear gaudy.

In one corner, there was a pianoforte that Duchess Margaret or one of her new ladies could play on to occupy the ladies' time while they sat in the room. There were several columns superimposed onto the walls gilded with small flowers and vines. Between the columns were small golden garlands. At the top of the columns, there were leaves that were also golden.

Vojvo briefly wondered what the bedroom looked like if the sitting room was this large and extravagant. He stood quickly when Duchess Margaret entered the room. She was wearing a crimson gown with a plain skirt. All the beauty was held in the bodice, constructed of a crimson and gold brocade. At her neck was a ruby and citrine necklace.

Vojvo bowed quickly to her. "Your Grace, you look beautiful this evening."

Duchess Margaret smiled at him. "Thank you, Captain," she said graciously. "What brings you here?"

"Your Grace," Vojvo started, pausing to pull at the skin of his bottom lip with his teeth. He wasn't sure how to tell her without anyone else knowing what he was talking about. "I have seen something in the dungeons that concerns you."

"Oh?" Curiosity lit the duchess's face. "What would interest me in the dungeons?"

"A friend, ma'am. The one that you traveled with to Marbon," Vojvo said hurriedly in case anyone walked in to hear them, "he's here in the dungeons."

"*What?*" The color in Duchess Margaret's face drained. "When was he put there?"

"This evening," Vojvo said. "Not long before the guards were changed."

Duchess Margaret covered her mouth with one hand, the other resting on her hip. She began to pace. "We must get him out. My husband can help us create a diversion."

Right, her husband who had ensured Liam was locked up would help. He would be a great deal of help. "Ma'am, there's one other thing…" Vojvo did not wish to be the one imparting this information, but it was his duty to her. He would always put her above all others.

"What is it?" Duchess Margaret looked at him stricken. "Please, I'm not sure I can handle any more bad news."

Vojvo flattened his mouth. Now he really didn't want to tell her, but his loyalty was to her, and her alone. "It is about your hus—"

The door opened, the duke walking in, pausing when he saw them. "My dear, am I interrupting something?"

Duchess Margaret went to her husband, a desperate look on her face. "Rowan, my love, Liam has been captured!" She grabbed his arm with both hands, looking up at him. "We must help him. He'll be executed!"

Vojvo watched guilt flash across the duke's face that Duchess Margaret did not catch, no doubt because of her worry, before he put his eyes wide in feigned surprise.

"We were so careful going to him." Rowan shook his head. "I don't know how anyone would have found him."

She looked between Vojvo and her husband, her eyes glistening. "Please, we have to help him."

"The king has already captured him." The duke cupped her cheek. "Margaret, there isn't anything we can do for him."

Vojvo tried not to roll his eyes.

"We must!" she pleaded. "There must be something—you have no idea how important he is."

The duke shook his head in disbelief. "How *important* he is? Margaret, he is a traitor!"

"He is a *king*!" Duchess Margaret reeled back with a gasp, covering her mouth when she realized what she had said.

Vojvo's head snapped to the side, and he blinked rapidly in surprise. Liam, a king? He couldn't possibly be. He was a traitor, like the duke said.

"Excuse me?" the duke asked quietly, anger starting to grow on his face.

Of course, he would be upset; his cousin was the king. It was treason what she was saying, and she'd already done enough of that to last her a lifetime.

"His full name is Liam Fulton Triburn, the last of the line the Platiri family usurped," Duchess Margaret said quietly.

Vojvo started at her words. It had been forbidden long ago to talk about the fallen line of kings, though the common people still spoke of them in campfire stories. If it were true that the traitor was truly the rightful king, it explained why Duchess Margaret had been so fierce in her protection of Liam when Vojvo had threatened to turn him in.

"We must help him," Duchess Margaret pleaded quietly. "We must if he's to have a chance to keep the people from suffering under His Majesty."

"What you're saying is treason," the duke reminded his wife coldly.

"I am already a traitor, darling." Duchess Margaret shrugged, shaking her head. "You knew this before you married me. I have already helped Liam and incurred the charge of traitor by His Majesty. Helping him now makes no difference to his ruling."

"You will bring the king's wrath down upon the both of us—and Samuel," Rowan spat. "Is that what you want? Do you want my poor boy—*our* boy—to be locked away and treated as a criminal for the rest of his life?"

"Do you want to live with yourself when you can help a man that has a real chance to change the world we live in for the better? To have a king that would never do to others what he did to me?" Duchess Margaret countered. "We have to help him for the sake of the rest of Anatalia."

Vojvo felt pride welling in his chest at Duchess Margaret's words. She would help the people of Anatalia no matter the cost for herself, and he would follow her example. He wanted a better Anatalia—he wanted an Anatalia that Jorren would have loved. The savagery with which the Platiri family ruled the country was unacceptable. Vojvo would not stand by and let it continue now that he knew who Liam was.

"Your Grace," Vojvo said quietly.

She turned around, looking as if she had forgotten he was there.

He knelt on one knee in front of her, her husband's betrayal forgotten. "I will do all I can to help you free him and make a better Anatalia."

Duchess Margaret smiled at him, tears starting to well in her eyes. He should not have been the one to make the first proclamation. She helped him stand. "I will happily accept your help, Captain."

37

Tension built between her shoulders as Margaret watched the captain leave their chambers. It was risky what she had done, but she knew it was now or never. She turned to Rowan. She could feel the frustration boiling off him. "Rowan?"

He looked at her, mouth in a firm line. His brows knitted together as he slowly inhaled. "Yes, Margaret?" Anger thrummed under the surface of his voice, ready to break through at any moment.

She had Vojvo on her side, but she needed her husband for this too. They wouldn't be able to pull off something this large without him. They couldn't simply break him out of the dungeons. They would need something corroborating his identity—one that wasn't Liam Fulton.

Margaret closed the distance between them, wrapping her arms around his waist. Tension ran through him as she pressed her fingers into his back. "My love, surely, you must see what your cousin has done to this country."

Rowan wrapped his arms around her in turn, a little tighter than was comfortable. "I cannot betray my family."

"I am your family too." Margaret looked up at him, her mouth turning downward. "Would you betray me?"

He stiffened, pulling her even tighter to him. "No, my beloved, I would not betray you."

"Then will you help me?" She looked at him pleadingly.

"Why not me?" Rowan asked.

Margaret furrowed her brow. "What do you mean?"

"Why not me to replace the king?" He shook his head, his mouth a tight frown. "I'm only two steps away from being king myself."

Wetting her lips, she rubbed them together. He was as close as one could be to the crown without being the direct heir, and she knew Sorren didn't want Gareth as an heir anyway. "You wouldn't even be able to ask that question if you knew about the cruelty of your family. Do you know what they did?"

Rowan shook his head.

"They murdered every member of Liam's family that they could find, just to make sure no one could refute them." Margaret's shoulders dropped as she sighed. "Children included, Rowan. No Platiri should be on the throne—ever. Including you."

"I—"

"Do you even want to be king, or is this because you don't want *Liam* to be king?"

"No." Rowan sighed, searching her face. "But what will happen once Liam becomes king?"

"What do you mean?" Margaret furrowed her brows.

"Will you not once again be the object of a king's desire and fall under the pressure?"

Margaret tried to pull away from him. "How *dare* you!" That was a low comment. She had not fallen under the pressure; she had been pushed.

Rowan held on to her tightly. "I'm sorry, beloved," he said quickly. "I am just worried that his affections for you will turn out the same way that my cousin's did."

"Liam would never do something like that to me!" Margaret snapped. "He would never do something like that to anyone."

"You have feelings for him, Margaret," Rowan said quietly. "I know that you do. otherwise, you would not be asking us to betray our king to help yours."

"I…" Margaret started weakly. "I want to do what is right for Anatalia and give her a king that will nourish and care for her, not let a king remain who would brutalize the people whom he claims to protect."

"I know you better than that, Margaret." Rowan gave her a sad but knowing look. "You're willing to risk your life, *all* of our lives, for him. You wouldn't do so so boldly without having feelings for him."

"I am your wife, Rowan," Margaret said vehemently. "It doesn't matter what past affections I have or have not had. I am devoted to you. I will not defile our marriage vows."

He looked only slightly appeased by her words. "And what if Liam demands you as his wife?"

"He can demand all he wants, Rowan. I am your wife, and your wife alone." The tone in Margaret's voice made clear this argument was quickly coming to a close. "Will you help me right the wrongs that your family had done to our Anatalia?"

Rowan let out a defeated sigh before finally saying, "I will help you, my love."

Margaret rewarded him with a bright smile. "I knew that I could count on you."

Margaret went down to the dungeons with Captain Vojvo. He had arranged for men loyal to him to be on duty for her visit so no word would get back to the king. Liam had been in the dungeon for almost a week, and she had wanted to see him immediately. She wore only a simple house dress and a cowl over her head to conceal her face.

Even in her plain clothes, Margaret's stomach tightened in fear every time she passed someone in the halls. She didn't want to be caught and reported back to the king.

"Your Grace." Captain Vojvo bowed to her when he saw her. "This way, please."

"Captain," she greeted quietly.

Margaret followed him through the maze of the prison, looking around in horror. It smelled dank and she saw standing water in some of the cells. Margaret could not believe the conditions that were common here, and she could not believe these were supposed to be better than other dungeons throughout Aratia. She nearly retched at the smell of one man who had smeared his defecation on the walls. She covered her hand with her mouth, eyes watering.

The captain stopped in front of the cell, pulling her away from the filth that she balked at. "He is just ahead," he whispered quietly to her.

Margaret quickly left Vojvo behind, going to Liam's cell. She saw him lying on his small cot with his arm resting over his eyes as she pushed the cowl back from her head. He moved only slightly when her ring clinked on the bars as she grasped them.

"Go away, Sorren," Liam said. "I wish to hear no more taunting."

"Liam," Margaret called out to him. "Liam it's me, Margaret."

Liam quickly rose from his cot, shock washing over his face. "Maggie!"

He looked far more weary than he had on her wedding day. Scruff covered his jaw and bags hung under his eyes. His clothes even seemed looser. Was he even being fed? She didn't have time to wonder.

"Hush," Margaret said harshly. "No one but the captain knows I'm down here."

Liam went to the bars, clasping his hands over hers. "What are you even doing here, Maggie?" he asked her in a quieter tone. "Do you know how dangerous it is for you to be seen down here?"

"I do," Margaret said, looking up at him. "I wanted to see you and tell you the news."

Liam had a reserved look on his face. "What news would that be?"

"My husband has told me that he will help you escape for my sake," Margaret told him. "For your sake, as well," she added quietly.

"Your husband—"

"And the captain has also agreed to help," Margaret informed him, quickly cutting off the angry tone that had rung from Liam's lips. "And we will all escape to Fradure where we can hide you from the king. You'll play the role of a servant with new papers and a new identity until we're safe."

"And if we're caught?" Liam asked, his brows raised high. "Do you know what will happen to you?"

"Yes," Margaret said, "I know full well what the consequences are. I've already faced some of them."

Liam reached between the bars to cup her cheek in his hand. "I know you have, Maggie."

"As soon as the papers are ready, Captain Vojvo will sneak you out of your cell with a guard's uniform to make you less conspicuous."

"How long until the papers are done?" Liam asked her, his hand still on her cheek. "The executioner will be here in a week."

"I will press Rowan to acquire them with haste," Margaret said confidently. "He's happy to help."

A dark look passed over Liam's face at the mention of her husband. Margaret assumed it was because she had a husband and had chosen Rowan over Liam. "It is good to see you," Liam said quietly.

"There will be many more days that you will see me," Margaret told him with a smile. "And very soon."

"Your Grace," the captain said, coming up to her side. "It's time for you to go."

Margaret caught the longing look on Liam's face at the mention of her departure. "I will see you again soon, Liam."

"I look forward to it." Liam pulled away from the bars and her, his face falling.

Margaret gave him one last look before she pulled up her cowl to shadow her face. She nodded to the captain before he guided her back through the dungeons. She wanted nothing more than to go back to the cell and help him escape this dank prison now. Instead, she went to her chambers to change for the evening meal.

38

Rowan rubbed his eyes with the tips of his fingers before dragging them down his face. He shouldn't even be doing this.

It was treason.

He let out a sharp breath, shaking his head. He promised Margaret he would help, and he would. Especially after she gutted him with the question of betraying her. He had for her own good, but he couldn't tell her that.

Side stepping filth on the street, Rowan's mouth curled. He'd asked his valet where to find false papers, and he was directed to Riamly Street nearly at the edge of Jalmar. It was the filthiest place he'd ever seen—and not one he'd like to go back to any time soon.

How the valet knew of this place, Rowan wouldn't ask. He didn't want to know.

Once he reached the correct number on the door, he pounded on it with his fist.

It opened quickly, a disheveled man with ink-stained fingers stood at the door, one eye squinted at him.

"What do you want?" he asked.

"I—"

"Well?"

"I'm in need of an identity." Was that even what he was supposed to say? He didn't deal with people like this.

The man pulled Rowan into the room by his elbow. "What the hell's wrong with you, Man? You can't just go 'round sayin' you need an identity."

Rowan pulled his arm from his grip, shaking out his shoulders. "Are you the person who can help me with that?"

"I am."

The place was as filthy inside as it was out. He didn't want to bump into anything. "What's your name?"

"No names, you dolt." The man glared at him. "Do you want the papers for you or someone else?"

Rowan inhaled deeply to calm himself. "Someone else."

"How real do you need it to be?" The man shuffled to a workspace piled with papers. "And when do you need it by?"

"As real as you can make it—"

"Ooh, that'll cost you." The man shook his head, grin on his face.

Rowan frowned before continuing, "And I need it no later than three days from now."

The man laughed. "That'll cost you even more!"

He contemplated for a moment telling Margaret it would be impossible to get the papers as quickly as she wanted them. Instead, he asked, "How much?"

"Eight tholar."

Rowan furrowed his brow. He supposed that would have been a lot for a normal person needing a new identity. "Let's make it an even tal if you get it to me before the three days is up."

The man's eyes widened. "You one of them fancy folk?"

"No details." Rowan tried not to grin when the man looked disappointed.

"Come back in two days when it's dark." The man waved his hand, mouth pursed. "You can go now."

Rowan dug five tholar out of his pocket, holding it out to the man. "Half up front, half when I get the papers."

The man snatched it from his hand lightning fast. "Go on now."

He didn't need to be told again. Rowan left, returning to the palace quickly. When he reached the rooms he shared with Margaret, he stripped the top layer of his clothes. He should burn them for just walking near what he saw on the streets. He'd wait until he went back for the papers before doing it though—no sense in burning two sets of clothes.

Margaret came out of their bedroom, hands to her ear as she put in an earring. "Were you able to hire someone?"

He could tell her he couldn't, and all of his problems could go away when the executioner arrived. But then Margaret would try something even more rash to save Liam. Wadding his clothes in his hands, Rowan let out a sigh. "I did."

"I'm very pleased to hear it, my love." She rewarded him with a broad smile. "Will it be done in time?"

He nodded slowly. "They should be."

Margaret came to his side, kissing his cheek before she wrinkled her nose. "You should bathe before dinner."

He dropped his clothes on the floor away from them. He was definitely burning them. "I will."

Somehow it was worse at night.

The smells were stronger, the puddles slimier. Rowan covered his mouth and nose with a kerchief as he turned onto Riamly Street. He stopped while still in the light of the torches. There were none lit on the street, keeping it ensconced in darkness.

Easier to do crime in the dark, Rowan supposed.

Sighing, he trudged forward, squinting at each door until he came to the correct number. He knocked, and it quickly opened, wafting a stink toward him.

"Inside," the man said.

Rowan walked in, his nose scrunching as the smell grew stronger. "Do you have the papers?"

The man went to a table, lifting several pages before pulling one out. "Money first, then you'll get it."

Rowan dug the remaining five tholar from his pocket, holding it up where the man could see it. "I'll not give it to you until I see that the new identity is done properly."

The man lit a candle to bring more light to the room, holding the paper up tightly between two hands. "Come and examine it then."

Rowan brought the candle up, squinting at the papers. They were almost as good as his own—they easily looked like they could have just been made in a provincial town by someone who simply did their best while making the original. "I'll take it."

The man let go of the paper with one hand, holding it out for the money. "It was a pleasure."

Grabbing the paper at the same time he handed him the money, Rowan said, "I hope never to see you again."

"Most say the same."

Rowan only nodded before leaving, tucking the fabricated papers into the inside breast pocket of his vest. He nearly sprinted to the end of the street to be within the lighted torches again, shaking out his shoulders when he was finally illuminated. He wouldn't be going back there again—ever.

He made it back to the palace quicker the second time, keeping his head down and coming in through the servant's entrance to avoid seeing anyone who might ask why he was out so late in the night.

Rowan traveled mostly through the servant's corridors that kept them hidden from the residents of the palace, garnering a few odd looks from those he passed. It didn't matter. He wouldn't see any of them again if he could help it.

When he entered his shared chambers, he didn't see Margaret anywhere. She'd likely gone to bed without him—he didn't mind. It gave him a chance to clean away the filth he'd been subjected to.

He stuffed Liam's new identity into the writing desk before he removed all of his clothes, leaving them on the floor to be disposed of at some point, before making his way into the bedroom where there was a wash basin he could use.

Once he was clean, Rowan put on a night shirt and climbed into the bed next to Margaret.

She shifted, inhaling deeply. After a few slow blinks, she asked, "Were you able to get it?"

"No." Rowan furrowed his brows, surprised at himself. Why would he tell her that?

"Did he say when it would be done?" Margaret sat up on her elbow looking concerned. "We leave in two days. It would be suspicious if we stayed longer than that with Liam in the dungeons."

"The king doesn't know we know," Rowan pointed out.

Margaret sighed. "He'd figure it out quickly if we delayed. He knows how much I want to leave."

He couldn't turn back on his lie now. "He'll try for tomorrow, but we gave him a very short window, my love."

"I know." Margaret sank back into the bed, covering her face with her hands. "I wish he had stayed where he was—where it was safe."

Rowan couldn't have agreed more. "I know. But you can't worry about that now." He kissed her quickly when she pulled her hands from her face. "Let's see what tomorrow has in store for us, all right?"

Margaret nodded slowly. "All right."

Rowan looked around the room before putting Liam's papers in his breast pocket. He didn't want her to find them by accident—that would cause a whole host of problems he was unwilling to deal with.

"I'll be back later," Rowan said.

"Are you leaving so soon?" Margaret put down the book she was reading. "The servants will be here any minute to finish packing our things."

Rowan nodded. "I've a few things left yet to do before we leave tomorrow," he lied.

"All right," she said. "Hurry back if you can."

He kissed her cheek. "I'm not sure how long it'll be, but I'll try."

Rowan really didn't know what he was going to do—everything had already been taken care of for their departure; Margaret was overseeing their things being packed, and he had no councils to sit on since they were leaving in the morning.

Aimlessly walking the corridors, he found himself going to the hall where the other nobles would be. He'd make his goodbyes for the both of them—Margaret certainly wouldn't want to. Those vipers had been nothing but cruel to her through her years at the palace.

Rowan stopped when he saw the king was there, flirting with some of the unmarried women. At least it wasn't the married ones, he supposed. He flinched when Sorren spotted him, nodding in his direction.

There wasn't much he could do now but face him one last time before they left. Rowan had avoided Sorren at all costs, not wanting to let slip that Margaret knew Liam was in the dungeons and they were actively trying to get him out of them. Well—Margaret was, at least.

He put his hand to his breast pocket. Rowan should have been as well, but he didn't have the heart. He wanted Liam gone for whatever hold he had over Margaret's heart. It wouldn't end until he was.

Rowan made a few rounds, talking empty pleasantries with other nobles in the room before approaching the king. "Your Majesty," he said with a stiff bow of his head.

"Your Grace, it's nice to see you socializing. You can't be spending all of your time with your new wife." Sorren leaned in, giving him a sly smile. "Not that I can blame you. I wouldn't l want to be without her company for some time."

Rowan tried not to curl his lip. Every word that came out of Sorren's mouth made him sick. "Her Grace and I have been consumed with preparations for returning to Fradure tomorrow."

"Ah, yes, yes." Sorren nodded. "You're leaving us for how long again?"

Rowan hoped for good, but he couldn't say that. "As long as you'll allow."

"Why don't we discuss it with Her Grace tonight? At dinner?" Sorren gripped his shoulder tightly. "I'd like to have her clearly in my mind before she goes."

Rowan flinched away from him. "We'd be delighted to attend and say goodbye together."

"Wonderful." Sorren grinned. "I look forward to it."

Rowan bowed his head to the king before leaving, waiting until he was in the corridor before shaking out his shoulders and arms. How Margaret dealt with him alone all those years, he didn't know. It was no wonder she despised his family.

He went back to his chambers, not wanting to delay telling her they would dine with the king tonight. It would take some preparation for her to get ready, and he didn't want her caught out.

Rowan leaned against the open door, watching Margaret instruct each servant without missing a beat. He stood up straight when she turned and spotted him.

"Back so soon?" She smiled, coming to him.

"His Majesty has requested we dine with him tonight to say our goodbyes."

Her face fell, shoulders slumping. "I was wondering if we could escape without one last encounter."

Rowan pulled his mouth into a flat line. He hated how Sorren affected her. He knew only one thing would cheer her up. "And" —he pulled her in close, tapping his hand on his breast pocket— "I have what we need."

"Really?" Margaret looked up at him, eyes wide.

Rowan nodded. "They were left for me at the palace gates this morning."

She furrowed her brows. "Isn't that a little reckless?"

"I don't think he particularly cared." Rowan shrugged. He wanted to drop it before he told her even more lies. "I think you and Sarah should pick out a dress for tonight, and I'll mind the packing."

"We should." Margaret kissed him quickly before heading toward their bedchamber at the end of the apartment.

Sighing, he looked around the room. Servants were in nearly every corner of the room, putting things delicately in trunks.

Whatever came, he'd done it to himself.

 **39**

aptain Vojvo hurried to Duchess Margaret's room with her summons. When he was let in, he bowed deeply to the duke and duchess. "Your Graces," he said respectfully.

"Tonight's the night." Duchess Margaret inhaled deeply, giving him a nervous smile. "The papers are here."

Vojvo looked between the two of them. "Tonight?"

"You can accomplish this, can you not?" Worry flashed across her face before she looked back at her husband, who shared the same expression. "His Majesty has invited us to dinner tonight, and we'll be asking to leave tomorrow to start our marriage tour."

"I can, Your Grace," Vojvo said. It was just cutting it close.

"We plan to leave in the morning with Liam in our cache of servants before anything has been discovered." She smiled delightedly. "I have faith in you, Captain." She handed him a small bundle of parchment.

He took the papers, looking over them carefully. They were good forgeries— if he hadn't known they were fake, he would have believed them. Until they were in a safe place, Liam would be called Matthew Brown. It was an innocuous name that would not bring attention to himself. "I will do my best, Your Grace."

The duke touched her, brows knit together. "We need to go to dinner, my dear."

Duchess Margaret gave Vojvo another smile. "Don't let me down," she said before they left.

Vojvo tucked Liam's new identity into his breast pocket, closing his eyes and taking in a slow deep breath to calm the nerves bubbling up. If this didn't succeed, Duchess Margaret would be sent to the block, him alongside her. He waited a few more moments before leaving their chambers in search of Sarah. They had come up with a plan together on how to take care of the guards without much fuss, and now she had to be ready to play her part.

He found her in the servants' dining hall in the lower levels of the palace already seated for dinner. Vojvo motioned for her to come to him when she caught sight of him.

"Is everything all right, Captain?" she asked quietly.

"Her Grace has informed me that tonight is the night." He leaned in close to her ear to ensure no one would hear him. "Make your excuses as soon as you can without raising suspicion and then come down to the dungeon."

Sarah nodded. "I'll tell them Her Grace has requested something or another that takes more time than usual. No one will bat an eye."

"I'll see you soon," he said before leaving.

Vojvo went to check the small alcove near Liam's cell. He had placed an old guard's uniform there so no one would find it, and he wouldn't have to search for one when the time came. Relieved it was still there, he went to stand at his post near Liam's cell.

They were lucky the number of guards hadn't been increased on this block. No doubt the king didn't want to raise suspicions of who was there by flooding the block with guards—if no one knew, no one could help him escape. This was supposed to be an area with no one in it. There were only the three of them—Theodore Allen, Thomas Flory, and himself.

While Vojvo waited for Sarah to come to the dungeons, he ran through their plan: she was to bring down a tray of wine goblets for the men guarding the cells in his row. The wine would be dosed with a sleeping draught that would make short work of his fellow guards. Once they were unconscious, the captain would hide the men in an empty cell in an abandoned portion of the dungeon. It was a simple plan that should easily succeed, but the old soldier was still anxious.

Vojvo turned his head when he heard light footsteps coming down the hall. It was Sarah coming down for her part in the escape. She held the tray in front of her, three glasses and a pitcher of wine on it, and a small pile of sweets. Vojvo was relieved she wasn't shaking to raise any suspicion. She stopped in front of the first guard with a flirtatious smile on her face.

"A gift from His Majesty," Sarah said in a tone that he had never heard her use before. It was not timid as she normally was, but the tone of a woman who knew how to use her charms as a weapon. "For your unwavering duty in guarding this most egregious traitor." Sarah went to Flory first, her eyes heated.

"Are you a gift along with it?"

"Leave it," Vojvo said sternly.

"You're no fun, old man." Flory took his glass before Sarah moved on to Theodore.

"I don't know if I should," Theodore said, looking between the two other guards.

Vojvo shook his head. "Turning down free wine from the king?"

Sarah lifted the tray higher. "At least if you won't take the wine, take the sweets." She smiled at him, one corner turned higher than the other. "I made them myself."

"Go on, Theo," Vojvo encouraged. "I doubt the king will ever think of us again."

216

Theodore reluctantly took the wine and a sweet, thanking Sarah as she moved on.

Vojvo took his goblet from her. "Go on now, before you're missed." He turned to the other guards, lifting his glass. "To His Majesty!"

They repeated it, taking a large drink. No one would dare not drink to the king.

Vojvo watched the other men drink theirs, dumping his out when no one was looking. Vojvo turned to see Liam staring intently at him from his cell. Did he suspect what they were attempting to do when he heard Sarah's voice? Vojvo stared back just as intently, waiting for the drug to take effect.

It was not long before the other guards were yawning intermittently. Soon after, their eyes were starting to droop. Vojvo hoped Sarah did not overdose his fellow guards. Liam stood at the bars of the cell, watching with curiosity the effect the men watching him were suffering.

Flory started to slump first, sliding down the wall with slowly blinking eyes.

Theodore shook his head, trying to clear it. He stumbled forward toward the corridor leading to the next level of the dungeon. "Sound the alarm," he slurred before stumbling to the ground. He struggled to get up, falling back onto his chest before he stilled.

Looking at the other men, Vojvo let out a sigh. He didn't like that he had to do it, but it couldn't be avoided. It was drugging them or hurting them, and he much preferred the option where he wouldn't get caught.

Vojvo hastily grabbed the spare uniform he had hidden away for Liam. "Put this on and hide your clothes somewhere unnoticeable," he said quickly, sliding the clothing between the bars. He handed Liam his new identity papers to keep on him just in case they had to split up. "And this is who you are."

Vojvo grabbed the keys for the cell from Theodore before he pulled the two guards to another row of cells on their block that were unoccupied. He unlocked two empty cells and pulled them into their own. Vojvo closed the doors behind him, making sure they were locked. They'd be found easily enough when someone went looking, but no one would see them if they were going to Liam's cell.

When he returned, Liam was dressed in his disguise. Vojvo unlocked his prison cell. "Quickly, before anyone becomes suspicious."

Liam looked at him pointedly. Vojvo had made no secret of how he had felt about Liam the last time they spoke. He'd threatened to turn him in until the then Lady Margaret left Marbon to come to the capital. "Why are you helping me?"

It was a fair question. "For Duchess Margaret," he said. "Now go out quickly, and I will follow shortly."

Vojvo waited for Liam to round the corner and he could hear him take slow steps so as to not alert the rest of the men in the dungeon anything was amiss with a hurried pace. Vojvo looked around to see if there was anything he left behind that would incriminate Duchess Margaret or himself before he followed behind. He didn't want to follow too closely in case he needed to hide Liam again.

When Vojvo rounded a corner, Liam was walking back toward him, his eyes wide. Vojvo stopped short when he heard familiar voices. He let out a sharp breath and pulled Liam into another hallway corridor of the dungeon, backing up into the shadows.

"We have to split up."

40

Sorren was nearly giddy as he was readied for dinner. He couldn't wait to see Margaret's face when he showed her. There would be no escape for Liam this time, and his problems would be solved. And she wouldn't be able to help him, not this time.

As Christian put on his dinner jacket, another servant entered the room. "Your Majesty, Their Graces have arrived for dinner."

"Hurry up, Christian," Sorren commanded.

Christian came around to the front of him, fastened his buttons at a measured pace. "Yes, Your Majesty."

The longer Christian took, the more frustrated Sorren became. He slapped Christian's hands away, finishing the buttons himself. "See?" He motioned to his buttons. "It doesn't take as long as you're taking, Christian."

"Yes, Your Majesty," he said with a bow of his head.

Sorren rolled his eyes, leaving his chambers for the dinner. He chose a small out of the way room near the dungeon entrance where they would have plenty of privacy. When he entered, the couple looked tense.

Margaret quickly stood, smiling at him. She curtsied low, not looking directly at him. "Your Majesty."

"Your Graces." Sorren motioned to the table. "Please, sit," he said before sitting down at the head of the table.

Margaret and Rowan sat on the same side of the table, Rowan sitting between Sorren and Margaret. "We were honored to receive your invitation," Rowan said.

He tried not to be annoyed—he was hoping Margaret would be within arm's reach. Sorren looked her over slowly. "Duchess, you look beautiful this evening." She had a healthy glow about her, despite how tense she was.

"Thank you, Your Majesty," Margaret responded demurely.

A footman poured wine for the table before backing up against the wall, looking straight ahead.

Sorren took a drink of his wine, letting out a breath with the comfortable burn from his throat to stomach. "When will you be leaving for your home, Rowan?" Sorren asked, looking between the two of them.

"Tomorrow morning, if Your Majesty will allow it," Rowan told him.

"I will." Sorren nodded. "And wish you swift travels. I know Her Grace is looking forward to acquainting herself with the staff and lands."

"They loved her on our tour, and I know they will love her even more now she's their lady." Rowan smiled at Margaret, extending his hand to her.

Margaret smiled at him tenderly, squeezing his hand. "I certainly hope I'll deserve their love."

Sorren scowled at his cup but said nothing. It was so saccharine that he could hardly believe they were serious.

The dinner went smoothly, though it was shorter than usual, their conversation lacking as each course was served. He couldn't help it; he was too excited to show them his conquest. Sorren didn't want to blurt anything out to him, keeping instead to simple topics about their travel and packing.

As the dessert was served, Sorren couldn't help but grin. It was almost time. "I have a surprise for you, my dear," Sorren said, looking at Margaret.

"Oh?" Margaret's brows knitted together. "Is it a wedding gift?"

"Of sorts," Sorren said cryptically.

"Is it more jewels?" She touched the necklace she wore—one of the ones he had given her. "Your gifts after the wedding were too much, Majesty."

"Nonsense," Sorren said with a wave of his hand, "and it is not more jewels. Guess again." He smirked behind his wine, leaning back in his seat.

"A new house—one in the city for us to stay in while we're at court?"

"No." His grin grew wider, pleased she could not guess.

"A horse?" Margaret asked desperately.

As much as he liked watching her squirm, it was time for the reveal. "You'll never guess." Sorren stood, making them stand with him. "I'll just show you."

Margaret looked at Rowan, eyes widening. "Where will we be going?"

"You'll see," Sorren said with almost childlike joy.

They followed behind him when he left the room. It took all he had in him to calmly walk toward the dungeon entrance. Sorren debated on whether he should tell Margaret of her husband's part in Liam's capture, but he decided against it. The least he could do for her after all these years was to not hurt her new marriage.

It would be over soon enough, after all.

"Your Majesty," Margaret said quietly, "why are we going to the dungeons?"

He looked over his shoulder, a grin on his face. "In due time, my dear," Sorren said, once again cryptic.

Sorren went down the familiar path to Liam's cell. He passed a guard who turned into another corridor without bowing to him. An annoyance, but one he couldn't bother with at the moment. He led Margaret and Rowan down each level of the dungeon until they reached the near empty one where Liam was housed.

Strangely, there were no guards down the row of cells that Liam inhabited, as he knew there should be. Sorren swallowed hard as they stepped closer to the cell, praying to Theotes he would be in there.

Sorren stood in front of the cell, clenching his fists in front of him. He wasn't there.

The bastard *wasn't there*.

How had he escaped?

Sorren had been so careful to keep any news of the traitor's imprisonment a secret. He reached out to the cell, testing if it would open. It was even locked behind him when he escaped.

"What were you wanting to show me?" Margaret asked.

Sorren turned to her with a stiff smile. "The cell that Liam Fulton will occupy when we capture him. We have located him in The Whistling Squire, and he will soon be in our custody." He couldn't tell her that it *was* the cell Liam Fulton had been in.

Margaret covered her mouth with both hands as she backed away from the cell. Margaret uncovered her mouth, her eyes wide. "I—"

"We will continue with our plans to travel tomorrow," Rowan said firmly, cutting off his wife. "We won't let this traitor affect us any longer."

"As you wish." Sorren gave Rowan a pointed look. They would certainly be talking later. He was the only other one in this group to know Liam was in the dungeons since he was the one to inform on Liam. "This time he will be executed promptly."

"Do with him as you will." Rowan held his hand up in front of Margaret to cut off any arguments. "He will not affect our lives any longer."

Margaret pursed her lips, brows furrowing. "As my husband commands."

Sorren looked at the empty cell once more before leaving the couple alone in the dungeon. "How dare he make a fool out of me again," he muttered to himself.

He returned to his chambers. When the door closed, he let out a roar of frustration. Vases flew as his anger raged. He threw everything that was in sight. He could not believe his misfortune of having the traitor once again escape from his dungeons. And to think that he was trying to show off his capture of the convict to Margaret. How *incompetent* he felt!

"Christian!" Sorren yelled.

Christian came in, his face pale. "Yes, Your Majesty?"

"Get me the guards that were watching the traitor," Sorren growled.

"Yes, Your Majesty," Christian said, bowing out of the room to retrieve the guards.

Sorren poured himself a whisky when Christian left and downed it.

Christian returned with his face even paler than before. "The guards cannot be found, Your Majesty."

Sorren threw his glass at the wall. "They cannot be *found?*"

"Yes, Your Majesty," Christian said quietly. "They are nowhere to be found."

"Well then *find them!*" Sorren lashed out, hitting Christian. "Search this entire palace!"

Christian jumped when the king threw another glass in his direction.

"And summon the Duke of Fradure—*now!*" That bastard had probably told Margaret Liam was in the dungeons and she arranged his escape. She had helped him once, and she would help him again. "Don't let him out of your sight!"

"Yes, Your Majesty." He scurried from the room.

Sorren let out a growl as he flopped back into his chair. His rage simmered only momentarily. He looked around—there wasn't anything else close to him he could throw.

41

Split up? Was Vojvo mad?

Liam furrowed his brow at the captain. "Why?" He didn't know where he was going in the palace. He couldn't just wander around hoping he found the right place before he was caught walking into the wrong woman's chambers and recaptured.

"Did you not just see the king pass with the duke and duchess?" Vojvo's brows furrowed as he threw his hands out. "If we're caught together and either one of us is recognized, it will bring it back to Duchess Margaret." He shook his head. "Neither of us want that."

It was fair enough—Liam had already done enough to bring harm to Margaret, and he didn't want to do it again. Even if she was the one who had orchestrated his jail break. "I don't know where her chambers are now," Liam said.

Vojvo paused, pulling his lips between his teeth before releasing them. "They're on the other side of the palace…in the west wing, two corridors farther down from the room you went to on her wedding day."

Liam frowned. "That still doesn't help." Not to mention, with the size of the palace, that was at least a quarter-mile from where they were now, if not further. It was plenty of time for him to get caught. "I can't knock on each door hoping it's the right one."

"I'll stand outside on guard duty as I would have before I was sent to the dungeons." Vojvo looked around before pulling out a knife from one of his pockets. "Find a place to shave. You'll stand out with your scruff if you're walking in the open."

Liam hadn't shaved without a mirror since his days in the field as a soldier. He'd be lucky if he wasn't a bloody mess by the end of it. "I'll do my best."

"You'll have to take the outside entrance—Corporal Lane will know you're not one of his." Vojvo inhaled deeply, his brows furrowing. "I don't know how long the king will take at your cell, and if you'll be reported missing just yet."

Liam nodded. They didn't have any time to waste. "I'll see you there." He didn't feel so confident he would make it, but if he could escape on his own through the sewers, he could do this.

Vojvo clapped him on the shoulders. "May Theotes guide you," he said before leaving Liam in the darkened row of cells.

Liam backed further into the cell block, looking round for anyone else. Several of the locks had rusted through on the cells—there must have been something that happened on this row for them to be abandoned like this.

Using his fingers as guide, Liam used the knife to shave. He'd be lucky if he didn't nick his fingers or his face—or both. He took the time he knew he didn't have to be careful. Liam didn't want to make himself look like anything other than an ordinary palace guard. When he finished, he tucked the knife away and headed toward the end of the row.

He stopped short at the intersection of corridors, bowing his head deeply and taking a step further back.

It was the king, his angry footsteps pounding against the stone floor.

"...make a fool of me..." was all Liam could hear as the king passed.

There was no question now. He'd been discovered missing. Liam's stomach clenched. From here on out, it would be a fight for his life at every turn.

Liam waited until he could no longer hear the angry steps of the king before leaving the corridor.

He tried to remember the layout of the palace grounds and the dungeon from his days living in the barracks and working in the city guard. It had been so long ago—fifteen years to the month since he'd left the palace to go to war with Salatia. Liam made his way to the entrance to the dungeon, scanning the area for the outside exit. Vojvo was right—he couldn't chance going straight through the palace.

Spotting it, he tested the door. It was unlocked. Furrowing his brow, Liam couldn't remember if it was always unlocked so guards could come in from the barracks or not. He slowly pushed it open, looking to see if anyone was there.

No one.

His shoulders relaxed as he stepped fully outside, breathing in the night air. It was the freshest he'd smelled since the last time he escaped from these dungeons. At least this time, it wasn't tinged with sewage and salt water.

Liam couldn't let this small spot of luck lower his guard. He still had a long way to go before he was safe again. And that wouldn't be until they were in Margaret's lands—either her old or her new as the Duchess of Fradure.

Liam walked further away from the palace so he could orient himself. Things looked vaguely familiar to him. All of the buildings on the property were left mostly unadorned so as to not detract from the grandeur of the palace. The barracks with its plain design and its crenulated roof were behind him to the east, so the west wing would be in front of him. He rolled his shoulders back, standing up straighter. All he had to do was walk with confidence like he was meant to be there, and people would believe he should be.

He kept careful watch of anyone who was outdoors as he passed, nodding to them as he would have when he lived in the barracks. So far, he'd seen no other guards, only people who would barely notice his presence as the help. He could see the center of the palace, its great staircase leading to a balcony and to the interior. With as easily as things were going for him, he thought of chancing using that entrance.

But it was only a matter of time before his luck would run out on him, and he didn't want it to be this soon.

Liam walked past the grand staircase, scanning the exterior for any entrances he could use without raising suspicion.

"Ho to the guard!"

Stomach clenching, Liam froze. He slowly turned around. It was another guard.

"What are you doing out here?"

"I got a little turned around," Liam said, giving him a shy grin. "I've only been on the guard for a few days."

"Where were you trying to go?" The other guard crossed his arms over his chest, frowning.

"The royal barracks." Liam tried to stay calm while his stomach churned. If this guard would just give him directions back, he could shake him quick enough.

The guard nodded with a small laugh. "That's an easy enough mistake to make—especially when it's dark out." He stepped closer to Liam. "You went west instead of east—let me show you where they are."

Ice trickled down his spine while he smiled. "That would be greatly appreciated."

# 42

"You have to remain calm," Rowan whispered against Margaret's ear once they left the dungeons. "You can't look like anything is amiss."

Margaret nodded, swallowing. "I know...I just—" She stopped short as people approached.

Rowan greeted one of their peers as they passed, waiting for them to be out of earshot before he said anything else. "I know. It'll be all right."

Margaret inhaled deeply, linking her arm with his. "It has to be."

They walked at a measured pace to their chambers—nothing could be shown as amiss. They were too deep in it now to be caught. When they turned the corner, Vojvo was standing outside their door, hands clasped behind his back in a casual but guarded pose.

Margaret let go of Rowan's arm, going to him hurriedly. "Is he...?"

Vojvo shook his head. "Not as of yet, Your Grace. I promised I would stand guard at the door until he arrived so he would know he had the right one."

Rowan furrowed his brow. "Why?"

Looking between the two of them, Vojvo settled on Margaret guiltily. "We had to split up...the king brought you down as we were escaping, and we didn't want to be found together to bring it back on you, Your Grace."

Margaret worried at her bottom lip, clenching her hands together in front of her. "And you don't—"

Vojvo shook his head silently.

Rowan turned as hurried footsteps slapped toward them. Margaret moved closer to Vojvo, her eyes widening. Surely, they hadn't been caught already.

Christian rounded the corner, breathing hard, though only one side of his face was red. He stood straight before addressing Rowan, "Your Grace, the king requests your presence."

Rowan kept his expression neutral, even with ice spreading down his spine. The king knew. Or at least he suspected. "I'll be there in a moment," he said. There wasn't anything Rowan could do now except go.

Christian hesitated. "I'm sorry, Your Grace, but...the king has requested you not leave my sight."

Margaret stepped forward, her mouth open to protest. Rowan raised his hand. "It's all right, my dear. I'm sure the king just wants to make sure he doesn't run out of time to say something to me."

"If you will, Your Grace?" Christian motioned toward the main corridor that would bring them to the king's chambers.

Rowan quickly kissed Margaret. "I'll be right back," he said before heading toward the king's chambers.

He was lucky it would take several minutes for him to get there. Sorren needed the time to cool down—it looked like he'd already taken some of his anger out on Christian if the red mark on his face was any indication.

Once they reached the closed door, Christian lightly knocked.

"Enter," they heard called.

Christian opened the door with Rowan behind him. "The Duke of Fradure, Your Majesty."

Sorren stood. "Get out, Christian."

Rowan swallowed, shifting on his feet. Sorren looked ready to murder him. "Is there something I can do for you, Your Majesty?"

"Why the hell would you tell Margaret about Liam?" Sorren demanded. "Now he's gone!"

"Me?" Rowan pointed to himself, looking incredulous. "Do you really think I would say anything and let there be any sort of chance my wife would find out that I betrayed her trust to get rid of someone who could hold any of her affection?"

Sorren still looked suspicious of him. "Then who?"

Rowan shrugged. He wanted to seem as nonchalant as possible. "I don't know. I don't want anything to do with that man. If I had my way, he'd have been dead in that cell." And that certainly wasn't a lie. Rowan would be much happier if Liam *was* in the cell instead of somewhere on his way to his and Margaret's chambers.

"I'll have guards on order soon enough to search this whole palace top to bottom, and the surrounding area." Sorren raised his brows at Rowan, looking like he was testing his resolve.

"By all means, search our apartments first. Take us right to the chopping block if you find him there." Rowan shook his head. He had to stand his ground to be believable and just hope that the king wouldn't take him up on his offer. "Like I said, I want nothing to do with him, and nowhere near my wife."

"Don't be surprised if I do," Sorren warned. He waved his hand to dismiss Rowan. "You may go."

Rowan bowed to him, leaving. Once the doors closed behind him, he let out a shaky breath. What had he done? That bluff could cost them everything.

He hurried back to his rooms with Margaret. Vojvo still stood guard outside, which meant Liam hadn't arrived yet. Good.

Vojvo nodded to him as he passed, saying nothing.

Rowan found Margaret pacing back and forth in front of the fireplace, Sarah standing off to the side watching her nervously. When she spotted him, she stopped her pacing. "Well?"

He shook his head. "He told me that Liam was supposed to be in the cell and told me to keep a careful eye on you since Liam is in your favor." What else could he say that wouldn't reveal the king knew Rowan would have known Liam was supposed to be in the cell already because he had told the king Liam was in the city? "He said he had a guard searching for Liam."

Margaret paused, rubbing her fingers together in front of her as she often did when she was nervous. "What did you say?"

"I told him he was welcome to search our chambers first for him, and that he could take us straight to the block if he was found." Rowan held a hand up when she gasped and stepped toward him. "I don't think he'll search our rooms, Margaret." He hoped his bluff was enough to steer the king away from them.

"But what if he does, Rowan?" Margaret rubbed her hand over her mouth, shaking her head. "And if it's *after* Liam arrives?"

"It's a risk we're going to have to take to prove we want nothing to do with him." Rowan's stomach quivered even as he said it. It was a big risk he was taking on their behalf—possibly one as big as Margaret had done.

Margaret swallowed hard, shaking her head. "Let's pray to Theotes he doesn't like the idea you've put in his head."

Rowan sighed. Indeed, they should. It would be all his fault if he got them killed by guards searching their rooms after Liam showed up.

 **43**

Liam glanced back over his shoulder at the west wing of the palace. The further he got from it, the more nervous he became. There was only so much time he had left before he would be caught out in the open like this. The only benefit he had now was looking less suspicious walking outside with another guard—most patrolled in twos around the palace, with larger groups in the city.

"You said you've only been a guard a few days?" the guard asked.

Liam looked at him with a furrowed brow, pulled from his thoughts. "Yes, I'm still new. I don't know anyone here." He swallowed hard. It was something he had said when he had first joined the Anatalian army all those years ago—at least until he had met Jorren.

The guard held a hand out to Liam. "Cedric Yomick."

"Matthew Br— Brindleson." Liam grimaced as he shook his hand. He'd almost given the name on his fake papers—he couldn't risk being seen as a guard by that name and then someone else by the same tomorrow morning when they left.

Cedric shook his hand firmly. "Now you know someone," he said with a grin.

Liam gave him a small smile back. He hoped he could just lose Cedric once they reached the royal barracks. Liam didn't want to hurt him—he reminded him too much of Jorren and the way he took Liam under his wing so easily. But he couldn't risk being caught, even for sentimentality.

That had already gotten him enough trouble over the last several months coming to the capital to save Margaret, who in the end didn't need him to save her. She'd done it herself with her new husband, and Liam had complicated matters. As he always did.

"Where do you hail from, Matthew?" Cedric asked as they walked.

"A bit north of here," Liam said. "From Seling, by the mountains."

"I'm from right here in Jalmar." Cedric seemed unperturbed Liam had not returned the question. He launched into telling Liam about his time in the guard and his family in the city, and Liam was happy to let him talk.

The less Liam said, the better.

Liam looked over his shoulder again—the west wing of the palace was nearly out of sight now. It was going to take him a while to get to Margaret's—hopefully before they ran out of time to leave safely.

As they approached the barracks, a commotion was starting. Guards and soldiers were starting to gather outside, orders being called out.

Cedric furrowed his brows at Liam, tapping his chest with the back of his hand. "Come on," he said before he started jogging toward the crowd.

Liam inhaled deeply, debating whether he could start running the other way without looking suspicious. Letting out a sigh, he started jogging toward the royal barracks. He could try to blend in with the chaos.

"What's happening?" Cedric asked once they reached another guard.

"A prisoner has escaped from the dungeons," he said. "The king has ordered a search of the grounds and the palace."

"I'll find my unit," Liam said hurriedly, slapping Cedric on the shoulder. He ran into the barracks before Cedric could say anything.

The barracks were vaguely familiar to him. He fought against the stream of soldiers and guards heading outside. Liam kept his head down as he pushed through, looking for any other exit he could escape from.

"He's tall for a man—over six feet—brown hair, blue eyes. He may or may not have a beard—"

Liam ducked into an empty room, putting his back against the wall a few steps down away from the doorway. If they were circulating his description, he would have to wait until the barracks had cleared.

It had been an unfortunate mistake, but at least the barracks would be the last place he would be expected to be. Liam closed his eyes, leaning his head back against the wall as he tried to control his breathing. It wouldn't be long, and then he could try to sneak into the west wing to hide in relative safety.

When he could no longer hear boots pounding against the floor of the barracks, Liam poked his head out of the door.

No one was in sight.

He slipped out into the hallway, looking for the back exit. Liam had nearly walked the whole of the bottom floor before he found a door that didn't lead to a room with four cots. He put his ear to the seam of the door, listening for any commotion outside. When he didn't hear anything, he slowly opened it, cautiously stepping out as he looked around.

No one.

Liam closed his eyes, inhaling deeply.

Now just to get to Margaret without being caught. It seemed an impossible task.

Edging to the corner of the building, he looked around. Groups of three and four were spreading out across the palace grounds, some heading inside by several different doors. He frowned as he thought. If he could sneak into a group of three…

No, that was idiotic. Who did he think he was, Aliem, Rodovan's deity who could walk invisible as the wind? Liam shook his head. There was another way. He just had to find it.

He folded his arms over his chest, leaning his shoulder against the wall as he thought. Liam would have to wait it out a little longer until more of the guards disappeared on their—

"Matthew?"

Liam whirled around, panic racing through him. "Cedric." He hadn't even heard him walk up.

"What are you—" Cedric looked at him more closely, squinting in the dim light. "You're—"

Liam didn't have any time to think. He grabbed Cedric by the arm with one hand, bringing his closed fist to Cedric's jaw. He stumbled backward but didn't go down like Liam had expected.

"Ho to—"

"I don't want to kill you, Cedric," Liam said as he advanced toward him. "But I will if you bring other guards here. I won't be taken prisoner again."

Cedric hesitated only a moment before opening his mouth again.

Liam lunged forward, hitting Cedric at his temple harder than he had before, hoping it would be enough to knock him out this time. He really didn't want to kill Cedric.

Cedric toppled backward, falling into a heap.

Liam let out a relieved breath before he went back to the corner of the building. Cedric hadn't alerted anyone to his presence, even having yelled the first time. He had to move quickly—unlike Matthew Brindleson, people would notice an actual guard missing.

There were still a few lingering guards, but if he kept his head down and walked with purpose, Liam might be able to fool them into thinking he was joining the search. He was already in the uniform for it, at least. No one besides Vojvo and the now unconscious Cedric knew that he had one.

It was now or never. Liam looked back to Cedric to make sure he was still on the ground before jogging toward the palace. He stayed as stooped as he could to look like he wasn't as tall as he was, keeping his head lowered enough to be partially obscured by his hat.

Few paid him mind, only one or two of the guards giving him a second glance as he passed. He slowed as he got closer to the west wing of the palace, ducking into the first door that he could to get inside.

He hoped with all of this that Captain Vojvo was still standing guard at Margaret's room. Liam looked down each side of the corridor before heading further into the west wing. He walked with a steady pace, his shoulders back. He belonged there.

Liam avoided eye contact with anyone in the hall, keeping his eyes forward. He belonged there.

If he believed it, they would believe it.

The further into the west wing he got, the faster his breathing became. He was so close now, and this would all be over until morning when they left the palace.

He belonged there.

Liam passed another corridor branching off the main hall. That was the one Margaret's room was on when he first came here. Vojvo said it was only two further down—he was so close now.

Keeping his pace steady, Liam continued on. He belong—

Liam stopped short when he got to the second corridor. Guards were walking into the room to search for him.

Vojvo was still standing outside for him. He looked calm, his hands behind his back, until he saw Liam. His eyes went wide, his body rigid.

Liam couldn't go in there. Not until they were gone. He waited until the door was closed before approaching Vojvo.

"Where the hell have you been?" he whispered harshly.

"The barracks." Liam glanced around the hall, watching for any other guards.

"The *bar*—" Vojvo stopped himself, lowering his voice before continuing, "the barracks?"

Liam nodded. "I got caught by a guard, who escorted me back to the barracks when I said I was new and had gotten lost."

"You can't stay here—you'll be caught for sure." Vojvo scanned the hall as he spoke. "You have to go until they leave."

"Where?" Liam spread his arms out, looking around. "There's nowhere to hide in here."

Vojvo pursed his lips, looking down the hall again. "There should be a servant's corridor here."

"That's likely even *less* safe," Liam protested.

"Figure it out," Vojvo snapped. "Her Grace's safety is my priority, not yours."

Liam frowned at him. Vojvo was right—it should be both of their priorities. "Find a way to tell me when they're gone," he said before heading down the corridor.

44

Margaret started when a heavy knock sounded at the door. She looked at Rowan with wide eyes. "Do you think…?"

Rowan inhaled deeply, closing his eyes. "I wouldn't put it past him," he said before getting up and going to the door. When he opened it, four guards stood in view, Vojvo slightly behind them with his brow furrowed. "May we help you?"

"Your Grace" —the guard at the front put a hand to his chest— "I am Pike, and these are Harris, Nelson, and Leonard." Pike pointed to each guard respectively. "We are here to search your rooms for an escaped prisoner by order of the king."

Margaret joined Rowan at the door, frowning. "An escaped prisoner?"

"Yes, Your Grace." Pike nodded. "The whole palace and grounds are being searched as we speak."

Margaret looked up at Rowan briefly before stepping out of the way of the door. "You're more than welcome to search. You won't find anyone here but us and our servants."

"Thank you, ma'am." Pike looked to Rowan, questioning.

Rowan stepped aside, extending his arm toward their rooms. "Yes, of course. We won't impede you from your duty."

Margaret watched the guards pile into the sitting room who would search their rooms for Liam.

Liam who was heading their way and could get there at any moment.

She inhaled deeply through her nose, letting a breath out from her mouth. She stepped close to Rowan after he closed the door. He wrapped an arm around her easily, looking as though this wasn't a bother to them.

She wished he had never put the idea in the king's head to search their rooms, knowing full well that Liam could have been there by the time Rowan returned from his audience and gotten them all killed.

"Who are you searching for again?" Margaret asked when Leonard came close enough to her.

"An escaped prisoner, Your Grace."

So, they either didn't know it was Liam specifically, or they wouldn't tell her. Neither matter—they were already here searching. Margaret touched her lips with the tips of her fingers, widening her eyes. "I certainly hope you find him—and quickly."

"As do we, ma'am," Harris said from across the room.

"How long will this take?" Rowan motioned to the room.

"It shouldn't be too long, Your Grace." Pike started opening the trunks. "We will have to do a thorough search to make sure he isn't hiding in here."

Margaret furrowed her brows as he started to move things around in the trunk. She supposed it made sense—their trunks were large enough a person could fit them if they were small enough. Liam would be incredibly cramped, but he could fit if he tried hard enough.

Margaret looked to the door when it opened, expecting another guard to come search their items. She frowned when it was Vojvo, furrowing her brows at him.

Vojvo bowed his head to them before approaching. He was stiff, walking with nervous energy radiating off of him. He leaned in close before speaking. "He's here."

Margaret nodded, trying to keep her face neutral. "Thank you. Let the servants know the wagons are ready, please. Once the guards have gone, we can start loading the wagons for the morning."

"Of course, Your Grace," Vojvo said before retreating from the room.

"Are you going on a trip, Your Graces?" Pike asked as he closed a trunk.

"We're going home," Rowan answered for them. "For our honeymoon."

"Many congratulations to you both," the guard said. "May Theotes bless your marriage."

Margaret smiled at him. "Thank you."

Nelson started opening the drawers of their writing desk, shuffling papers around.

"What are you doing?" Margaret demanded. "You certainly won't find your prisoner in there."

Nelson looked to Pike for a moment before turning to Margaret and Rowan. "We were also told to look for any evidence of aid given to the prisoner, Your Grace."

"Aid?"

Nelson nodded. "Any letters, paperwork—anything that could prove someone helped the prisoner escape."

Rowan stiffened next to her, keeping his eyes intent on the guard, though he said nothing.

"I see." Margaret swallowed. She didn't know what had been packed away from the writing desk. She had saved only two of Liam's letters over the years, burning the rest after she'd read them.

She shouldn't have kept any of them—she knew how dangerous it was. She could only hope they had already been packed away by Sarah in a place that would not be easy for the guards to find in their search.

Sarah came to wait a step behind Margaret as Harris and Leonard moved on to the bedroom. When Pike opened another trunk, pulling out a small chest, she whispered, "That one contains your gifts from the lord general."

Margaret cleared her throat to get Pike's attention. "Please be careful with that one." She hardly needed someone to find a letter addressed to the King of Salatia and a forbidden book within her things.

"Of course, Your Grace." Pike nodded, balancing the chest on the corner of the larger trunk.

"Surely you've seen enough to know no one is hiding in these chambers?" Rowan asked.

Nelson paused, giving Rowan a chagrined look. "We were asked to be especially thorough with your chambers, Your Grace."

Margaret looked up at Rowan. He was stiff, the corners of his mouth turned downward. He shouldn't have taunted the king with his bluff of them not helping Liam, and he knew it.

Pike turned, knocking the small chest to the ground. It toppled open, spilling its contents. Sarah rushed forward to gather the contents, but Pike was already cleaning it up. He looked at each item carefully as he put it back in the chest, pausing at the letter. "Why do you have a letter addressed to the King of Salatia" —Pike turned it over, raising his brows— "with the seal of the deceased Lord General Crompton?"

Rowan looked at her sharply, his brows furrowed.

It took everything Margaret had not to start pulling her fingers nervously in front of her. She had to come up with a plausible lie—and quickly. "He was friends, of sorts, with King Peralta, and I asked if he would help me negotiate terms of a sale for a portion of my tobacco to go to Salatia."

"But it was never sent?" Pike squinted at her as he held the letter tightly between his fingers.

"His Majesty graciously negotiated on my behalf instead," Margaret said slowly. "I wanted to keep the letter as a reminder of the kindness Lord General Crompton showed me. Especially after his tragic death—may Theotes keep his soul at rest."

Sighing, it seemed Pike decided it was a harmless letter. He put it back in the chest, closing it. "We should be done here shortly, Your Graces."

Margaret looked up at Rowan, wetting her lips. "Why don't you see how the guards are doing in our bedchamber?"

Rowan looked at her with a gelid stare. He said nothing, but went to check on them, nonetheless.

Margaret swallowed hard. It seemed they would be having a discussion about the letter Pike found once the guards left.

Sarah came back to stand at Margaret's side, watching with her as Nelson and Pike continued to search the sitting room. A few moments later, Leonard and Harris came out of the bedchamber with Rowan following behind.

Pike looked to the other two guards, brows raised. When Harris shook his head, Pike closed the last trunk. "Thank you for your cooperation, Your Graces. We'll leave you to your evening."

Relief washed over Margaret. She would be glad when they were gone, and Liam could try again to come to their chambers. "Once again, we hope that you find this prisoner soon so we can all feel safe again," she said.

Rowan walked them to the door, only speaking when they were all outside of the room. "Safe searching."

"Thank you, Your Graces," Pike said.

Rowan waited until the door was closed before turning to Margaret, his arms crossed in front of him. "You have a letter to the King of Salatia from my cousin—my *dead* cousin?"

Margaret rubbed her forefingers and thumbs together as her stomach tightened. She should have told him about the letter at the same time she'd told him of Liam's heritage. "Yes."

"*Why?*" Rowan demanded.

"I…" Margaret rubbed her lips together and inhaled deeply. "It's a letter to ask King Peralta to support Liam when he tries to take his rightful place."

"From my cousin?" Rowan ran a hand through his hair, looking at her in disbelief. "How long have you been planning this, Margaret? Crompton has been dead for *two years* now!"

"I gave up the plan when he died." Margaret looked down at her hands. "We'd only been planning six months when the king killed him."

Rowan reeled backward, shaking his head. "I beg your pardon?"

Margaret looked to Sarah for support, but there was none she could give. She turned back to Rowan, nodding. "He came to my chambers after he did it and told me that was what happened to people who tried to take what was his."

Inhaling deeply, Rowan closed his eyes. He ran his hands over his face a few times before pulling them away. "And what was the plan you two had hatched together?"

"Crompton wanted me to marry Liam to add legitimacy to his campaign." Margaret looked down at her hands, unable to face her husband's stare. "If he had a wife from the Anatalian nobility, Crompton thought it might bring some of the other nobles to the cause."

"And you were going to?" Rowan asked.

Margaret nodded, still unable to look at her husband. "I would have done anything to escape Sorren at that point. Crompton could have put himself on the throne, and I would have gladly helped."

Rowan sighed heavily. "And now?"

Margaret looked up at him, brows furrowed. "What do you mean?"

"Would you still marry him now?" Rowan asked slowly.

Closing the distance between them, Margaret grabbed his hands. "Of course not," she said fervently. "I won't be parted from you until Theotes takes you from me himself.

Rowan squeezed her hands, leaning his forehead against hers. "It relieves me to hear it."

"I promise you, there's nothing between Liam and I now but friendship." Margaret brought Rowan's hands up, kissing each one. "And that's all there will ever be so long as you and I are married, which I hope to be for a very long time."

Rowan let out a sigh, his shoulders sinking as he relaxed. "We should try to rest while we can. Captain Vojvo will make sure he gets into the room safely."

Margaret nodded. She could only hope that Liam wouldn't be caught before he could safely make it back from wherever it was he had to hide once the guards were here.

～⊙ 45 ⊙～

Sarah looked around the room for something to occupy her—anywhere but the duke and duchess as they spoke. There was nothing left except to ready Duchess Margaret for bed. She didn't know where the duke's valet was—she couldn't say she particularly cared. If they didn't think him trustworthy enough to know what was going on, Sarah didn't want him around.

"Shall I change you for bed, Your Grace?" Sarah asked when the duke mentioned getting some rest.

Duchess Margaret nodded, her shoulders drooping as she sighed.

"I'll join you in a moment." The duke went to pour himself a drink from one of the the decanters left in the room.

Sarah followed the duchess into the bedchamber, closing the door behind them. "I already have your travel clothes laid out for when morning comes," she said as she started unlacing Duchess Margaret's bodice. "I know we want to move as quickly as we can tomorrow."

The duchess nodded. "Have you spoken to George yet?"

Sarah shook her head. "Not yet. I was waiting for a calm moment after everything was in place."

"He doesn't know at all that we're leaving?"

Sarah took in a slow breath. She'd been keeping her distance from George for the last week—she didn't want him caught up in any of this. "He knows that we're going to Fradure for your honeymoon…he just doesn't know we might not come back."

Duchess Margaret grabbed her hands, squeezing them tightly. "I can finish this if you want to go."

Sarah shook her head, keeping her eyes down. "I don't mind, Your Grace."

Duchess Margaret held onto Sarah's hands until she looked at her. "Sarah, I know this is dangerous…it could get us all killed if we don't succeed. There are no guarantees in the service of a traitor."

"I know." Sarah nodded, swallowing. "We're all traitors now."

"If you want to stay with George so you can have a life with him, I'll support your choice," Duchess Margaret said quickly, her mouth trembling slightly. "And I'll keep you as safe as I can if you come with us. But I want the choice to be yours, and yours alone."

It hadn't crossed her mind to leave the duchess. As she had said, they were all traitors now, and Sarah had helped Captain Vojvo execute Liam's escape.

"Go to George now while you can." Duchess Margaret smiled at her sadly. "With our rooms having been searched already, the guards won't pay attention to us any longer."

"I'll let you know when I come back," Sarah said.

"Don't make your decision now. Make it with George." Duchess Margaret pulled her into a tight hug that felt like she was savoring it in case it was their last. "If I don't see you again, know that I've cherished all our time together."

Cold crept into her chest the duchess pulled away, like the loss of something wonderful. "I have as well, Your Grace."

Sarah left the duchess's chambers, taking servant's halls to the outside of the palace. She hadn't seen any sign of Liam hiding away, nor any guards searching these private halls. No doubt, like many of the others, they didn't care to see the servants behind the walls.

The city streets were crowded with people who were running errands or done with their work for the day. Sarah weaved her way through the throng of people, coveting the way they walked about unawares of the treachery happening in the palace. She knew of only two places that George would be at this time of day, and that was either in The Whistling Squire or in the flower market. She would first try the flower market, walking the path that she thought that George had taken her down on one of their evenings together. She did not quite remember the way, searching this way and that.

When she finally reached the flower market, she saw a familiar swathe of red hair. It was George putting together a bouquet of flowers, no doubt for one of his sisters in the city. His thoughtfulness made her want to wrap herself in it as long as was allowed. Sarah went to him, gently touching his arm.

George grinned when he saw her. "Lamb, what are you doing out in the city?"

Duchess Margaret's offer to stay with George with her blessing rang through her ears when he looked at her like that. "I had to see you." Sarah smiled with an effort she didn't feel.

"That sounds like a perfectly reasonable explanation to me," George said mischievously, wrapping his arms around her.

Sarah wanted to lean against him, wanted to stay in his arms, but she couldn't. There were no guarantees in the service of a traitor, and she couldn't guarantee even if she left the duchess's service that she would be safe. That George would be safe with her as his wife—the king knew her face, knew her name. Knew that she was in the service of Duchess Margaret.

Instead, Sarah pulled back, her face dropping into a frown. "George, I'm leaving tomorrow morning…and I don't know for how long."

George looked at her sharply. "You're what?"

"I can't tell you why, but their Graces are wanting to leave for Fradure before His Majesty rescinds permission for them to go. It's no longer a trip for their honeymoon." Sarah couldn't look at him, guilt weighing heavily in her chest. "It's not safe for us to stay here any longer."

"What do you mean it's not safe?" George tilted her chin up, looking at her with furrowed brows.

"I can't tell you," Sarah told him. She didn't know what to do about anything. If any of them were found to be helping Liam escape that night, they would all be executed.

"Stay here with me," George suggested. "We can get married as soon as possible, and I can keep you safely with me."

Sarah shook her head, tears coming to her eyes. "I cannot leave Her Grace, not during this."

"Then let me come with you, Lamb." George tried to pull her into his arms.

Sarah pulled away from him again. "I can't let you do that George," she said despondently. "It's too dangerous for you to come with us."

"If it's too dangerous for me to go, it's too dangerous for you to go." George grabbed onto her shoulders, squeezing them. "Please, Sarah. Don't go."

Pain shot through her chest. He never used her name—he only called her Lamb. He wasn't making this choice any easier for her, but she had to keep him safe from what they were doing. "I must go with Duchess Margaret, George. She is going to need me, and I will not leave her."

"And where does that leave you and me?" George demanded, his mouth going flat.

Sarah let out a small, choking sob. "I cannot become your wife anymore."

George looked at her shocked. "Lamb—"

"I'm sorry, I have to go," Sarah said, her voice thick. She had to leave before she changed her mind.

"Lamb!" George grabbed her hand as she turned to leave, eyes beseeching her to stay.

Her eyes stung as tears gathered. Sarah looked back at him briefly and squeezed his hand before pulling away from him. She turned to look at him once, her eyes bright with tears.

"Sarah!" he yelled, voice cracking.

She disappeared into the throng of people, letting them engulf her. Sarah didn't care as she was pushed this way and that as people ran into her. She'd left her future behind her, readily heading into uncertainty.

She knew it was for the best…it was either leave him safely behind and choose a different path to spare his life, or lose him and be forced onto another.

But it didn't hurt any less.

46

L iam tried to keep his breathing calm as he waited in the servants' hallway in a cabinet he couldn't even guess what it was used for. They'd been nicer than he expected, decorated much like the main corridors, but without any paintings. Time seemed to creep at an eternity's pace as he listened for any sort of sign from Captain Vojvo that it was safe to emerge from his hiding place. He wished they'd at least formed a code word before parting to make it easier.

Slow, heavy footsteps started from somewhere behind him. He tried not to hold his breath, knowing it would make no difference. It was loud enough no one could hear him breathing anyway.

"I need an extra hand for Her Grace," a vaguely familiar voice called. "One familiar with her."

Did he chance it? If it wasn't Vojvo, all of this would be over soon. He shifted silently, putting his ear to the door to listen for anything else.

"I'm looking for someone familiar with Jorren as well."

Liam swallowed. Vojvo's son...his friend. He hadn't heard the name in some time. It was him. He slowly opened the door to the cabinet, scanning the area for Vojvo.

Vojvo was just ahead of him, his back rigid. He turned when the hinges of the cabinet squeaked. "Hurry up, we don't have time to waste," he said quietly.

Liam nodded, climbing out of the cabinet and closing it behind him. "Lead the way.

Vojvo turned, heading in the opposite direction, his footsteps nearly silent now. So those had been to put Liam on alert he was coming.

Liam followed, relief rolling from his shoulders. He wouldn't get excited yet, but he was close to being done with his hiding for good.

It didn't take long for them to go from the servants' hallway to the main corridor near Margaret's rooms. Vojvo halted at the doorway, holding up his hand for Liam to wait. He walked through slowly, holding the door open for Liam.

They quickly crossed the main corridor, going to Margaret's rooms. Vojvo opened the door, carefully scanning the hall as he ushered Liam into the room.

Liam stopped short a few steps into the room. He was flabbergasted at the opulence that he saw around him. Even filled with travel trunks, it was the grandest room he'd seen besides the throne room. He ran his fingers over the tables and plucked a few notes out on the pianoforte as he walked the room.

How could Margaret have lived in this kind of opulence every day and been so humble and accepting of living in Marbon with the Gollacks', or even in Silvica in the country home that he had found her in? Their humble start had been nothing close to what he now saw in these rooms.

"I don't see Sarah anywhere," Vojvo commented as he walked toward the closed door on the far side of the room. "Her Grace will want to know you're here safely, though."

Liam quickly found a mirror, trying to straighten his hair with his fingers after taking off his guardsman's hat.

"You don't have to impress her," Vojvo said. "She's already spoken for."

Liam paused at his words. Vojvo was right, of course. He did not need to impress Margaret, but he wanted to nonetheless. Liam wanted her to see him looking better than she had in the dungeons, better than he had been when they had traveled together.

"I know," he said shortly.

Vojvo knocked on the door lightly, taking a step back as he waited for the door to open.

Liam heard muffled voices on the other side of the door before two sets of feet walked toward the door. He dreaded seeing her husband up close, especially knowing how he'd betrayed Margaret.

Margaret opened the door, and the breath went out of him. She nearly glowed against her dark dressing gown, a warm smile on her face. "Liam, I am so thrilled that you've made it safely."

"Maggie—"

"Your Grace," Rowan cut him off tersely.

Liam tried not to scowl at Margaret's husband. He was the reason Liam had been captured in the first place. "Your Grace," Liam corrected through clenched teeth. "I'm honored that you were once again willing to risk everything to help me."

"You're too important to me to let you stay in that cell," Margaret said brightly, picking up his hands.

Liam stole a glance at her husband, seeing a dark look on his face. Good. It was arrogant of him to taunt him now, but he didn't care. Liam brought Margaret's hands to his mouth, kissing her knuckles. "I'm very glad that you feel that way."

"Duchess Margaret," the captain said behind him. "When will we be leaving?"

"We'll be leaving at first light—before that, if we can," Margaret said. "And you two will be staying in our bedchamber until we leave so that neither one of you will be seen."

Her husband blanched at the statement. "My dear, may I speak with you?"

Margaret turned to look at him. "Rowan, our rooms have been searched already, but who's to say Sorren won't try again? At least our room has a balcony they could climb over if it came to it."

The duke did not look happy but conceded to her. "As you wish, darling."

"I have arranged for you both to have clothes brought here, and we will leave the room for you to change," Margaret said as she walked into her bedroom. "Would you like to clean yourself up before you change?"

Liam followed behind, looking around the room. "I would, thank you."

The bedchamber had been similar to the sitting room, large and opulent. At the far end of the room was the largest bed he had ever seen. The frame was elaborately wrought with golden vines, venturing out from the center of the frame where a large flower rested that matched the Radovian rug. It amazed Liam how tailored everything was to each other. Every aspect of the room matched in some fashion to the room-sized Radovian rug in the sitting room.

Margaret retrieved a basin and pitcher, pouring the water into the large ceramic bowl. She laid a cloth on the side of the bowl for him to use. "Clothes for the two of you are already set out on the trunk in the corner. We'll be in the sitting room if you need anything."

"Thank you, Maggie." Liam gently squeezed her arm, garnering a glare from Rowan.

"You shouldn't provoke him," Vojvo said once the door was closed. "Her Grace might have her way now, but he could easily ruin it for all of us."

Liam sighed, nodding. "I know. He just…he makes me want to provoke him."

"Buck up and move on." Vojvo shook his head. "Don't risk our lives for the chance to be petty to her husband."

Frowning, Liam picked up the cloth and dipped it into the basin. "You're right, Captain," he said with a sigh. "I'll try to stop—I really will."

As Liam changed, he could hear the couple arguing. It didn't make him happy that he was causing discord between Margaret and her husband. Liam didn't want Margaret to have any trouble in her marriage, despite the fact he hated she was married to someone else. He knocked on the door before going through. Margaret looked at him surprised. She stood quickly.

"Are your clothes adequate?" Margaret asked.

"They are, thank you," Liam assured her.

"If you wouldn't mind waiting in here, we'll arrange places for the two of you to sleep tonight," Margaret said.

"Of course, Maggie." Liam gave her a smile. It would almost be like it was in Marbon with him sleeping on the floor of her room. He couldn't say it was under better circumstances, per se, but more favorable for her than the last time they'd slept that way.

Vojvo gave him a stern look as he settled on one of the mats.

Liam grimaced. He'd already done it again. He didn't know if he'd actually be able to stop until they'd parted ways again. He could hardly wait until they were out of the capital, and he could put all of this behind him again.

Margaret and her husband climbed into the large bed, blowing out the candles on their bedside tables. It didn't make much difference with a fire going in the fireplace. It was Mamonat and warm, but the evening still got colder than what was comfortable sleeping without a fire.

Liam settled near the fireplace for the night, reveling in its warmth. The smell of it reminded him of Jossnon and his smithy, making him relax. He'd see him again one day—just like he'd promised Jossnon when Liam told him he was leaving to make good on a promise.

Liam looked to the bed, softly illuminated by the fire. He could see Margaret restlessly tossing while Rowan lay still, wishing that he still had the connection that he used to have with her. It brought home how much their time apart had affected the both of them; they had both grown apart in so many ways.

Margaret looked at him from the bed, a frown on her face. She slipped out of the bed, going to him. "Is there something wrong, Liam?"

"No," he whispered back. "I'm just processing this all."

"Would you like to talk?" she asked, sitting in the chair next to him.

Liam glanced back at the bed. "I don't want to disturb your husband."

"We can talk in the sitting room, so we don't wake him if you'd like," Margaret countered. "I wouldn't mind catching up with you."

Liam sat up and looked at her. "I would like that."

Margaret smiled, leading the way to the sitting room. She lit the candles on one of the candelabras, setting it on the table next to the large, unlit fireplace. She sighed as she sat, wrapping a shawl around her shoulders. Liam sat close to her on the plush couch, watching her slightly uneasy look.

"I have some terrible news for you," Margaret said slowly, her face starting to redden.

"What is it?"

"I don't know if you ever got my letter, but Elizabeth died a year ago." Her voice was thick with unreleased tears. "She, um, she wanted me to tell you that she loves you." Her lips were in a thin line, eyes sad.

Liam wanted nothing more than to pull her into his arms, but he knew that it would no longer be appropriate. He opted instead to grab her hand and squeeze it. "I know," he said gently. "Aram told me."

"You talked to Aram?" Margaret asked hopefully.

It was Liam's turn to look sad. "Maggie... Aram died not long before I came here," Liam said, knowing better than to tell her that he had given Aram enough poppy's milk to kill a bull.

"He what?" Tears were starting to well in her eyes as she was comprehending the news. "When?"

Liam squeezed her hand. "Not long before I arrived in Marbon to travel here," he lied gently.

Her tears were freely flowing now. "Poor Aram," she was barely able to say.

Liam grabbed both of her hands and kissed them gently. "Maggie, he's with Beth now. He's much better off."

Margaret nodded, wiping away her tears. "I know," she choked out.

Liam couldn't help himself any longer and pulled her against him. It felt good to have her in his arms once again. He gently rubbed her back to calm her down, telling her of his time in Numetra she wouldn't have known yet. He couldn't bring himself to tell her about Eli's death and his part in it—not now. Not while it was still fresh for him. He would carry that burden on his own for a while longer, and maybe once they were safe he would tell her all that happened to him.

She soon fell asleep against him, and Liam sighed. He easily picked her up and put her back into her bed. He tucked a strand of hair behind her ear, letting out another sigh. He could have been doing that to Gretta now in their bed had he not left; had he not chosen Margaret over her.

But he had, and now he was putting not just Margaret in danger with her helping him, but everyone in this room. Everyone who would be in their party in the morning. It weighed heavily on him, and he would leave again as soon as they were safe. He couldn't keep putting her and everyone else in danger because he couldn't stay away.

She was safe now with her new husband, and she would be safer still without him around anymore.

47

Margaret lay awake in the early morning hours. It was still dark outside, though the embers of the fire told her only hours had passed since she'd fallen asleep in Liam's arms. It would be another hour yet before Sarah came to ready her for their journey—if she decided to stay, that was. Margaret hoped she had, but her hope was small after not seeing her when she got up with Liam.

She had slept fitfully after hearing of Aram's death and suspected she wouldn't sleep well until they were all in her and Rowan's lands where they would be safe. Where they could tell Liam the truth of his heritage and make a plan for a better Anatalia.

Regret filled her chest. She should have summoned Aram like she had promised. It saddened her that Aram had died alone, with no family around him as Elizabeth had. She wished that she could have been there for him or that he had even told her that he was ill.

Sitting up, Margaret saw Liam sleeping peacefully by the dying fire. It was a familiar sight to her, having seen it for several weeks while they traveled together, both before and after the Gollacks. It had been some time, but it was burned in her memory. Margaret looked at her husband in the bed next to her. She sighed heavily; it was unfair to him, the way she felt. Seeing Liam again had brought back the butterflies in her stomach that she had in her time in Marbon—the excitement she felt when Crompton had said she was going to marry Liam and become queen when he took the throne.

The longing for a life with him when he had kissed her the first time.

When Margaret caught herself touching her lips, she decided to get up and ready herself. It would save time, wanting to leave as early as they could to avoid Sorren entirely, and she could hide the letter Crompton had left her on her person without anyone knowing where it was. The fewer people who knew about it, the better.

Once she was dressed, Margaret sat in the drawing room to collect her thoughts. Their clothes had been packed while they were at dinner the night before, but there was more yet to be done. She would have happily left it all behind to get away and have her things either lost or sent for once they reached Rowan's home, Craneswile, in Fradure.

Margaret was ready to leave the capital—to be as far away from Sorren as possible. It made her skin crawl every time she saw him knowing that her husband knew of their previous relationship. She could only imagine what Rowan thought when he saw them together, and now he had concerns about her and Liam.

Margaret looked up when the door to the bedchamber opened. Liam poked his head out of the room, coming out when he saw her. "Are you all right?"

Margaret nodded, tucking her feet under her on the couch. "How did you sleep?"

"Uneasily." Liam sat next to her. "I feel I won't sleep well until we're safe in your lands."

Margaret gave him a slight smile. "I know what you mean. I could barely sleep last night."

Liam looked at her seriously. "Are you happy, Maggie?"

The question took her by surprise. "Of course." She furrowed her brow at him. "I have a wonderful husband and now I have a son that I adore."

"Is he good to you?" Liam rubbed his lips together, leaning back against the couch. "Your husband, I mean."

"He's a very good man," Margaret told Liam. "He's very protective of me."

"I've gathered that." Liam kept his eyes on his hands. "I'm glad you're happy...even if it's with someone else."

Margaret knew of Liam's feelings for her, though she hoped he didn't know about her feelings for him. "We should probably wake up the captain and Rowan."

Liam nodded, looking her over slowly as if to access her person, making sure that she was truly all right. "The captain and I will rouse the servants to leave earlier."

Margaret offered him a grateful smile. "Thank you, Liam."

She rose with his help and went into her bedchamber with him. Margaret immediately went to Rowan. She gently cupped his cheek and kissed him lightly to wake him. She briefly caught Liam watching her as he woke Captain Vojvo. "My darling," she said quietly, "we need to leave soon."

Rowan inhaled deeply, pulling her against him and stroking her hair. "What time is it?"

"About an hour before dawn," Margaret told him, gently stroking his cheek. "I'll ready you this morning—I want to leave as early as possible."

Rowan pulled her into a fierce kiss, grabbing her face. "Anything you want, beloved."

Margaret took another look at Liam, noting the stiffness of his turned back. She knew that Rowan was purposefully exaggerating his affections. She pulled away from her husband. "I'll wait for you in the sitting room."

The captain had already dressed in the short time Margaret was trying to wake Rowan. "You can stay here, my lady. Liam can wait in the sitting room, and I will return once the servants are awake."

Margaret nodded. "Thank you, Captain."

Rowan waited until the door was closed before he spoke. "Where were you last night?"

Margaret furrowed her brow. "I was either in bed with you or in the sitting room."

Rowan inhaled deeply, taking a moment before saying, "I woke up and you weren't there…and neither was Liam."

"I was talking with him last night in the sitting room." Margaret crossed her arms over her chest. "We were talking about Elizabeth's death. And he told me that Aram had died as well."

"I don't want you to be alone with him." Rowan's mouth formed a flat line. "I don't want him to get the wrong impression."

"There's no impression to give, Rowan." Margaret tried not to roll her eyes as she turned to get Rowan's clothes. "I told you last night, and I'll tell you again: there's nothing between Liam and me. Not while we're married."

"Does he know that?" Rowan raised his brows.

"He does, and so should you," Margaret snapped.

She waited until Rowan was dressed before opening the door to the sitting room. Margaret was startled when she caught sight of Liam. "What's happened to your face?"

"I thought he could use a bit of a disguise, Your Grace," Sarah said shyly. "People don't like to look at those who are different for long."

Margaret stopped, happiness blossoming in her chest. Sarah decided to stay after all. She went to her, grabbing up Sarah's hands, squeezing them tightly. "I'm glad you're here."

Sarah gave her a sad smile. "As am I, Your Grace."

Margaret turned to look closer at Liam. She would certainly say he was a different person if she didn't know him so well. Sarah had drawn a port-wine stain that covered one of Liam's eyes and traveled all the way down to his neck. Margaret looked away, unsettled by how different Liam looked with it. "I'm certain it'll do the trick, Sarah." And it was, since she could barely look at him. He wasn't her Liam, looking like that.

Rowan wrapped an arm around her. "Shall we?"

Margaret nodded, waiting until Liam and the servants left for their wagons and carriage before she and Rowan went to get Samuel from the palace nursery.

They didn't want to draw too much attention to them by having him stay in their room when they already had all the servants preparing for their departure.

Margaret tried not to let worry consume her as they walked past several guards still searching the palace. She had no idea what would happen as the servants made their way to the wagons, and if they would be stopped and searched for Liam. She couldn't let it affect her—she couldn't look nervous in the palace as they were leaving.

Rowan had her wait outside the room while he talked to the nanny, coming out with a sleeping Samuel draped over his shoulder. "He would have been wide awake if you did it," he said quietly to Margaret. "I want him to sleep until we're out of the city."

She agreed—they needed all the stealth they could muster for their trip out of the city.

When they reached the stables, several servants were still loading the wagons. Margaret was relieved they weren't being questioned as to what they were doing. They'd come too far to be caught now.

Rowan got into the carriage with Samuel, gently laying him down on the plush bench opposite where they'd sit so he could continue sleeping. It was an open carriage for anyone to see in—no doubt the choice had been deliberate on Rowan's part to show they had nothing to hide as they rode through the city.

Once all the wagons had been loaded and the ties secured, the traveling party slowly went through the city streets to keep from drawing suspicion to them. The horses' hooves were deafening to Margaret as they bounced against the buildings lining the street. She looked back at Liam. He was driving one of their wagons, looking calm and collected. Like he really was one of their servants and he was supposed to be there. If only he knew the truth.

"Hold!" Margaret's stomach sank when they were stopped at the gate by a soldier raising his hand. "Every party must be checked."

"Of course." Rowan waved his hand to their group. "You're welcome to look anywhere you like."

Margaret grabbed Rowan's free hand as the soldier approached to keep hers from trembling. It was daring to have Liam directly in the open.

Each servant handed over their papers and gave a cursory nod when they were given back. The soldier stared at Liam, looking away quickly to glance at his papers.

Theotes bless Sarah and her quick thinking.

Margaret let out a silent breath when the soldier handed Liam back his papers without a word and returned to the front of the party. "Theotes bless your travels, Your Graces," he said before motioning the other soldiers to open the gate.

"Ride on!" Captain Vojvo called out, leading them out into the country.

Margaret happily squeezed Rowan's hand, letting her head fall back against the cushioned seat of their carriage.

The group stopped for the night in the late Duke of Rivack's lands. They had stopped earlier for lunch, sending the majority of the servants ahead so their things would already be in Fradure when they arrived. It was a clear night and Margaret felt the weight of her troubles starting to lift. Liam would be safe now, safer even when they reached her new home. Margaret knew that the king would focus his attention in the city first.

Margaret sat between Rowan and Liam. Both of them sat stiffly, eyeing the other across the fire. It saddened her that the two people she had any real affection for had such a strong dislike for the other. It would not change, she knew. They were both jealous men and while Liam would concede to the fact she had committed herself to someone else, Rowan was as possessive as his cousin. Margaret did not want the two of them warring over her.

"It's nice to be traveling again," Margaret said tentatively.

"This is much more relaxed than how we traveled," Liam said. "Very luxurious."

Rowan bristled beside her.

Margaret smiled, putting her hand on her husband's knee. "I like this way of travel much better. You'll remember how much I hated sleeping on the ground."

"Speaking of sleep," Rowan said, standing and holding his hand out to Margaret. "We're going to bed."

Margaret looked up at Rowan and then back to Liam. "I am rather tired," she said. "Goodnight, Liam. We'll see you in the morning."

"Goodnight, Maggie," Liam said, despite the angry look on Rowan's face.

Rowan helped Margaret up, pulling her back to their tent.

Their traveling party took a nearly straight path toward Fradure to get there as quickly as they could. Margaret requested a stop in Silvica to see her old country home—they would pass close by anyway, and it wouldn't add much extra time to their journey. The last time she and Rowan had gone to Silvica in their pilgrimage, she had not gone to the actual home.

Margaret wanted to see what condition the home was in and whether or not it should be remodeled and sold, or just closed until she and Rowan wanted to stay in it. With what was to come, she didn't know when they would be able to see it again. Whatever choice they made, it would be difficult for her to do anything with her father's favorite home. She wanted to remember it with him in it.

She inhaled deeply, the smell of wildflowers reaching her. They weren't far off now, the field of flowers a familiar land marker. Margaret patted Duchess's neck as she started to prance—she knew where they were. Margaret had elected to ride her to the cottage while Rowan and Samuel stayed in the carriage, wanting to revel in the nostalgia of long-gone days.

Margaret slowed Duchess to a halt the closer she got to the home. She didn't know how she would handle seeing the cottage again. It'd been three years since she'd last seen it with the king.

"Maggie?" Liam rode up next to her, a worried look etched into his face, now free of the faux blemish. "Are you all right?"

Margaret nodded. "Just nervous."

"I'll be here by your side. For whatever you need." Liam stayed next to her, waiting for her to move first.

Margaret smiled slightly, her face falling quickly as she thought of going inside. It had been hard enough the first time. She pulled her mare to a stop when she reached the trail leading to her country home. Her stomach swirled, threatening to come up. So much had happened there, the worst of it because of the man riding next to her.

But she couldn't hold that against him. She played an equal part in the mess that followed. Margaret inhaled deeply and nudged her mare forward to go down the trail. She let Duchess walk at her own pace. It was all too familiar, Duchess speeding up the closer they got to the house, her ears twitching forward. At least Duchess only had good memories there. Margaret reluctantly stopped at the front of the home, wanting nothing more than to turn around and leave.

Her garden was severely overgrown, ivy growing up the side of the house. The paint was starting to chip, and there was a small part of the roof that was starting to fall in. How had all that happened in three short years? She should have sent someone to care for it in her absence.

Margaret slid off of Duchess and stood in front of the home as the rest of the traveling party pulled up. Rowan and Liam came to stand next to her, each on a different side. Liam was the one who gently touched her side to show his support.

"I'd like to go in on my own," she said, leaving them both behind before they could answer.

The halls were filled with dust that stirred when her skirts dragged through it. Margaret coughed slightly when the dust flew around her, waving it away with an impatient hand. She worked her way through the house, stopping in her room and running her hands on all the dresses that she had left behind. She scoffed at herself. She had never arranged for someone to pack the things for her like she said she would—she was too upset while they were in Dorcia, and her life had been irreparably shattered by the king when they returned to the capital.

Margaret pulled out one of the sleeves—it had had holes chewed into it, ravaged by moths. None of them had been remarkably fine as the ones that she now wore as a duchess. She longed for the days that were simple once more as she stood in the country home. Margaret wished that she could go back to the days when her father was still alive and she had never been forced into maneuvering her way through court as the king's mistress.

Margaret stopped in the hallway in front of her father's room. She had not been able to go inside his room when she was there with the king to move her father's body for burial in Dorcia. She rested her hand on the doorknob. Her stomach clenched at the thought of going in, but she had no choice. She had to put it behind her now.

Inhaling deeply, Margaret opened the door. The vase that Nicholas Oliphant had broken against the wall still lay in pieces around the room. She touched the cheek he'd slapped with her fingertips, feeling a phantom sting from his hand.

Memories of the day flooded back to her. She looked at the bed where her father had died, the sheets that he had been lying on were gone. Margaret knew they had been wrapped around him for his burial shroud. She closed her eyes tightly to block out the blood that had soaked through to the bed after she had left him there.

She quickly wiped her eyes free of the tears that fell. Margaret looked around the rest of the room, starting to leave when Liam came in. He looked almost as sad as she felt.

"Maggie?"

Margaret quickly wiped her face again. "I'm sorry, Liam, I didn't see you there," she said, her voice thick.

Liam pulled her into his arms, holding her close. "It's all right, Maggie."

Margaret buried her face into his shoulder, clinging to him giving into her tears.

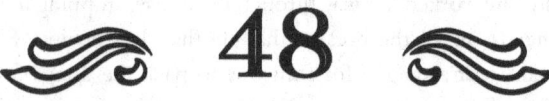 **48**

"And she just left?"

George leaned his elbows on the table, covering his face with his hands. "She said she was leaving with her lady and didn't know when—or if—she would ever be back and broke our engagement."

His sister rubbed his arm until he exposed his face. "What are you going to do?"

"The only thing I can do." George leaned back in his chair with a sigh. "I have to go after her. She's the love of my life, Moira."

"What about the shop?" Moira poured them both another drink, taking a small sip of hers.

"Paul and David can handle it until I return." George smiled wryly. "Mary will keep them to task, no doubt."

Moira laughed. "As if telling them what to do isn't her favorite thing."

"I need to go. I have to get to selling some things." George downed his drink. "I'll need money for the road and a horse."

"Ben and I can help you," Moira said. "We have a little saved."

"You need it more than I do." George stood, kissing her forehead and putting a hand to her stomach. "But thank you."

George was able to sell the majority of his possessions within a few days. He sat in his almost empty room at his sister's home, tapping his fingers restlessly on his legs. He could hardly wait for the morning so he could go after Sarah. He would not give up on her so easily—nor would he let her give up on him. She was the love of his life. She couldn't just leave without another word without him going after her. As soon as the sun came up, he would leave on the horse he'd bought last night. He lay down on the floor with his head on his pack to sleep.

George rode his horse hard as soon as the gates of the city opened in the morning—not that the guards made it easy on him. He was stopped nearly every other street, asking what his business was riding so fast and if he was hiding anything.

George could hardly hide another man in just a sack of food and a horse.

Once he was out of the city, he tried to take the most traveled roads. Their traveling party couldn't have gotten far—they would have been a large group. It should be easy enough to follow their trail.

George followed a diagonal trail through Rivack straight toward Silvica. There was no chance they wouldn't stop there to refresh their supplies. It was one of the first towns Duchess Margaret had on her lands if they were going to Fradure.

As a single rider, it would only take him four days of hard riding to get to Silvica. He would have to stop at inns and trade for new horses so he wouldn't kill the beasts. It was worth it to him so he could get to Sarah and finally talk some sense into her.

He shook his head, squinting against the glaring light of the sun. How could she just up and leave him?

George was slumped on his horse's neck when he heard voices talking. He sat up with his red rimmed eyes squinting against the light. He hadn't slept for more than a few hours since he left Jalmar several days ago. He needed sleep, but he wanted to see Sarah more.

He urged his horse into a trot, becoming slightly more awake at the prospect of seeing her. He heard several women chatting together and George hoped that in his closeness to Silvica it would be Sarah and whomever she was traveling with.

A canopy was set up near a cottage where the women were talking together as they were unpacking food stores and placing them on a long table. It was early afternoon, and they were surely getting ready for a meal. He had to find out quickly who they were—if Sarah was among them. He dismounted and nearly stumbled from exhaustion.

"Sarah?" he called out as he started forward. George looked around briefly before he collapsed.

George groaned as he was shaken awake by small but not so gentle hands. "Wake up, you clothead!" He heard a familiar voice tell him sternly.

George groaned again, struggling to open his eyes. "Sarah?"

"Yes, Sarah!" she yelled while slapping her hands against his chest. "What were you trying to do, kill yourself?"

"I was tryin' to get to you." George gave her a weak grin. "You are to be my wife, after all."

Sarah let out a reluctant laugh, helping him sit up. "When did you leave to get here?"

"Four days ago," George said, reveling in her arms around him.

"Four days!" Sarah yelled, making him look at her. "It should have taken you at least a week!"

"I didn't have a week." He pulled her closer to him. "If this really is as dangerous as you say it is, then I wanted to be here to protect you."

Sarah rested her hand on his cheek, a small smile on her face. "Oh, George."

"Now can you tell me what it is you're all doin' that's so dangerous?"

Sarah sighed before she started talking. "Do you remember when I told you that Duchess Margaret was forced into her affair with the king?"

George nodded, furrowing his brow.

"It was because she helped a criminal…Liam Fulton. He was arrested in Jalmar not long before we left, and Captain Vojvo and I helped him escape from the cells, and we all left the capital the next morning with him in our traveling party," Sarah said quietly. "We're going to the duke's lands where we can keep him safe."

So that was why there were so many soldiers in the city. He furrowed his brow as his mind caught up. Her lady had gotten her involved in this—put her in danger unnecessarily, and for what? "Why in the world are you helping a traitor?" George demanded harshly.

Sarah held her hand up to quiet George. "I can't tell you that yet, but I can tell you that he's not a traitor and those charges were false."

George still frowned in disapproval. "I still don't know if I approve of you stayin' with the Duchess Margaret if she's goin' to be constantly putting you in danger like this."

"I trust Duchess Margaret and so should you, George. She's a good woman," Sarah said vehemently.

"I'll trust you, Sarah, but don't ask me to trust her," George told her just as passionately. "Not yet."

Sarah nodded slowly. "We need to get moving as soon as luncheon is done, and you need sleep. The wagon should be suitable for you to sleep in. I'll ask Their Graces if you can stay."

George stood up slowly, resting his arm around her shoulders. "Lead the way, Lamb."

49

"Why is Mother crying?"

What was Samuel talking about? Rowan had been paying attention to the ruckus by the table set up for luncheon while Margaret was exploring the cottage. It was something he'd have to deal with later, though it at least seemed that Sarah knew the man who'd come upon their small camp.

"I don't know, Sam." Rowan looked back toward the cottage. His stomach sank when he saw Margaret crying into Liam's chest, his arms wrapped tightly around her. Rowan should have been the one she came to to cry on. He should have been the one to follow her into the cottage and not Liam. "Why don't you go to Diana and see if she'll give you a sweet?"

She always had treats at the ready for Samuel whenever he wanted them. Rowan had tried to stop her, but she kept it up anyway to make Samuel happy.

"Where is she?" Samuel brightened, looking for Diana.

"She's probably with the other servants." Rowan gently urged him forward. "Go on. I'll see what's wrong with Mother."

Rowan waited until Samuel had run to the servants before approaching the pair. Had he known it would be so emotional for her here, he never would have allowed her to stop here to check on the cottage's state. Rowan pulled Margaret away from Liam, holding her close to him. He gave Liam a harsh stare before turning his attention to Margaret. "Beloved, why don't we take a moment to eat, and then we'll leave? It's obviously upsetting you. The servants have already started serving luncheon."

Margaret nodded, letting him lead her away from the country home.

Rowan looked back at Liam. He was frowning, arms crossed over his chest. It seemed Rowan made the right decision pulling Margaret away from him. "What can I do to make you feel better?"

"I just need a moment." Margaret sniffled.

"Why don't you spend some time with Samuel, and I'll have plates made for all of us?" Rowan suggested, grabbing her hand and kissing it. "He's been missing you with all the time you've been spending with Liam."

"I'm sorry." Margaret looked chagrined when she glanced up at him. "It's been four years since I've seen Liam, and I've been trying to catch up. But that's not an excuse to ignore Sam."

"Samuel would really love it if you gave him some special attention," Rowan said. He was trying to be supportive of her, but it was hard watching her with Liam. They clearly had a deep bond he and Margaret didn't have yet.

He couldn't help but wish he'd never taken Vojvo out of her service. If he hadn't, she never would have discovered Liam was in the dungeons, and even if the king had shown her Liam, she wouldn't have had time to help him before they left. His betrayal of her was coming around in strange ways to bite him.

Rowan relaxed a little more once Margaret was sitting with Samuel, smiling and laughing with him. That was the type of trip they should be having, the same as when they were on tour.

Once they reached his estate and Liam was told where his family came from, Rowan would tell Margaret Liam had to go. If he wanted to do anything with the information of being a Triburn of the royal line, that would be his business and he could do it away from them.

Liam could not, and would not, be staying with them. Rowan knew it would eventually break them, and he wouldn't allow that to happen.

"Your Grace?" Sarah asked as she approached.

Margaret looked up from Samuel, shading her eyes with one hand. "What is it, Sarah?"

"George has followed us, Your Grace," she said hesitantly.

Margaret furrowed her brow. "I thought you ended your engagement to him."

"I did." Sarah nodded. "He has decided he doesn't like that arrangement..." She looked between Margaret and Rowan, worrying at her bottom lip. "Please don't make me send him away, Your Graces."

Rowan looked to Margaret. "Do you know him?"

Margaret shook her head. "I've seen him only once, but I trust Sarah."

"He'll not say anything," Sarah assured them. "He...he doesn't like what the king is doing to the people."

Margaret rubbed her lips together as she thought. "Perhaps he could be an asset to Liam knowing how the common people feel..."

Rowan sighed. "If you can vouch for him, he can stay."

Sarah nodded vigorously, a smile spreading across her face. "I can, Your Grace."

Margaret held out her hand to Sarah, squeezing it when her hand was offered in return. "I'm pleased for you, Sarah. If you would like to exchange vows when we reach Craneswile, we'll arrange it."

"Thank you," Sarah said. "I think we would like that."

This was the Margaret he enjoyed being around—the generous soul of her people. Not the treason-planning woman she'd been the last several weeks—and for who knows how long to come.

Rowan looked to the horizon. "We should leave soon. We'll not get much farther before we need to camp for the night."

Margaret nodded. She kissed Samuel's cheek before standing him up from her lap. "Why don't you and I go help Sarah clean up so we can go faster?"

Samuel nodded excitedly.

Margaret held her hands out to Rowan, and he helped her stand, pulling her against him. He couldn't help but grin back when she gave him a sweet smile.

With the help of everyone, they were able to pack quickly and get on the road. He was anxious to get to Craneswile. Even in their lands, Rowan wouldn't feel his family was safe until they were in his home where they could keep the king out if they had to.

Liam rode next to the carriage as they journeyed to their next stop. Margaret held Samuel on her lap, pointing out familiar things and telling him of her time in Silvica with her father.

Rowan smiled as Samuel excitedly listened, hanging on to her every word. This is how he wanted their lives to be—not whatever was to come after helping Liam escape. He looked over to Liam—he was quiet, lost in his own thoughts.

When the sun started to sink on the horizon, they stopped for the night. As Rowan suspected, they didn't make it too much further, only about ten miles outside of Silvica.

Once camp had been set up, several fires were built so all of the remaining servants could have a warm fire to sit around while they ate. Liam, Captain Vojvo, and Sarah joined them at their fire. It was an unusual arrangement, but he didn't mind how close Margaret was to her servants. They were all she had until he and Samuel came along.

"Where is George?" Margaret asked when Sarah sat.

"Still sleeping, Your Grace." Sarah smiled slightly. "I don't suspect we'll see him awake until the morning."

"He's lucky he didn't kill himself riding like that." Vojvo shook his head.

"Love will make you do foolish things." Liam's shoulders sank as he looked into the fire.

Liam wasn't wrong in that, and Rowan suspected he was speaking from personal experience. He himself had certainly done some foolish things in the name of love for both Margret and his late wife Clairance.

Rowan wanted to make an effort for Margaret's sake. She was trying hard to bridge the gap between Liam and himself since they left the capital. "What will you do with your newfound freedom?"

"I'm not sure." Liam snagged a long stem of grass from the ground beside him, tearing it up and throwing it into the fire. "Likely go back to Salatia. Anatalia holds nothing for me now that Margaret has released me from my bond."

He put his family in danger for a man who wanted to forswear his homeland? He inhaled deeply in an attempt to keep his anger from bubbling over. "Margaret, may I speak to you privately?" Rowan kept his eyes on Liam, brow furrowed. "In the tent, please."

"I— Yes." She stood, shaking out her skirts. "Please excuse us," she said to Liam before going into the tent.

Rowan followed her, releasing the binding on the tent flaps so they closed. It wasn't much privacy, but if they talked quietly enough. He turned to Margaret, inhaling deeply to give himself a moment to calm his rising anger.

"Why him, Margaret?" Rowan shook his head. "He's unattached to anything in Anatalian but you. He doesn't even want to stay here."

"He'll change his mind once I tell him he's the rightful king." Margaret's mouth went flat. "You don't know him."

"Neither do you!" Rowan snapped before lowering his voice again. "Not really. You spent a year with him and then what?" He threw his arms into the air before returning his hands to his hips. "Some letters here and there? You don't know if he'll make a good king, and you're willing to throw all of Anatalia into a civil war for him?"

"Rowan—"

"Him being in love with you isn't enough reason to support his claim to the throne." Rowan put a hand to his brow, rubbing it as he sighed. And her being in love with him wasn't a reason either, but he couldn't bring himself to say it. "He doesn't know the people, the politics—anything that's really happened since the war."

"Then we'll help him," Margaret said quietly. "I wish I could make you see what I see in him."

"And I wish that you could see how blinded you are by attachment." Rowan moved closer, gently grabbing her shoulders. "We're in this now because of our actions, but Margaret, you have to be sensible. You cannot help him to the throne on blind hope."

Margaret looked down as she swallowed. "I promise that I'll try, if you promise that you'll not be blinded to his potential because of your jealousy."

Irritation rippled through him as he frowned. He was jealous of the way Margaret behaved around him, but his hesitation about Liam becoming a king of Anatalia wasn't based solely on it. He would still make an effort, and if there was nothing worthy of the throne in Liam, he would put himself forward as an alternative again.

"I'll try," he sighed.

50

Excitement bubbled in Margaret's stomach. After being on the road for nearly two weeks, they weren't far from Craneswile. They only had a few days left to go. She couldn't wait to explore its sumptuousness. She hadn't much time her first visit there, but this time she could explore as much as she wanted. It was her home now too.

Margaret sought Liam out in their camp. She smiled at him almost timidly. She knew he was a sore point with her husband and was trying to make sure she didn't spend too much time with Liam. "I've asked Rowan if we could make a stop in Marbon to pay our respects to Aram and Elizabeth—it will only add a day to our journey."

Liam looked up from the piece of wood he was whittling. "Oh?"

"He said yes." She pressed her lips together. "But it will have to be a short trip."

"That's all we'll need—it won't be the same without them there, anyway." Liam gave her a sad smile. "You should rest, it's been a long day."

Margaret nodded, going to her tent. She hoped going to visit the Gollacks' graves would give her some closure. Rowan was seated in the small sitting area their large tent afforded them, drink in hand and a book in his lap.

Rowan looked back at her when she approached. "I presume you've told him?"

Margaret nodded. She picked up his hand, holding it in both of hers. "Thank you for letting me stop there, even though I know you want to return to Craneswile as quickly as possible."

And she was thankful. They had been tense with each other since their argument over whether Liam would make a good king or not when they camped outside of Silvica.

"I just want us to be safe." He squeezed her hands, pulling his away. "He puts us all in danger, but we'll be much safer there."

Margaret pressed her lips together. She knew how much danger she'd had put them in. She'd lived with the consequences of it until Rowan came to her rescue. "I want us safe too. I promise this will be for the best."

"Will it?" Rowan sighed. "I'm trying to believe you, Margaret, but it seems unlikely. We don't know if he'll make a good king, and you still haven't shown me any proof that what you say is true."

Margaret inhaled deeply, trying not to let his distrust bother her. It's not like she didn't deserve it for how long she lied about sleeping with the king—directly to his face, no less. "I can show you proof once we reach Craneswile and have actual privacy."

"If you say so, Margaret." Rowan gave her a tight smile before going back to his book.

Margaret rode on Duchess with Samuel sitting in front of her as they came close to Marbon. She pointed out a few animals along the trail to make him smile. It didn't take long before he was pointing out animals back to her.

She looked to Liam on her left, smile fading. He tightly gripped something to his chest she couldn't see, his face doleful. She held Samuel tighter to her, almost as if she could ward off Liam's sorrow with the fresh smell off Samuel's hair. "Liam?"

Liam turned to her, quickly avoiding her eyes. "Yes?"

"Are you all right?" Worry started to nag between her shoulder blades.

He nodded silently.

Margaret wet her lips before rubbing them together. "We're almost to Marbon," she said. "Do you need a moment before we get there?"

"No." Liam shook his head, still avoiding her gaze.

She frowned. Had Rowan said something to him when she wasn't looking?

"Mother?"

Margaret turned her attention back to Samuel. "What is it, my darling?"

"You missed a big deer." He pouted, crossing his arms. "You have to pay attention."

"I'm sorry." She grinned at him. "Whoever sees the next one first gets a sweet."

Samuel's eyes widened, and he quickly turned his gaze back to the road.

Margaret looked at Liam again, still grinning, deflating when he looked even more anguished than before. She decided to let him be until they were at the town's border.

When the familiar town came into view, she pulled Duchess to a stop. "I'll tell Rowan that we would like to visit the graves on our own and have a camp set up outside of the city—either on this side or the other."

Liam nodded. "I'll wait here for you."

Margaret helped Samuel down, then slid from Duchess. She handed Liam the reins before she took Samuel's hand and walked back to the carriage, where Rowan rode.

Rowan looked at her with his brows raised. "Is everything all right?"

"Liam and I would like to pay our respects alone." Margaret opened the door, letting Samuel in.

Rowan furrowed his brow. "Margaret, I—"

"They were like parents to us, Rowan." She inhaled deeply, closing her eyes. "There's nothing going on between us. As long as you're my husband, there will never be anything between anyone else and me."

"I'm sorry." Rowan's shoulders drooped, pulling Samuel into his side. "We'll set up camp here and wait for you. We'll leave in the morning for Craneswile."

"Thank you." She stood on her toes and kissed him before going back to Liam and mounting Duchess again.

"Are you ready for this?" Liam asked.

"I think so." Margaret urged Duchess forward.

The town didn't feel the same, as if the presence of the Gollacks was what made Marbon, *Marbon*. It felt lifeless—cold. Like any other town they passed through. She and Liam rode silently to the cemetery.

Margaret let out a heavy sigh as she slid down from Duchess. "I can't believe they're gone."

"I know, but they're much better off, Maggie." Liam took the reins of both horses before letting her take his arm as they walked to their graves.

"I know," she said quietly. "I know."

Both graves were covered with grass, the freshness of burial long gone. Margaret's shoulders fell as she looked at them. The Gollacks would be forgotten in time, living only in their memories.

Liam handed Margaret the horses' reins before he knelt between the two graves. He rested his hand on Aram's grave, his head down. "I'm sorry," he whispered. "I love you. I pray you've found him."

Margaret had to look away, her eyes stinging. Had she done better by them, maybe they would still be there. She was so preoccupied with her life that she hadn't checked in with them enough to even find out they were ill. Even if she couldn't have come herself or brought them to the capital, she could have sent a servant to look after them in their old age. They could've had someone there to help with things they couldn't do and get them help when they refused it for themselves.

Liam stood, looking back at Margaret. "One last look at the river?"

A small smile lifted her face. "I'd like that."

It would be a nice end to their time there. It was unlikely they would ever set foot in the town again together, much less go to their spot. Margaret urged Duchess faster, relaxing more the closer they got to the river where they had spent so much time together. They set the horses to graze before sitting under their shady tree, just listening to the water.

Margaret touched her fingertips to her lips—the river brought back memories of the first time he kissed her. It still gave her butterflies. She leaned her head against Liam's shoulder, staring out at the river. "It's so peaceful here."

Liam held her close to his side, resting his head on top of hers. "I'm glad that I get to see it with you again."

"I am too." Margaret sighed. "Do you ever wish you could go back to this—to here?"

"Sometimes." Liam dropped his arm from her. "But no, I don't wish that I could. We've come too far from the people we were here."

He was right, as he so often was. She was happily married, and he was going to go on to do great things…at least, she hoped he would when she finally told him he was meant to be king.

"Liam?" She sat up straighter, looking at him.

"Yes, Maggie?"

"Who did you hope Aram found?"

Liam sighed, pulling a wooden duck from his pocket. He gently stroked its face with his thumb. "My boy, Eli."

Margaret's brows furrowed. He sounded so sad. "What happened to him?"

"It was a hunting accident." Liam held the duck so tightly in his hands that his knuckles turned white. "I killed him."

"It was an accident." Margaret tentatively put her hand over his, giving it a gentle squeeze. "I know you. You'd never do it on purpose."

"Gretta said the same." Liam swallowed hard, eyes still intent on the duck. "I called him Duck, the same as my mother called me, and he loved it. I had carved one like this for his funeral pyre, but I couldn't bear to part with it…" —he started stroking its face again— "until I buried Aram with it and asked him to watch over Eli until I could. This duck was…for me."

Margaret put a hand to her mouth, choking back a noise. She quickly wiped away her tears before saying, "I'm sorry, Liam."

He looked down at her, gently wiping away her fresh tears with his thumb. "Once I see you back to your home and your new life, I need to go back and make things right with Gretta—with all of my family."

Swallowing back the rest of her tears, Margaret stood, brushing the dirt from her skirts. "We should get back to our traveling party." She'd thought about sneaking away to visit the orphans with Liam instead of Rowan, but they didn't have time for that. They didn't need to see her—and she would only cause trouble with Rowan if she went.

Liam looked across the river toward Salatia longingly. "How long until we reach your home?"

"Another two weeks or so." Margaret smiled sadly at him. "I think you'll like it there."

"I shouldn't stay long—just long enough to rest for a few days and gather supplies."

Margaret tried not to blurt out the secret she'd been trying to tell him for years. It was the perfect opportunity now—they were somewhere comfortable with each other, and they knew one another well. But she wanted to wait until it was safe to take out her proof. "We can talk about what happens next once we're somewhere safe," she said instead.

"If it isn't much trouble for everyone, I'd like to continue on today." Liam helped her on to Duchess before mounting Ashka. "The sooner you're safe and I know it, the better."

"Rowan will certainly like that." Margaret let out a small laugh. "He's been saying the same since we left the city."

"I think that means you've found someone I'll approve of for you." Liam gave her a sad smile. "And that you won't need me to look after you anymore."

Margaret wanted to remind him that he hadn't looked after her since they left the Gollacks together years ago, but she knew he fully intended on being able to help her if he could. "We'll see."

Margaret let out a relieved sigh when Craneswile came into view. She was almost home—it wasn't something she hadn't felt in a long time. She looked back to Rowan, a grin on her face. She held up her reins in question.

Rowan chuckled. "Go on."

Margaret loosened Duchess's reins, letting her gallop to the steps of Craneswile. A servant was already there to greet her, taking Duchess from her when she dismounted. "Where is the housekeeper?"

"She should be in the foyer, Your Grace."

Margaret hurried up the steps, letting out a heavy breath. She'd forgotten how many there were. She walked inside, struck once more by the age and enormity of it.

"Your Grace!" the housekeeper curtsied quickly. "We weren't expecting you for a while yet."

When Margaret caught her breath, she said, "I galloped ahead, so I could make a request of you."

"Anything, Your Grace."

"We have a guest traveling with us, and I would like for him to have the nicest room at Craneswile." Margaret wanted Liam situated somewhere befitting his station when she told him his heritage.

"Of course, Your Grace. I'll have one of the maids make sure it's ready for him."

Margaret thanked her and made her plan while she waited for the rest of the party. Should she tell him right away? Allow everyone to rest and get out of their traveling clothes? She wished she'd done it by the river now. It would have been less complicated, but Margaret seemed never to have the right timing for anything.

When Rowan entered the foyer, a smile split his face. This was the happiest she'd seen him since she'd made him agree to help Liam. "I would very much like to take my wife upstairs and see no one else for the rest of the evening."

"Is that so?" She tried not to balk at the openness—they were married after all.

He pulled her into his arms, resting his forehead against hers. "It is."

She guessed she would see how quickly Sarah could retrieve her book of proof from her trunks and see where that took them. "I suppose we'll have to see how possible that is."

"I'm sure we'll figure something out." He kissed her, pulling her closer. "Sam is with Dianna, and the only thing left is to manage the servants, but that will be the housekeeper's job."

"Can you give me an hour?" Margaret smiled. "And then I'm all yours for the rest of our lives."

"The rest of our lives?" Rowan grinned. "I think I can give you an hour then."

She pulled away from him, heading up the stairs to their room. Margaret hoped Sarah would already be there. Since Rowan stayed with the party, the servants would have arrived the same time he did. The hall was familiar, the wooden floors creaking under her feet. The room she had stayed in the first time was only a few doors down from where she would be with Rowan now that they were married.

The door opened when Margaret reached out to grab it, and a surprised squeak followed. "Your Grace!"

"Sarah, you were just who I was looking for." Margaret motioned her back inside the room, closing the door behind them. "Do you know where the trunk you packed my important documents in is?"

Margaret didn't want to outright say, "Do you have the proof Crompton gave me to help overthrow the king?" in this house. She could have no idea who was where and who could hear what.

"It was the first thing I brought in." Sarah went to the bed, pulling the chest out from under the bed. "I didn't know the safest place for it yet, so I put it here."

Margaret opened it, rifling through until she found the book containing the portrait of Liam's however-many-times-great-grandfather. There would be no denying what she was saying when he saw this. She flipped through the pages until she found what she was looking for.

She ran her hand over the face of the long-gone king; Liam was almost an exact match. There wasn't anything to argue when someone could look at this and see there was a clear family resemblance.

"Thank you, Sarah." Margaret stuck her finger in the book to save the page and closed it. "I'll be right back."

"He's in the room you were in," Sarah said as Margaret left.

Excitement ran through her stomach. She'd finally be able to tell him. Margaret paused at the door a moment before knocking.

"Come in."

Margaret walked in, feeling at home in the familiar room. Liam was standing in front of the windows overlooking the front lawn with the lake. "How do you like it?"

Liam turned to face her. "Why did you help me again, Maggie?" He gestured around the room and to the outside. "Why would you put all of this in jeopardy for me?"

"Because you give me hope." Margaret looked up at him, book close to her chest.

Liam's brow furrowed. "Hope?"

Margaret looked at Liam with a seriousness he had never seen before. "Yes, Liam, hope. You have the power to change the world that we live in for the better, and I can think of no better man to do it."

Liam shook his head, the wrinkles in his forehead deepening further. Her words only confused him more. "Maggie, what are you talking about?"

She handed him the book, open to the right page. "You are the rightful heir to the Anatalian throne."

THE ANATALIAN KING

"I'm *what?*"

CONTINUE THE STORY!

THE ANATALIAN QUEEN

272

About the Author

Rebecca Mikkelson has been writing fantasy stories since her early teens for fun and was thrilled to turn her dream into a reality when she was published for the first time in an anthology. She currently lives in Maryland with her husband and three cats.

In her free time, Rebecca likes to cross stitch to relax when her cats aren't hogging the embroidery floss. She also enjoys reading a wide variety of books, ranging from non-fiction biographies of historical figures and families to high fantasy.

As well as being an author, Rebecca works as the editor-in-chief at Authors 4 Authors Publishing, which she helped start in 2018.

Follow her online:

RebeccaMikkelson.com
TikTok: **@zebookverm**
Twitter: **@zebookverm**
Instagram/Threads: **@authorRebeccaMikkelson**
Facebook: **@RebeccaMikkelsonAuthor**

Authors 4 Authors Publishing

A publishing company for authors, run by authors, blending the best of traditional and independent publishing

We specialize in speculative fiction: science fiction, fantasy, paranormal, and romance. Get lost in another world!

Check out our collection at https://books2read.com/rl/a4a or visit Authors4AuthorsPublishing.com/books

For updates, scan the QR code or visit our website to join our semi-monthly newsletter!

Want more historical fantasy? We recommend:

One Thousand and One Days
by Renee Frey

Sutaita, daughter of the Sultan's vizier, planned on a life of quiet study. But when she learns she and her sister must be the next two brides for the bloodthirsty Sultan Shahryar al'Mamun, Sutaita decides to change their fortune. Staying alive by telling stories every night, she must buy enough time to solve the mysteries surrounding the Sultan's edict. In this retelling of the Arabian Nights frame story, can Sutaita slip past the walls around the Sultan's heart and soul? Or will she end up like so many brides before—with her head on a chopping block?

books2read.com/1001Days